Praise for Appendix N

"Another wonderful exploration of the surprising, revelatory and just plain weird literary origins of the world of D&D. Come take a walk through Gygax's mind."

— Patton Oswalt, actor; *Parks and Recreation*, *Bojack Horseman*, *Archer*, *The Sandman*

"Here be the treasure that influenced a generation of game designers and their players."

— Mike Mason, Creative Director, Call of Cthulhu

"An exquisite gateway into the netherworlds of Weird Fiction."

— David Blandy, artist and creator of Eco-Mofos!!!

Appendix N

Weird Tales From the Roots of Dungeons & Dragons

Edited by Peter Bebergal

Appendix N

Weird Tales From the Roots of Dungeons & Dragons

Edited by Peter Bebergal

ISBN: 9781913689933

Foreword © 2024 Adrian Tchaikovsky

Introduction © 2024 Peter Bebergal

Afterword © 2020 Ann VanderMeer

First Published by Strange Attractor Press 2020, this revised edition 2024

Cover: *When The Mind Is Open The Tower Will Appear* by Arik Roper

Texts Copyright © 2024 The Authors & Their Estates

Interior Artwork by Alex Crispin

Layout by Bea Turner & Jamie Sutcliffe

A CIP catalogue record for this book is available from the British Library.

Distributed by The MIT Press, Cambridge, Massachusetts.
And London, England.

Issued as a special edition hardback limited to 500 copies, and an unlimited paperback edition.

Strange Attractor Press
BM SAP, London, WC1N 3XX, UK
www.strangeattractor.co.uk

Contents

Key to Secret Passage

Dungeon Module GG1
Descent into the Temple of Appendix N
An Adventure for Character Levels 1-4

When the adventurers first arrive in the village, they can already hear whispers of the strange and terrible happenings in the ruins of the nearby hills. They learn from the villagers of a rumor that after a recent earthquake, a hole opened revealing a previously unknown passage into a lost and buried temple that many believe is filled with great treasure. A few of the more stalwart villagers attempted to explore the area but have disappeared. Since then, the villagers report monstrous shadows, winged horrors gliding silently in the moonlight, and the echo of necromantic spells being uttered from the area of the ruins. From the nearby cemetery there have been sightings of wights and vampires. The villagers are desperate and offer that the adventurers may keep whatever treasure they can find if they can rescue the lost men and seal up the evils they believe have been unearthed.

Notes for the Dungeon Master only:

On their way to investigate, the players may meet a number of non-player characters that would make for excellent companions, including the brave swordsman Ryre; a barbarian known as Conan; two slightly untrustworthy but good natured thieves Fafhrd and the Gray Mouser; a cunning adventurer called Cyrion; a survivor of the lost-city of Atlantis named Kardios; the Viking Hauk, among others. A full list with character statistics can be found below. Also note the series of wandering monster tables for skeletons, zombies, demons, liches, gnolls, and Tharagavverug, a dragon-crocodile. Lastly, mapping may be difficult for the players, so use the keys below in full to describe the temple and the encounters therein.

Foreword

A brief introduction, not for the purpose of autotrumpetry, but to give context to what I have to say about D&D. I'm an author, still best known for writing about Giant Spiders From Outer Space (*Children of Time*) but with over 50 novels and novellas under my belt, plus short stories. I have, as the writing world goes, writ good. And everything I have as a writer, I owe to role-playing games, Dungeons and Dragons in particular.

I have been a reader of genre fiction from a very young age. I cut my teeth on Dr Who novelizations before going on to raid the (mostly yellow-jacketed) contents of the Science Fiction section at what was, in retrospect, the remarkably well-stocked Horncastle public library. Many of the authors in this collection—and some of the specific stories—had already passed before my eyes long before I ever rolled a d20. I was, in this, following in the reading footsteps of the pioneers who would create the first role-playing games.

Around the age of 13, I first ran into the games themselves. Initially this was a chaotic free-for-all during lunch break where you could turn up with a character scrawled on a piece of scrap paper and they'd fit you into the initiative order somewhere. Later, those who stuck

FOREWORD

with it gravitated to one another and formed insular cliques plodding through roughly-sketched dungeons and failing saving throws against poison. And those books I had grown up with, the swords, the sorcery, the quests, the monsters—RPGs felt like the motherlode, the magic portal, the way that you could actually step into those worlds, even a little bit. And more than step—you could create your own. I gravitated more and more to the role of Dungeon Master (/Games Master/ Keeper etc. as by then other games were starting to creep into the mix). How long did this particular craze last for me, you may ask? As I write this, at the age of five decades and change, I am GMing one campaign and playing in two others, thank you very much.

So what does this have to do with writing? Because it would be very narratively neat and convenient if I could somehow bring things around and forge a Ring of Power with all of this personal anecdotage, concerning fiction into games into fiction. Well...

I never stopped reading voraciously, through all this. At the age of around 16-17 I ran into some of TSR's literary ventures in the form of the *Dragonlance Chronicles* by Weiss and Hickman, a series I'll still vouch for. But as well as fantastical spectacle and engaging characters (Raistlin!), these books had one other key element. They were—very obviously—a write-up of someone's D&D campaign. That was, for me, a lightbulb moment. If they can do that, why can't I...? And, right after that, I started writing. And found out that, in fact, I couldn't do it, because writing's a skill that takes time and practice. But at least I was on the long and winding road to getting into print.

In this, my past as a player and a GM was inordinately useful. There are a lot of transferable skills, from gamer to writer. When creating a world to be adventured within, one learns to build something robust, consistent and wide-ranging, because otherwise the players are frankly going to pull it apart like a flock of keas (you know, those parrots that can dismantle your car). When playing a character—or, as a GM, playing a world full of them—you learn a lot about how to filter your perceptions, thoughts and speech through someone—or something—else's point of view. All of this feeds directly into writing, and a few years of gaming is admirable preparation. There's more, though. As a player, working within a group; as a GM, creating for a party of players, you are not simply working in a vacuum. Everything you make, every performance you give, is specifically tailored for an audience. You become very used to the idea of creating for others. For players or, say, for readers. Despite its occasional reputation as a dive of antisocial nerds, RPGs can teach a great many social and empathy skills. As someone to whom human contact honestly never came naturally, I doubt I could have written for a wider audience without that training ground of creating worlds and stories at the gaming table.

I suspect I'm not alone in any of this. Certainly the vast majority of writers of my generation, and a fair number of the generation before, are from a gaming background. It is a hobby that unlocks the imagination—and explicitly primes you to present its products to others—in a way that is invaluable to the aspiring writer.

Many of the stories in this book arise from a dim and early past, before SF, fantasy and horror were even common currency as genre terms. Along with Tolkien's more formal myth-making, they were the mainspring of inspiration to a great many later authors, and to the creators of the earliest RPGs. These are the pulp writers who rose and fell with their medium in the early 20th century. Then the New Weird authors like Moorcock who built and expanded on their legacy, and took it off in wild new directions. (Moorcock is one of those later authors whose influence, often underacknowledged, is shot all through gaming.) They are authors whose work set me on the path to both gaming and writing in my early reading years, and who have been in and out of vogue and print over the decades. From the early pulp pioneers like Howard and Moore, through to carriers of the torch like Tanith Lee, one can track their influence in and out of both gaming and fiction all the way to the present day.

Adrian Tchaikovsky, 2024

Editor's Introduction

In the early 1970s, the young game designer and wargame aficionado Gary Gygax had the idea to add fantasy elements to medieval wargaming, developing a system called *Chainmail*, the 1971 precursor to what would become Dungeons & Dragons. In 1974, along with Dave Arneson, another game designer who had already developed a simple role-playing system known as *Blackmoor*, Gygax wrote and illustrated the first edition of "Dungeons & Dragons," a box set including the three pamphlets "Men & Magic," "Monsters & Treasure," and "Underworld & Wilderness Adventures," and started the company called Tactical Studies Rules (TSR). TSR soon began producing supplements to the game in response to a swell of interest from a burgeoning gaming community taken with this novel game. It was a DIY endeavor with a punk sensibility, an ethos that was not constrained by any preconceived ideas, expectations, or bottom lines. Gygax and company were able to take risks and fill in the details in whatever way they wanted, contrary to current gaming protocols. It would reach a turning point in 1977 when TSR published what would increasingly become a cultural force: The Basic Dungeons & Dragons boxed set, concurrently with the Advanced Dungeons & Dragons *Monster Manual*. Over the next two years, the *Players Handbook* and *Dungeon Masters Guide* would complete the Advanced Dungeons & Dragons gaming experience. It would set the standard for tabletop role-playing games for all subsequent generations of players.

EDITOR'S INTRODUCTION

Gygax was a wargamer, a hobby that demands patience, a certain knowledge of history, an ability to understand complex rules, and a giant table to spread out massive maps and hundreds of miniature playing pieces. He conceived of D&D, however, as needing only paper, pencils, and dice. This game would be different from a night spent pushing tiny Allied troops into position. Critically, rather than the factual details required for accuracy in wargaming play, Gygax put aside his history books to call up another set of influences shaping his imagination. In the 1974 D&D booklet, "Men and Magic" Gygax writes:

> These rules are strictly fantasy. Those wargamers who lack imagination, those who don't care for Burroughs' Martian adventures where John Carter is groping through black pits, who feel no thrill upon reading Howard's Conan saga, who do not enjoy the de Camp & Pratt fantasies or Fritz Leiber's Fafhrd and the Gray Mouser pitting their swords against evil sorceries will not be likely to find Dungeons & Dragons to their taste. But those whose imaginations know no bounds will find that these rules are the answer to their prayers. With this last bit of advice we invite you to read on and enjoy a "world" where the fantastic is fact and magic really works!

Such an emphasis on the fantasy fiction behind D&D was further elucidated in the first edition of the 1979 Dungeons Masters Guide, which included an Appendix N: Inspirational and Educational Reading, where Gygax describes growing up immersed in magical stories told by his father, as well as fairy tales, comic books, and science fiction and fantasy films. "Upon such a base," he writes, "I built my interest in fantasy, being an avid reader of all science fiction and fantasy literature since 1950." The authors and works listed in Gygax's Appendix N are a collection of epic fantasy fiction, supernatural and adventure novels and stories, weird science, and the pulpy weirdness of Sword & Sorcery. While Appendix N is almost a footnote, it is a reminder that D&D was originally conceived as a sandbox of ideas, a playable representation of pulp, science fiction, and fantasy literature.

Appendix N is also a revealing look into the mind and heart of D&D's creator. Gygax's nostalgia for a child's wonder of stories, and how this grew into a love of telling stories of his own, shows us that D&D is not simply about imagination, but about the power of imagination combined with play and narrative story development. Appendix N might be easily overlooked when flipping through the first edition of the *Dungeon Masters Guide*, but it is arguably the key to unlocking the treasure box holding the true origins of a game that has forever changed the pop culture landscape.

What Appendix N is not, however, is a map to D&D rules, monsters, or gameplay. In fact, some of Gygax's sources seem puzzling, such as the traditional science fiction adventures of Stanley Weinbaum and Fredric Brown. It is, however, a full list of the works Gygax cites as inspirations. Moreover, while none are mentioned by name, Gygax points out that horror movies, comic books, and fairy tales also occupy rooms in the vast dungeon of his imagination. Gygax's Appendix N is also not the last word on literature and D&D. In the 1981 edition of the Basic D&D set, editor Tom Moldvay included an "Inspirational Source Material," his own list of what he describes as "useful" to "improve a dungeon, flesh out a scenario, and provide inspiration for a campaign." So while Gygax offers a selection of what shaped his youthful interest in fantasy leading to his creation of D&D, two years later Moldvay would offer what players might look to for gaming stimulation.

It's worth noting none of the subsequent versions of Dungeons & Dragons included an Appendix N-like section. Even the 1983 Basic set revised and edited by Frank Mentzer, and one of the bestselling D&D products, did away with Moldvay's "Inspirational Source Material." Thankfully, the tradition of citing influential sources was reinstated with "Appendix E: Inspirational Reading" found in the 5th edition released in 2013 that includes Gygax's original picks as well as a number of other books that have influenced generations of gamers and developers.

The challenge of creating a single anthology of source readings based on the original Appendix N is multifold. First, many of the texts are novel length and I wanted to avoid reprinting excerpts. It is nigh impossible to capture a single excerpt from many of these classic works that would be satisfying to read on its own. Second, while Gygax's list reflects those stories he found inspirational, many of those named do not directly relate to the particular kind of fantasy weirdness found in the actual *Dungeon Masters Guide* or other core books and modules of that time. This meant that in some cases I chose to include stories by the same authors, rather than the specific texts listed by Gygax, where doing so was better fitted for the scope and tenor of this collection. Lastly, editing from an already tightly curated list meant that I was inclined to choose the stories that I found resonant and reflective of my own idea of what D&D is about. To this end, the book you are holding is my own Appendix N, a collection of stories drawn from the original, but selected because they are tales that feel like dungeon dwelling in dark and dreadful places, where both magic swords and astral horrors can be found. The stories here are the ones where a quick death may be the result of a misfired spell or trap. Lastly, some stories were simply not available due to various copyright issues or other unforeseeable restrictions. But what is omitted here should not be overlooked and to this end, Gygax's original Appendix N is included here at the end of the anthology.

I also looked briefly at Moldvay's "Inspirational Source Material" to round out a few of the stories I believed were criminally missing from Gygax's original. Also, while Appendix N is a window into Gygax's pulp-infested consciousness, the "Inspirational Source

Material" section in the Moldvay arises out of a player's sensibility. If Appendix N is the Ur temple of D&D, the primal dwelling of where to find its soul, "Inspirational Source Material" is the outer court, where the people are playing the game. So many additional novels and stories here read like the stuff of modules and offer a wealth of gaming resources.

Deservedly so, this Appendix N opens with "How Sargoth Lay Siege to Zaremm," a tale by Lin Carter. While Gygax names Carter's World's End series, his impact is much greater than any one of his many novels. Carter is best known as an editor of countless fantasy anthologies, as well as the essential Ballantine Fantasy series that introduced readers of the 1970s to figures like Clark Ashton Smith, Lord Dunsany, Hope Mirrlees, and even the medieval romances of the designer and utopian William Morris. As noted, part of what made D&D stick in the 1970s was the growing interest in Sword & Sorcery and high fantasy. Carter was the single most important promoter of Conan during the time and wrote numerous overly faithful imitations of the famed barbarian. "How Sargoth Lay Siege to Zaremm" is a pastiche of Lord Dunsany and offers a minor masterpiece of set and setting for entering a state of role-playing consciousness. Herein, an unconquerable fortress held strong by rumors of dark magic should tempt any hardy adventurer in search of glory and gold.

There is, I hope, a little bit of forgivable unoriginality here in my choices. Robert E. Howard's Conan tale "Tower of the Elephant" can be found in numerous collections and anthologies. Nevertheless, its inclusion here is not only because it showcases wonderful dungeon dwelling elements I wanted for my own take on Appendix N. Gygax was clear about the influence of Conan on the creation of D&D. In *Dragon* #63 from 1982, Gygax bemoans the film directed by John Milius and written by Oliver Stone, released that same year, writing that "if there is any resemblance between the cinema version of Conan the Barbarian and that of Robert E. Howard, it is purely coincidental."

H. P. Lovecraft is another overly anthologized writer, but no one named in Appendix N has had greater impact and reach across all aspects of gaming and popular culture, inspiring uncountable novels, short stories, films, and a wide range of non-D&D RPG games and supplements. Lovecraft also helped make early D&D weird. Look at the 1976 supplement known as "Eldritch Wizardry," where you will find the bizarre: Liches and invisible stalkers, Goetic-like demons and intellect devourers, Cerebral Parasites and Thought Eaters. There is even a Lovecraftian alien artifact, the Mighty Servant of Leuk-o, described as "a towering automaton of metal, crystal and some fibrous material of unknown origins." For this anthology, I chose "The Doom that Came to Sarnath," a story that takes place in Lovecraft's "dreamlands," a perfect location to find the stuff of legends and arcane treasures to furnish an RPG campaign.

Some stories here are essential to not only getting at the heart of what Gygax was putting forth in the game, but as fantasy tales on their own, such as "The Jewels of the Forest" by Fritz Leiber, the award-winning writer of fantasy, science fiction, and horror. It's remarkable that a tale published in 1932 could so perfectly capture what an RPG dungeon crawl escapade can feel like. "The Jewels in the Forest" is the first Fafhrd and the Gray Mouser story, Fritz Leiber's unlikely companions. The huge barbarian and the small rogue represent the best of an adventuring party. Why would these two be together except for their shared love of questing, danger, and treasure? And with each knife's edge success, their friendship only deepens. This story, along with the subsequent Fafhrd and the Gray Mouser tales, might be only second to Conan in terms of influence on Gygax and company. This story was also turned into an actual D&D adventure, published in 1985 as part of the Lankhmar setting in the adventure module *Swords of the Undercity*.

I'll have to admit a bit of favoritism here with Michael Moorcock's first Elric story, "The Dreaming City," a tale of magic swords, demons, and terrible sorceries. The story is the perfect entry into the world of the albino, drug addicted emperor of Melniboné. Elric also presents a master class on thinking about the unwieldy D&D rules related to alignment (chaotic good, lawful evil, etc). Elric is the protagonist you root for but would have to be played as with "evil" alignment to be true to the character. He is the great fantasy anti-hero, seemingly avenging injustice, but using whatever dark resources necessary to win. Moorcock's Elric tales are a drop in a vast oeuvre that has spanned decades, but his demon-sword wielding hero has had particular influence as far reaching as other RPGs and rock and roll.

There is hardly anything listed in Appendix N that made it directly into the actual gameplay of D&D except for Jack Vance's Dying Earth series, one of the few named that can be found in the very rules. Vance's overall influence on Gygax is profound. He once called Vance "very best of all the authors of imaginative fiction," and his magic system has shaped the core rules of D&D and other RPGs as well. Essentially, magic users must prepare a set number of spells before each encounter, and once used, these are "forgotten" until the next day. In the Dying Earth tales, this makes magic feel rare and precious. Casting a spell (of which there are only a hundred known) must be done only when absolutely necessary. For Gygax, it seems his adoption of what he called "Vancian" magic is so that magic users would not become fire-ball cannons, unbalancing the game and making magic ridiculously potent. It's also possible he wanted magic, and magic users, to resonate in the way they might in a Conan story. Mages are singular beings of immense power whose arcane knowledge is mysterious, yet formidable. Any number of Vance's stories would do, but I have a fondness for the first adventure of the wizard known as "Turjan of Miir."

One of the more perplexing entries in Appendix N is the 1978 anthology *Swords Against Darkness III*, edited by Andrew J. Offutt. Its overall presence is a great addition to the list, as it contains a stellar selection of Sword & Sorcery tales. What is curious is that

Gygax chose to include only Volume III and not the first two as well. (The entire series would see five volumes altogether, but the last two would not have been available until after the *Dungeon Masters Guide* went to print.) In any case, I decided to look at all the volumes in search of Appendix N treasures and chose four stories from the series.

First is "The Tale of Hauk" by the Hugo and Nebula-winning author Poul Anderson, which appeared in the initial volume of *Swords Against Darkness*. Gygax specifically calls out Poul Anderson's *Three Hearts and Three Lions* and *The Broken Sword*, among many others, as his choice texts, but "The Tale of Hauk" reads like a rousing night at the gaming table. Moreover, it showcases Anderson's prowess at mixing history and fantasy. There are Vikings here—the main people of his novel *The Broken Sword*—their long boats sailing towards Europe and beyond, only to return to a village tormented by a supernatural foe they both fear and love.

The first volume of *Swords Against Darkness* also includes "Straggler from Atlantis" by Manly Wade Wellman. This is the first tale of Kardios, the only survivor of sunken Atlantis. Kardios finds himself washed up on the shores of a strange land where he meets a clutch of giants in desperate need of a hero of their own. While Kardios is a formidable warrior, he is also a bard, a class that Gygax would bring into the game. Wellman's better-known protagonist is Silver John the Balladeer, a guitarist/occult investigator who roams the Appalachian Mountains, and if either was the influence for "bard" class in D&D, it would more likely be John, as he appeared a decade or more before Kardios. Nevertheless, "Straggler from Atlantis" has all the essentials for an Appendix N story: a quest offered and accepted, a mighty weapon, and a fiendish adversary with a mysterious origin.

Gygax was certainly not wrong in highlighting *Swords Against Darkness III*. This an essential collection, and in some ways stands out as a micro Appendix N as it is replete with dynamite adventures, and I can imagine they all resonated perfectly with the evolution of the game by the time *Swords Against Darkness III* was published in 1978. There is no better example of this than Ramsey Campbell's story "Pit of Wings." Campbell—not specifically named in Appendix N—considered by many to be one of the most important living horror writers—is best known for his tales of terror and Cthulhu-esque stories. In the 1970s he wrote a series of fantasy tales—most of which appeared in the *Swords Against Darkness* series and featured the swordsman Ryre. In "Pit of Wings," Ryre encounters an enslaved people in thrall to both their cruel masters and a monstrous force that demands sacrifice.

Another standout tale from *Swords Against Darkness III*, and a highlight of my own choices, is David Madison's "Tower of Darkness," a heart-quickening tale featuring the adventuring couple Marcus and Diana. Madison is likely the least known of any of the authors here, and who died tragically when he was 27, the year this story appeared. Madison's overall output is brief, but "Tower of Darkness" reveals a young writer who would have likely become a formidable voice in fantasy fiction had he lived.

Swords Against Darkness also turned me on to Tanith Lee, a writer I have known about but had never read before now. Tanith Lee was a prolific author, having written over a dozen series and multiple short stories. I decided, though, that instead of using one of the stories found in the *Swords Against Darkness* series, her tales of Cyrion, the blond adventurer whose ability at deduction is as sharp as his sword, fall easily into the kind of fantasy tales that Gygax would cite. And while Lee is not mentioned by name in Appendix N, she does—like Ramsey Campbell—make it into Moldvay's list. "Hero at the Gates" has strong D&D timbre, especially by 1981 when the look and feel of the game was starting to congeal. Cyrion might not be the best character to play at the gaming table: with high stats in all his attributes and a number of bonuses on his saves, he would easily thread his way through most difficulties in your average dungeon crawl.

EDITOR'S INTRODUCTION

From the pen of fantasist Margaret St. Clair, I chose her delightfully strange "The Man Who Sold Rope to the Gnoles," and like Lin Carter's "How Sargoth Lay Siege to Zaremm," it is also a nod to the Lord Dunsany story "How Nuth Would Have Practiced His Art Upon the Gnoles." In this St. Clair story, your adventuring hero is instead a salesman naïve enough to believe his techniques for marketing rope would keep him from a bitter end. There is a dungeon adventure here of sorts, but it doesn't involve clashing swords or misfired traps. As quests go, it all seems a little polite and well mannered, despite the horror.

Fred Saberhagen's *Changeling Earth* appears in Appendix N as the only novel of his mentioned by name, but I preferred to note the "et al" after the title to look at Saberhagen's *Books of Swords* series, because, well, magic swords. Saberhagen's *Sword* books are typical of the "dying earth" subgenre of fantasy literature, where in the far future technology has given way to magic. A quest for what are known as the twelve swords of power drives the plot of the novels, each represented in the poem included here.

Seven of the authors contained herein cite Lord Dunsany as being an influence on their work. While not as well-known as folks like Lovecraft and J. R. R. Tolkien, Lord Dunsany created his own mythologies that almost demand we read them over and over again so as to never forget. Any number of Lord Dunsany's tales would have fit in this anthology, but the "The Fortress Unvanquishable, Save for Sacnoth" from 1908 is timeless, a phantasmagoria of what are now fantasy tropes; dragons, wizards, magic swords, towering citadels, sorcery, a frightened populace, and a hero rising to the challenge.

In *Dragon* magazine #94, published in March of 1985, Gary Gygax offered up a short essay on the little influence J.R.R. Tolkien's work had on the development of Dungeons & Dragons. Instead, Gygax writes, it was authors such as Robert E. Howard, Fritz Leiber, Poul Anderson, H. P. Lovecraft, as well as the often overlooked A. Merritt. Merritt is of course also named in the original Appendix N as well as in the proto-Appendix "Fantasy/ Swords & Sorcery: Recommended Reading" Gygax wrote for *Dragon* #4 in 1976. In Merritt's story "The People of the Pit," a pair of explorers are travelling in an unnamed wilderness when they discover a man desperately crawling towards them, dragging along with him a tale of the undreamt of horrors he unwittingly discovered at the bottom of a chasm. Originally published in 1918, the tale did not likely stand out among the myriad other pulp adventures of the time, except that Merritt had already distinguished himself has being particularly adept at writing about forgotten and alien peoples that inhabit the bowels of the Earth. Merritt—a devoted reader and collector of occult texts—was interested in the theosophical roots of many of these theories and in a strange turn, would influence those who believed his fictions contained hidden truths such as Richard Shaver, an author known for his "true-life-tales" in which he claims to have discovered ancient and advanced technologies hidden in the mysterious recesses of earth's substrata.

Andre Norton, one of the most prolific of the authors listed in Gygax's Appendix N, is best known for her *Witch World* series, a collection of novels and short stories about a planet in another universe where the laws of magic are akin to science. Norton was likely the only Appendix N author to actually play D&D with Gygax, and she would go on to publish *Quag Keep* in 1978, a novel in which a group of gamers are transported to the world of Greyhawk. (An excerpt from this novel appeared in *Dragon* magazine #12.) For this collection I chose "Legacy From Sorn Fen," one of the lesser-known *Witch World* tales. Herein is the strange fate of an ambitious warlord who tries to steal power that he neither earns or deserves. The story contains minor quests, rewards for good deeds, and even better, is told by a bard.

It's unfortunate for us that Gygax does not list any of the specific comic books that influenced him. Nevertheless, one of the named authors was also a comic book writer. Gardner Fox, whose sword and sorcery stories starring Kothar the Barbarian and Kyrik the "Warlock

Sorcerer" are name checked in Appendix N, was even better known as one of the creators of the Golden Age Flash, Hawkman, Doctor Fate, and the magician Zatanna. Before Kothar, however, Fox tried his hand at another barbarian, this one named Crom, who appeared as a comic strip in two issues of *Out of This World Adventures* from 1950. As a way of paying respect to both Gygax's list and Fox's career as a comic book writer, I chose to include the first Crom the Barbarian story, illustrated by John Giunta.

I also turned to Moldvay's "Inspirational Source Material" for the two authors I have convinced myself Gygax read and influenced D&D, but for some inscrutable reason chose to leave out: Clark Ashton Smith and C. L. Moore.

Choosing a Smith story was easy. In an unimaginable future, beyond all histories, sits the lone continent of Zothique. Built on top of countless tombs and burial sites, the land is populated by decadent nobles, foul sorcerers, desert nomads, and of course, necromancers. "Empire of the Necromancers" is the first in a series of stories known as the Zothique cycle, and first appeared in *Weird Tales*, September 1932. There, the editors describe the tale as "An endless army of plague-eaten bodies, of tattered skeletons, poured in ghastly torrents through the city streets." Smith is not mentioned in the original Appendix N, but I am going to assume that was simply an oversight. It's impossible to imagine the lurid undead creatures found in the *Monster Manual* and other materials weren't born from Gygax's reading of Smith.

It is also surprising to not see C. L. Moore in the original Appendix N (even Moldvay only mentions her in passing), as she was likely one the authors Gygax would have encountered in his reading of the pulps. Sword & Sorcery has long skirted on the edge of what is usually termed "weird" fiction, due in large part to Robert E. Howard's friendship with H. P. Lovecraft and his subsequent stories related to the Cthulhu mythos. While Howard's Conan does not encounter the Old Ones or other mythos-horrors, the famed barbarian is often found dealing with infernal geometric bending magic, strange gods, and lost languages. From out of the imagination of C. L. Moore, Gygax might not only have found the uncanny blend of sword and spiritual madness, but a heroine named Jirel, a woman of deep courage, fighting prowess, and religious conviction. In "Black God's Kiss," Jirel is forced to accept a satanic gift to destroy a conquering king squatting in her castle. Gygax makes special note in the first edition of the *Players Handbook* that playable characters can be men or women, and I like to think he had Jirel of Joiry as his model for what a female character might look like.

I propose that the term Appendix N has come to mean anyone's list of texts and media that influence their own roleplaying experiences. For myself, I came of age with D&D in the late 1970s when I found my way to one of the first gaming stores. In 1978 my older brother drove me to the Compleat Strategist in Hollywood, Florida. He had heard from some friends about this odd new game, Dungeons & Dragons, and took me over to see if they carried it. This was my first exposure to not only D&D, but to wargames and RPGs more generally. The proprietor looked a lot like me, only he was 20 years older and about two feet taller. He had blond greasy hair, thick glasses, and he kept his fingernails long and manicured, which I later learned was so he could easily pick up the die-cut pieces of the massive war games he sold and played: *PanzerBlitz*, *Wooden Ships & Iron Men*, *Starship Troopers*. Over the next year. I was in the store every Sunday and roamed the floor, looking at the D&D miniatures, supplements and third-party modules. At home, when I wasn't playing with my small gaming group, I pored over the D&D rules, mapped out dungeons, and painted lead figurines.

My imagination was awash with the resurgent interest in Sword & Sorcery stories that helped to populate the landscape of the 1970s with comic books like *Kull*, *John Carter* and *Savage Sword of Conan*. There was also a post-1960s psychedelic haze that still lingered even into the later part of the decade. Dr. Strange was travelling the astral planes to save our realm from demons and other evil magics, Frank Frazetta's warriors and sorcerers donned the covers of the comic magazines *Creepy* and *Eerie*. My dungeons for D&D games were—in the theater of my mind—populated by Ray Harryhausen's skeletons, my wizards looked like Gandalf from the 1977 animated version of *The Hobbit* by Arthur Rankin Jr. and Jules Bass, and the orcs marched to the beat of Rush.

To this end, I offer what I hope to be a preview of the next volume of this anthology, one that is representative of the books and comics that came to define the D&D of my own childhood. "The Sword of Dragonus," written and illustrated by Frank Brunner—best known for his work on *Doctor Strange* for Marvel Comics in the 1970s—first appeared in 1971 in the fanzine *Phase* #1, a prime example of the heyday of fantasy and science fiction small-press magazines of the late 1960s and 1970s. The story would later be reprinted in the Marvel Comics magazine *Monsters Unleashed* #2, from September 1973.

My own Appendix N would look very little like Gygax's original, but much of what impacted my own experiences with D&D are simply the later narratives that are only possible because of the selection found in the *Dungeon Masters Guide*. So just as D&D—born out of an imagination steeped in pulp and weird fantasy—would carve out an immense cavern of wonders related to RPGs and pop culture, so too would those very same texts influence uncountable fiction writers, filmmakers and game designers. Appendix N is not simply a list of texts that Gygax thought highly of. Rather, it's a monument to the triumph of fantasy literature in every aspect of pop culture.

Peter Bebergal, Cambridge, Massachusetts, 2024

KEY TO UPPER LEVEL

How Sargoth Lay Siege To Zaremm

Lin Carter (1930-1988)

They say in Simrana: when Sargoth ruled in Thole there was never such a mighty man of war.

He took Yarz with his spears, and Darbool with his archers, and Naraba he quelled with one bright glimpse of his sword.

As for Aj, that tall-towered city, it fell before the terror of his awful name, whispered once before the gates thereof.

O never was there such a man of war!

Filled with the glory he had won from Yarz and Darbool, and also Naraba, and moreover Aj of the Towers, he rested for a time. The mornings he passed lolling in his tent of tapestries taken in war; the afternoons he sat in a terrible throne fashioned of the skulls of all the warriors and champions he had bested and slain; the evenings he sprawled on many fat cushions stuffed with the beards of conquered kings, listening to harpers sing of his prowess.

He drank very much wine from cups of silver and gold, from goblets of onyx and jade, from ewers of chalcedony.

Once each hour, at the changing of the guard, all his host would strike their swords against their shields like stricken bells, and cry out with one voice: Hail to Sargoth, that mighty man of war, for never was there such as he!

One evening as the Moon rose, a globe of pallid opal, very fair against the purple sky, he drowsed upon his many cushions, and mayhap he slept a little, and the harpers stilled their song and spake quietly one to the other.

And one harper said: A mighty man of war is our Lord; there be none greater.

Aye, aye, the harpers nodded, and one said: He is very great, for he hath taken Yarz; Darbool, too, hath he whelmed with his archers; and Naraba, and even many-towered Aj.

But another said: He hath not taken Zaremm. Zaremm stands and is unconquered in war. No man hath ever taken Zaremm.

And the harpers shook their heads and sighed, one to the other, and that softly: Nay, he be mighty in war, our Lord; but of course he hath not taken Zaremm.

And with dawn Sargoth arose and did on his armor of blazing gold, his great cloak the color of manblood, and his plumed helm the Gnomes had fashioned in the likeness of the visage of Death.

As captive princes knelt in the dust to do on his greaves, he spake in a negligent and careless tone to his captains: There be a town near about, and its name be Zaremm. Know ye aught of it?

And the captains nodded, and stroked their great beards and said: Aye, dread Lord, the name be known to us. It lies beyond the hills, thus and so.

Then let us go up against Zaremm, quoth Sargoth, while the widows of emperors did on his spurs.

Dread Lord, said the captains, hurriedly, and not looking him full in the eye, mayhap it would be better to wend south away, to Araboul, where there be sapphires, or north to Hurz, where the spikenard tree groweth.

Mayhap, said he, and mayhap not. Is the King of Zaremm, then, so mighty a man of war as I?

Great Sargoth, said the captains, and very quickly, there be no king in Zaremm. There, it is told, the Magicians rule.

Ah! Then let us forth to Zaremm, quoth he, for I fear no wise men. There is no wisdom hath a sharper edge than this my great sword! And he mounted his destrier, while the orphaned daughters of extinguished dynasties held the reins.

And greatly daring, one of the older captains knelt, and put his grey beard in the dust before him, saying: O Sargoth, there is a name for Zaremm.

What name is that? He asked carelessly, taking up his great spear.

And the old captain whispered: Men call it The City That May Not Be Taken In War.

It is a goodly name, he smiled, and all the trumpets screamed.

As the host drew about the walls of Zaremm, Sargoth, that mighty man of war, looked forth and saw it was a goodly town. The walls they were tall and strong and set about with carven monsters of stone like mighty gargoyles.

He saw also that no warriors manned those walls, and this interested him the more.

He lifted his left hand very slightly, and a thousand men in black main strode forth under great shields, loudly calling the folk of Zaremm to pray unto their Gods, for their doom was at hand. But no sounds arose from the city, which slumbered beneath the noon, and no bugles cried warning; naught chanced in any wise.

He lifted his right hand ever so little, and a thousand men in burnished bronze stepped forth bearing mighty rams and engines wherewith to force the gates and topple the walls. He saw now that a few aged men had strayed forth upon the battlements, and stood, leaning upon their elbows, gazing down at the great glittering host encamped below their walls

They were lean and old, with snowy beards adown their breasts. Wrapped in voluminous robes of mystic purple were they, scrawled all over with strange signs in gleaming silver. They leaned idly, looking down, and one of them yawned.

HOW SARGOTH LAY SIEGE TO ZAREMM

And Sargoth reined his restive steed with an iron hand, mailed in gold, and raised his flashing sword to signal the assault, and in that same moment one of the sleepy old men of the battlements above spoke out, lazily, a certain Word.

The hills shuddered at the sound of it, and the earth groaned beneath their feet at the hearing thereof.

And, as the first stone wing unfolded and the first mighty claw of granite scraped and squealed against the battlements, and the first stone dragon lifted its terribly-horned head ere it launched itself forth from the walls like a titanic juggernaut to crush and kill, then it was that Sargoth knew why they called Zaremm The City That May Not Be Taken In War.

And the Siege of Zaremm was the briefest in all the annals of war. Or so they tell the tale in Simrana.

The Tale of Hauk

Poul Anderson (1926-2001)

A man called Geirolf dwelt on the Great Fjord in Raumsdal. His father was Bui Hardhand, who owned a farm inland near the Dofra Fell. One year Bui went in viking to Finnmark and brought back a woman he dubbed Gydha. She became the mother of Geirolf. But because Bui already had children by his wife, there would be small inheritance for this by-blow.

Folk said uncanny things about Gydha. She was fair to see, but spoke little, did no more work than she must, dwelt by herself in a shack out of sight of the garth, and often went for long stridings alone on the upland heaths, heedless of cold, rain, and rovers. Bui did not visit her often. Her son Geirolf did. He too was a moody sort, not much given to playing with others, quick and harsh of temper. Big and strong, he went abroad with his father already when he was twelve, and in the next few years won the name of a mighty though ruthless fighter.

Then Gydha died. They buried her near her shack, and it was whispered that she spooked around it of nights. Soon after, walking home with some men by moonlight from a feast at a neighbor's, Bui clutched his breast and fell dead. They wondered if Gydha had called him, maybe to accompany her home to Finnmark, for there was no more sight of her.

Geirolf bargained with his kin and got the price of a ship for himself. Thereafter he gathered a crew, mostly younger sons and a wild lot, and fared west. For a long while he harried Scotland, Ireland, and the coasts south of the Channel, and won much booty. With some of this he bought his farm on the Great Fjord. Meanwhile he courted Thyra, a daughter of the yeoman Sigtryg Einarsson, and got her.

They had one son early on, Hauk, a bright and lively lad. But thereafter five years went by until they had a daughter who lived, Unn, and two years later a boy they called Einar. Geirolf was in viking every summer, and sometimes wintered over in the Westlands. Yet he was a kindly father, whose children were always glad to see him come roaring home. Very tall and broad in the shoulders, he had long red-brown hair and a full beard around a broad blunt-nosed face whose eyes were ice blue and slanted. He liked fine clothes and heavy gold rings, which he also lavished on Thyra.

Then the time came when Geirolf said he felt poorly and would not fare elsewhere that season. Hauk was fourteen years old and had been wild to go. "I'll keep my promise to you as well as may be," Geirolf said, and sent men asking around. The best he could do was get his son a bench on a ship belonging to Ottar the Wide-Faring from Haalogaland in the north, who was trading along the coast and meant to do likewise overseas.

Hauk and Ottar took well to each other. In England, the man got the boy prime-signed so he could deal with Christians. Though neither was baptized, what he heard while they wintered there made Hauk thoughtful. Next spring they fared south to trade among the Moors, and did not come home until late fall.

Ottar was Geirolf's guest for a while, though he scowled to himself when his host broke into fits of deep coughing. He offered to take Hauk along on his voyages from now on and start the youth toward a good livelihood.

"You a chapman—the son of a viking?" Geirolf sneered. He had grown surly of late.

Hauk flushed. "You've heard what we did to those Vikings who set on us," he answered.

"Give our son his head," was Thyra's smiling rede, "or he'll take the bit between his teeth."

The upshot was that Geirolf grumbled agreement, and Hauk fared off. He did not come back for five years.

Long were the journeys he took with Ottar. By ship and horse, they made their way to Uppsala in Svithjodh, thence into the wilderness of the Keel after pelts; amber they got on the windy strands of jutland, salt herring along the Sound; seeking beeswax, honey, and tallow, they pushed beyond Holmgard to the fair at Kiev; walrus ivory lured them past North Cape, through bergs and floes to the land of the fur-clad Biarmians; and they bore many goods west. They did not hide that the wish to see what was new to them drove them as hard as any hope of gain.

In those days King Harald Fairhair went widely about in Norway, bringing all the land under himself. Lesser kings and chieftains must either plight faith to him or meet his wrath; it crushed whomever would stand fast. When he entered Raumsdal, he sent men from garth to garth as was his wont, to say he wanted oaths and warriors.

"My older son is abroad," Geirolf told these, "and my younger still a stripling. As for myself—" He coughed, and blood flecked his beard. The king's men did not press the matter.

But now Geirolf's moods grew worse. He snarled at everybody, cuffed his children and housefolk, once drew a dagger and stabbed to death a thrall who chanced to spill some soup on him. When Thyra reproached him for this, he said only, "Let them know I am not altogether hallowed out. I can still wield blade." And he looked at her so threateningly from beneath his shaggy brows that she, no coward, withdrew in silence.

A year later, Hauk Geirolfsson returned to visit his parents.

That was on a chill fall noontide. Whitecaps chopped beneath a whistling wind and cast spindrift salty onto lips. Clifftops on either side of the fjord were lost in mist. Above blew cloud wrack like smoke. Hauk's ship, a wide-beamed knorr, rolled, pitched, and creaked as it beat its way under sail. The owner stood in the bows, wrapped in a flame-red cloak, an uncommonly big young man, yellow hair tossing around a face akin to his father's, weatherbeaten though still scant of beard. When he saw the arm of the fjord that he wanted to enter, he pointed with a spear at whose head he had bound a silk pennon. When he saw Disafoss pouring in a white stream down the blue-gray stone wall to larboard, and beyond the waterfall at the end of that arm lay his old home, he shouted for happiness.

Geirolf had rich holdings. The hall bulked over all else, heavy-timbered, brightly painted, dragon heads arching from rafters and gables. Elsewhere around the yard were cookhouse, smokehouse, bathhouse, storehouses, workshop, stables, barns, women's bower. Several cabins for hirelings and their families were strewn beyond. Fishing boats lay on the strand near a shed which held the master's dragonship. Behind the steading, land sloped sharply upward through a narrow dale, where fields were walled with stones grubbed out of them and now stubbled after harvest. A bronze-leaved oakenshaw stood untouched not far from the buildings; and a mile inland, where hills humped themselves toward the mountains, rose a darkling wall of pinewood.

Spearheads and helmets glimmered ashore. But men saw it was a single craft bound their way, white shield on the mast. As the hull slipped alongside the little wharf, they lowered their weapons. Hauk sprang from bow to dock in a single leap and whooped.

Geirolf trod forth. "Is that you, my son?" he called. His voice was hoarse from coughing; he had grown gaunt and sunken-eyed; the ax that he bore shivered in his hand.

"Yes, father, yes, home again," Hauk stammered. He could not hide his shock.

Maybe this drove Geirolf to anger. Nobody knew; he had become impossible to get along with. "I could well-nigh have hoped otherwise," he rasped. "An unfriend would give me something better than straw-death."

The rest of the men, housecarls and thralls alike, flocked about Hauk to bid him welcome. Among them was a burly, grizzled yeoman whom he knew from aforetime, Leif Egilsson, a neighbor come to dicker for a horse. When he was small, Hauk had often wended his way over a woodland trail to Leif's garth to play with the children there.

He called his crew to him. They were not just Norse, but had among them Danes, Swedes, and English, gathered together over the years as he found them trustworthy. "You brought a mickle for me to feed," Geirolf said. Luckily, the wind bore his words from all but Hauk. "Where's your master Ottar?"

The young man stiffened. "He's my friend, never my master," he answered. "This is my own ship, bought with my own earnings. Ottar abides in England this year. The West Saxons have a new king, one Alfred, whom he wants to get to know."

"Time was when it was enough to know how to get sword past a Westman's shield," Geirolf grumbled.

Seeing peace down by the water, women and children hastened from the hall to meet the newcomers. At their head went Thyra. She was tall and deep-bosomed; her gown blew around a form still straight and freely striding. But as she neared, Hauk saw that the gold of her braids was dimmed and sorrow had furrowed her face. Nonetheless she kindled when she knew him. "Oh, thrice welcome, Hauk!" she said low. "How long can you bide with us?"

After his father's greeting, it had been in his mind to say he must soon be off. But when he spied who walked behind his mother, he said, "We thought we might be guests here the winter through, if that's not too much of a burden."

"Never—" began Thyra. Then she saw where his gaze had gone, and suddenly she smiled.

Alfhild Leifsdottir had joined her widowed father on this visit. She was two years younger than Hauk, but they had been glad of each other as playmates. Today she stood a maiden grown, lissome in a blue wadmal gown, heavily crowned with red locks above great green eyes, straight nose, and gently curved mouth. Though he had known many a woman, none struck him as being so fair.

He grinned at her and let his cloak flap open to show his finery of broidered, fur-lined tunic, linen shirt and breeks, chased leather boots, gold on arms and neck and sword-hilt. She paid them less heed than she did him when they spoke.

Thus Hauk and his men moved to Geirolf's hall. He brought plentiful gifts, there was ample food and drink, and their tales of strange lands—their songs, dances, games, jests, manners—made them good housefellows in these lengthening nights.

Already on the next morning, he walked out with Alfhild. Rain had cleared the air, heaven and fjord sparkled, wavelets chuckled beneath a cool breeze from the woods. Nobody else was on the strand where they went.

"So you grow mighty as a chapman, Hauk," Alfhild teased. "Have you never gone in viking... only once, only to please your father?"

"No," he answered gravely, "I fail to see what manliness lies in falling on those too weak to defend themselves. We graders must be stronger and more war-skilled than any who may seek to plunder us." A thick branch of driftwood, bleached and hardened, lay nearby. Hauk picked it up and snapped it between his hands. Two other men would have had trouble doing that. It gladdened him to see Alfhild glow at the sight. "Nobody has tried us twice," he said.

They passed the shed where Geirolf's dragon lay on rollers. Hauk opened the door for a peek at the remembered slim shape. A sharp whiff from the loom within brought his nose wrinkling. "Whew!" he snorted. "Dry rot."

"Poor Fireworm has long lain idle," Alfhild sighed. "In later years, your father's illness has gnawed him till he doesn't even see to the care of his ship. He knows he will never take it a-roving again."

"I feared that," Hauk murmured.

"We grieve for him on our own garth too," she said. "In former days, he was a staunch friend to us. Now we bear with his ways, yes, insults that would make my father draw blade on anybody else."

"That is dear of you," Hauk said, staring straight before him. "I'm very thankful."

"You have not much cause for that, have you?" she asked. "I mean, you've been away so long... Of course, you have your mother. She's borne the brunt, stood like a shield before your siblings—" She touched her lips, "I talk too much."

"You talk as a friend," he blurted. "May we always be friends."

They wandered on, along a path from shore to fields. It went by the shaw. Through boles and boughs and falling leaves, they saw Thor's image and altar among the trees. "I'll make offering here for my father's health." Hauk said, "though truth to tell, I've more faith in my own strength than in any gods."

"You have seen lands where strange gods rule," she nodded.

"Yes, and there too, they do not steer things well," he said. "It was in a Christian realm that a huge wolf came raiding flocks, on which no iron would bite. When it took a baby from a hamlet near our camp, I thought I'd be less than a man did I not put an end to it."

"What happened?" she asked breathlessly, and caught his arm.

"I wrestled it barehanded—no foe of mine was ever more fell— and at last broke its neck." He pulled back a sleeve to show scars of terrible bites.

"Dead, it changed into a man they had outlawed that year for his evil deeds. We burned the lich to make sure it would not walk again, and thereafter the folk had peace. And... we had friends, in a country otherwise wary of us."

She looked on him in the wonder he had hoped for.

Erelong she must return with her father. But the way between the garths was just a few miles, and Hauk often rode or skied through the woods. At home, he and his men helped do what work there was, and gave merriment where it had long been little known.

Thyra owned this to her son, on a snowy day when they were by themselves. They were in the women's bower, whither they had gone to see a tapestry she was weaving. She wanted to know how it showed against those of the Westlands; he had brought one such, which hung above the benches in the hall. Here, in the wide quiet room, was dusk, for the day outside had become a tumbling whiteness. Breath steamed from lips as the two of them spoke. It smelled sweet; both had drunk mead until they could talk freely.

"You did better than you knew when you came back," Thyra said. "You blew like a spring into this winter of ours. Einar and Unn were withering; they blossom again in your nearness."

"Strangely has our father changed," Hauk answered sadly. "I remember once when I was small, how he took me by the hand on a frost-clear night, led me forth under the stars, and named for me the pictures in them, Thor's Wain, Freyja's Spindle—how wonderful he made them, how his deep slow laughterful voice filled the dark."

"A wasting illness draws the soul inward," his mother said. "He... has no more manhood... and it tears him like fangs that he will die helpless in bed. He must strike out at someone, and here we are."

She was silent a while before she added: "He will not live out the year. Then you must take over."

"I must be gone when weather allows," Hauk warned. "I promised Ottar."

"Return as soon as may be," Thyra said. "We have need of a strong man, the more so now when yonder King Harald would reave their freehold rights from yeomen."

"It would be well to have a hearth of my own." Hauk stared past her, toward the unseen woods. Her worn face creased in a smile.

Suddenly they heard yells from the yard below. Hauk ran out onto the gallery and looked down. Geirolf was shambling after an aged carl named Atli. He had a whip in his hand and was lashing it across the white locks and wrinkled cheeks of the man who could not run fast either and who sobbed.

"What is this?" broke from Hauk. He swung himself over the rail, hung, and let go. The drop would at least have jarred the wind out of most. He, though, bounced from where he landed, ran behind his father, caught hold of the whip and wrenched it from Geirolf's grasp. "What are you doing?"

Geirolf howled and struck his son with a doubled fist. Blood trickled from Hauk's mouth. He stood fast. Atli sank to hands and knees and fought not to weep.

"Are you also a heelbiter of mine?" Geirolf bawled.

"I'd save you from your madness, father," Hauk said in pain. "Atli followed you to battle ere I was born—he dandled me on his knee—and he's a free man. What has he done, that you'd bring down on us the anger of his kinfolk?"

"Harm not the skipper, young man," Atli begged. "I fled because I'd sooner die than lift hand against my skipper."

"Hell swallow you both!" Geirolf would have cursed further, but the coughing came on him. Blood drops flew through the snowflakes, down onto the white earth, where they mingled with the drip from the heads of Hauk and Atli. Doubled over, Geirolf let them half lead, half carry him to his shut-bed. There he closed the panel and lay alone in darkness.

"What happened between you and him?" Hauk asked.

"I was fixing to shoe a horse," Atli said into a ring of gaping onlookers. "He came in and wanted to know why I'd not asked his leave. I told him 'twas plain Kilfaxi needed new shoes. Then he hollered, 'I'll show you I'm no log in the woodpile!' and snatched yon whip off the wall and took after me!" The old man squared his shoulders. "We'll speak no more of this, you hear?" he ordered the household.

Not did Geirolf, when next day he let them bring him some broth.

For more reasons than this, Hauk came to spend much of this time at Leif's garth. He would return in such a glow that even the reproachful looks of his young sister and brother, even the sullen or the weary greeting of his father, could not dampen it.

At last, when lengthening days and quickening blood bespoke seafarings soon to come, that happened which surprised nobody. Hauk told them in the hall that he wanted to marry Alfhild Leifsdottir, and prayed Geirolf press the suit for him. "What must be, will be," said his father, a better grace than awaited. Union of the families was clearly good for both.

Leif Egilsson agreed, and Alfhild had nothing but aye to say. The betrothal feast crowded the whole neighborhood together in cheer. Thyra hid the trouble within her, and Geirolf himself was calm if not blithe.

Right after, Hauk and his men were busking themselves to fare. Regardless of his doubts about gods, he led in offering for a safe voyage to Thor, Aegir, and St. Michael. But Alfhild found herself a quiet place alone, to cut runes on an ash tree in the name of Freyja.

When all was ready, she was there with the folk of Geirolf's stead to see the sailors off. That morning was keen, wind roared in trees and skirled between cliffs, waves ran green and white beneath small flying clouds. Unn could not but hug her brother who was going, while Einar gave him a handclasp that shook. Thyra said, "Come home hale and early, my son." Alfhild mostly stored away the sight of Hauk. Atli and others of the household mumbled this and that.

Geirolf shuffled forward. The cane on which he leaned rattled among the stones of the beach. He was hunched in a hairy cloak against the sharp air. His locks fell tangled almost to the coal-smoldering eyes. "Father, farewell," Hauk said, taking his free hand.

"You mean 'fare far,' don't you?" Geirolf grated. "'Fare far and never come back.' You'd like that, wouldn't you? But we will meet again. Oh, yes, we will meet again."

16

Hauk dropped the hand. Geirolf turned and sought the house. The rest behaved as if they had not heard, speaking loudly, amidst yelps of laughter, to overcome those words of foreboding. Soon Hauk called his orders to begone.

Men scrambled aboard the laden ship. Its sail slatted aloft and filled, the mooring lines were cast loose, the hull stood out to sea. Alfhild waved until it was gone from sight behind the bend where Disafoss fell.

The summer passed—plowing, sowing, lambing, calving, farrowing, hoeing, reaping, flailing, butchering—rain, hail, sun, stars, loves, quarrels, births, deaths—and the season wore toward fall. Alfhild was seldom at Geirolf's garth, nor was Leif; for Hauk's father grew steadily worse. After midsummer he could no longer leave his bed. But often he whispered, between lung-tearing coughs, to those who tended him, "I would kill you if I could."

On a dark day late in the season, when rain roared about the hall and folk and hounds huddled close to fires that hardly lit the gloom around, Geirolf awoke from a heavy sleep. Thyra marked it and came to him. Cold and dankness gnawed their way through her clothes. The fever was in him like a brand. He plucked restlessly at his blanket, where he half sat in his short shut-bed. Though flesh had wasted from the great bones, his fingers still had strength to tear the wool. The mattress rustled under him. "Straw-death, straw-death," he muttered.

Thyra laid a palm on his brow. "Be at ease," she said.

It dragged from him: "You'll not be rid... of me... so fast... by straw-death." An icy sweat broke forth and the last struggle began.

Long it was, Geirolf's gasps and the sputtering flames the only noises within that room, while rain and wind ramped outside and night drew in. Thyra stood by the bedside to wipe the sweat off her man, blood and spittle from his beard. A while after sunset, he rolled his eyes back and died.

Thyra called for water and lamps. She cleansed him, clad him in his best, and laid him out. A drawn sword was on his breast.

THE TALE OF HAUK

In the morning, thralls and carls alike went forth under her orders. A hillock stood in the fields about half a mile inland from the house. They dug a grave chamber in the top of this, lining it well with timber. "Won't you bury him in his ship?" asked Atli.

"It is rotten, unworthy of him," Thyra said. Yet she made them haul it to the barrow, around which she had stones to outline a hull. Meanwhile folk readied a grave-ale, and messengers bade neighbors come.

When all were there, men of Geirolf's carried him on a litter to his resting place and put him in, together with weapons and a jar of Southland coins. After beams had roofed the chamber, his friends from aforetime took shovels and covered it well. They replaced the turfs of sere grass, leaving the hillock as it had been save that it was now bigger. Einar Thorolfsson kindled his father's ship. It burned till dusk, when the horns of the new moon stood over the ford. Meanwhile folk had gone back down to the garth to feast and drink. Riding home next day, well gifted by Thyra, they told each other that this had been an honorable burial.

The moon waxed. On the first night that it rose full, Geirolf came again.

A thrall named Kark had been late in the woods, seeking a strayed sheep. Coming home, he passed near the howe. The moon was barely above the pines; long shivery beams of light ran on the water, lost themselves in shadows ashore, glinted wanly anew where a bedewed stone wall snaked along a stubblefield. Stars were few. A great stillness lay on the land, not even an owl hooted, until all at once dogs down in the garth began howling. It was not the way they howled at the moon; across the mile between, it sounded ragged and terrified. Kark felt the chill close in around him, and hastened toward home.

Something heavy trod the earth. He looked around and saw the bulk of a huge man coming across the field from the barrow. "Who's that?" he called uneasily. No voice replied, but the weight

18

of those footfalls shivered through the ground into his bones. Kark swallowed, gripped his staff, and stood where he was. But then the shape came so near that moonlight picked out the head of Geirolf. Kark screamed, dropped his weapon, and ran.

Geirolf followed slowly, clumsily behind.

Down in the garth, light glimmered red as doors opened. Folk saw Kark running, gasping for breath. Atli and Einar led the way out, each with a torch in one hand, a sword in the other. Little could they see beyond the wild flame-gleam. Kark reached them, fell, writhed on the hard-beaten clay of the yard, and wailed.

"What is it, you lackwit?" Atli snapped, and kicked him. Then Einar pointed his blade.

"A stranger—" Atli began.

Geirolf rocked into sight. The mould of the grave clung to him. His eyes stared unblinking, unmoving, blank in the moonlight, out of a gray face whereon the skin crawled. The teeth in his tangled beard were dry. No breath smoked from his nostrils. He held out his arms, crook-fingered.

"Father!" Einar cried. The torch hissed from his grip, flickered weakly at his feet, and went out. The men at his back jammed the doorway of the hall as they sought its shelter.

"The skipper's come again," Atli quavered. He sheathed his sword, though that was hard when his hand shook, and made himself step forward. "Skipper, d'you know your old shipmate Atli?"

The dead man grabbed him, lifted him, and dashed him to earth. Einar heard bones break. Atli jerked once and lay still. Geirolf trod him and Kark underfoot. There was a sound of cracking and rending. Blood spurted forth.

Blindly, Einar swung blade. The edge smote but would not bite. A wave of grave-chill passed over him. He whirled and bounded back inside.

Thyra had seen. "Bar the door," she bade. The windows were

already shuttered against frost. "Men, stand fast. Women, stoke up the fires."

They heard the lich groping about the yard. Walls creaked where Geirolf blundered into them. Thyra called through the door, "Why do you wish us ill, your own household?" But only those noises gave answer. The hounds cringed and whined.

"Lay iron at the doors and under every window," Thyra commanded. "If it will not cut him, it may keep him out."

All that night, then, folk huddled in the hall. Geirolf climbed onto the roof and rode the ridgepole, drumming his heels on the shakes till the whole building boomed. A little before sunrise, it stopped. Peering out by the first dull dawnlight, Thyra saw no mark of her husband but his deep-sunken footprints and the wrecked bodies he had left.

"He grew so horrible before he died," Unn wept. "Now he can't rest, can he?"

"We'll make him an offering," Thyra said through her weariness. "It may be we did not give him enough when we buried him."

Few would follow her to the howe. Those who dared, brought along the best horse on the farm. Einar, as the son of the house when Hauk was gone, himself cut its throat after a sturdy man had given the hammer-blow. Carls and wenches butchered the carcass, which Thyra poured what was left over the bones, upon the grave.

Two ravens circled in sight, waiting for folk to go so they could take the food. "Is that a good sign?" Thyra sighed. "Will Odin fetch Geirolf home?"

That night everybody who had not fled to neighboring steads gathered in the hall. Soon after the moon rose, they heard the footfalls come nearer and nearer. They heard Geirolf break into the storehouse and worry the laid-out bodies of Atil and Kark. They heard him kill cows in the barn. Again he rode the roof.

In the morning Leif Egilsson arrived, having gotten the news. He found Thyra too tired and shaken to do anything further.

"The ghost did not take your offering," he said, "but maybe the gods will."

In the oakenshaw, he led the giving of more beasts. There was talk of a thrall for Odin, but he said that would not help if this did not. Instead, he saw to the proper burial of the slain, and of those kine which nobody would dare eat. That night he abode there.

And Geirolf came back. Throughout the darkness, he tormented the home which had been his.

"I will bide here one more day," Leif said next sunrise. "We all need rest—though ill is it that we must sleep during daylight when we've so much readying for winter to do."

By that time, some other neighborhood men were also on hand. They spoke loudly of how they would hew the lich asunder.

"You know not what you boast of," said aged Grim the Wise. "Einar smote, and he strikes well for a lad, but the iron would not bite. It never will. Ghost-strength is in Geirolf, and all the wrath he could not set free during his life."

That night folk waited breathless for moonrise. But when the gnawed shield climbed over the pines, nothing stirred. The dogs, too, no longer seemed cowed. About midnight, Grim murmured into the shadows, "Yes, I thought so. Geirolf walks only when the moon is full."

"Then tomorrow we'll dig him up and burn him!" Leif said.

"No," Grim told them. "That would spell the worst of luck for everybody here. Don't you see, the anger and unpeace which will not let him rest, those would be forever unslaked? They could not but bring doom on the burners."

"What then can we do?" Thyra asked dully.

"Leave this stead," Grim counselled, "at least when the moon is full."

"Hard will that be," Einar sighed. "Would that my brother Hauk were here."

"He should have returned erenow," Thyra said. "May we in our woe never know that he has come to grief himself."

THE TALE OF HAUK

In truth, Hauk had not. His wares proved welcome in Flanders, where he bartered for cloth that he took across to England. There Ottar greeted him, and he met the young King Alfred. At that time there was no war going on with the Danes, who were settling into the Danelaw and thus in need of household goods. Hauk and Ottar did a thriving business among them. This led them to think they might do as well in Iceland, whither Norse folk were moving who liked not King Harald Fairhair. They made a voyage to see. Foul winds hampered them on the way home. Hence fall was well along when Hauk's ship returned.

The day was still and cold. Low overcast turned sky and water the hue of iron. A few gulls cruised and mewed, while under them sounded creak and splash of oars, swearing of men, as the knorr was rowed. At the end of the fjord-branch, garth and leaves were tiny splashes of color, lost against rearing cliffs, brown fields, murky wildwood. Straining ahead from afar, Hauk saw that a bare handful of men came down to the shore, moving listlessly more than watchfully. When his craft was unmistakable, though a few women—no youngsters—sped from the hall as if they could not wait. Their cries came to him more thin than the gulls'.

Hauk lay alongside the dock. Springing forth, he called merrily, "Where is everybody? How fares Alfhild?" His words lost themselves in silence. Fear touched him. "What's wrong?"

Thyra trod forth. Years might have gone by during his summer abroad, so changed was she. "You are barely in time," she said in an unsteady tone. Taking his hands, she told him how things stood.

Hauk stared long into emptiness. At last, "Oh, no," he whispered. "What's to be done?"

"We hoped you might know that, my son," Thyra answered. "The moon will be full tomorrow night."

His voice stumbled. "I am no wizard. If the gods themselves would not lay this ghost, what can I do?"

Einar spoke, in the brashness of youth: "We thought you might deal with him as you did with the werewolf."

"But that was—No, I cannot!" Hauk croaked. "Never ask me."

"Then I fear we must leave," Thyra said. "For aye. You see how many have already fled, thrall and free alike, though nobody else has a place for them. We've not enough left to farm these acres. And who would buy them of us? Poor must we go, helpless as the poor ever are."

"Iceland—" Hauk wet his lips. "Well, you shall not want while I live." Yet he had counted on this homestead, whether to dwell on or sell.

"Tomorrow we move over to Leif's garth, for the next three days and nights," Thyra said.

Unn shuddered. "I know not if I can come back," she said. "This whole past month here, I could hardly ever sleep." Dulled skin and sunken eyes bore her out.

"What else would you do?" Hauk asked.

"Whatever I can," she stammered, and broke into tears. He knew: wedding herself too young to whoever would have her dowryless, poor though the match would be—or making her way to some town to turn whore, his little sister.

"Let me think on this," Hauk begged. "Maybe I can hit on something."

His crew were also daunted when they heard. At eventide they sat in the hall and gave only a few curt words about what they had done in foreign parts. Everyone lay down early on bed, bench, or floor, but none slept well.

Before sunset, Hauk had walked forth alone. First he sought the grave of Atli. "I'm sorry, dear old friend," he said. Afterward he went to Geirolf's howe. It loomed yellow-gray with withered grass wherein grinned the skull of the slaughtered horse. At its foot were strewn the charred bits of the ship, inside stones which outlined a greater but unreal hull. Around reached stubblefields and walls, hemmed in by woods on one side and water on the other, rock lifting sheer beyond. The chill and the quiet had deepened.

THE TALE OF HAUK

Hauk climbed to the top of the barrow and stood there a while, head bent downward. "Oh, father," he said, "I learned doubt in Christian lands. What's right for me to do?" There was no answer. He made a slow way back to the dwelling.

All were up betimes next day. It went slowly over the woodland path to Leif's, for animals must be herded along. The swine gave more trouble than most. Hauk chuckled once, not very merrily, and remarked that at least this took folk's minds off their sorrows. He raised no mirth.

But he had Alfhild ahead of him. At the end of the way, he sprinted shouting into the yard. Leif owned less land than Geirolf, his buildings were smaller and fewer, most of his guests must house outdoors in sleeping bags. Hauk paid no heed. "Alfhild!" he called "I'm here!"

She left the dough she was kneading and sped to him. They hugged each other hard and long, in sight of the whole world. None thought that shame, as things were. At last she said, striving not to weep, "How we've longed for you! Now the nightmare can end."

He stepped back. "What mean you?" he uttered slowly, knowing full well.

"Why—" She was bewildered. "Won't you give him his second death?"

Hauk gazed past her for some heartbeats before he said: "Come aside with me."

Hand in hand, they wandered off. A meadow lay hidden from the garth by a stand of aspen. Elsewhere around, pines speared into a sky that today was bright. Clouds drifted on a nipping breeze. Far off, a stag bugled.

Hauk spread feet apart, hooked thumbs in belt, and made himself meet her eyes. "You think over-highly of my strength," he said.

"Who has more?" she asked. "We kept ourselves going by saying you would come home and make things good again."

"What if the drow is too much for me?" His words sounded raw through the hush. Leaves dropped yellow from their boughs.

She flushed. "Then your name will live."

"Yes—" Softly he spoke the words of the High One:

> "Kine die, kinfolk die,
> and so at last oneself.
> This I know that never dies;
> how dead men's deeds are deemed."

"You will do it!" she cried gladly.

His head shook before it drooped. "No. I will not. I dare not."

She stood as if he had clubbed her.

"Won't you understand?" he began.

The wound he had dealt her hopes went too deep. "So you show yourself a nithing!"

"Hear me," he said, shaken. "Were the lich anybody else's—"

Overwrought beyond reason, she slapped him and choked, "The gods bear witness, I give them my holiest oath, never will I wed you unless you do this thing. See, by my blood I swear." She whipped out her dagger and gashed her wrist. Red rills coursed out and fell in drops on the fallen leaves.

He was aghast. "You know not what you say. You're too young, you've been too sheltered. Listen."

She would have fled from him, but he gripped her shoulders and made her stand. "Listen," went between his teeth. "Geirolf is still my father—my father who begot me, reared me, named the stars for me, weaponed me to make my way in the world. How can I fight him? Did I slay him, what horror would come upon me and mine?"

"O-o-oh," broke from Alfhild. She sank to the ground and wept as if to tear loose her ribs.

He knelt, held her, gave what soothing he could. "Now I know,' she mourned. "Too late."

"Never," he murmured. "We'll fare abroad if we must, take new land, make new lives together."

"No," she gasped. "Did I not swear? What doom awaits an oath-breaker?"

Then he was long still. Heedlessly though she had spoken, her blood lay in the earth, which would remember.

He too was young. He straightened. "I will fight," he said.

Now she clung to him and pleaded that he must not. But an iron calm had come over him. "Maybe I will not be cursed," he said. "Or maybe the curse will be no more than I can bear."

"It will be mine too, I who brought it on you," she plighted herself. Hand in hand again, they went back to the garth. Leif spied the haggard look on them and half guessed what had happened. "Will you fare to meet the drow, Hauk?" he asked. "Wait till I can have Grim the Wise brought here. His knowledge may help you."

"No," said Hauk. "Waiting would weaken me. I go this night."

Wide eyes stared at him—all but Thyra's; she was too torn.

Toward evening he busked himself. He took no helm, shield, or byrnie, for the dead man bore no weapons. Some said they would come along, armored themselves well, and offered to be at his side. He told them to follow him, but no farther than to watch what happened. Their iron would be of no help, and he thought they would only get in each other's way, and his, when he met the over-human might of the drow. He kissed Alfhild, his mother, and his sister, and clasped hands with his brother, bidding them stay behind if they loved him.

Long did the few miles of path seem, and gloomy under the pines. The sun was on the world's rim when men came out in the open. They looked past fields and barrow down to the empty garth, the fjordside cliffs, the water where the sun lay as half an ember behind a trail of blood. Clouds hurried on a wailing wind through a greenish sky. Cold struck deep. A wolf howled.

"Wait here," Hauk said.

"The gods be with you," Leif breathed.

"I've naught tonight but my own strength," Hauk said. "Belike none of us ever had more."

His tall form, clad in leather and wadmal, showed black athwart

26

the sunset as he walked from the edge of the woods, out across plowland toward the crouching howe. The wind fluttered his locks, a last brightness until the sun went below. Then for a while the evenstar alone had light.

Hauk reached the mound. He drew sword and leaned on it, waiting. Dusk deepened. Star after star came forth, small and strange. Clouds blowing across them picked up a glow from the still unseen moon.

It rose at last above the treetops. Its ashen sheen stretched gashes of shadow across earth. The wind loudened.

The grave groaned. Turves, stones, timbers swung aside. Geirolf shambled out beneath the sky. Hauk felt the ground shudder under his weight. There came a carrion stench, though the only sign of rotting was on the dead man's clothes. His eyes peered dim, his teeth gnashed dry in a face at once well remembered and hideously changed. When he saw the living one who waited, he veered and lumbered thitherward.

"Father," Hauk called. "It's I, your eldest son."

The drow drew nearer.

"Halt, I beg you," Hauk said unsteadily. "What can I do to bring you peace?"

A cloud passed over the moon. It seemed to be hurtling through heaven. Geirolf reached for his son with fingers that were ready to clutch and tear. "Hold," Hauk shrilled. "No step farther."

He could not see if the gaping mouth grinned. In another stride, the great shape came well-nigh upon him. He lifted his sword and brought it singing down. The edge struck truly, but slid aside. Geirolf's skin heaved, as if to push the blade away. In one more step, he laid grave-cold hands around Hauk's neck.

Before that grip could close, Hauk dropped his useless weapon, brought his wrists up between Geirolf's, and mightily snapped them apart. Nails left furrows, but he was free. He sprang back, into a wrestler's stance.

Geirolf moved in, reaching. Hauk hunched under those arms

and himself grabbed waist and thigh. He threw his shoulder against a belly like rock. Any live man would have gone over, but the lich was too heavy.

Geirolf smote Hauk on the side. The blows drove him to his knees and thundered on his back. A foot lifted to crush him. He rolled off and found his own feet again. Geirolf lurched after him. The hastening moon linked their shadows. The wolf howled anew, but in fear. Watching men gripped spear shafts till their knuckles stood bloodless.

Hauk braced his legs and snatched for the first hold, around both of Geirolf's wrists. The drow strained to break loose and could not; but neither could Hauk bring him down. Sweat ran moon-bright over the son's cheeks and darkened his shirt. The reek of it was at least a living smell in his nostrils. Breath tore at his gullet. Suddenly Geirolf wrenched so hard that his right arm tore from between his foe's fingers. He brought that hand against Hauk's throat. Hauk let go and slammed himself backward before he was throttled.

Geirolf stalked after him. The drow did not move fast. Hauk sped behind and pounded on the broad back. He seized an arm of Geirolf's and twisted it around. But the dead cannot feel pain. Geirolf stood fast. His other hand groped about, got Hauk by the hair, and yanked. Live men can hurt. Hauk stumbled away. Blood ran from his scalp into his eyes and mouth, hot and salt.

Geirolf turned and followed. He would not tire. Hauk had no long while before strength ebbed. Almost, he fled. Then the moon broke through to shine full on his father. "You... shall not... go on... like that," Hauk mumbled while he snapped after air.

The drow reached him. They closed, grappled, swayed, stamped to and fro, in wind and flicker moonlight. Then Hauk hooked an ankle behind Geirolf's and pushed. With a huge thud, the drow crashed to earth. He dragged Hauk along.

Hauk's bones felt how terrible was the grip upon him. He let go his own hold. Instead, he arched his back and pushed himself away. His clothes ripped. But he burst free and reeled to his feet.

Geirolf turned over and began to crawl up. His back was once more to Hauk. The young man sprang. He got a knee hard in between the shoulderblades, while both his arms closed on the frosty head before him.

He hauled. With the last and greatest might that was in him, he hauled. Blackness went in tatters before his eyes.

There came a loud snapping sound. Geirolf ceased pawing behind him. He sprawled limp. His neck was broken, his jawbone wrenched from the skull. Hauk climbed slowly off him, shuddering. Geirolf stirred, rolled, half rose. He lifted a hand toward Hauk. It traced a line through the air and a line growing from beneath that. Then he slumped and lay still.

Hauk crumpled too.

"Follow me who dare!" Leif roared, and went forth across the field. One by one, as they saw nothing move ahead of them, the men came after. At last they stood hushed around Geirolf—who was only a harmless dead man now, though the moon shone bright in his eyes—and on Hauk, who had begun to stir.

"Bear him carefully down to the hall," Leif said. "Start a fire and tend it well. Most of you, take from the woodpile and come back here. I'll stand guard meanwhile... though I think there is no need."

And so they burned Geirolf there in the field. He walked no more.

In the morning, they brought Hauk back to Leif's garth. He moved as if in dreams. The others were too awestruck to speak much. Even when Alfhild ran to meet him, he could only say, "Hold clear of me. I may be under a doom."

"Did the drow lay a weird on you?" she asked, spear-stricken.

"I know not," he answered. "I think I fell into the dark before he was wholly dead."

"What?" Leif well-nigh shouted. "You did not see the sign he drew?"

"Why, no," Hauk said. "How did it go?"

"Thus. Even afar and by moonlight, I knew." Leif drew it.

"That is no ill-wishing!" Grim cried. "That's naught but the Hammer."

Life rushed back into Hauk. "Do you mean what I hope?"

"He blessed you," Grim said. "You freed him from what he had most dreaded and hated—his straw-death. The madness in him is gone, and he has wended hence to the world beyond."

Then Hauk was glad again. He led them all in heaping earth over the ashes of his father, and in setting things right on the farm. That winter, at the feast of Thor, he and Alfhild were wedded. Afterward he became well thought of by King Harald, and rose to great wealth. From him and Alfhild stem many men whose names are still remembered. Here ends the tale of Hauk the Ghost Slayer.

The Jewels in the Forest

Fritz Leiber (1910-1992)

It was the Year of the Behemoth, the Month of the Hedgehog, the Day of the Toad. A hot, late summer sun was sinking down toward evening over the somber, fertile land of Lankhmar. Peasants toiling in the endless grain fields paused for a moment and lifted their earth-stained faces and noted that it would soon be time to commence lesser chores. Cattle cropping the stubble began to move in the general direction of home. Sweaty merchants and shopkeepers decided to wait a little longer before enjoying the pleasures of the bath. Thieves and astrologers moved restlessly in their sleep, sensing that the hours of night and work were drawing near.

At the southernmost limit of the land of Lankhmar, a day's ride beyond the village of Soreev, where the grain fields give way to rolling forests of maple and oak, two horsemen cantered leisurely along a narrow, dusty road. They presented a sharp contrast. The larger wore a tunic of unbleached linen, drawn tight at the waist by a very broad leather belt. A fold of linen cloak was looped over his head as a protection against the sun. A longsword with a pomegranate-shaped golden pommel was strapped to his side. Behind his right shoulder a quiver of arrows jutted up. Half sheathed in a saddlecase was a thick yew bow, unstrung. His great, lean muscles, white skin, copper hair, green eyes, and above all the pleasant yet untamed expression of his massive countenance, all hinted at a land of origin colder, rougher, and more barbarous than that of Lankhmar.

Even as everything about the larger man suggested the wilderness, so the general appearance of the smaller man—and he was considerably smaller—spoke of the city. His dark face was that of a jester. Bright, black eyes, snub nose, and little lines of irony about the mouth. Hands of a conjurer. Something about the set of his wiry frame betokening exceptional competence in street fights and tavern brawls. He was clad from head to foot in garments of gray silk, soft and curiously loose of weave. His slim sword, cased in gray mouseskin, was slightly curved toward the tip. From his belt hung a sling and a pouch of missiles.

Despite their many dissimilarities, it was obvious that the two men were comrades, that they were united by a bond of subtle mutual understanding, woven of melancholy, humor, and many another strand. The smaller rode a dappled gray mare; the larger, a chestnut gelding.

They were nearing a point where the narrow road came to the end of a rise, made a slight turn and wound down into the next valley. Green walls of leaves pressed in on either side. The heat was considerable, but not oppressive. It brought to mind thoughts of satyrs and centaurs dozing in hidden glades.

Then the gray mare, slightly in the lead, whinnied. The smaller man tightened his hold on the reins, his black eyes darting quick, alert glances, first to one side of the road and then to the other. There was a faint scraping sound, as of wood on wood.

Without warning the two men ducked down, clinging to the side harness of their horses. Simultaneously came the musical twang of bowstrings, like the prelude of some forest concert, and several arrows buzzed angrily through the spaces that had just been vacated. Then the mare and the gelding were around the turn and galloping like the wind, their hooves striking up great puffs of dust.

From behind came excited shouts and answers as the pursuit got underway. There seemed to have been fully seven or eight men in the ambuscade—squat, sturdy rogues wearing chain-mail shirts and steel caps. Before the mare and the gelding had gone a stone's throw down the road, they were out and after, a black horse in the lead, a black-bearded rider second.

But those pursued were not wasting time. The larger man rose to a stand in his stirrups, whipping the yew bow from its case. With his left hand he bent it against the stirrup, with his right he drew the upper loop of the string into place. Then his left hand slipped down the bow to the grip and his right reached smoothly back over his shoulder for an arrow. Still guiding his horse with his knees, he rose even higher and turned in his saddle and sent an eagle-feathered shaft whirring. Meanwhile his comrade had placed a small leaden ball in his sling, whirled it twice about his head, so that it hummed stridently, and loosed his cast.

Arrow and missile sped and struck together. The one pierced the shoulder of the leading horseman and the other smote the second on his steel cap and tumbled him from his saddle. The pursuit halted abruptly in a tangle of plunging and rearing horses. The men who had caused this confusion pulled up at the next bend in the road and turned back to watch.

"By the Hedgehog," said the smaller, grinning wickedly, "but they will think twice before they play at ambuscades again!"

"Blundering fools," said the larger. "Haven't they even learned to shoot from their saddles? I tell you, Gray Mouser, it takes a barbarian to fight his horse properly."

"Except for myself and a few other people," replied the one who bore the feline nickname of Gray Mouser. "But look, Fafhrd, the rogues retreat bearing their wounded, and one gallops far ahead. *Tcha*, but I dinted black beard's pate for him. He hangs over his nag like a bag of meal. If he'd have known who we were, he wouldn't have been so hot on the chase."

There was some truth to this last boast. The names of the Gray Mouser and the Northerner Fafhrd were not unknown in the lands around Lankhmar—and in proud Lankhmar, too. Their taste for strange adventure, their mysterious comings and goings, and their odd sense of humor were matters that puzzled almost all men alike.

Abruptly Fafhrd unstrung his bow and turned forward in his saddle.

"This should be the very valley we are seeking," he said. "See, there are the two hills, each with two close-set humps, of which the document speaks. Let's have another look at it, to test my guess."

The Gray Mouser reached into his capacious leather pouch and withdrew a page of thick vellum, ancient and curiously greenish. Three edges were frayed and worn; the fourth showed a clean and recent cut. It was inscribed with the intricate hieroglyphs of Lankhmarian writing, done in the black ink of the squid. But it was not to these that the Mouser turned his attention, but to several faint lines of diminutive red script, written into the margin. These he read.

"Let kings stack their treasure houses ceiling-high, and merchants burst their vaults with hoarded coin, and fools envy them. I have a treasure that outvalues theirs. A diamond as big as a man's skull. Twelve rubies each as big as the skull of a cat. Seventeen emeralds each as big as the skull of a mole. And certain rods of crystal and bars of orichalcum. Let Overlords swagger jewel-bedecked and queens load themselves with gems, and fools adore them. I have a treasure that will outlast theirs. A treasure house have I builded for it in the far southern forest, where the two hills hump double, like sleeping camels, a day's ride beyond the village of Soreev.

"A great treasure house with a high tower, fit for a king's dwelling—yet no king may dwell there. Immediately below the keystone of the chief dome my treasure lies hid, eternal as the glittering stars. It will outlast me and my name, I, Urgaan of Angarngi. It is my hold on the future. Let fools seek it. They shall win it not. For although my treasure house be empty as air, no deadly creature in rocky lair, no sentinel outside anywhere, no pitfall, poison, trap, or snare, above and below the whole place bare, of demon or devil not a hair, no serpent lethal-fanged yet fair, no skull with mortal eye a-glare, yet have I left a guardian there. Let the wise read this riddle and forbear."

"The man's mind runs to skulls," muttered the Mouser. "He must have been a gravedigger or a necromancer."

"Or an architect," observed Fafhrd thoughtfully, "in those past days when graven images of the skulls of men and animals served to bedeck temples."

"Perhaps," agreed the Mouser. "Surely the writing and ink are old enough. They date at least as far back as the Century of the Wars with the East—five long lifespans."

The Mouser was an accomplished forger, both of handwriting and of objects of art. He knew what he was talking about.

Satisfied that they were near the goal of their quest, the two comrades gazed through a break in the foliage down into the valley. It was shaped like the inside of a pod—shallow, long, and narrow. They were viewing it from one of the narrow ends. The two peculiarly humped hills formed the long sides. The whole of the valley was green with maple and oak, save for a small gap toward the middle. That, thought the Mouser, might mark a peasant's dwelling and the cleared space around it.

Beyond the gap he could make out something dark and squarish rising a little above the treetops. He called his companion's attention to it, but they could not decide whether it was indeed a tower such as the document mentioned, or just a peculiar shadow, or perhaps even the dead, limbless trunk of a gigantic oak. It was too far away.

"Almost sufficient time has passed," said Fafhrd, after a pause, "for one of those rogues to have sneaked up through the forest for another shot at us. Evening draws near."

They spoke to their horses and moved on slowly. They tried to keep their eyes fixed on the thing that looked like a tower, but since they were descending, it almost immediately dropped out of sight below the treetops. There would be no further chance of seeing it until they were quite close at hand.

The Mouser felt a subdued excitement running through his flesh. Soon they would discover if there was a treasure to be had or not. A diamond as big as a man's skull... rubies... emeralds... He found an almost nostalgic delight in prolonging and savoring to the full this last, leisurely stage of their quest. The recent ambuscade served as a necessary spice.

He thought of how he had slit the interesting-looking vellum page from the ancient book on architecture that reposed in the library of the rapacious and overbearing Lord Rannarsh. Of how, half in jest, he had sought out and interrogated several peddlers from the South. Of how he had found one who had recently passed through a village named Soreev. Of how that one had told him of a stone structure in the forest south of Soreev, called by the peasants the House of Angarngi and reputed to be long deserted. The peddler had seen a high tower rising above the trees. The Mouser recalled the man's wizened, cunning face and chuckled. And that brought to mind the greedy, sallow face of Lord Rannarsh, and a new thought occurred to him.

"Fafhrd," he said, "those rogues we just now put to flight—what did you take them for?"

The Northerner grunted humorous contempt.

"Run-of-the-manger ruffians. Waylayers of fat merchants. Pasture bravos. Bumpkin bandits!"

"Still, they were all well armed, and armed alike—as if they were in some rich man's service. And that one who rode far ahead. Mightn't he have been hastening to report failure to some master?"

"What is your thought?"

The Mouser did not reply for some moments.

"I was thinking," he said, "that Lord Rannarsh is a rich man and a greedy one, who slavers at the thought of jewels. And I was wondering if he ever read those faint lines of red lettering and made a copy of them, and if my theft of the original sharpened his interest."

The Northerner shook his head.

"I doubt it. You are oversubtle. But if he did, and if he seeks to rival us in this treasure quest, he'd best watch each step twice—and choose servitors who can fight on horseback."

They were moving so slowly that the hooves of the mare and the gelding hardly stirred up the dust. They had no fear of danger from the rear. A well-laid ambuscade might surprise them, but not a man or horse in motion. The narrow road wound along in a purposeless fashion. Leaves brushed their faces, and occasionally they had to swing their bodies out of the way of encroaching branches. The ripe scent of the late summer forest was intensified now that they were below the rim of the valley. Mingled with it were whiffs of wild berries and aromatic shrubs. Shadows imperceptibly lengthened.

"Nine chances out of ten," murmured the Mouser dreamily, "the treasure house of Urgaan of Angarngi was looted some hundred years ago, by men whose bodies are already dust."

"It may be so," agreed Fafhrd. "Unlike men, rubies and emeralds do not rest quietly in their graves."

This possibility, which they had discussed several times before, did not disturb them now, or make them impatient. Rather did it impart to their quest the pleasant melancholy of a lost hope. They drank in the rich air and let their horses munch random mouthfuls of leaves. A jay called shrilly from overhead and off in the forest a catbird was chattering, their sharp voices breaking in on the low buzzing and droning of the insects. Night was drawing near. The almost-horizontal rays of the sun gilded the treetops. Then Fafhrd's sharp ears caught the hollow lowing of a cow.

A few more turns brought them into the clearing they had spied. In line with their surmise, it proved to contain a peasant's cottage—a neat little low-eaved house of weathered wood, situated in the midst of an acre of grain. To one side was a bean patch; to the other, a woodpile which almost dwarfed the house. In front of the cottage stood a wiry old man, his skin as brown as his homespun tunic. He had evidently just heard the horses and turned around to look.

"Ho, father," called the Mouser, "it's a good day to be abroad in, and a good home you have here."

The peasant considered these statements and then nodded his head in agreement.

"We are two weary travelers," continued the Mouser.

Again the peasant nodded gravely.

"In return for two silver coins will you give us lodging for the night?"

The peasant rubbed his chin and then held up three fingers.

"Very well, you shall have three silver coins," said the Mouser, slipping from his horse. Fafhrd followed suit.

Only after giving the old man a coin to seal the bargain did the Mouser question casually, "Is there not an old, deserted place near your dwelling called the House of Angarngi?" The peasant nodded.

"What's it like?"

The peasant shrugged his shoulders.

"Don't you know?"

The peasant shook his head.

"But haven't you ever seen the place?" The Mouser's voice carried a note of amazement he did not bother to conceal.

He was answered by another head-shake.

"But, father, it's only a few minutes' walk from your dwelling, isn't it?"

The peasant nodded tranquilly, as if the whole business were no matter for surprise.

A muscular young man, who had come from behind the cottage to take their horses, offered a suggestion.

"You can see tower from other side the house. I can point her out."

At this the old man proved he was not completely speechless by saying in a dry, expressionless voice: "Go ahead. Look at her all you want."

And he stepped into the cottage. Fafhrd and the Mouser caught a glimpse of a child peering around the door, an old woman stirring a pot, and someone hunched in a big chair before a tiny fire.

The upper part of the tower proved to be barely visible through a break in the trees. The last rays of the sun touched it with deep red. It looked about four or five bowshots distant. And then, even as they watched, the sun dipped under and it became a featureless square of black stone.

"She's an old place," explained the young man vaguely. "I been all around her. Father, he's just never bothered to look."

"You've been inside?" questioned the Mouser.

The young man scratched his head.

"No. She's just an old place. No good for anything."

"There'll be a fairly long twilight," said Fafhrd, his wide green eyes drawn to the tower as if by a lodestone. "Long enough for us to have a closer look."

"I'd show the way," said the young man, "save I got water to fetch."

"No matter," replied Fafhrd. "When's supper?"

"When the first stars show."

They left him holding their horses and walked straight into the woods. Immediately it became much darker, as if twilight were almost over, rather than just begun. The vegetation proved to be somewhat thicker than they had anticipated. There were vines and thorns to be avoided. Irregular, pale patches of sky appeared and disappeared overhead.

The Mouser let Fafhrd lead the way. His mind was occupied with a queer sort of reverie about the peasants. It tickled his fancy to think how they had stolidly lived their toilsome lives, generation after generation, only a few steps from what might be one of the greatest treasure-troves in the world. It seemed incredible. How could people sleep so near jewels and not dream of them? But probably they never dreamed.

So the Gray Mouser was sharply aware of few things during the journey through the woods, save that Fafhrd seemed to be taking a long time—which was strange, since the barbarian was an accomplished woodsman.

Finally a deeper and more solid shadow loomed up through the trees, and in a moment they were standing in the margin of a small, boulder-studded clearing, most of which was occupied by the bulky structure they sought. Abruptly, even before his eyes took in the details of the place, the Mouser's mind was filled with a hundred petty perturbations. Weren't they making a mistake in leaving their horses with those strange peasants? And mightn't those rogues have followed them to the cottage? And wasn't this the Day of the Toad, an unlucky day for entering deserted houses? And shouldn't they have a short spear along, in case they met a leopard? And wasn't that a whippoorwill he heard crying on his left hand, an augury of ill omen?

The treasure house of Urgaan of Angarngi was a peculiar structure. The main feature was a large, shallow dome, resting on walls that formed an octagon. In front, and merging into it, were two lesser domes. Between these gaped a great square doorway. The tower rose asymmetrically from the rear part of the chief dome. The eyes of the Mouser sought hurriedly through the dimming twilight for the cause of the salient peculiarity of the structure, and decided it lay in the utter simplicity. There were no pillars, no outjutting cornices, no friezes, no architectural ornaments of any sort, skull-embellished or otherwise. Save for the doorway and a few tiny windows set in unexpected places, the House of Angarngi was a compact mass of uniformly dark gray stones most closely joined.

But now Fafhrd was striding up the short flight of terraced steps that led toward the open door, and the Mouser followed him, although he would have liked to spy around a little longer. With every step he took forward he sensed an odd reluctance growing within him. His earlier mood of pleasant expectancy vanished as suddenly as if he'd stepped into quicksand. It seemed to him that the black doorway yawned like a toothless mouth. And then a little shudder went through him, for he saw the mouth had a tooth—a bit of ghostly white that jutted up from the floor. Fafhrd was reaching down toward the object.

"I wonder whose skull this may be?" said the Northerner calmly.

The Mouser regarded the thing, and the scattering of bones and fragments of bone beside it. His feeling of uneasiness was fast growing toward a climax, and he had the unpleasant conviction that, once it did reach a climax, something would happen. What was the answer to Fafhrd's question? What form of death had struck down that earlier intruder? It was very dark inside the treasure house. Didn't the manuscript mention something about a guardian? It was hard to think of a flesh-and-blood guardian persisting for three hundred years, but there were things that were immortal or nearly immortal. He could tell that Fafhrd was not in the least affected by any premonitory disquietude, and was quite capable of instituting an immediate search for the treasure. That must be prevented at all costs. He remembered that the Northerner loathed snakes.

"This cold, damp stone," he observed casually. "Just the place for scaly, cold-blooded snakes."

"Nothing of the sort," replied Fafhrd angrily. "I'm willing to wager there's not a single serpent inside. Urgaan's note said, 'No deadly creature in rocky lair,' and to cap that, 'no serpent lethal-fanged yet fair.'"

"I am not thinking of guardian snakes Urgaan may have left here," the Mouser explained, "but only of serpents that may have wandered in for the night. Just as that skull you hold is not one set there by Urgaan 'with mortal eye a-glare,' but merely the brain-case of some unfortunate wayfarer who chanced to perish here."

"I don't know," Fafhrd said, calmly eyeing the skull.

"Its orbits might glow phosphorescently in absolute dark."

A moment later he was agreeing it would be well to postpone the search until daylight returned, now that the treasure house was located. He carefully replaced the skull.

As they re-entered the woods, the Mouser heard a little inner voice whispering to him, *Just in time. Just in time.* Then the sense of uneasiness departed as suddenly as it had come, and he began to feel somewhat ridiculous. This caused him to sing a bawdy ballad of his own invention, wherein demons and other supernatural agents were ridiculed obscenely. Fafhrd chimed in good-naturedly on the choruses.

It was not as dark as they expected when they reached the cottage. They saw to their horses, found they had been well cared for, and then fell to the savory mess of beans, porridge, and pot herbs that the peasant's wife ladled into oak bowls. Fresh milk to wash it down was provided in quaintly carved oak goblets. The meal was a satisfying one and the interior of the house was neat and clean, despite its stamped earthen floor and low beams, which Fafhrd had to duck.

There turned out to be six in the family, all told. The father, his equally thin and leathery wife, the older son, a young boy, a daughter, and a mumbling grandfather, whom extreme age confined to a chair before the fire. The last two were the most interesting of the lot.

The girl was in the gawkish age of mid-adolescence, but there was a wild, coltish grace in the way she moved her lanky legs and slim arms with their prominent elbows. She was very shy, and gave the impression that at any moment she might dart out the door and into the woods.

In order to amuse her and win her confidence, the Mouser began to perform small feats of legerdemain, plucking copper coins out of the ears of the astonished peasant, and bone needles from the nose of his giggling wife. He turned beans into buttons and back again into beans, swallowed a large fork, made a tiny wooden manikin jig on the palm of his hand, and utterly bewildered the cat by pulling what seemed to be a mouse out of its mouth.

The old folks gaped and grinned. The little boy became frantic with excitement. His sister watched everything with concentrated interest, and even smiled warmly when the Mouser presented her with a square of fine, green linen he had conjured from the air, although she was still too shy to speak.

Then Fafhrd roared sea-chanteys that rocked the roof and sang lusty songs that set the old grandfather gurgling with delight. Meanwhile the Mouser fetched a small wineskin from his saddlebags, concealed it under his cloak, and filled the oak goblets as if by magic. These rapidly fuddled the peasants, who were unused to so potent a beverage, and by the time Fafhrd had finished telling a bloodcurdling tale of the frozen north, they were all nodding, save the girl and the grandfather.

The latter looked up at the merry-making adventurers, his watery eyes filled with a kind of impish, senile glee, and mumbled, "You two be right clever men. Maybe you be beast-dodgers." But before this remark could be elucidated, his eyes had gone vacant again, and in a few moments he was snoring.

Soon all were asleep, Fafhrd and the Mouser keeping their weapons close at hand, but only variegated snores and occasional snaps from the dying embers disturbed the silence of the cottage.

The Day of the Cat dawned clear and cool. The Mouser stretched himself luxuriously and, catlike, flexed his muscles and sucked in the sweet, dewy air. He felt exceptionally cheerful and eager to be up and doing. Was not this his day, the day of the Gray Mouser, a day in which luck could not fail him?

His slight movements awakened Fafhrd and together they stole silently from the cottage so as not to disturb the peasants, who were oversleeping with the wine they had taken. They refreshed their faces and hands in the wet grass and visited their horses. Then they munched some bread, washed it down with drafts of cool well water flavored with wine, and made ready to depart.

This time their preparations were well thought out. The Mouser carried a mallet and a stout iron pry-bar, in case they had to attack masonry, and made certain that candles, flint, wedges, chisels, and several other small tools were in his pouch. Fafhrd borrowed a pick from the peasant's implements and tucked a coil of thin, strong rope in his belt. He also took his bow and quiver of arrows.

THE JEWELS IN THE FOREST

The forest was delightful at this early hour. Bird cries and chatterings came from overhead, and once they glimpsed a black, squirrel-like animal scampering along a bough. A couple of chipmunks scurried under a bush dotted with red berries. What had been shadow the evening before was now a variety of green-leafed beauty. The two adventurers trod softly.

They had hardly gone more than a bowshot into the woods when they heard a faint rustling behind them. The rustling came rapidly nearer, and suddenly the peasant girl burst into view. She stood breathless and poised, one hand touching a treetrunk, the other pressing some leaves, ready to fly away at the first sudden move. Fafhrd and the Mouser stood as stock-still as if she were a doe or a dryad. Finally she managed to conquer her shyness and speak.

"You go there?" she questioned, indicating the direction of the treasure house with a quick, ducking nod. Her dark eyes were serious.

"Yes, we go there," answered Fafhrd, smiling.

"Don't." This word was accompanied by a rapid head-shake.

"But why shouldn't we, girl?" Fafhrd's voice was gentle and sonorous, like an integral part of the forest. It seemed to touch some spring within the girl that enabled her to feel more at ease. She gulped a big breath and began.

"Because I watch it from edge of the forest, but never go close. Never, never, never. I say to myself there be a magic circle I must not cross. And I say to myself there be a giant inside. Queer and fearsome giant." Her words were coming rapidly now, like an undammed stream. "All gray he be, like the stone of his house. All gray—eyes and hair and fingernails, too. And he has a stone club as big as a tree. And he be big, bigger than you, twice as big." Here she nodded at Fafhrd. "And with his club he kills, kills, kills. But only if you go close. Every day, almost, I play a game with him. I pretend to be going to cross the magic circle. And he watches from inside the door, where I can't see him, and he thinks I'm going to cross. And I dance through the forest all around the house, and he follows me, peering from the little windows. And I get closer and closer to the circle, closer and closer. But I never cross. And he be very angry and gnash his teeth, like rocks rubbing rocks, so that the house shakes. And I run, run, run away. But you mustn't go inside. Oh, you mustn't."

She paused, as if startled by her own daring. Her eyes were fixed anxiously on Fafhrd. She seemed drawn toward him. The Northerner's reply carried no overtone of patronizing laughter.

"But you've never actually seen the gray giant, have you?"

"Oh, no. He be too cunning. But I say to myself he must be there inside. I know he be inside. And that's the same thing, isn't it? Grandfather knows about him. We used to talk about him, when I was little. Grandfather calls him the beast. But the others laugh at me, so I don't tell."

Here was another astounding peasant-paradox, thought the Mouser with an inward grin. Imagination was such a rare commodity with them that this girl unhesitatingly took it for reality.

"Don't worry about us, girl. We'll be on the watch for your gray giant," he started to say, but he had less success than Fafhrd in keeping his voice completely natural or else the cadence of his words didn't chime so well with the forest setting.

The girl uttered one more warning. "Don't go inside, oh, please," and turned and darted away. The two adventurers looked at each other and smiled. Somehow the unexpected fairy tale, with its conventional ogre and its charmingly naive narrator added to the delight of the dewy morning. Without a comment they resumed their soft-stepping progress. And it was well that they went quietly, for when they had gotten within a stone's throw of the clearing, they heard low voices that seemed to be in grumbling argument. Immediately they cached the pick and pry-bar and mallet under a clump of bushes, and stole forward, taking advantage of the natural cover and watching where they planted their feet.

THE JEWELS IN THE FOREST

On the edge of the clearing stood half a dozen stocky men in black chain-mail shirts, bows on their backs, shortswords at their sides. They were immediately recognizable as the rogues who had laid the ambuscade. Two of them started for the treasure house, only to be recalled by a comrade. Whereupon the argument apparently started afresh.

"That red-haired one," whispered the Mouser after an unhurried look. "I can swear I've seen him in the stables of Lord Rannarsh. My guess was right. It seems we have a rival."

"Why do they wait, and keep pointing at the house?" whispered Fafhrd. "Is it because some of their comrades are already at work inside?"

The Mouser shook his head. "That cannot be. See those picks and shovels and levers they have rested on the ground? No, they wait for someone—for a leader. Some of them want to examine the house before he arrives. Others counsel against it. And I will bet my head against a bowling ball that the leader is Rannarsh himself. He is much too greedy and suspicious to entrust a treasure quest to any henchmen."

"What's to do?" murmured Fafhrd. "We cannot enter the house unseen, even if it were the wise course, which it isn't. Once in, we'd be trapped."

"I've half a mind to loose my sling at them right now and teach them something about the art of ambuscade," replied the Mouser, slitting his eyes grimly. "Only then the survivors would flee into the house and hold us off until, mayhap, Rannarsh came, and more men with him."

"We might circle part way around the clearing," said Fafhrd, after a moment's pause, "keeping to the woods. Then we can enter the clearing unseen and shelter ourselves behind one of the small domes. In that way we become masters of the doorway, and can prevent their taking cover inside. Thereafter I will address them suddenly and try to frighten them off, you meanwhile staying hid and giving substance to my threats by making enough racket for ten men."

This seemed the handiest plan to both of them, and they managed the first part of it without a hitch. The Mouser crouched behind the small dome, his sword, sling, daggers, and a couple of sticks of wood laid ready for either noise-making or fight. Then Fafhrd strode briskly forward, his bow held carelessly in front of him, an arrow fitted to the string. It was done so casually that it was a few moments before Rannarsh's henchmen noticed him. Then they quickly reached for their own bows and as quickly desisted when they saw that the huge newcomer had the advantage of them. They scowled in irritated perplexity.

"Ho, rogues!" began Fafhrd. "We allow you just as much time as it will take you to make yourselves scarce, and no more. Don't think to resist or come skulking back. My men are scattered through the woods. At a sign from me they will feather you with arrows."

Meanwhile the Mouser had begun a low din and was slowly and artistically working it up in volume. Rapidly varying the pitch and intonation of his voice and making it echo first from some part of the building and then from the forest wall, he created the illusion of a squad of bloodthirsty bowmen. Nasty cries of "Shall we let fly?" "You take the redhead," and "Try for the belly shot; it's surest," kept coming now from one point and now another, until it was all Fafhrd could do to refrain from laughing at the woebegone, startled glances the six rogues kept darting around. But his merriment was extinguished when, just as the rogues were starting to slink shamefacedly away, an arrow arched erratically out of the woods, passing a spear's length above his head.

"Curse that branch!" came a deep, guttural voice the Mouser recognized as issuing from the throat of Lord Rannarsh. Immediately after, it began to bark commands.

"At them, you fools! It's all a trick. There are only the two of them. Rush them!"

Fafhrd turned without warning and loosed point-blank at the voice, but did not silence it. Then he dodged back behind the small dome and ran with the Mouser for the woods.

The six rogues, wisely deciding that a charge with drawn swords would be overly heroic, followed suit, unslinging their bows as they went. One of them turned before he had reached sufficient cover, nocking an arrow. It was a mistake. A ball from the Mouser's sling took him low in the forehead, and he toppled forward and was still.

The sound of that hit and fall was the last heard in the clearing for quite a long time, save for the inevitable bird cries, some of which were genuine, and some of which were communications between Fafhrd and the Mouser. The conditions of the death-dealing contest were obvious. Once it had fairly begun, no one dared enter the clearing, since he would become a fatally easy mark; and the Mouser was sure that none of the five remaining rogues had taken shelter in the treasure house. Nor did either side dare withdraw all its men out of sight of the doorway, since that would allow someone to take a commanding position in the top of the tower, providing the tower had a negotiable stair. Therefore it was a case of sneaking about near the edge of the clearing, circling and counter-circling, with a great deal of squatting in a good place and waiting for somebody to come along and be shot.

The Mouser and Fafhrd began by adopting the latter strategy, first moving about twenty paces nearer the point at which the rogues had disappeared. Evidently their patience was a little better than that of their opponents. For after about ten minutes of nerve-racking waiting, during which pointed seed pods had a queer way of looking like arrowheads, Fafhrd got the red-haired henchman full in the throat just as he was bending his bow for a shot at the Mouser. That left four besides Rannarsh himself. Immediately the two adventurers changed their tactics and separated, the Mouser circling rapidly around the treasure house and Fafhrd drawing as far back from the open space as he dared.

Rannarsh's men must have decided on the same plan, for the Mouser almost bumped into a scar-faced rogue as soft-footed as himself. At such close range, bow and sling were both useless—in their normal function. Scarface attempted to jab the barbed arrow he held into the Mouser's eye. The Mouser weaved his body to one side, swung his sling like a whip, and felled the man senseless with a blow from the horn handle. Then he retreated a few paces, thanked the Day of the Cat that there had not been two of them, and took to the trees as being a safer, though slower method of progress. Keeping to the middle heights, he scurried along with the sure-footedness of a rope walker, swinging from branch to branch only when it was necessary, making sure he always had more than one way of retreat open.

He had completed three-quarters of his circuit when he heard the clash of swords a few trees ahead. He increased his speed and was soon looking down on a sweet little combat. Fafhrd, his back to a great oak, had his broadsword out and was holding off two of Rannarsh's henchmen, who were attacking with their shorter weapons. It was a tight spot and the Northerner realized it. He knew that ancient sagas told of heroes who could best four or more men at swordplay. He also knew that such sagas were lies, providing the hero's opponents were reasonably competent.

And Rannarsh's men were veterans. They attacked cautiously but incessantly, keeping their swords well in front of them and never slashing wildly. Their breath whistled through their nostrils, but they were grimly confident, knowing the Northerner dared not lunge strongly at one of them because it would lay him wide open to a thrust by the other. Their game was to get one on each side of him and then attack simultaneously.

Fafhrd's counter was to shift position quickly and attack the nearer one murderously before the other could get back in range. In that way he managed to keep them side by side, where he could hold their blades in check by swift feints and crosswise sweeps. Sweat beaded his face and blood dripped from a scratch on his left thigh. A fearsome grin showed his white teeth, which occasionally parted to let slip a base, primitive insult.

The Mouser took in the situation at a glance, descended rapidly to a lower bough, and poised himself, aiming a dagger at the back of one of Fafhrd's adversaries. He was, however, standing very close to the thick trunk, and around this trunk darted a horny hand tipped with a short sword. The third henchman had also thought it wise to take to the trees. Fortunately for the Mouser, the man was uncertain of his footing and therefore his thrust, although well aimed, came a shade slow. As it was the little gray-clad man only managed to dodge by dropping off.

Thereupon he startled his opponent with a modest acrobatic feat. He did not drop to the ground, knowing that would put everyone at the mercy of the man in the tree. Instead, he grabbed hold of the branch on which he had been standing, swung himself smartly up again, and grappled. Steadying themselves now with one hand, now another, they drove for each other's throats, ramming with knees and elbows whenever they got a chance. At the first onset both dagger and sword were dropped, the latter sticking point-down in the ground directly between the two battling henchmen and startling them so that Fafhrd almost got home an attack.

The Mouser and his man surged and teetered along the branch away from the trunk, inflicting little damage on each other since it was hard to keep balance. Finally they slid off at the same time, but grabbed the branch with their hands. The puffing henchman aimed a vicious kick. The Mouser escaped it by yanking up his body and doubling up his legs. The latter he let fly violently, taking the henchman full in the chest, just where the ribs stop. The unfortunate retainer of Rannarsh fell to the ground, where he had the wind knocked out of him a second time.

At the same moment one of Fafhrd's opponents tried a trick that might have turned out well. When his companion was pressing the Northerner closely, he snatched for the shortsword sticking in the ground, intending to hurl it underhanded as if it were a javelin. But Fafhrd, whose superior endurance was rapidly giving him an advantage in speed, anticipated the movement and simultaneously made a brilliant counterattack against the other man. There were two thrusts, both lightninglike, the first a feint at the belly, the second a slicing stab that sheared through the throat to the spine. Then he whirled around and, with a quick sweep, knocked both weapons out of the hands of the first man, who looked up in bewilderment and promptly collapsed into a sitting position, panting in utter exhaustion, though with enough breath left to cry, "Mercy!"

To cap the situation, the Mouser dropped lightly down, as if out of the sky. Fafhrd automatically started to raise his sword, for a backhand swipe. Then he stared at the Mouser for as long a time as it took the man sitting on the ground to give three tremendous gasps. Then he began to laugh, first uncontrollable snickers and later thundering peals. It was a laughter in which the battle-begotten madness, completely sated anger, and relief at escape from death were equally mingled.

"Oh, by Glaggerk and by Kos!" he roared. "By the Behemoth! Oh, by the Cold Waste and the guts of the Red God! Oh! Oh! Oh!" Again the insane bellowing burst out. "Oh, by the Killer Whale and the Cold Woman and her spawn!" By degrees the laughter died away, choking in his throat. He rubbed his forehead with the palm of his hand and his face became starkly grave. Then he knelt beside the man he had just slain, and straightened his limbs, and closed his eyes, and began to weep in a dignified way that would have seemed ridiculous and hypocritical in anyone but a barbarian.

Meanwhile the Mouser's reactions were nowhere near as primitive. He felt worried, ironic, and slightly sick. He understood Fafhrd's emotions, but knew that he would not feel the full force of his own for some time yet, and by then they would be deadened and somewhat choked. He peered about anxiously, fearful of an anticlimactic attack that would find his companion helpless. He counted over the tally of their opponents. Yes, the six henchmen were all accounted for. But Rannarsh himself, where was Rannarsh? He fumbled in his pouch to make sure he had not lost his good-luck talismans and amulets. His lips moved rapidly as he murmured two or three prayers and cantrips. But all the while he held his sling ready, and his eyes never once ceased their quick shifting.

From the middle of a thick clump of bushes he heard a series of agonized gasps, as the man he had felled from the tree began to regain his wind. The henchman whom Fafhrd had disarmed, his face ashy pale from exhaustion rather than fright, was slowly edging back into the forest. The Mouser watched him carelessly, noting the comical way in which the steel cap had slipped down over his forehead and rested against the bridge of his nose. Meanwhile the gasps of the man in the bushes were taking on a less agonized quality. At almost the same instant, the two rose to their feet and stumbled off into the forest.

The Mouser listened to their blundering retreat. He was sure that there was nothing more to fear from them. They wouldn't come back. And then a little smile stole into his face, for he heard the sounds of a third person joining them in their flight. That would be Rannarsh, thought the Mouser, a man cowardly at heart and incapable of carrying on single-handed. It did not occur to him that the third person might be the man he had stunned with his sling handle.

Mostly just to be doing something, he followed them leisurely for a couple of bowshots into the forest. Their trail was impossible to miss, being marked by trampled bushes and thorns bearing tatters of cloth. It led in a beeline away from the clearing. Satisfied, he returned, going out of his way to regain the mallet, pick, and pry-bar.

He found Fafhrd tying a loose bandage around the scratch on his thigh. The Northerner's emotions had run their gamut and he was himself again. The dead man for whom he had been somberly grieving now meant no more to him than food for beetles and birds. Whereas for the Mouser it continued to be a somewhat frightening and sickening object.

"And now do we proceed with our interrupted business?" the Mouser asked.

Fafhrd nodded in a matter-of-fact manner and rose to his feet. Together they entered the rocky clearing. It came to them as a surprise how little time the fight had taken. True, the sun had moved somewhat higher, but the atmosphere was still that of early morning. The dew had not dried yet. The treasure house of Urgaan of Angarngi stood massive, featureless, grotesquely impressive.

"The peasant girl predicted the truth without knowing it," said the Mouser with a smile. "We played her game of 'circle-the-clearing and don't-cross-the-magic circle,' didn't we?"

The treasure house had no fears for him today. He recalled his perturbations of the previous evening, but was unable to understand them. The very idea of a guardian seemed somewhat ridiculous. There were a hundred other ways of explaining the skeleton inside the doorway.

So this time it was the Mouser who skipped into the treasure house ahead of Fafhrd. The interior was disappointing, being empty of any furnishings and as bare and unornamented as the outside walls. Just a large, low room. To either side square doorways led to the smaller domes, while to the rear a long hallway was dimly apparent, and the beginnings of a stair leading to the upper part of the main dome.

With only a casual glance at the skull and the broken skeleton, the Mouser made his way toward the stair.

"Our document," he said to Fafhrd, who was now beside him, "speaks of the treasure as resting just below the keystone of the chief dome. Therefore we must seek in the room or rooms above."

"True," answered the Northerner, glancing around. "But I wonder, Mouser, just what use this structure served. A man who builds a house solely to hide a treasure is shouting to the world that he has a treasure. Do you think it might have been a temple?"

The Mouser suddenly shrank back with a sibilant exclamation. Sprawled a little way up the stair was another skeleton, the major bones hanging together in lifelike fashion. The whole upper half of the skull was smashed to bony shards paler than those of a gray pot. "Our hosts are overly ancient and indecently naked," hissed the Mouser, angry with himself for being startled. Then he darted up the stairs to examine the grisly find. His sharp eyes picked out several objects among the bones. A rusty dagger, a tarnished gold ring that looped a knucklebone, a handful of horn buttons, and a slim, green-eaten copper cylinder. The last awakened his curiosity. He picked it up, dislodging hand-bones in the process, so that they fell apart, rattling dryly. He pried off the cap of the cylinder with his dagger point, and shook out a tightly rolled sheet of ancient parchment. This he gingerly unwound. Fafhrd and he scanned the lines of diminutive red lettering by the light from a small window on the landing above.

Mine is a secret treasure. Orichalcum have I, and crystal, and blood-red amber. Rubies and emeralds that demons would war for, and a diamond as big as the skull of a man. Yet none have seen them save I. I, Urgaan of Angarngi, scorn the flattery and the envy of fools. A fittingly lonely treasure house have I built for my jewels. There, hidden under the keystone, they may dream unperturbed until earth and sky wear away. A day's ride beyond the village of Soreev, in the valley of the two double-humped hills, lies that house, trebly-domed and single-towered. It is empty. Any fool may enter. Let him. I care not.

"The details differ slightly," murmured the Mouser, "but the phrases have the same ring as in our document."

"The man must have been mad," asserted Fafhrd, scowling. "Or else why should he carefully hide a treasure and then, with equal care, leave directions for finding it?"

"We thought our document was a memorandum or an oversight," said the Mouser thoughtfully. "Such a notion can hardly explain two documents." Lost in speculation, he turned toward the remaining section of the stair, only to find still another skull grinning at him from a shadowy angle. This time he was not startled, yet he experienced the same feeling that a fly must experience when, enmeshed in a spider's web, it sees the dangling, empty corpses of a dozen of its brothers. He began to speak rapidly.

"Nor can such a notion explain three or four or mayhap a dozen such documents. For how came these other questers here, unless each had found a written message? Urgaan of Angarngi may have been mad, but he sought deliberately to lure men here. One thing is certain: this house conceals—or did conceal—some deadly trap. Some guardian. Some giant beast, say. Or perhaps the very stones distill a poison. Perhaps hidden springs release sword blades which stab out through cracks in the walls and then return."

"That cannot be," answered Fafhrd. "These men were killed by great, bashing blows. The ribs and spine of the first were splintered. The second had his skull cracked open. And that third one there. See! The bones of his lower body are smashed."

The Mouser started to reply. Then his face broke into an unexpected smile. He could see the conclusion to which Fafhrd's arguments were unconsciously leading—and he knew that that conclusion was ridiculous. What thing would kill with great, bashing blows? What thing but the gray giant the peasant girl had told them about? The gray giant twice as tall as a man, with his great stone club—a giant fit only for fairy tales and fantasies.

And Fafhrd returned the Mouser's smile. It seemed to him that they were making a great deal of fuss about nothing. These skeletons were suggestive enough, to be sure, but did they not represent men who had died many, many years ago—centuries ago? What guardian could outlast three centuries? Why, that was a long enough time to weary the patience of a demon! And there were no such things as demons, anyhow. And there was no earthly use in mucking around about ancient fears and horrors that were as dead as dust. The whole matter, thought Fafhrd, boiled down to something very simple. They had come to a deserted house to see if there was a treasure in it.

Agreed upon this point, the two comrades made their way up the remaining section of stair that led to the dimmer regions of the House of Angarngi. Despite their confidence, they moved cautiously and kept sharp watch on the shadows lying ahead. This was wise.

Just as they reached the top, a flash of steel spun out of the darkness. It nicked the Mouser in the shoulder as he twisted to one side. There was a metallic clash as it fell to the stone floor. The Mouser, gripped by a sudden spasm of anger and fright, ducked down and dashed rapidly through the door from which the weapon had come, straight at the danger, whatever it was.

"Dagger-tossing in the dark, eh, you slick-bellied worm?" Fafhrd heard the Mouser cry, and then he, too, had plunged through the door.

Lord Rannarsh cowered against the wall, his rich hunting garb dusty and disordered, his black, wavy hair pushed back from his forehead, his cruelly handsome face a sallow mask of hate and extreme terror. For the moment the latter emotion seemed to predominate and, oddly enough, it did not appear to be directed toward the men he had just assailed, but toward something else, something unapparent.

"O gods!" he cried. "Let me go from here. The treasure is yours. Let me out of this place. Else I am doomed. The thing has played at cat and mouse with me. I cannot bear it. I cannot bear it!"

"So now we pipe a different tune, do we?" snarled the Mouser. "First dagger-tossing, then fright and pleas!"

"Filthy coward tricks," added Fafhrd. "Skulking here safe while your henchmen died bravely."

"Safe? Safe, you say? O gods!" Rannarsh almost screamed. Then a subtle change became apparent in his rigid-muscled face. It was not that his terror decreased. If anything, that became greater. But there was added to it, over and above, a consciousness of desperate shame, a realization that he had demeaned himself ineradicably in the eyes of these two ruffians. His lips began to writhe, showing tight-clenched teeth. He extended his left hand in a gesture of supplication.

"Oh, mercy, have mercy," he cried piteously, and his right hand twitched a second dagger from his belt and hurled it underhand at Fafhrd.

The Northerner knocked aside the weapon with a swift blow of his palm, then said deliberately, "He is yours, Mouser. Kill the man."

And now it was cat against cornered rat. Lord Rannarsh whipped a gleaming sword from its gold-worked scabbard and rushed in, cutting, thrusting, stabbing. The Mouser gave ground slightly, his slim blade flickering in a defensive counterattack that was wavering and elusive, yet deadly. He brought Rannarsh's rush to a standstill. His blade moved so quickly that it seemed to weave a net of steel around the man. Then it leaped forward three times in rapid succession. At the first thrust it bent nearly double against a concealed shirt of chain mail. The second thrust pierced the belly. The third transfixed the throat. Lord Rannarsh fell to the floor, spitting and gagging, his fingers clawing at his neck. There he died.

"An evil end," said Fafhrd somberly, "although he had fairer play than he deserved, and handled his sword well. Mouser, I like not this killing, although there was surely more justice to it than the others."

The Mouser, wiping his weapon against his opponent's thigh, understood what Fafhrd meant. He felt no elation at his victory, only a cold, queasy disgust. A moment before he had been raging, but now there was no anger left in him. He pulled open his gray jerkin and inspected the dagger wound in his left shoulder. A little blood was still welling from it and trickling down his arm.

"Lord Rannarsh was no coward," he said slowly. "He killed himself, or at least caused his own death, because we had seen him terrified and heard him cry in fright."

And at these words, without any warning whatsoever, stark terror fell like an icy eclipse upon the hearts of the Gray Mouser and Fafhrd. It was as if Lord Rannarsh had left them a legacy of fear, which passed to them immediately upon his death. And the unmanning thing about it was that they had no premonitory apprehension, no hint of its approach. It did not take root and grow gradually greater. It came all at once, paralyzing, overwhelming. Worse still, there was no discernible cause. One moment they were looking down with something of indifference upon the twisted corpse of Lord Rannarsh. The next moment their legs were weak, their guts were cold, their spines prickling, their teeth clicking, their hearts pounding, their hair lifting at the roots.

Fafhrd felt as if he had walked unsuspecting into the jaws of a gigantic serpent. His barbaric mind was stirred to the deeps. He thought of the grim god Kos brooding alone in the icy silence of the Cold Waste. He thought of the masked powers Fate and Chance, and of the game they play for the blood and brains of men. And he did not will these thoughts. Rather did the freezing fear seem to crystallize them, so that they dropped into his consciousness like snowflakes.

Slowly he regained control over his quaking limbs and twitching muscles. As if in a nightmare, he looked around him slowly, taking in the details of his surroundings. The room they were in was semicircular, forming half of the great dome. Two small windows, high in the curving ceiling, let in light.

An inner voice kept repeating, *Don't make a sudden move. Slowly. Slowly. Above all, don't run. The others did. That was why they died so quickly. Slowly. Slowly.*

He saw the Mouser's face. It reflected his own terror. He wondered how much longer this would last, how much longer he could stand it without running amuck, how much longer he could passively endure this feeling of a great invisible paw reaching out over him, span by span, implacably.

The faint sound of footsteps came from the room below. Regular and unhurried footsteps. Now they were crossing into the rear hallway below. Now they were on the stairs. And now they had reached the landing, and were advancing up the second section of the stairs.

The man who entered the room was tall and frail and old and very gaunt. Scant locks of intensely black hair straggled down over his high-domed forehead. His sunken cheeks showed clearly the outlines of his long jawbone, and waxy skin was pulled tight over his small nose. Fanatical eyes burned in deep, bony sockets. He wore the simple, sleeveless robe of a holy man. A pouch hung from the cord round his waist.

He fixed his eyes upon Fafhrd and the Gray Mouser.

58

"I greet you, you men of blood," he said in a hollow voice. Then his gaze fell with displeasure upon the corpse of Rannarsh.

"More blood has been shed. It is not well."

And with the bony forefinger of his left hand he traced in the air a curious triple square, the sign sacred to the Great God.

"Do not speak," his calm, toneless voice continued, "for I know your purposes. You have come to take treasure from this house. Others have sought to do the same. They have failed. You will fail. As for myself, I have no lust for treasure. For forty years I have lived on crusts and water, devoting my spirit to the Great God." Again he traced the curious sign. "The gems and ornaments of this world and the jewels and gauds of the world of demons cannot tempt or corrupt me. My purpose in coming here is to destroy an evil thing.

"I"—and here he touched his chest— "I am Arvlan of Angarngi, the ninth lineal descendant of Urgaan of Angarngi. This I always knew, and sorrowed for, because Urgaan of Angarngi was a man of evil. But not until fifteen days ago, on the Day of the Spider, did I discover from ancient documents that Urgaan had built this house, and built it to be an eternal trap for the unwise and venturesome. He has left a guardian here, and that guardian has endured.

"Cunning was my accursed ancestor, Urgaan, cunning and evil. The most skillful architect in all Lankhmar was Urgaan, a man wise in the ways of stone and learned in geometrical lore. But he scorned the Great God. He longed for improper powers. He had commerce with demons, and won from them an unnatural treasure. But he had no use for it. For in seeking wealth and knowledge and power, he lost his ability to enjoy any good feeling or pleasure, even simple lust. So he hid his treasure, but hid it in such a way that it would wreak endless evil on the world, even as he felt men and one proud, contemptuous, cruel woman—as heartless as this fane—had wreaked evil upon him. It is my purpose and my right to destroy Urgaan's evil.

"Seek not to dissuade me, lest doom fall upon you. As for me, no harm can befall me. The hand of the Great God is poised above me, ready to ward off any danger that may threaten his faithful servant. His will is my will. Do not speak, men of blood! I go to destroy the treasure of Urgaan of Angarngi."

And with these words, the gaunt holy man walked calmly on, with measured stride, like an apparition, and disappeared through the narrow doorway that led into the forward part of the great dome.

Fafhrd stared after him, his green eyes wide, feeling no desire to follow or to interfere. His terror had not left him but it was transmuted. He was still aware of a dreadful threat, but it no longer seemed to be directed against him personally.

Meanwhile, a most curious notion had lodged in the mind of the Mouser. He felt that he had just now seen, not a venerable holy man, but a dim reflection of the centuries-dead Urgaan of Angarngi. Surely Urgaan had that same high-domed forehead, that same secret pride, that same air of command. And those locks of youthfully black hair, which contrasted so ill with the aged face also seemed part of a picture looming from the past. A picture dimmed and distorted by time, but retaining something of the power and individuality of the ancient original.

They heard the footsteps of the holy man proceed a little way into the other room. Then for the space of a dozen heartbeats there was complete silence. Then the floor began to tremble slightly under their feet, as if the earth were quaking, or as if a giant were treading near. Then there came a single quavering cry from the next room, cut off in the middle by a single sickening crash that made them lurch. Then, once again, utter silence.

Fafhrd and the Mouser looked at one another in blank amazement—not so much because of what they had just heard but because, almost at the moment of the crash, the pall of terror had lifted from them completely. They jerked out their swords and hurried into the next room.

It was a duplicate of the one they had quitted, save that instead of two small windows, there were three, one of them near the floor. Also, there was but a single door, the one through which they had just entered. All else was closely mortised stone—floor, walls, and hemidomed ceiling.

Near the thick center wall, which bisected the dome, lay the body of the holy man. Only "lay" was not the right word. Left shoulder and chest were mashed against the floor. Life was fled. Blood puddled around.

Fafhrd's and the Mouser's eyes searched wildly for a being other than themselves and the dead man and found none—no, not one gnat hovering amongst the dust motes revealed by the narrow shafts of sunlight shooting down through the windows. Their imaginations searched as wildly and as much in vain for a being that could strike such a man-killing blow and vanish through one of the three tiny orifices of the windows. A giant, striking serpent with a granite head...

Set in the wall near the dead man was a stone about two feet square, jutting out a little from the rest. On this was boldly engraved, in antique Lankhmarian hieroglyphs: "Here rests the treasure of Urgaan of Angarngi."

The sight of that stone was like a blow in the face to the two adventurers. It roused every ounce of obstinacy and reckless determination in them. What matter that an old man sprawled smashed beside it? They had their swords! What matter they now had proof some grim guardian resided in the treasure house? They could take care of themselves! Run away and leave that stone unmoved, with its insultingly provocative inscription? No, by Kos, and the Behemoth! They'd see themselves in Nehwon's hell first!

Fafhrd ran to fetch the pick and the other large tools, which had been dropped on the stairs when Lord Rannarsh tossed his first dagger. The Mouser looked more closely at the jutting stone. The cracks around it were wide and filled with a dark, tarry mixture. It gave out a slightly hollow sound when he tapped it with his sword hilt. He calculated that the wall was about six feet thick at this point—enough to contain a sizable cavity. He tapped experimentally along the wall in both directions, but the hollow ring quickly ceased.

Evidently the cavity was a fairly small one. He noted that the crevices between all the other stones were very fine, showing no evidence of any cementing substance whatsoever. In fact, he couldn't be sure that they weren't false crevices, superficial cuts in the surface of solid rock. But that hardly seemed possible. He heard Fafhrd returning, but continued his examination.

The state of the Mouser's mind was peculiar. A dogged determination to get at the treasure overshadowed other emotions. The inexplicably sudden vanishing of his former terror had left certain parts of his mind benumbed. It was as if he had decided to hold his thoughts in leash until he had seen what the treasure cavity contained. He was content to keep his mind occupied with material details, and yet make no deductions from them.

His calmness gave him a feeling of at least temporary safety. His experiences had vaguely convinced him that the guardian, whatever it was, which had smashed the holy man and played cat and mouse with Rannarsh and themselves, did not strike without first inspiring a premonitory terror in its victims.

Fafhrd felt very much the same way, except that he was even more single-minded in his determination to solve the riddle of the inscribed stone.

They attacked the wide crevices with chisel and mallet. The dark tarry mixture came away fairly easily, first in hard lumps, later in slightly rubbery, gouged strips. After they had cleared it away to the depth of a finger, Fafhrd inserted the pick and managed to move the stone slightly. Thus the Mouser was enabled to gouge a little more deeply on that side. Then Fafhrd subjected the other side of the stone to the leverage of the pick. So the work proceeded, with alternate pryings and gougings.

They concentrated on each detail of the job with unnecessary intensity, mainly to keep their imaginations from being haunted by the image of a man more than two hundred years dead. A man with high-domed forehead, sunken cheeks, nose of a skull—that is, if the dead thing on the floor was a true type of the breed of Angarngi. A man who had somehow won a great treasure, and then hid it away from all eyes, seeking to obtain neither glory nor material profit from it. Who said he scorned the envy of fools, and who yet wrote many provocative notes in diminutive red lettering in order to inform fools of his treasure and make them envious. Who seemed to be reaching out across the dusty centuries, like a spider spinning a web to catch a fly on the other side of the world.

And yet, he was a skillful architect, the holy man had said. Could such an architect build a stone automaton twice as tall as a tall man? A gray stone automaton with a great club? Could he make a hiding place from which it could emerge, deal death, and then return? No, no, such notions were childish, not to be entertained! Stick to the job in hand. First find what lay behind the inscribed stone. Leave thoughts until afterward.

The stone was beginning to give more easily to the pressure of the pick. Soon they would be able to get a good purchase on it and pry it out.

Meanwhile an entirely new sensation was growing in the Mouser—not one of terror at all, but of physical revulsion. The air he breathed seemed thick and sickening. He found himself disliking the texture and consistency of the tarry mixture gouged from the cracks, which somehow he could only liken to wholly imaginary substances, such as the dung of dragons or the solidified vomit of the Behemoth. He avoided touching it with his fingers, and he kicked away the litter of chunks and strips that had gathered around his feet. The sensation of queasy loathing became difficult to endure.

He tried to fight it, but had no more success than if it had been seasickness, which in some ways it resembled. He felt unpleasantly dizzy. His mouth kept filling with saliva. The cold sweat of nausea beaded his forehead. He could tell that Fafhrd was unaffected, and he hesitated to mention the matter; it seemed ridiculously out of place, especially as it was unaccompanied by any fear or fright. Finally the stone itself began to have the same effect on him as the tarry mixture, filling him with a seemingly causeless, but none the less sickening revulsion. Then he could bear it no longer. With a vaguely apologetic nod to Fafhrd, he dropped his chisel and went to the low window for a breath of fresh air.

This did not seem to help matters much. He pushed his head through the window and gulped deeply. His mental processes were overshadowed by the general indifference of extreme nausea, and everything seemed very far away. Therefore when he saw that the peasant girl was standing in the middle of the clearing, it was some time before he began to consider the import of the fact. When he did, part of his sickness left him; or at least he was enabled to overpower it sufficiently to stare at her with gathering interest.

Her face was white, her fists were clenched, her arms held rigid at her sides. Even at the distance he could catch something of the mingled terror and determination with which her eyes were fixed on the great doorway. Toward this doorway she was forcing herself to move, one jerking step after another, as if she had to keep screwing her courage to a higher pitch. Suddenly the Mouser began to feel frightened, not for himself at all, but for the girl. Her terror was obviously intense, and yet she must be doing what she was doing—braving her "queer and fearsome gray giant"—for his sake and Fafhrd's. At all costs, he thought, she must be prevented from coming closer. It was wrong that she be subjected for one moment longer to such a horribly intense terror.

His mind was confused by his abominable nausea, yet he knew what he must do. He hurried toward the stairs with shaky strides, waving Fafhrd another vague gesture. Just as he was going out of the room he chanced to turn up his eyes, and spied something peculiar on the ceiling. What it was he did not fully realize for some moments.

Fafhrd hardly noticed the Mouser's movements, much less his gestures. The block of stone was rapidly yielding to his efforts. He had previously experienced a faint suggestion of the Mouser's nausea, but perhaps because of his greater single-mindedness, it had not become seriously bothersome. And now his attention was wholly concentrated on the stone. Persistent prying had edged it out a palm's breadth from the wall. Seizing it firmly in his two powerful hands, he tugged it from one side to the other, back and forth. The dark, viscous stuff clung to it tenaciously, but with each sidewise jerk it moved forward a little.

The Mouser lurched hastily down the stairs, fighting vertigo. His feet kicked bones and sent them knocking against the walls. What was it he had seen on the ceiling? Somehow, it seemed to mean something. But he must get the girl out of the clearing. She mustn't come any closer to the house. She mustn't enter.

Fafhrd began to feel the weight of the stone, and knew that it was nearly clear. It was damnably heavy—almost a foot thick. Two carefully gauged heaves finished the job. The stone overbalanced. He stepped quickly back. The stone crashed ponderously on the floor. A rainbow glitter came from the cavity that had been revealed. Fafhrd eagerly thrust his head into it.

The Mouser staggered toward the doorway. It was a bloody smear he had seen on the ceiling. And just above the corpse of the holy man. But why should that be? He'd been smashed against the floor, hadn't he? Was it blood splashed up from his lethal clubbing? But then why smeared? No matter. The girl. He must get to the girl. He must. There she was, almost at the doorway. He could see her. He felt the stone floor vibrating slightly beneath his feet. But that was his dizziness, wasn't it?

Fafhrd felt the vibration, too. But any thought he might have had about it was lost in his wonder at what he saw. The cavity was filled to a level just below the surface of the opening, with a heavy metallic liquid that resembled mercury, except that it was night-black. Resting on this liquid was a more astonishing group of gems than Fafhrd had ever dreamed of.

In the center was a titan diamond, cut with a myriad of oddly angled facets. Around it were two irregular circles, the inner formed of twelve rubies, each a decahedron, the outer formed of seventeen emeralds, each an irregular octahedron. Lying between these gems, touching some of them, sometimes connecting them with each other, were thin, fragile-looking bars of crystal, amber, greenish tourmaline, and honey-pale orichalchum. All these objects did not seem to be floating in the metallic liquid so much as resting upon it, their weight pressing down the surface into shallow depressions, some cup-shaped, others troughlike. The rods glowed faintly, while each of the gems glittered with a light that Fafhrd's mind strangely conceived to be refracted starlight.

His gaze shifted to the mercurous heavy fluid, where it bulged up between, and he saw distorted reflections of stars and constellations which he recognized, stars and constellations which would be visible now in the sky overhead, were it not for the concealing brilliance of the sun. An awesome wonder engulfed him. His gaze shifted back to the gems. There was something tremendously meaningful about their complex arrangement, something that seemed to speak of overwhelming truths in an alien symbolism. More, there was a compelling impression of inner movement, of sluggish thought, of inorganic consciousness. It was like what the eyes see when they close at night—not utter blackness, but a shifting, fluid pattern of many-colored points of light. Feeling that he was reaching impiously into the core of a thinking mind, Fafhrd gripped with his right hand for the diamond as big as a man's skull.

The Mouser blundered through the doorway. There could be no mistaking it now. The close-mortised stones were trembling. That bloody smear, as if the ceiling had champed down upon the holy man, crushing him against the floor, or as if the floor had struck upward. But there was the girl, her terror-wide eyes fastened upon him, her mouth open for a scream that did not come. He must drag her away, out of the clearing.

But why should he feel that a fearful threat was now directed at himself as well? Why should he feel that something was poised above him, threatening? As he stumbled down the terraced steps, he looked over his shoulder and up. The tower. The tower! It was falling. It was falling toward him. It was dipping at him over the dome. But there were no fractures along its length. It was not breaking. It was not falling. It was bending.

Fafhrd's hand jerked back, clutching the great, strangely faceted jewel, so heavy that he had difficulty in keeping his hold upon it. Immediately the surface of the metallic, star-reflecting fluid was disturbed. It bobbled and shook. Surely the whole house was shaking, too. The other jewels began to dart about erratically, like water insects on the surface of a puddle. The various crystalline and metallic bars began to spin, their tips attracted now to one jewel and now to another, as if the jewels were lodestone and the bars iron needles. The whole surface of the fluid was in a whirling, jerking confusion that suggested a mind gone mad because of loss of its chief part.

For an agonizing instant the Mouser stared up in amazement— frozen at the clublike top of the tower, hurling itself down upon him. Then he ducked and lunged forward at the girl, tackling her, rapidly rolling over and over with her. The tower top struck a sword's length behind them, with a thump that jolted them momentarily off the ground. Then it jerked itself up from the pitlike depression it had made.

Fafhrd tore his gaze away from the incredible, alien beauty of the jewel-confused cavity. His right hand was burning. The diamond was hot. No, it was cold beyond belief. By Kos, the room was changing shape! The ceiling was bulging downward at a point. He made for the door, then stopped dead in his tracks. The door was closing like a stony mouth. He turned and took a few steps over the quaking floor toward the small, low window. It snapped shut, like a sphincter. He tried to drop the diamond. It clung painfully to the inside of his hand. With a snap of his wrist he whipped it away from him. It hit the floor and began to bounce about, glaring like a living star.

The Mouser and the peasant girl rolled toward the edge of the clearing. The tower made two more tremendous bashes at them, but both went yards wide, like the blows of a blind madman. Now they were out of range. The Mouser lay sprawled on his side, watching a stone house that hunched and heaved like a beast, and a tower that bent double as it thumped grave-deep pits into the ground.

It crashed into a group of boulders and its top broke off, but the jaggedly fractured end continued to beat the boulders in wanton anger, smashing them into fragments. The Mouser felt a compulsive urge to take out his dagger and stab himself in the heart. A man had to die when he saw something like that.

Fafhrd clung to sanity because he was threatened from a new direction at every minute and because he could say to himself, "I know. I know. The house is a beast, and the jewels are its mind. Now that mind is mad. I know. I know." Walls, ceiling, and floor quaked and heaved, but their movements did not seem to be directed especially at him. Occasional crashes almost deafened him. He staggered over rocky swells, dodging stony advances that were half bulges and half blows, but that lacked the speed and directness of the tower's first smash at the Mouser. The corpse of the holy man was jolted about in grotesque mechanical reanimation.

Only the great diamond seemed aware of Fafhrd. Exhibiting a fretful intelligence, it kept bounding at him viciously, sometimes leaping as high as his head. He involuntarily made for the door as his only hope. It was champing up and down with convulsive regularity.

Watching his chance, he dived at it just as it was opening, and writhed through. The diamond followed him, striking at his legs. The carcass of Rannarsh was flung sprawling in his path. He jumped over it, then slid, lurched, stumbled, fell down stairs in earthquake, where dry bones danced. Surely the beast must die, the house must crash and crush him flat. The diamond leaped for his skull, missed, hurtled through the air, and struck a wall. Thereupon it burst into a great puff of iridescent dust.

Immediately the rhythm of the shaking of the house began to increase. Fafhrd raced across the heaving floor, escaped by inches the killing embrace of the great doorway, plunged across the clearing—passing a dozen feet from the spot where the tower was beating boulders into crushed rock—and then leaped over two pits in the ground. His face was rigid and white. His eyes were vacant.

He blundered bull-like into two or three trees, and only came to a halt because he knocked himself flat against one of them.

The house had ceased most of its random movements, and the whole of it was shaking like a huge dark jelly. Suddenly its forward part heaved up like a behemoth in death agony. The two smaller domes were jerked ponderously a dozen feet off the ground, as if they were the paws. The tower whipped into convulsive rigidity. The main dome contracted sharply, like a stupendous lung. For a moment it hung there, poised. Then it crashed to the ground in a heap of gigantic stone shards. The earth shook. The forest resounded. Battered atmosphere whipped branches and leaves. Then all was still. Only from the fractures in the stone a tarry, black liquid was slowly oozing, and here and there iridescent puffs of air suggested jewel-dust.

Along a narrow, dusty road two horsemen were cantering slowly toward the village of Soreev in the southernmost limits of the land of Lankhmar. They presented a somewhat battered appearance. The limbs of the larger, who was mounted on a chestnut gelding, showed several bruises, and there was a bandage around his thigh and another around the palm of his right hand. The smaller man, the one mounted on a gray mare, seemed to have suffered an equal number of injuries.

"Do you know where we're headed?" said the latter, breaking a long silence. "We're headed for a city. And in that city are endless houses of stone, stone towers without numbers, streets paved with stone, domes, archways, stairs. Tcha, if I feel then as I feel now, I'll never go within a bowshot of Lankhmar's walls."

His large companion smiled.

"What now, little man? Don't tell me you're afraid of earthquakes?"

Empire of the Necromancers

Clark Ashton Smith (1893-1961)

The legend of Mmatmuor and Sodosma shall arise only in the latter cycles of Earth, when the glad legends of the prime have been forgotten. Before the time of its telling, many epochs shall have passed away, and the seas shall have fallen in their beds, and new continents shall have come to birth. Perhaps, in that day, it will serve to beguile for a little the black weariness of a dying race, grown hopeless of all but oblivion. I tell the tale as men shall tell it in Zothique, the last continent, beneath a dim sun and sad heavens where the stars come out in terrible brightness before eventide.

I

Mmatmuor and Sodosma were necromancers who came from the dark isle of Naat, to practice their baleful arts in Tinarath, beyond the shrunken seas. But they did not prosper in Tinarath: for death was deemed a holy thing by the people of that gray country; and the nothingness of the tomb was not lightly to be desecrated; and the raising up of the dead by necromancy was held in abomination.

So, after a short interval, Mmatmuor and Sodosma were driven forth by the anger of the inhabitants, and were compelled to flee toward Cincor, a desert of the south, which was peopled only by the bones and mummies of a race that the pestilence had slain in former time.

EMPIRE OF THE NECROMANCERS

The land into which they went lay drear and leprous and ashen below the huge, ember-colored sun. Its crumbling rocks and deathly solitudes of sand would have struck terror to the hearts of common men; and, since they had been thrust out in that barren place without food or sustenance, the plight of the sorcerers might well have seemed a desperate one. But, smiling secretly, with the air of conquerors who tread the approaches of a long-coveted realm, Sodosma and Mmatmuor walked steadily on into Cincor

Unbroken before them, through fields devoid of trees and grass, and across the channels of dried-up rivers, there ran the great highway by which travelers had gone formerly between Cincor and Tinarath. Here they met no living thing; but soon they came to the skeletons of a horse and its rider, lying full in the road, and wearing still the sumptuous harness and raiment which they had worn in the flesh. And Mmatmuor and Sodosma paused before the piteous bones, on which no shred of corruption remained; and they smiled evilly at each other.

"The steed shall be yours," said Mmatmuor, "since you are a little the elder of us two, and are thus entitled to precedence; and the rider shall serve us both and be the first to acknowledge fealty to us in Cincor."

Then, in the ashy sand by the wayside, they drew a threefold circle; and standing together at its center, they performed the abominable rites that compel the dead to arise from tranquil nothingness and obey henceforward, in all things, the dark will of the necromancer. Afterward they sprinkled a pinch of magic powder on the nostril-holes of the man and the horse; and the white bones, creaking mournfully, rose up from where they had lain and stood in readiness to serve their masters.

So, as had been agreed between them, Sodosma mounted the skeleton steed and took up the jeweled reins, and rode in an evil mockery of Death on his pale horse; while Mmatmuor trudged on beside him, leaning lightly on an ebon staff; and the skeleton of the man, with its rich raiment flapping loosely, followed behind the two like a servitor.

After a while, in the gray waste, they found the remnant of another horse and rider, which the jackals had spared and the sun had dried to the leanness of old mummies. These also they raised up from death; and Mmatmuor bestrode the withered charger; and the two magicians rode on in state, like errant emperors, with a lich and a skeleton to attend them. Other bones and charnel remnants of men and beasts, to which they came anon, were duly resurrected in like fashion; so that they gathered to themselves an everswelling train in their progress through Cincor.

Along the way, as they neared Yethlyreom, which had been the capital, they found numerous tombs and necropoli, inviolate still after many ages, and containing swathed mummies that had scarcely withered in death. All these they raised up and called from sepulchral night to do their bidding. Some they commanded to sow and till the desert fields and hoist water from the sunken wells; others they left at diverse tasks, such as the mummies had performed in life. The century-long silence was broken by the noise and tumult of myriad activities; and the lank liches of weavers toiled at their shuttles; and the corpses of plowmen followed their furrows behind carrion oxen.

Weary with their strange journey and their oft-repeated incantations, Mmatmuor and Sodosma saw before them at last, from a desert hill, the lofty spires and fair, unbroken domes of Yethlyreom, steeped in the darkening stagnant blood of ominous sunset.

"It is a goodly land," said Mmatmuor, "and you and I will share it between us, and hold dominion over all its dead, and be crowned as emperors on the morrow in Yethlyreom."

"Aye," replied Sodosma, "for there is none living to dispute us here; and those that we have summoned from the tomb shall move and breathe only at our dictation, and may not rebel against us."

So, in the blood-red twilight that thickened with purple, they entered Yethlyreom and rode on among the lofty, lampless mansions, and installed themselves with their grisly retinue in that stately and abandoned palace, where the dynasty of Nimboth emperors had reigned for two thousand years with dominion over Cincor.

In the dusty golden halls, they lit the empty lamps of onyx by means of their cunning sorcery, and supped on royal viands, provided from past years, which they evoked in like manner. Ancient and imperial wines were poured for them in moonstone cups by the fleshless hands of their servitors; and they drank and feasted and reveled in phantasmagoric pomp, deferring till the morrow the resurrection of those who lay dead in Yethlyreom.

They rose betimes, in the dark crimson dawn, from the opulent palace-beds in which they had slept; for much remained to be done. Everywhere in that forgotten city, they went busily to and fro, working their spells on the people that had died in the last year of the pest and had lain unburied. And having accomplished this, they passed beyond Yethlyreom into that other city of high tombs and mighty mausoleums, in which lay the Nimboth emperors and the more consequential citizens and nobles of Cincor.

Here they bade their skeleton slaves to break in the sealed doors with hammers; and then, with their sinful, tyrannous incantations, they called forth the imperial mummies, even to the eldest of the dynasty, all of whom came walking stiffly, with lightless eyes, in rich swathings sewn with flame-bright jewels. And also, later, they brought forth to a semblance of life many generations of courtiers and dignitaries.

Moving in solemn pageant, with dark and haughty and hollow faces, the dead emperors and empresses of Cincor made obeisance to Mmatmuor and Sodosma, and attended them like a train of captives through all the streets of Yethlyreom. Afterward, in the immense throne-room of the palace, the necromancers mounted the high double throne, where the rightful rulers had sat with their consorts. Amid the assembled emperors, in gorgeous and funereal state, they were invested with sovereignty by the sere hands of the mummy of Hestaiyon, earliest of the Nimboth line, who had ruled in half-mythic years. Then all the descendants of Hestaiyon, crowding the room in a great throng, acclaimed with toneless, echo-like voices the dominion of Mmatmuor and Sodosma.

Thus did the outcast necromancers find for themselves an empire and a subject people in the desolate, barren land where the men of Tinarath had driven them forth to perish. Reigning supreme over all the dead of Cincor, by virtue of their malign magic, they exercised a baleful despotism. Tribute was borne to them by fleshless porters from outlying realms; and plague-eaten corpses, and tall mummies scented with mortuary balsams, went to and fro upon their errands in Yethlyreom, or heaped before their greedy eyes, from inexhaustible vaults, the cobweb-blackened gold and dusty gems of antique time.

Dead laborers made their palace-gardens to bloom with long-perished flowers; liches and skeletons toiled for them in the mines, or reared superb, fantastic towers to the dying sun. Chamberlains and princes of old time were their cupbearers, and stringed instruments were plucked for their delight by the slim hands of empresses with golden hair that had come forth untarnished from the night of the tomb. Those that were fairest, whom the plague and the worm had not ravaged overmuch, they took for their lemans and made to serve their necrophilic lust.

II

In all things, the people of Cincor performed the actions of life at the will of Mmatmuor and Sodosma. They spoke, they moved, they ate and drank as in life. They heard and saw and felt with a similitude of the senses that had been theirs before death; but their brains were enthralled by a dreadful necromancy. They recalled but dimly their former existence; and the state to which they had been summoned was empty and troublous and shadow-like. Their blood ran chill and sluggish, mingled with water of Lethe; and the vapors of Lethe clouded their eyes.

Dumbly they obeyed the dictates of their tyrannous lords, without rebellion or protest, but filled with a vague, illimitable weariness such as the dead must know, when having drunk of eternal sleep, they are called back once more to the bitterness of mortal being. They knew no passion or desire, or delight, only the black languor of their awakening from Lethe, and a gray, ceaseless longing to return to that interrupted slumber.

Youngest and last of the Nimboth emperors was Illeiro, who had died in the first month of the plague. and had lain in his high-built mausoleum for two hundred years before the coming of the necromancers.

Raised up with his people and his fathers to attend the tyrants, Illeiro had resumed the emptiness of existence without question and had felt no surprise. He had accepted his own resurrection and that of his ancestors as one accepts the indignities and marvels of a dream. He knew that he had come back to a faded sun, to a hollow and spectral world, to an order of things in which his place was merely that of an obedient shadow. But at first he was troubled only, like the others, by a dim weariness and pale hunger for the lost oblivion.

Drugged by the magic of his overlords, weak from the age-long nullity of death, he beheld like a somnambulist the enormities to which his fathers were subjected. Yet, somehow, after many days, a feeble spark awoke in the sodden twilight of his mind.

Like something lost and irretrievable, beyond prodigious gulfs, he recalled the pomp of his reign in Yethlyreom, and the golden pride and exultation that had been his in youth. And recalling it, he felt a vague stirring of revolt, a ghostly resentment against the magicians who had haled him forth to this calamitous mockery of life. Darkly he began to grieve for his fallen state, and the mournful plight of his ancestors and his people.

Day by day, as a cupbearer in the halls where he had ruled aforetime, Illeiro saw the doings of Mmatmuor and Sodosma. He saw their caprices of cruelty and lust, their growing drunkenness and gluttony. He watched them wallow in their necromantic luxury, and become lax with indolence, gross with indulgence. They neglected the study of their art, they forgot many of their spells. But still they ruled, mighty and formidable; and, lolling on couches of purple and rose, they planned to lead an army of the dead against Tinarath.

Dreaming of conquest, and of vaster necromancies, they grew fat and slothful as worms that have installed themselves in a charnel rich with corruption. And pace by pace with their laxness and tyranny, the fire of rebellion mounted in the shadowy heart of Illeiro, like a flame that struggles with Lethean damps. And slowly, with the waxing of his wrath, there returned to him something of the strength and firmness that had been his in life. Seeing the turpitude of the oppressors, and knowing the wrong that had been done to the helpless dead, he heard in his brain the clamor of stifled voices demanding vengeance.

Among his fathers, through the palace-halls of Yethlyreom, Illeiro moved silently at the bidding of the masters, or stood awaiting their command. He poured in their cups of onyx the amber vintages, brought by wizardry from hills beneath a younger sun; he submitted to their contumelies and insults. And night by night he watched them nod in their drunkenness, till they fell asleep, flushed and gross, amid their arrogated splendor.

There was little speech among the living dead; and son and father, daughter and mother, lover and beloved, went to and fro without sign of recognition, making no comment on their evil lot. But at last, one midnight, when the tyrants lay in slumber, and the flames wavered in the necromantic lamps, Illeiro took counsel with Hestaiyon, his eldest ancestor, who had been famed as a great wizard in fable and was reputed to have known the secret lore of antiquity.

Hestaiyon stood apart from the others, in a corner of the shadowy hall. He was brown and withered in his crumbling mummy-cloths; and his lightless obsidian eyes appeared to gaze still upon nothingness. He seemed not to have heard the questions of Illeiro; but at length, in a dry, rustling whisper, he responded:

"I am old, and the night of the sepulcher was long, and I have forgotten much. Yet, groping backward across the void of death, it may be that I shall retrieve something of my former wisdom; and between us we shall devise a mode of deliverance." And Hestaiyon searched among the shreds of memory, as one who reaches into a place where the worm has been and the hidden archives of old time have rotted in their covers; till at last he remembered, and said:

"I recall that I was once a mighty wizard; and among other things, I knew the spells of necromancy; but employed them not, deeming their use and the raising up of the dead an abhorrent act. Also, I possessed other knowledge; and perhaps, among the remnants of that ancient lore, there is something which may serve to guide us now. For I recall a dim, dubitable prophecy, made in the primal years, at the founding of Yethlyreom and the empire of Cincor. The prophecy was, that an evil greater than death would befall the emperors and the people of Cincor in future times; and that the first and the last of the Nimboth dynasty, conferring together, would effect a mode of release and the lifting of the doom. The evil was not named in the prophecy: but it was said that the two emperors would learn the solution of their problem by the breaking of an ancient clay image that guards the nethermost vault below the imperial palace in Yethlyreom."

Then, having heard this prophecy from the faded lips of his forefather, Illeiro mused a while, and said:

"I remember now an afternoon in early youth, when searching idly through the unused vaults of our palace, as a boy might do, I came to the last vault and found therein a dusty, uncouth image of clay, whose form and countenance were strange to me. And, knowing not the prophecy, I turned away in disappointment, and went back as idly as I had come, to seek the moted sunlight."

Then, stealing away from their heedless kinfolk, and carrying jeweled lamps they had taken from the hall, Hestaiyon and Illeiro went downward by subterranean stairs beneath the palace; and, threading like implacable furtive shadows the maze of nighted corridors, they came at last to the lowest crypt.

Here, in the black dust and clotted cobwebs of an immemorial past, they found, as had been decreed, the clay image, whose rude features were those of a forgotten earthly god. And Illeiro shattered the image with a fragment of stone; and he and Hestaiyon took from its hollow center a great sword of unrusted steel, and a heavy key of untarnished bronze, and tablets of bright brass on which were inscribed the various things to be done, so that Cincor should be rid of the dark reign of the necromancers and the people should win back to oblivious death.

So, with the key of untarnished bronze, Illeiro unlocked, as the tablets had instructed him to do, a low and narrow door at the end of the nethermost vault, beyond the broken image; and he and Hestaiyon saw, as had been prophesied, the coiling steps of somber stone that led downward to an undiscovered abyss, where the sunken fires of earth still burned. And leaving Illeiro toward the open door, Hestaiyon took up the sword of unrusted steel in his thin hand, and went back to the hall where the necromancers slept, lying a-sprawl on their couches of rose and purple, with the wan, bloodless dead about them in patient ranks.

Upheld by the ancient prophecy and the lore of the bright tablets, Hestaiyon lifted the great sword and struck off the head of Mmatmuor and the head of Sodosma, each with a single blow. Then, as had been directed, he quartered the remains with mighty strokes. And the necromancers gave up their unclean lives, and lay supine, without movement, adding a deeper red to the rose and a brighter hue to the sad purple of their couches.

Then, to his kin, who stood silent and listless, hardly knowing their liberation, the venerable mummy of Hestaiyon spoke in sere murmurs, but authoritatively, as a king who issues commands to his children. The dead emperors and empresses stirred, like autumn leaves in a sudden wind, and a whisper passed among them and went forth from the palace, to be communicated at length, by devious ways, to all the dead of Cincor.

All that night, and during the blood-dark day that followed, by wavering torches or the light of the failing sun, an endless army of plague-eaten liches, of tattered skeletons, poured in a ghastly torrent through the streets of Yethlyreom and along the palace-hall where Hestaiyon stood guard above the slain necromancers. Unpausing, with vague, fixed eyes, they went on like driven shadows, to seek the subterranean vaults below the palace, to pass through the open door where Illeiro waited in the last vault, and then to wend downward by a thousand thousand steps to the verge of that gulf in which boiled the ebbing fires of earth. There, from the verge, they flung themselves to a second death and the clean annihilation of the bottomless flames.

But, after all had gone to their release, Hestaiyon still remained, alone in the fading sunset, beside the cloven corpses of Mmatmuor and Sodosma. There, as the tablets had directed him to do, he made trial of those spells of elder necromancy which he had known in his former wisdom, and cursed the dismembered bodies with that perpetual life-in-death which Mmatmuor and Sodosma had sought to inflict upon the people of Cincor. And maledictions came from the pale lips, and the heads rolled horribly with glaring eyes, and the limbs and torsos writhed on their imperial couches amid clotted blood. Then, with no backward look, knowing that all was done as had been ordained and predicted from the first, the mummy of Hestaiyon left the necromancers to their doom, and went wearily through the nighted labyrinth of vaults to rejoin Illeiro.

So, in tranquil silence, with no further need of words, Illeiro and Hestaiyon passed through the open door of the nether vault, and Illeiro locked the door behind them with its key of untarnished bronze. And thence, by the coiling stairs, they wended their way to the verge of the sunken flames and were one with their kinfolk and their people in the last, ultimate nothingness.

But of Mmatmuor and Sodosma, men say that their quartered bodies crawl to and fro to this day in Yethlyreom, finding no peace or respite from their doom of life-indeath, and seeking vainly through the black maze of nether vaults the door that was locked by Illeiro.

Turjan of Miir

Jack Vance (1916-2013)

Turjan sat in his workroom, legs sprawled out from the stool, back against and elbows on the bench. Across the room was a cage; into this Turjan gazed with rueful vexation. The creature in the cage returned the scrutiny with emotions beyond conjecture.

It was a thing to arouse pity—a great head on a small spindly body, with weak rheumy eyes and a flabby button of a nose. The mouth hung slackly wet, the skin glistened waxy pink. In spite of its manifest imperfection, it was to date the most successful product of Turjan's vats.

Turjan stood up, found a bowl of pap. With a long-handled spoon he held food to the creature's mouth. But the mouth refused the spoon and mush trickled down the glazed skin to fall on the rickety frame.

Turjan put down the bowl, stood back and slowly returned to his stool. For a week now it had refused to eat. Did the idiotic visage conceal perception, a will to extinction? As Turjan watched, the white-blue eyes closed, the great head slumped and bumped to the floor of the cage. The limbs relaxed; the creature was dead.

Turjan sighed and left the room. He mounted winding stone stairs and at last came out on the roof of his castle Miir, high above the river Derna. In the west the sun hung close to old earth; ruby shafts, heavy and rich as wine, slanted past the gnarled boles of the archaic forest to lay on the turfed forest floor. The sun sank in accordance with the old ritual; latter-day night fell across the forest, a soft, warm darkness came swiftly, and Turjan stood pondering the death of his latest creature.

He considered its many precursors: the thing all eyes, the boneless creature with the pulsing surface of its brain exposed, the beautiful female body whose intestines trailed out into the nutrient solution like seeking fibrils, the inverted inside-out creatures…Turjan sighed bleakly. His methods were at fault; a fundamental element was lacking from his synthesis, a matrix ordering the components of the pattern.

As he sat gazing across the darkening land, memory took Turjan to a night of years before, when the Sage had stood beside him.

"In ages gone," the Sage had said, his eyes fixed on a low star, "a thousand spells were known to sorcery and the wizards effected their wills. Today, as Earth dies, a hundred spells remain to man's knowledge, and these have come to us through the ancient books… But there is one called Pandelume, who knows all the spells, all the incantations, cantraps, runes, and thaumaturgies that have ever wrenched and molded space…" He had fallen silent, lost in his thoughts.

"Where is this Pandelume?" Turjan had asked presently.

"He dwells in the land of Embelyon," the Sage had replied, "but where this land lies, no one knows."

"How does one find Pandelume, then?"

The Sage had smiled faintly. "If it were ever necessary, a spell exists to take one there."

Both had been silent a moment; then the Sage had spoken, staring out over the forest.

"One may ask anything of Pandelume, and Pandelume will answer—provided that the seeker performs the service Pandelume requires. And Pandelume drives a hard bargain."

Then the Sage had shown Turjan the spell in question, which he had discovered in an ancient portfolio, and kept secret from all the world.

Turjan, remembering this conversation, descended to his study, a long low hall with stone walls and stone floor deadened by a thick russet rug. The tomes which held Turjan's sorcery lay on the long table of black skeel or were thrust helter-skelter into shelves. These were volumes compiled by many wizards of the past, untidy folios collected by the Sage, leather-bound librams setting forth the syllables of a hundred powerful spells, so cogent that Turjan's brain could know but four at a time.

Turjan found a musty portfolio, turned the heavy pages to the spell the Sage had shown him, the Call to the Violent Cloud. He stared down at the characters and they burned with an urgent power, pressing off the page as if frantic to leave the dark solitude of the book.

Turjan closed the book, forcing the spell back into oblivion. He robed himself with a short blue cape, tucked a blade into his belt, fitted the amulet holding Laccodel's Rune to his wrist. Then he sat down and from a journal chose the spells he would take with him. What dangers he might meet he could not know, so he selected three spells of general application: the Excellent Prismatic Spray, Phandaal's Mantle of Stealth, and the Spell of the Slow Hour.

He climbed the parapets of his castle and stood under the far stars, breathing the air of ancient Earth...How many times had this air been breathed before him? What cries of pain had this air experienced, what sighs, laughs, war shouts, cries of exultation, gasps...

The night was wearing on. A blue light wavered in the forest. Turjan watched a moment, then at last squared himself and uttered the Call to the Violent Cloud.

All was quiet; then came a whisper of movement swelling to the roar of great winds. A wisp of white appeared and waxed to a pillar of boiling black smoke. A voice deep and harsh issued from the turbulence.

"At your disturbing power is this instrument come; whence will you go?"

"Four Directions, then One," said Turjan. "Alive must I be brought to Embelyon."

The cloud whirled down; far up and away he was snatched, flung head over heels into incalculable distance. Four directions was he thrust, then one, and at last a great blow hurled him from the cloud, sprawled him into Embelyon.

Turjan gained his feet and tottered a moment, half-dazed. His senses steadied; he looked about him.

He stood on the bank of a limpid pool. Blue flowers grew about his ankles and at his back reared a grove of tall blue-green trees, the leaves blurring on high into mist. Was Embelyon of Earth? The trees were Earth-like, the flowers were of familiar form, the air was of the same texture... But there was an odd lack to this land and it was difficult to determine. Perhaps it came of the horizon's curious vagueness, perhaps from the blurring quality of the air, lucent and uncertain as water. Most strange, however, was the sky, a mesh of vast ripples and cross-ripples, and these refracted a thousand shafts of colored light, rays which in mid-air wove wondrous lace, rainbow nets, in all the jewel hues. So as Turjan watched, there swept over him beams of claret, topaz, rich violet, radiant green. He now perceived that the colors of the flowers and the trees were but fleeting functions of the sky, for now the flowers were of salmon tint, and the trees a dreaming purple. The flowers deepened to copper, then with a suffusion of crimson, warmed through maroon to scarlet, and the trees had become sea-blue.

"The Land None Knows Where," said Turjan to himself. "Have I been brought high, low, into a pre-existence or into the after-world?" He looked toward the horizon and thought to see a black curtain raising high into the murk, and this curtain encircled the land in all directions.

The sound of galloping hooves approached; he turned to find a black horse lunging break-neck along the bank of the pool. The rider was a young woman with black hair streaming wildly. She wore loose white breeches to the knee and a yellow cape flapping in the wind.

One hand clutched the reins, the other flourished a sword.

Turjan warily stepped aside, for her mouth was tight and white as if in anger, and her eyes glowed with a peculiar frenzy. The woman hauled back on the reins, wheeled her horse high around, charged Turjan, and struck out at him with her sword.

Turjan jumped back and whipped free his own blade. When she lunged at him again, he fended off the blow and leaning forward, touched the point to her arm and brought a drop of blood. She drew back startled; then up from her saddle she snatched a bow and flicked an arrow to the string. Turjan sprang forward, dodging the wild sweep of the sword, seized her around the waist, and dragged her to the ground.

She fought with a crazy violence. He had no wish to kill her, and so struggled in a manner not entirely dignified. Finally he held her helpless, her arms pinioned behind her back.

"Quiet, vixen!" said Turjan, "Lest I lose patience and stun you!"

"Do as you please," the girl gasped. "Life and death are brothers."

"Why do you seek to harm me?" demanded Turjan. "I have given you no offense."

"You are evil, like all existence." Emotion ground the delicate fibers of her throat. "If power were mine, I would crush the universe to bloody gravel, and stamp it into the ultimate muck."

Turjan in surprise relaxed his grip, and she nearly broke loose. But he caught her again.

"Tell me, where may I find Pandelume?"

The girl stilled her exertion, twisted her head to stare at Turjan. Then: "Search all Embelyon. I will assist you not at all."

If she were more amiable, thought Turjan, she would be a creature of remarkable beauty.

"Tell me where I may find Pandelume," said Turjan, "else I find other uses for you."

She was silent for a moment, her eyes blazing with madness. Then she spoke in a vibrant voice.

"Pandelume dwells beside the stream only a few paces distant."

Turjan released her, but he took her sword and bow.

"If I return these to you, will you go your way in peace?"

For a moment she glared; then without words she mounted her horse and rode off through the trees.

Turjan watched her disappear through the shafts of jewel colors, then went in the direction she had indicated. Soon he came to a long low manse of red stone backed by dark trees. As he approached the door swung open. Turjan halted in mid-stride.

"Enter!" came a voice. "Enter, Turjan of Miir!"

So Turjan wonderingly entered the manse of Pandelume. He found himself in a tapestried chamber, bare of furnishing save a single settee. No one came to greet him. A closed door stood at the opposite wall, and Turjan went to pass through, thinking perhaps it was expected of him.

"Halt, Turjan," spoke the voice. "No one may gaze on Pandelume. It is the law."

Turjan, standing in the middle of the room, spoke to his unseen host.

"This is my mission, Pandelume," he said. "For some time I have been striving to create humanity in my vats. Yet always I fail, from ignorance of the agent that binds and orders the patterns. This master-matrix must be known to you; therefore I come to you for guidance."

"Willingly will I aid you," said Pandelume. "There is, however, another aspect involved. The universe is methodized by symmetry and balance; in every aspect of existence is this equipoise observed. Consequently, even in the trivial scope of our dealings, this equivalence must be maintained, thus and thus. I agree to assist you; in return, you perform a service of equal value for me. When you have completed this small work, I will instruct and guide you to your complete satisfaction."

"What may this service be?" inquired Turjan.

"A man lives in the land of Ascolais, not far from your Castle Miir. About his neck hangs an amulet of carved blue stone. This you must take from him and bring to me."

Turjan considered a moment.

"Very well," he said. "I will do what I can. Who is the man?"

Pandelume answered in a soft voice.

"Prince Kandive the Golden."

"Ah," exclaimed Turjan ruefully, "you have gone to no pains to make my task a pleasant one… But I will fulfill your requirements as best I can."

"Good," said Pandelume. "Now I must instruct you. Kandive wears this amulet hidden below his singlet. When an enemy appears, he takes it out to display on his chest, such is the potency of the charm. No matter what else, do not gaze on this amulet, either before or after you take it, on pain of most hideous consequence."

"I understand," said Turjan. "I will obey. Now there is a question I would ask—providing the answer will not involve me in an undertaking to bring the Moon back to Earth, or recover an elixir you inadvertently spilled in the sea."

Pandelume laughed loud. "Ask on," he responded, "and I will answer."

Turjan put his question.

"As I approached your dwelling, a woman of insane fury wished to kill me. This I would not permit and she departed in rage. Who is this woman and why is she thus?"

Pandelume's voice was amused. "I, too," he replied, "have vats where I mold life into varied forms. This girl T'sais I created, but I wrought carelessly, with a flaw in the synthesis. So she climbed from the vat with a warp in her brain, in this manner: what we hold to be beautiful seems to her loathsome and ugly, and what we find ugly is to her intolerably vile, in a degree that you and I cannot understand. She finds the world a bitter place, peopled with shapes of direst malevolence."

"So this is the answer," Turjan murmured. "Pitiable wretch!"

"Now," said Pandelume, "you must be on your way to Kaiin; the auspices are good…In a moment open this door, enter, and move to the pattern of runes on the floor."

Turjan performed as he was bid. He found the next room to be circular and high-domed, with the varying lights of Embelyon pouring down through sky-transparencies. When he stood upon the pattern in the floor, Pandelume spoke again.

"Now close your eyes, for I must enter and touch you. Heed well, do not try to glimpse me!"

Turjan closed his eyes. Presently a step sounded behind him. "Extend your hand," said the voice. Turjan did so and felt a hard object placed therein. "When your mission is accomplished, crush this crystal and at once you will find yourself in this room." A cold hand was laid on his shoulder.

"An instant you will sleep," said Pandelume. "When you awake you will be in the city Kaiin."

The hand departed. A dimness came over Turjan as he stood awaiting the passage. The air had suddenly become full of sound: clattering, a tinkling of many small bells, music, voices. Turjan frowned, pursed his lips: A strange tumult for the austere home of Pandelume!

A woman's voice sounded close by.

"Look, O Santanil, see the man-owl who closes his eyes to merriment!"

There was a man's laughter, suddenly hushed. "Come. The fellow is bereft and possibly violent. Come."

Turjan hesitated, then opened his eyes. It was night in white-walled Kaiin, and festival time. Orange lanterns floated in the air, moving as the breeze took them. From the balconies dangled flower chains and cages of blue fireflies. The streets surged with the wine-flushed populace, costumed in a multitude of bizarre modes. Here was a Melantine bargeman, here a warrior of Valdaran's Green Legion, here another of ancient times wearing one of the old helmets. In a little cleared space a garlanded courtesan of the Kauchique littoral danced the Dance of the Fourteen Silken Movements to the music of flutes. In the shadow of a balcony a girl barbarian of East Almery embraced a man blackened and in leather harness as a

Deodand of the forest. They were gay, these people of waning Earth, feverishly merry, for infinite night was close at hand, when the red sun should finally flicker and go black.

Turjan melted into the throng. At a tavern he refreshed himself with biscuits and wine; then he made for the palace of Kandive the Golden.

The palace loomed before him, every window and balcony aglow with light. Among the lords of the city there was feasting and revelry. If Prince Kandive were flushed with drink and unwary, reflected Turjan, the task should not be too difficult. Yet, entering boldly, he might be recognized, for he was known to many in Kaiin. So, uttering Phandaal's Mantle of Stealth, he faded from the sight of all men.

Through the arcade he slipped, into the grand salon, where the lords of Kaiin made merry like the throngs of the street. Turjan threaded the rainbow of silk, velour, sateen, watching the play with amusement. On a terrace some stood looking into a sunken pool where a pair of captured Deodands, their skins like oiled jet, paddled and glared; others tossed darts at the spread-eagled body of a young Cobalt Mountain witch. In alcoves beflowered girls offered synthetic love to wheezing old men, and elsewhere others lay stupefied by dream-powders. Nowhere did Turjan find Prince Kandive. Through the palace he wandered, room after room, until at last in an upper chamber he came upon the tall golden-bearded prince, lolling on a couch with a masked girl-child who had green eyes and hair dyed pale green.

Some intuition or perhaps a charm warned Kandive when Turjan slipped through the purple hangings. Kandive leapt to his feet.

"Go!" he ordered the girl. "Out of the room quickly! Mischief moves somewhere near and I must blast it with magic!"

The girl ran hastily from the chamber. Kandive's hand stole to his throat and pulled forth the hidden amulet. But Turjan shielded his gaze with his hand.

Kandive uttered a powerful charm which loosened space free of all warp. So Turjan's spell was void and he became visible.

TURJAN OF MIIR

"Turjan of Miir skulks through my palace!" snarled Kandive.

"With ready death on my lips," spoke Turjan. "Turn your back, Kandive, or I speak a spell and run you through with my sword."

Kandive made as if to obey, but instead shouted the syllables bringing the Omnipotent Sphere about him.

"Now I call my guards, Turjan," announced Kandive contemptuously, "and you shall be cast to the Deodands in the tank."

Kandive did not know the engraved band Turjan wore on his wrist, a most powerful rune, maintaining a field solvent of all magic. Still guarding his vision against the amulet, Turjan stepped through the Sphere. Kandive's great blue eyes bulged.

"Call the guards," said Turjan. "They will find your body riddled by lines of fire."

"Your body, Turjan!" cried the Prince, babbling the spell. Instantly the blazing wires of the Excellent Prismatic Spray lashed from all directions at Turjan. Kandive watched the furious rain with a wolfish grin, but his expression changed quickly to consternation. A finger's breadth from Turjan's skin the fire-darts dissolved into a thousand gray puffs of smoke.

"Turn your back, Kandive," Turjan ordered. "Your magic is useless against Laccodel's Rune." But Kandive took a step toward a spring in the wall.

"Halt!" cried Turjan. "One more step and the Spray splits you thousandfold!"

Kandive stopped short. In helpless rage he turned his back and Turjan, stepping forward quickly, reached over Kandive's neck, seized the amulet and raised it free. It crawled in his hand and through the fingers there passed a glimpse of blue. A daze shook his brain, and for an instant he heard a murmur of avid voices…His vision cleared. He backed away from Kandive, stuffing the amulet in his pouch. Kandive asked, "May I now turn about in safety?"

"When you wish," responded Turjan, clasping his pouch. Kandive, seeing Turjan occupied, negligently stepped to the wall and placed his hand on a spring.

"Turjan," he said, "you are lost. Before you may utter a syllable, I will open the floor and drop you a great dark distance. Can your charms avail against this?"

Turjan halted in mid-motion, fixed his eyes upon Kandive's red and gold face. Then he dropped his eyes sheepishly. "Ah, Kandive," he fretted, "you have outwitted me. If I return you the amulet, may I go free?"

"Toss the amulet at my feet," said Kandive, gloating. "Also Laccodel's Rune. Then I shall decide what mercy to grant you."

"Even the Rune?" Turjan asked, forcing a piteous note to his voice.

"Or your life."

Turjan reached into his pouch and grasped the crystal Pandelume had given him. He pulled it forth and held it against the pommel of his sword.

"Ho, Kandive," he said, "I have discerned your trick. You merely wish to frighten me into surrender. I defy you!"

Kandive shrugged. "Die then." He pushed the spring. The floor jerked open, and Turjan disappeared into the gulf. But when Kandive raced below to claim Turjan's body, he found no trace, and he spent the rest of the night in temper, brooding over wine.

Turjan found himself in the circular room of Pandelume's manse. Embelyon's many-colored lights streamed through the sky-windows upon his shoulder—sapphire blue, the yellow of marigolds, blood red. There was silence through the house. Turjan moved away from the rune in the floor, glancing uneasily to the door, fearful lest Pandelume, unaware of his presence, enter the room.

"Pandelume!" he called. "I have returned!"

There was no response. Deep quiet held the house. Turjan wished he were in the open air where the odor of sorcery was less strong. He looked at the doors; one led to the entrance hall, the other he knew not where. The door on the right hand must lead outside; he laid his hand on the latch to pull it open. But he paused. Suppose he were mistaken, and Pandelume's form were revealed? Would it be wiser to wait here?

A solution occurred to him. His back to the door, he swung it open.

"Pandelume!" he called.

A soft intermittent sound came to his ears from behind, and he seemed to hear a labored breath. Suddenly frightened, Turjan stepped back into the circular room and closed the door.

He resigned himself to patience and sat on the floor.

A gasping cry came from the next room. Turjan leapt to his feet.

"Turjan? You are there?"

"Yes; I have returned with the amulet."

"Do this quickly," panted the voice. "Guarding your sight, hang the amulet over your neck and enter."

Turjan, spurred by the urgency of the voice, closed his eyes and arranged the amulet on his chest. He groped to the door and flung it wide.

Silence of a shocked intensity held an instant; then came an appalling screech, so wild and demoniac that Turjan's brain sang. Mighty pinions buffeted the air, there was a hiss and the scrape of metal. Then, amidst muffled roaring, an icy wind bit Turjan's face. Another hiss—and all was quiet.

"My gratitude is yours," said the calm voice of Pandelume. "Few times have I experienced such dire stress, and without your aid might not have repulsed that creature of hell."

A hand lifted the amulet from Turjan's neck. After a moment of silence Pandelume's voice sounded again from a distance.

"You may open your eyes."

Turjan did so. He was in Pandelume's workroom; amidst much else, he saw vats like his own.

"I will not thank you," said Pandelume. "But in order that a fitting symmetry be maintained, I perform a service for a service.

I will not only guide your hands as you work among the vats, but also will I teach you other matters of value."

In this fashion did Turjan enter his apprenticeship to Pandelume. Day and far into the opalescent Embelyon night he worked under Pandelume's unseen tutelage. He learned the secret of renewed youth, many spells of the ancients, and a strange abstract lore that Pandelume termed "Mathematics".

"Within this instrument," said Pandelume, "resides the Universe. Passive in itself and not of sorcery, it elucidates every problem, each phase of existence, all the secrets of time and space. Your spells and runes are built upon its power and codified according to a great underlying mosaic of magic. The design of this mosaic we cannot surmise; our knowledge is didactic, empirical, arbitrary. Phandaal glimpsed the pattern and so was able to formulate many of the spells which bear his name. I have endeavored through the ages to break the clouded glass, but so far my research has failed. He who discovers the pattern will know all of sorcery and be a man powerful beyond comprehension."

So Turjan applied himself to the study and learned many of the simpler routines.

"I find herein a wonderful beauty," he told Pandelume. "This is no science, this is art, where equations fall away to elements like resolving chords, and where always prevails a symmetry either explicit or multiplex, but always of a crystalline serenity."

In spite of these other studies, Turjan spent most of his time at the vats, and under Pandelume's guidance achieved the mastery he sought. As a recreation he formed a girl of exotic design, whom he named Floriel. The hair of the girl he had found with Kandive on the night of the festival had fixed in his mind, and he gave his creature pale green hair. She had skin of creamy tan and wide emerald eyes. Turjan was intoxicated with delight when he brought her wet and perfect from the vat. She learned quickly and soon knew how to speak with Turjan. She was one of dreamy and wistful habit, caring for little but wandering among the flowers of the meadow, or sitting silently by the river; yet she was a pleasant creature and her gentle manners amused Turjan.

But one day the black-haired T'sais came riding past on her horse, steely-eyed, slashing at flowers with her sword. The innocent Floriel wandered by and T'sais, exclaiming "Green-eyed woman— your aspect horrifies me, it is death for you!" cut her down as she had the flowers in her path.

Turjan, hearing the hooves, came from the workroom in time to witness the sword-play. He paled in rage and a spell of twisting torment rose to his lips. Then T'sais looked at him and cursed him, and in the pale face and dark eyes he saw her misery and the spirit that caused her to defy her fate and hold to her life. Many emotions fought in him, but at last he permitted T'sais to ride on. He buried Floriel by the river-bank and tried to forget her in intense study.

A few days later he raised his head from his work.

"Pandelume! Are you near?"

"What do you wish, Turjan?"

"You mentioned that when you made T'sais, a flaw warped her brain. Now I would create one like her, of the same intensity, yet sound of mind and spirit."

"As you will," replied Pandelume indifferently, and gave Turjan the pattern.

So Turjan built a sister to T'sais, and day by day watched the same slender body, and the same proud features take form.

When her time came, and she sat up in her vat, eyes glowing with joyful life, Turjan was breathless in haste to help her forth.

She stood before him wet and naked, a twin to T'sais, but where the face of T'sais was racked by hate, here dwelt peace and merriment; where the eyes of T'sais glowed with fury, here shone the stars of imagination.

Turjan stood wondering at the perfection of his own creation. "Your name shall be T'sain," said he, "and already I know that you will be part of my life."

He abandoned all else to teach T'sain, and she learned with marvelous speed.

"Presently we return to Earth," he told her, "to my home beside a great river in the green land of Ascolais."

"Is the sky of Earth filled with colors?" she inquired.

"No," he replied. "The sky of Earth is a fathomless dark blue, and an ancient red sun rides across the sky. When night falls the stars appear in patterns that I will teach you. Embelyon is beautiful, but Earth is wide, and the horizons extend far off into mystery. As soon as Pandelume wills, we return to Earth."

T'sain loved to swim in the river, and sometimes Turjan came down to splash her and toss rocks in the water while he dreamed. Against T'sais he had warned her, and she had promised to be wary.

But one day, as Turjan made preparations for departure, she wandered far afield through the meadows, mindful only of the colors at play in the sky, the majesty of the tall blurred trees, the changing flowers at her feet; she looked on the world with a wonder that is only for those new from the vats. Across several low hills she wandered, and through a dark forest where she found a cold brook. She drank and sauntered along the bank, and presently came upon a small dwelling.

The door being open, T'sain looked to see who might live here. But the house was vacant, and the only furnishings were a neat pallet of grass, a table with a basket of nuts, a shelf with a few articles of wood and pewter.

T'sain turned to go on her way, but at this moment she heard the ominous thud of hooves, sweeping close like fate. The black horse slid to a stop before her. T'sain shrank back in the doorway, all Turjan's warnings returning to her mind. But T'sais had dismounted and came forward with her sword ready. As she raised to strike, their eyes met, and T'sais halted in wonder.

It was a sight to excite the brain: the beautiful twins, wearing the same white waist-high breeches, with the same intense eyes and careless hair, the same slim pale bodies, the one wearing on her face hate for every atom of the universe, the other a gay exuberance.

T'sais found her voice.

"How is this, witch? You bear my semblance, yet you are not me. Or has the boon of madness come at last to dim my sight of the world?"

T'sain shook her head. "I am T'sain. You are my twin, T'sais, my sister. For this I must love you and you must love me."

"Love? I love nothing! I will kill you and so make the world better by one less evil." She raised her sword again.

"No!" cried T'sain in anguish. "Why do you wish to harm me? I have done no wrong!"

"You do wrong by existing, and you offend me by coming to mock my own hideous mold."

T'sain laughed. "Hideous? No. I am beautiful, for Turjan says so. Therefore you are beautiful, too."

T'sais' face was like marble.

"You make sport of me."

"Never. You are indeed very beautiful."

T'sais dropped the point of her sword to the ground. Her face relaxed into thought.

"Beauty! What is beauty? Can it be that I am blind, that a fiend distorts my vision? Tell me, how does one see beauty?"

"I don't know," said T'sain. "It seems very plain to me. Is not the play of colors across the sky beautiful?"

T'sais looked up in astonishment. "The harsh glarings? They are either angry or dreary, in either case detestable."

"See how delicate are the flowers, fragile and charming."

"They are parasites, they smell vilely."

T'sain was puzzled. "I do not know how to explain beauty. You seem to find joy in nothing. Does nothing give you satisfaction?"

"Only killing and destruction. So then these must be beautiful."

T'sain frowned. "I would term these evil concepts."

"Do you believe so?"

"I am sure of it."

T'sais considered. "How can I know how to act? I have been certain, and now you tell me that I do evil!"

T'sain shrugged. "I have lived little, and I am not wise. Yet I know that everyone is entitled to life. Turjan could explain to you easily."

"Who is Turjan?" inquired T'sais.

"He is a very good man," replied T'sain, "and I love him greatly. Soon we go to Earth, where the sky is vast and deep and of dark blue."

"Earth...If I went to Earth, could I also find beauty and love?"

"That may be, for you have a brain to understand beauty, and beauty of your own to attract love."

"Then I kill no more, regardless of what wickedness I see. I will ask Pandelume to send me to Earth."

T'sain stepped forward, put her arms around T'sais, and kissed her.

"You are my sister and I will love you."

T'sais' face froze. Rend, stab, bite, said her brain, but a deeper surge welled up from her flowing blood, from every cell of her body, to suffuse her with a sudden flush of pleasure. She smiled.

"Then—I love you, my sister. I kill no more, and I will find and know beauty on Earth or die."

T'sais mounted her horse and set out for Earth, seeking love and beauty.

T'sain stood in the doorway, watching her sister ride off through the colors. Behind her came a shout, and Turjan approached.

"T'sain! Has that frenzied witch harmed you?" He did not wait for a reply. "Enough! I kill her with a spell, that she may wreak no more pain."

He turned to voice a terrible charm of fire, but T'sain put her hand to his mouth.

"No, Turjan, you must not. She has promised to kill no more. She goes to Earth seeking what she may not find in Embelyon."

So Turjan and T'sain watched T'sais disappear across the many-colored meadow.

"Turjan," spoke T'sain.

"What is your wish?"

"When we come to Earth, will you find me a black horse like that of T'sais?"

"Indeed," said Turjan, laughing, as they started back to the house of Pandelume.

A Hero at the Gates

Tanith Lee (1947-2015)

The city lay in the midst of the desert.

At the onset it could resemble a mirage; next, one of the giant mesas that were the teeth of the desert, filmy blue with distance and heat. But Cyrion had found the road which led to the city, and taking the road, presently the outline of the place came clear. High walls and higher towers within, high gates of hammered bronze. And above, the high and naked desert sky, that reflected back from its sounding-bowl no sound at all from the city, and no smoke.

Cyrion stood and regarded the city. He was tempted to believe it a desert too, one of those hulks of men's making, abandoned centuries ago as the sands of the waste crept to their threshold. Certainly, the city was old. Yet it had no aspect of neglect, none of the indefinable melancholy of the unlived-in house.

Intuitively, Cyrion knew that as he stood regarding the city from without, so others stood noiselessly within, regarding Cyrion.

What did they perceive? This: a young man, tall and deceptively slim, deceptively elegant, which elegance itself was something of a surprise, for he had been months travelling in the desert, on the caravan routes and the rare and sand-blown roads. He wore the loose dark clothing of a nomad, but with the generous hood thrust back to show he did not have a nomad's pigmentation. At his side a sword was sheathed in red leather. The sunlight struck a silver-gold burnish on the pommel of the sword that was also the color of his hair. His left hand was mailed in rings which apparently no bandit had been able to relieve him of. If the watchers in the city had remarked that Cyrion was as handsome as the Arch-Demon himself, they would not have been the first to do so.

Then there came the booming scraping thunder of two bronze gates unbarred and dragged inward on their runners. The way into the city was exposed—yet blocked now by a crowd. Silent they were, and clad in black, the men and the women; even the children. And their faces were all the same, and gazed at Cyrion in the same way. They gazed at him as if he were the last bright day of their lives, the last bright coin in the otherwise empty coffer.

The sense of his dynamic importance to them was so strong that Cyrion swept the crowd a low, half-mocking bow. As he swept the bow, from his keen eyes' corner, Cyrion saw a man walk through the crowd and come out of the gate.

The man was as tall as Cyrion. He had a hard face, tanned but sallow, wings of black hair beneath a shaved crown, and a collar of swarthy gold set with gems. But his gaze also clung on Cyrion. It was like a lover's look. Or the starving lion's as it beholds the deer.

"Sir," said the black-haired man, "what brings you to this, our city?"

Cyrion gestured lazily with the ringed left hand. "The nomads have a saying: 'After a month in the desert, even a dead tree is an object of wonder.'"

"Only curiosity, then," said the man.

"Curiosity; hunger; thirst; loneliness; exhaustion," enlarged Cyrion. By looking at Cyrion, few would think him affected by any of these things.

"Food we will give you, drink and rest. Our story we may not give. To satisfy the curious is not our fate. Our fate is darker and more savage. We await a savior. We await him in bondage."

"When is he due?" Cyrion enquired.

"You, perhaps, are he."

"Am I? You flatter me. I have been called many things, never savior."

"Sir," said the black-haired man, "do not jest at the wretched trouble of this city, nor at its solitary hope."

"No jest," said Cyrion, "but I hazard you wish some service of me. Saviors are required to labor, I believe, in behalf of their people. What do you want? Let us get it straight."

"Sir," said the man, "I am Memled, prince of this city."

"Prince, but not savior?" interjected Cyrion, his eyes widening with the most insulting astonishment.

Memled lowered his gaze. "If you seek to shame me with that, it is your right. But you should know, I am prevented by circumstance."

"Oh, indeed. Naturally."

"I bear your gibe without complaint. I ask again if you will act for the city."

"And I ask you again what I must do."

Memled raised his lids and directed his glance at Cyrion once more. "We are in the thrall of a monster, a demon-beast. It dwells in the caverns beneath the city, but at night it roves at will. It demands the flesh of our men to eat; it drinks the blood of our women and our children. It is protected through ancient magic, by a pact made a hundred years before between the princes of the city (cursed be they!) and the hordes of the Fiend. None born of the city has power to slay the beast. Yet there is a prophecy. A stranger, a hero who ventures to our gates, will have the power."

"And how many heroes," said Cyrion gently, "have you persuaded to an early death with this enterprise, you and your demon-beast?"

"I will not lie to you. Upward of a score. If you turn aside, no one here will speak ill of you. Your prospects of success would be slight, should you set your wits and sword against the beast. And our misery is nothing to you."

Cyrion ran his eyes over the black-clad crowd. The arid faces were all still fixed towards his. The children, like miniature adults, just as arid, immobile, noiseless. If the tale were true, they had learned the lessons of fear and sorrow early, nor would they live long to enjoy their lessoning.

"Other than its dietary habits," Cyrion said, "what can you tell me of your beast?"

Memled shivered. His sallowness increased. "I can reveal no more. It is a part of the foul sorcery that binds us. We may say nothing to aid you, do nothing to aid you. Only pray for you, if you should decide to pit your skill against the devil."

Cyrion smiled. "You have a cool effrontery, my friend, that is altogether delightful. Inform me then merely of this. If I conquer your beast, what reward is there—other, of course, than the blessing of your people?"

"We have our gold, our silver, our jewels. You may take them all away with you, or whatever you desire. We crave safety, not wealth. Our wealth has not protected us from horror and death."

"I think we have a bargain," said Cyrion. He looked at the children again. "Providing the treasury tallies with your description."

It was noon, and the desert sun poured its merciless light upon the city. Cyrion walked in the company of Prince Memled and his guard—similarly black-clad men, but with weighty blades and daggers at their belts, none, presumably, ever stained by beast-blood. The crowd moved circumspectly in the wake of their prince. Only the rustle of feet shuffling the dust was audible, and no speech. Below the bars of overhanging windows, here and there, a bird cage had been set out in the violet shade. The birds in the cages did not sing.

They reached a marketplace, sun-bleached, unpeopled and without merchandise of any sort. A well at the market's center proclaimed the water which would, in the first instance, have caused the building of a city here. Further evidence of water lay across from the market, where a broad stairway, flanked by stone columns, led to a massive battlemented wall and doors of bronze this time plated by pure flashing gold.

Over the wall-top, the royal house showed its peaks and pinnacles, and the heads of palm trees. There was a green perfume in the air, heady as incense in the desert.

The crowd faltered in the marketplace. Memled, and his guard conducted Cyrion up the stairway. The gold-plated doors were opened. They entered a cool palace, blue as an under-sea cave, buzzing with slender fountains, sweet with the scent of sun-scorched flowers.

Black-garmented servants brought chilled wine. The food was poor and did not match the wine. Had the flocks and herds gone to appease the demon-beast? Cyrion had spied not a goat nor a sheep in the city. For that matter, not a dog, nor even the sleek lemon cats and striped marmosets rich women liked to nurse instead of babies.

After the food and drink, Memled, near wordless yet courteous, led Cyrion to a treasury where wealth lay as thick as dust, and spilling on the ground.

"I would have thought," said Cyrion, fastidiously investigating ropes of pearls and chains of rubies, "such stuff might have bought you a hero, had you sent for one."

"This, too, is our limitation. We may not send. He must come to us, by accident."

"As the nomads say," said Cyrion. charmingly, innocently, "'No man knows the wall better than he who built it.'"

At that instant, something thundered in the guts of the world.

It was a fearful bellowing cacophony. It sounded hot with violence and the lust for carnage. It was like a bull, or a pen of bulls, with throats of brass and sinews of molten iron, roaring in concert underground.

The floor shook a little. A sapphire tumbled from its heap and fell upon another heap below. Cyrion seemed interested rather than disturbed.

Certainly, there was nothing more than interest in his voice as he asked Prince Memled: "Can that be your beast, contemplating tonight's dinner?"

Memled's face took on an expression of the most absolute anguish and despair. His mouth writhed. He uttered a sudden sharp cry, as if a dreaded, well-remembered pain had seized him. He shut his eyes.

Intrigued, Cyrion observed: "It is fact then, you cannot speak of it? Calm yourself, my friend. It speaks very ably for itself."

Memled covered his face with his hands, and turned away.

Cyrion walked out through the door. Presently, pallid, but sufficiently composed, Memled followed his hero-guest. Black guards closed the treasury.

"Now," said Cyrion, "since I cannot confront your beast until it emerges from its caverns by night, I propose to sleep. My journey through the desert has been arduous, and, I am sure you agree, freshness in combat is essential."

"Sir," said Memled, "the palace is at your disposal. But, while you sleep, I and some others shall remain at your side."

Smiling, Cyrion assured him, "Indeed, my friend, you and they will not."

"Sir, it is best you are not left alone. Forgive my insistence."

"What danger is there? The beast is no threat till the sun goes down. There are some hours yet."

Memled seemed troubled. He spread his hand, indicating the city beyond the palace walls. "You are a hero, sir. Certain of the people may bribe the guard. They may enter the palace and disrupt your rest with questions and clamor."

"It seemed to me," said Cyrion, "your people are uncommonly quiet. But if not, they are welcome. I sleep deeply. I doubt if anything would wake me till sunset, when I trust you, Prince, or another, will do so."

Memled's face, such an index of moods, momentarily softened with relief. "That deeply do you sleep? Then I will agree to let you sleep alone. Unless, perhaps a girl might be sent to you?"

"You are too kind. However, I decline the girl. I prefer to select my own ladies, after a fight rather than before."

Memled smiled his own stiff and rusty smile. Behind his eyes, sluggish currents of self-dislike, guilt and shame stirred cloudily.

The doors were shut on the sumptuous chamber intended for Cyrion's repose. Aromatics burned in silver bowls. The piercing afternoon sun was excluded behind shutters of painted wood and embroidered draperies. Beyond the shut doors, musicians made sensuous low music on pipes, drums and ghirzas. All was conducive to slumber. Though not to Cyrion's.

In contrast to his words, he was a light sleeper. In the city of the beast, he had no inclination to sleep at all. Privacy was another case. Having secured the chamber doors on the inside, he prowled soundlessly, measuring the room for its possibilities. He prised open a shutter, and scanned across the blistering roofs of the palace into the dry green palm shade of the gardens.

All about, the city kept its tongueless vigil. Cyrion thoughtfully felt of its tension. It was like a great single heart, poised between one beat and the next. A single heart, or two jaws about to snap together—

"Cyrion," said a voice urgently.

To see him spin about was to discover something of the nature of Cyrion. A nonchalant idler at the window one second, a coiled spring let fly the split second after. The sword was ready in his bare right hand. He had drawn too fast almost for a man's eye to register. Yet he was not even breathing quickly. And, finding the vacant chamber before him, as he had left it, no atom altered in his stance.

"Cyrion," cried the voice again, out of nothing and nowhere. "I pray heaven you had the cunning to lie to them, Cyrion."

Cyrion appeared to relax his exquisite vigilance. He had not.

"Heaven, no doubt, enjoys your prayers," he said. "And am I to enjoy the sight of you?" The voice was female, expressive and very beautiful.

"I am in a prison," said the voice. There was the smallest catch in it, swiftly mastered. "I speak to warn you. Do not credit them, Cyrion."

Cyrion began to move about the room. Casually and delicately he lifted aside the draperies with his sword.

"They offered me a girl," he said reflectively. "But they did not offer you certain death."

Cyrion had completed his circuit of the room. He looked amused and entertained.

He knelt swiftly, then stretched himself flat. A circular piece was missing in the mosaic pattern of the floor. He set one acute eye there and looked through into a dim area, lit by one murky source of light beyond his view. Directly below, a girl lay prone on the darkness which must itself be a floor, staring up at him from luminous wild eyes. In the half-glow she was more like a bloom of light herself than a reality; a trembling crystalline whiteness on the air, hair like the gold chains in the treasury, a face like that of a carved goddess, the body of a beautiful harlot before she gets in the trade—still virgin— and at her waist, her wrists, her ankles, drawn taut to pegs in the ground, iron chains.

"So there you are."

"It is a device of the stonework that enabled you to hear me and I you. In former days, princes would sit in your room above, drinking and making love, listening to the cries of those being tortured in this dungeon, and sometimes they would peer through to increase their pleasure. But either Memled has forgotten, or he thought me past crying out. I glimpsed your shadow pass over the aperture. Earlier, the jailor spoke your name to me. Oh, Cyrion, I am to die, and you with me."

She stopped, and tears ran like drops of silver from her wild eyes.

"You have a captive audience, lady," said Cyrion.

"It is this way," she whispered. "The beast they have pretended to seek rescue from is, in fact, the familiar demon of the city. They love the brute, and commit all forms of beastliness in its name. How else do you suppose they have amassed such stores of treasure, here in the wilderness? And once a year they honor the beast by giving to it a beautiful maiden and a notable warrior. I was to have been the

106

bride of a rich and wise lord in a city by the sea. But I am thought beautiful; Memled heard of me. Men of this city attacked the caravan in which I rode, and carried me here, to this, where I have lingered a month. You arrived by unlucky destiny, unless some of Memled's sorcery enticed you here, unknowingly. Tonight, we shall share each other's fate."

"You are their prisoner, I am not. How do they plan to reconcile me to sacrifice?"

"That is but too simple. At dusk a hundred men will come. You do not seem afraid, but even fearless, before a hundred men you cannot prevail. They will take your sword, stun you, bind you. There is a trick door in the western wall that gives on a stairway. Through the door and down the stair they will thrust you. Below are the caverns where the beast roams, bellowing for blood. I too must pass that way to death."

"A fascinating tale," said Cyrion, "What prompts you to tell it me?"

"Are you not a hero?" the girl demanded passionately. "Have you not promised to slay the beast for them, to be their savior, though admittedly in return for gold. Can you not instead be your own savior, and mine?"

"Forgive me, lady," said Cyrion, in a tone verging subtly on naivete, "I am at a loss. Besides, our dooms seem written with a firm hand. Perhaps we should accept them."

Cyrion rose from the mosaic. On his feet he halted, just aside from the hole.

After a moment, the girl screamed: "You are a coward, Cyrion. For all your looks and your fine sword, for all your nomad's garments, the wear of those they name the Lions of the Desert—for all that— coward and fool."

Cyrion seemed to be considering.

After a minute, he said amiably: "I suppose I might open the trick door now, and seek the monster of my own volition, sword in hand and ready. Then, if I slay him, I might return for you, and free you."

The girl wept. Through her tears she said, with a knife for a voice: "If you are a man, you will do it."

"Oh no, lady. Only if I am your notion of a man."

The stair was narrow, and by design lightlessly invisible—save that Cyrion had filched one of the scented tapers from the room above to give him eyes. The trick door had been easy to discover, an ornamental knob that turned, a slab that slid. Thirty steps down, he passed another kind of door, of iron, on his right. Faintly, beyond the door, he heard a girl weeping.

The stair descended through the western wall of the palace, and proceeded underground. Deep in the belly of the caverns that sprawled, as yet unseen, at the end of the stair, no ominous rumor was manifested. At length, the stair reached bottom, and ceased. Ahead stretched impenetrable black, and from the black an equally black and featureless silence.

Cyrion advanced, the taper held before him. The dark toyed with the taper, surrendering a miniature oasis of half-seen things, such as trunks of rock soaring up towards the ceiling. The dark mouthed Cyrion. It licked him, rolled him around on its tongue. The lit taper was just a garnish to its palate; it liked the light with Cyrion, as a man might like salt with his meat.

Then there came a huge wind from out of the nothing ahead. A metallic heated blast, as if from a furnace. Cyrion stopped, pondering. The beast, closeted in the caverns, had sighed? An instant after, it roared.

Above, in the treasury, the roaring had seemed to stagger the foundations of the house. Here, it peeled even the darkness, and dissected it like a fruit. The broken pieces of the dark rattled on the trunks of rock. Shards erupted from the rock and rained to the ground. The caverns thrummed, murmured, fell dumb. The dark did not re-congeal.

There was a new light. A flawless round of light, pale, smoky red. Then it blinked. Then there were two. Two flawless rounds of simmering raw rose. Two eyes. Cyrion dropped the taper and put his heel on it.

This beast you witnessed by its own illumination. It swelled from the black as the eyes brightened with its interest. It was like no other beast; you could liken it to nothing else. It was like itself, unique. Only its size was comparable to anything. To a tower, a wall—one eye alone, that rosy window, could have fit tall Cyrion in its socket.

So radiant now, those eyes, the whole cavern was displayed, the mounting rocks, the floor piled with dusts, the dust curtains floating in the air. From the dust, the beast lifted itself. It gaped its mouth. Cyrion ducked, and the blast of burning though non-incendiary breath rushed over his head. It was not fetid breath, simply very hot. Cyrion planted his sword point down in the dust, and indolently leaned on it. He looked like a marvelous statue. For someone who could move like lightning, he had chosen now to become stone, and the pink fires settled on his pale hair, staining it the color of diluted wine.

In this fashion Cyrion watched the demon-beast, by the light of its vast eyes, slink towards him. He watched, motionless, leaning on his sword.

Then a sinewy taloned forefoot, lengthy as a column, struck at him, and Cyrion was no longer in that spot, motionless, leaning on his sword, as he had been an instant before. Away in the shadow, Cyrion stood again unmoving, sword poised, negligently waiting. Again, the batting of scythe-fringed death; again missing him.

The jaws clashed, and slaver exploded forth, like a waterfall. Cyrion was gone, out of reach. Stone had returned to lightning. The fourth blow was his. He neither laughed at the seriousness of his mission nor frowned. No meditation was needed, the target no challenge, facile… Cyrion swung back his arm, and sent the sword plummeting, like a straight white rent through the cavern. It met the beast's left eye, shattered it like pink glass, plunged to the brain.

Like a cat, Cyrion sprang to a ledge and crouched there.

Black ichor spouted to the cavern's top. Now, once more gradually, the light faded. The thunderous roaring ebbed like a colossal sea withdrawing from these dry caves beneath the desert.

On his ledge, Cyrion waited, pitiless and without triumph, for the beast, in inevitable stages, to fall, to be still, to die.

In the reiterated blackness, blind, but remembering infallibly his way, as he remembered all things, once disclosed, Cyrion went to the demon-beast and plucked out his sword, and returned with it up the pitchy stairway to the iron dungeon door set in the wall.

The iron door was bolted from without. He shot the bolts and pushed open the door.

He paused, just inside the prison, sword in hand, absorbing each detail. A stone box the prison was, described by dull fluttering torches. The girl lay on the floor, pegged and chained as he had regarded her through the peep-hole. He glanced towards the peep-hole, which was barely to be seen against the torch murk.

"Cyrion," the girl murmured, "the beast's black blood is on your sword, and you live."

Her white and lovely face was turned to him, the rich strands of golden hair swept across the floor, her silken breasts quivered to the tumult of her heart. Her tears fell again, but now her eyes were yielding. They showed no amazement or inquisition, only love. He went to her, and, raising his sword a second time, chopped the head from her body.

Thirty steps up, a door crashed wide. Cyrion stooped gracefully, straightened, took the thirty steps in a series of fine-flexed leaps. He stepped through the trick door and was in the upper chamber, the sword yet stark in his bare right hand. And in his left hand, mailed with rings, a woman's head held by its shining hair.

Opposite, in the forced doorway of the chamber, Memled stared with a face like yellow cinders. Then he collapsed on his knees, and behind him, the guards also dropped down.

Memled began to sob. The sobs were rough, racking him. He plainly could not keep them back, and his whole body shuddered.

Cyrion remained where he was, ignoring his bloody itinerary. Finally Memled spoke.

"After an eternity, heaven has heard our lament, replied to our entreaty. You, the hero of the city, after the eternity, our savior. But we were bound by the hell-pact, and could neither warn nor advise you. How did you fathom the truth?"

"And what is the truth?" asked Cyrion, with unbelievable sweetness, as he stood between blotched blade and dripping head.

"The truth—that the monster is illusion set to deceive those heroes who would fight for us, set to deceive by the bitch-sorceress whose head you have lopped. Year in and out, she has drained us, roaming by night, feasting on the flesh and blood of my people, unrelenting and vile she-wolf that she was. And our fragile chance, a prophecy, the solitary weakness in the hell-pact—that only if a heroic traveler should come to the gates and agree to rid us of our torment, might we see her slain. But always she bewitched and duped these heroes, appearing in illusory shackles, lying that we would sacrifice her, sending each man to slay a phantom beast that did not exist save while her whim permitted it. And then the hero would go to her, trustingly, and she would seize him and murder him too. Over a score of champions we sent to their deaths in this manner, because we were bound and could not direct them where the evil lay. And so, again, sir hero, how did you fathom truth in this sink of witchery?"

"Small things," said Cyrion laconically.

"But you will list them for me?" Memled proffered his face, all wet with tears, and brimming now with a feverish joy.

"Her proximity to me, which seemed unlikely if she were what she claimed. Her extreme beauty which had survived a month's imprisonment and terror, and her wrists and ankles which were unchafed by her chains. That, a stranger to this place, she knew so much of its by-ways and its history. More interesting, that she knew so much of me—besides my name, which I did not see why a jailor should have given her—for instance, that I wore a nomad's garment, and that she thought me presentable, though she could not have

111

seen me herself. She claimed she beheld my shadow pass over the peephole, but no more. She knew all our bargain, too, yours and mine, as if she had been listening to it. Would you hear more?"

"Every iota of it!"

"Then I will cite the beast, which patently was unreal. So huge a voice it could make the floors tremble, and yet the house was still intact. And the creature itself so untiny it could have shaken the city to flour but confined in a cavern where it had not even stirred the dust. And then, the absence of bones, and its wholesome breath, meant to impress by volume and heat, and which smelled of nothing else. A cat which chews rats will have a fouler odor. And this thing, which supposedly ate men and drank their blood and was big enough to fill the air with stink, clean as a scoured pot on the stove. Lastly, I came above and saw the peephole would show nothing of what went on in this room, let alone a shadow passing. And I noticed too, the lady's sharp teeth, if you like."

Memled got to his feet. Halfway to Cyrion, he checked and turned to the guards. "Inform the city our terror has ended."

The guards, round-eyed, rushed away.

Memled came to Cyrion, glaring at the head, which Cyrion had prudently set down in a convenient bowl, and which was beginning to crumble to a sort of rank powder.

"We are free of her," Memled cried. "And the treasury is yours to despoil. Take all I have. Take—take this, the royal insignia of the city," and he clutched the collar of swarthy gold at his throat.

"Unnecessary," said Cyrion lightly. He wiped his sword upon a drapery. Memled paid no heed. Cyrion sheathed the sword. Memled smiled, still rusty, but his face vivid with excitement. "The treasury, then," suggested Cyrion.

Cyrion dealt cannily in the treasury. The light of day was gone by now, and by the smooth amber of the lamps, Cyrion chose from among the ropes of jewels and skeins of metal, from the cups and gemmy daggers, the armlets and the armor. Shortly, there was sufficient to weigh down a leather bag, which Cyrion slung upon his back. Memled would have pressed further gifts on him. Cyrion declined.

"As the nomads say," said Cyrion, "'three donkeys cannot get their heads into the same bucket.' I have enough."

Outside in the city, now ablaze with windows under a sky ablaze with stars, songs and shouting of celebration rose into the cool hollow of the desert night.

"A night without blood and without horror," said Memled.

Cyrion walked down the palace stairway. Memled remained on the stair, his guards scattered loosely about him. In the marketplace a fire burned, and there was dancing. The black clothes were all gone; the women had put on their finery and earrings sparkled and clinked as they danced together. The men drank, eyeing the women.

Near the edge of the group, two children poised like small stones, dressed in their best, and Cyrion saw their faces.

A child's face, incorrigible calendar of the seasons of the soul. Men learn pretense, if they must. A child has not had the space to learn.

Cyrion hesitated. He turned about, and strolled back towards the steps of the palace, and softly up the steps.

"One last thing, my friend, the prince," he called to Memled.

"What is that?"

Cyrion smiled. "You were too perfect and I did not quite see it, till just now a child showed me." Cyrion swung the bag from his shoulder exactly into Memled's belly. Next second the sword flamed to Cyrion's hand, and Memled's black-winged head hopped down the stair.

Around the fire, the dancers had left off dancing. The guards were transfixed in stammering shock, though no hand flew to a blade. Cyrion wiped his own blade, this time on Memled's already trembling torso.

"That one, too," said Cyrion.

"Yes, sir," said the nearest of the guard, thickly. "There were the two of them."

"And they diced nightly over who should batten on the city, did they not, your prince-demon and his doxy. He could not avoid the prophecy, either, of a hero at the gates. He was obliged to court me, and, in any event, reckoned the lady would deal with me as with the others. But when she did not, he was content I should have killed her, if he could escape me and keep the city for himself to feed him. He rendered himself straightly. He never once uttered for his own demonic side. He acted as a man, as Memled, the prince—fear and joy. He was too good. Yet I should never have been sure but for the children's agonized blankness down there, in the crowd."

"You are undeniably a hero, and heaven will bless you," said the guard. It was easy to see he was a true human man, and the rest of them were human too. Unpredictable and bizarre was their relief at rescue, as with all true men, who do not get their parts by heart beforehand, when to cry or when to grin.

Cyrion laughed low at the glittering sky. "Then bless me, heaven."

He went down the stair again. Both children were howling now, as they had not dared do formerly, untrammeled, healthy. Cyrion opened the leather bag, and released the treasure on the square, for adults and children alike to play with.

Empty-handed, as he came, Cyrion went away into the desert, under the stars.

Tower of the Elephant

Robert E. Howard (1906-1936)

Torches flared murkily on the revels in the Maul, where the thieves of the east held carnival by night. In the Maul they could carouse and roar as they liked, for honest people shunned the quarters, and watchmen, well paid with stained coins, did not interfere with their sport. Along the crooked, unpaved streets with their heaps of refuse and sloppy puddles, drunken roisterers staggered, roaring. Steel glinted in the shadows where wolf preyed on wolf, and from the darkness rose the shrill laughter of women, and the sounds of scufflings and strugglings. Torchlight licked luridly from broken windows and wide-thrown doors, and out of those doors, stale smells of wine and rank sweaty bodies, clamor of drinking-jacks and fists hammered on rough tables, snatches of obscene songs, rushed like a blow in the face.

In one of these dens merriment thundered to the low smoke-stained roof, where rascals gathered in every stage of rags and tatters—furtive cut-purses, leering kidnappers, quick-fingered thieves, swaggering bravoes with their wenches, strident-voiced women clad in tawdry finery. Native rogues were the dominant element—dark-skinned, dark-eyed Zamorians, with daggers at their girdles and guile in their hearts. But there were wolves of half a dozen outland nations there as well. There was a giant Hyperborean renegade, taciturn, dangerous, with a broadsword strapped to his great gaunt frame—for men wore steel openly in the Maul. There was a Shemitish counterfeiter, with his hook nose and curled blue-black beard. There was a bold-eyed Brythunian wench, sitting on the knee of a tawny-haired Gunderman—a wandering mercenary soldier, a deserter from some defeated army. And the fat gross rogue whose bawdy jests were causing all the shouts of mirth was a professional kidnapper come up from distant Koth to teach woman-stealing to Zamorians who were born with more knowledge of the art than he could ever attain.

This man halted in his description of an intended victim's charms, and thrust his muzzle into a huge tankard of frothing ale. Then blowing the foam from his fat lips, he said, "By Bel, god of all thieves, I'll show them how to steal wenches: I'll have her over the Zamorian border before dawn, and there'll be a caravan waiting to receive her. Three hundred pieces of silver, a count of Ophir promised me for a sleek young Brythunian of the better class. It took me weeks, wandering among the border cities as a beggar, to find one I knew would suit. And is she a pretty baggage!"

He blew a slobbery kiss in the air.

"I know lords in Shem who would trade the secret of the Elephant Tower for her," he said, returning to his ale.

A touch on his tunic sleeve made him turn his head, scowling at the interruption. He saw a tall, strongly made youth standing beside him. This person was as much out of place in that den as a gray wolf among mangy rats of the gutters. His cheap tunic could not conceal the hard, rangy lines of his powerful frame, the broad heavy shoulders, the massive chest, lean waist and heavy arms. His skin was brown from outland suns, his eyes blue and smoldering; a shock of tousled black hair crowned his broad forehead. From his girdle hung a sword in a worn leather scabbard.

The Kothian involuntarily drew back; for the man was not one of any civilized race he knew.

"You spoke of the Elephant Tower," said the stranger, speaking Zamorian with an alien accent. "I've heard much of this tower; what is its secret?"

116

The fellow's attitude did not seem threatening, and the Kothian's courage was bolstered up by the ale, and the evident approval of his audience. He swelled with self-importance.

"The secret of the Elephant Tower?" he exclaimed. "Why, any fool knows that Yara the priest dwells there with the great jewel men call the Elephant's Heart, that is the secret of his magic."

The barbarian digested this for a space.

"I have seen this tower," he said. "It is set in a great garden above the level of the city, surrounded by high walls. I have seen no guards. The walls would be easy to climb. Why has not somebody stolen this secret gem?"

The Kothian stared wide-mouthed at the other's simplicity, then burst into a roar of derisive mirth, in which the others joined.

"Harken to this heathen!" he bellowed. "He would steal the jewel of Yara!—Harken, fellow," he said, turning portentously to the other, "I suppose you are some sort of a northern barbarian—"

"I am a Cimmerian," the outlander answered, in no friendly tone. The reply and the manner of it meant little to the Kothian; of a kingdom that lay far to the south, on the borders of Shem, he knew only vaguely of the northern races.

"Then give ear and learn wisdom, fellow," said he, pointing his drinking-jack at the discomfited youth. "Know that in Zamora, and more especially in this city, there are more bold thieves than anywhere else in the world, even Koth. If mortal man could have stolen the gem, be sure it would have been filched long ago. You speak of climbing the walls, but once having climbed, you would quickly wish yourself back again. There are no guards in the gardens at night for a very good reason—that is, no human guards. But in the watch-chamber, in the lower part of the tower, are armed men, and even if you passed those who roam the gardens by night, you must still pass through the soldiers, for the gem is kept somewhere in the tower above."

"But if a man could pass through the gardens," argued the Cimmerian, "why could he not come at the gem through the upper part of the tower and thus avoid the soldiers?"

Again the Kothian gaped at him.

"Listen to him!" he shouted jeeringly. "The barbarian is an eagle who would fly to the jeweled rim of the tower, which is only a hundred and fifty feet above the earth, with rounded sides slicker than polished glass!"

The Cimmerian glared about, embarrassed at the roar of mocking laughter that greeted this remark. He saw no particular humor in it, and was too new to civilization to understand its discourtesies. Civilized men are more discourteous than savages because they know they can be impolite without having their skulls split, as a general thing. He was bewildered and chagrined, and doubtless would have slunk away, abashed, but the Kothian chose to goad him further.

"Come, come!" he shouted. "Tell these poor fellows, who have only been thieves since before you were spawned, tell them how you would steal the gem!"

"There is always a way, if the desire be coupled with courage," answered the Cimmerian shortly, nettled.

The Kothian chose to take this as a personal slur. His face grew purple with anger.

"What!" he roared. "You dare tell us our business, and intimate that we are cowards? Get along; get out of my sight!" And he pushed the Cimmerian violently.

"Will you mock me and then lay hands on me?" grated the barbarian, his quick rage leaping up; and he returned the push with an open-handed blow that knocked his tormenter back against the rude-hewn table. Ale splashed over the jack's lip, and the Kothian roared in fury, dragging at his sword.

"Heathen dog!" he bellowed. "I'll have your heart for that!" Steel flashed and the throng surged wildly back out of the way. In their flight they knocked over the single candle and the den was plunged in darkness, broken by the crash of upset benches, drum of flying feet, shouts, oaths of people tumbling over one another, and a single strident yell of agony that cut the din like a knife. When a candle was relighted, most of the guests had gone out by doors and broken windows, and the rest huddled behind stacks of wine-kegs and under tables. The barbarian was gone; the center of the room was deserted except for the gashed body of the Kothian. The Cimmerian, with the unerring instinct of the barbarian, had killed his man in the darkness and confusion.

II

The lurid lights and drunken revelry fell away behind the Cimmerian. He had discarded his torn tunic, and walked through the night naked except for a loincloth and his high-strapped sandals. He moved with the supple ease of a great tiger, his steely muscles rippling under his brown skin.

He had entered the part of the city reserved for the temples. On all sides of him they glittered white in the starlight—snowy marble pillars and golden domes and silver arches, shrines of Zamora's myriad strange gods. He did not trouble his head about them; he knew that Zamora's religion, like all things of a civilized, long-settled people, was intricate and complex, and had lost most of the pristine essence in a maze of formulas and rituals. He had squatted for hours in the courtyard of the philosophers, listening to the arguments of theologians and teachers, and come away in a haze of bewilderment, sure of only one thing, and that, that they were all touched in the head.

His gods were simple and understandable; Crom was their chief, and he lived on a great mountain, whence he sent forth dooms and death. It was useless to call on Crom, because he was a gloomy, savage god, and he hated weaklings. But he gave a man courage at birth, and the will and might to kill his enemies, which, in the Cimmerian's mind, was all any god should be expected to do.

His sandaled feet made no sound on the gleaming pave. No watchmen passed, for even the thieves of the Maul shunned the temples, where strange dooms had been known to fall on violators.

TOWER OF THE ELEPHANT

Ahead of him he saw, looming against the sky, the Tower of the Elephant. He mused, wondering why it was so named. No one seemed to know. He had never seen an elephant, but he vaguely understood that it was a monstrous animal, with a tail in front as well as behind. This a wandering Shemite had told him, swearing that he had seen such beasts by the thousands in the country of the Hyrkanians; but all men knew what liars were the men of Shem. At any rate, there were no elephants in Zamora.

The shimmering shaft of the tower rose frostily in the stars. In the sunlight it shone so dazzlingly that few could bear its glare, and men said it was built of silver. It was round, a slim perfect cylinder, a hundred and fifty feet in height, and its rim glittered in the starlight with the great jewels which crusted it. The tower stood among the waving exotic trees of a garden raised high above the general level of the city. A high wall enclosed this garden, and outside the wall was a lower level, likewise enclosed by a wall. No lights shone forth; there seemed to be no windows in the tower—at least not above the level of the inner wall. Only the gems high above sparkled frostily in the starlight.

Shrubbery grew thick outside the lower, or outer wall. The Cimmerian crept close and stood beside the barrier, measuring it with his eyes. It was high, but he could leap and catch the coping with his fingers. Then it would be child's play to swing himself up and over, and he did not doubt that he could pass the inner wall in the same manner. But he hesitated at the thought of the strange perils which were said to await within. These people were strange and mysterious to him; they were not of his kind—not even of the same blood as the more westerly Brythunians, Nemedians, Kothians and Aquilonians, whose civilized mysteries had awed him in times past. The people of Zamora were very ancient, and, from what he had seen of them, very evil.

He thought of Yara, the high priest, who worked strange dooms from this jeweled tower, and the Cimmerian's hair prickled as he remembered a tale told by a drunken page of the court—how Yara had laughed in the face of a hostile prince, and held up a glowing, evil gem before him, and how rays shot blindingly from that unholy jewel, to envelop the prince, who screamed and fell down, and shrank to a withered blackened lump that changed to a black spider which scampered wildly about the chamber until Yara set his heel upon it.

Yara came not often from his tower of magic, and always to work evil on some man or some nation. The king of Zamora feared him more than he feared death, and kept himself drunk all the time because that fear was more than he could endure sober. Yara was very old—centuries old, men said, and added that he would live forever because of the magic of his gem, which men called the Heart of the Elephant, for no better reason than they named his hold the Elephant's Tower.

The Cimmerian, engrossed in these thoughts, shrank quickly against the wall. Within the garden someone was passing, who walked with a measured stride. The listener heard the clink of steel. So after all a guard did pace those gardens. The Cimmerian waited, expected to hear him pass again, on the next round, but silence rested over the mysterious gardens.

At last curiosity overcame him. Leaping lightly he grasped the wall and swung himself up to the top with one arm. Lying flat on the broad coping, he looked down into the wide space between the walls. No shrubbery grew near him, though he saw some carefully trimmed bushes near the inner wall. The starlight fell on the even sward and somewhere a fountain tinkled.

The Cimmerian cautiously lowered himself down on the inside and drew his sword, staring about him. He was shaken by the nervousness of the wild at standing thus unprotected in the naked starlight, and he moved lightly around the curve of the wall, hugging its shadow, until he was even with the shrubbery he had noticed. Then he ran quickly toward it, crouching low, and almost tripped over a form that lay crumpled near the edges of the bushes.

A quick look to right and left showed him no enemy in sight at least, and he bent close to investigate. His keen eyes, even in the dim starlight, showed him a strongly built man in the silvered armor and crested helmet of the Zamorian royal guard. A shield and a spear lay near him, and it took but an instant's examination to show that he had been strangled. The barbarian glanced about uneasily. He knew that this man must be the guard he had heard pass his hiding-place by the wall. Only a short time had passed, yet in that interval nameless hands had reached out of the dark and choked out the soldier's life.

Straining his eyes in the gloom, he saw a hint of motion through the shrubs near the wall. Thither he glided, gripping his sword. He made no more noise than a panther stealing through the night, yet the man he was stalking heard. The Cimmerian had a dim glimpse of a huge bulk close to the wall; felt relief that it was at least human; then the fellow wheeled quickly with a gasp that sounded like panic, made the first motion of a forward plunge, hands clutching, then recoiled as the Cimmerian's blade caught the starlight. For a tense instant neither spoke, standing ready for anything.

"You are no soldier," hissed the stranger at last. "You are a thief like myself."

"And who are you?" asked the Cimmerian in a suspicious whisper.

"Taurus of Nemedia."

The Cimmerian lowered his sword.

"I've heard of you. Men call you a prince of thieves."

A low laugh answered him. Taurus was as tall as the Cimmerian, and heavier; he was big-bellied and fat, but his every movement betokened a subtle dynamic magnetism, which was reflected in the keen eyes that glinted vitally, even in the starlight. He was barefooted and carried a coil of what looked like a thin, strong rope, knotted at regular intervals. "Who are you?" he whispered.

"Conan, a Cimmerian," answered the other. "I came seeking a way to steal Yara's jewel, that men call the Elephant's Heart."

Conan sensed the man's great belly shaking in laughter, but it was not derisive.

"By Bel, god of thieves!" hissed Taurus. "I had thought only myself had courage to attempt that poaching. These Zamorians call themselves thieves—bah! Conan, I like your grit. I never shared an adventure with anyone, but by Bel, we'll attempt this together if you're willing."

"Then you are after the gem, too?"

"What else? I've had my plans laid for months, but you, I think, have acted on a sudden impulse, my friend."

"You killed the soldier?"

"Of course. I slid over the wall when he was on the other side of the garden. I hid in the bushes; he heard me, or thought he heard something. When he came blundering over, it was no trick at all to get behind him and suddenly grip his neck and choke out his fool's life. He was like most men, half blind in the dark. A good thief should have eyes like a cat."

"You made one mistake," said Conan.

Taurus's eyes flashed angrily.

"I? I, a mistake? Impossible!"

"You should have dragged the body into the bushes."

"Said the novice to the master of the art. They will not change the guard until past midnight. Should any come searching for him now, and find his body, they would flee at once to Yara, bellowing the news, and give us time to escape. Were they not to find it, they'd go on beating up the bushes and catch us like rats in a trap."

"You are right," agreed Conan.

"So. Now attend. We waste time in this cursed discussion. There are no guards in the inner garden—human guards, I mean, though there are sentinels even more deadly. It was their presence which baffled me for so long, but I finally discovered a way to circumvent them."

"What of the soldiers in the lower part of the tower?"

"Old Yara dwells in the chambers above. By that route we will come—and go, I hope. Never mind asking me how. I have arranged a way. We'll steal down through the top of the tower and strangle old Yara before he can cast any of his accursed spells on us. At least we'll try; it's the chance of being turned into a spider or a toad, against the wealth and power of the world. All good thieves must know how to take risks."

"I'll go as far as any man," said Conan, slipping off his sandals.

"Then follow me." And turning, Taurus leaped up, caught the wall and drew himself up. The man's suppleness was amazing, considering his bulk; he seemed almost to glide up over the edge of the coping. Conan followed him, and lying flat on the broad top, they spoke in wary whispers.

"I see no light," Conan muttered. The lower part of the tower seemed much like that portion visible from outside the garden—a perfect, gleaming cylinder, with no apparent openings.

"There are cleverly constructed doors and windows," answered Taurus, "but they are closed. The soldiers breathe air that comes from above."

The garden was a vague pool of shadows, where feathery bushes and low spreading trees waved darkly in the starlight. Conan's wary soul felt the aura of waiting menace that brooded over it. He felt the burning glare of unseen eyes, and he caught a subtle scent that made the short hairs on his neck instinctively bristle as a hunting dog bristles at the scent of an ancient enemy. "Follow me," whispered Taurus, "keep behind me, as you value your life."

Taking what looked like a copper tube from his girdle, the Nemedian dropped lightly to the sward inside the wall. Conan was close behind him, sword ready, but Taurus pushed him back, close to the wall, and showed no indication to advance, himself. His whole attitude was of tense expectancy, and his gaze, like Conan's, was fixed on the shadowy mass of shrubbery a few yards away. This shrubbery was shaken, although the breeze had died down. Then two great eyes blazed from the waving shadows, and behind them other sparks of fire glinted in the darkness.

"Lions!" muttered Conan.

"Aye. By day they are kept in subterranean caverns below the tower. That's why there are no guards in this garden." Conan counted the eyes rapidly.

"Five in sight; maybe more back in the bushes. They'll charge in a moment—"

"Be silent!" hissed Taurus, and he moved out from the wall, cautiously as if treading on razors, lifting the slender tube. Low rumblings rose from the shadows and the blazing eyes moved forward. Conan could sense the great slavering jaws, the tufted tails lashing tawny sides. The air grew tense—the Cimmerian gripped his sword, expecting the charge and the irresistible hurtling of giant bodies. Then Taurus brought the mouth of the tube to his lips and blew powerfully. A long jet of yellowish powder shot from the other end of the tube and billowed out instantly in a thick green-yellow cloud that settled over the shrubbery, blotting out the glaring eyes.

Taurus ran back hastily to the wall. Conan glared without understanding. The thick cloud hid the shrubbery, and from it no sound came.

"What is that mist?" the Cimmerian asked uneasily.

"Death!" hissed the Nemedian. "If a wind springs up and blows it back upon us, we must flee over the wall. But no, the wind is still, and now it is dissipating. Wait until it vanishes entirely. To breathe it is death."

Presently only yellowish shreds hung ghostily in the air; then they were gone, and Taurus motioned his companion forward. They stole toward the bushes, and Conan gasped. Stretched out in the shadows lay five great tawny shapes, the fire of their grim eyes dimmed forever. A sweetish cloying scent lingered in the atmosphere.

"They died without a sound," muttered the Cimmerian. "Taurus, what was that powder?"

"It was made from the black lotus, whose blossoms wave in the lost jungles of Khitai, where only the yellow-skulled priests of Yun dwell. Those blossoms strike dead any who smell of them."

Conan knelt beside the great forms, assuring himself that they were indeed beyond power of harm. He shook his head; the magic of the exotic lands was mysterious and terrible to the barbarians of the north.

"Why can you not slay the soldiers in the tower in the same way?" he asked.

"Because that was all the powder I possessed. The obtaining of it was a feat which in itself was enough to make me famous among the thieves of the world. I stole it out of a caravan bound for Stygia, and I lifted it, in its cloth-of-gold bag, out of the coils of the great serpent which guarded it, without awaking him. But come, in Bel's name! Are we to waste the night in discussion?"

They glided through the shrubbery to the gleaming foot of the tower, and there, with a motion enjoining silence, Taurus unwound his knotted cord, on one end of which was a strong steel hook. Conan saw his plan, and asked no questions as the Nemedian gripped the line a short distance below the hook, and began to swing it about his head. Conan laid his ear to the smooth wall and listened, but could hear nothing. Evidently the soldiers within did not suspect the presence of intruders, who had made no more sound than the night wind blowing through the trees. But a strange nervousness was on the barbarian; perhaps it was the lion-smell which was over everything.

Taurus threw the line with a smooth, ripping motion of his mighty arm. The hook curved upward and inward in a peculiar manner, hard to describe, and vanished over the jeweled rim. It apparently caught firmly, for cautious jerking and then hard pulling did not result in any slipping or giving.

"Luck the first cast," murmured Taurus. "I—"

It was Conan's savage instinct which made him wheel suddenly; for the death that was upon them made no sound. A fleeting glimpse showed the Cimmerian the giant tawny shape, rearing upright against the stars, towering over him for the death-stroke. No civilized man could have moved half so quickly as the barbarian moved. His sword flashed frostily in the starlight with every ounce of desperate nerve and thew behind it, and man and beast went down together.

Cursing incoherently beneath his breath, Taurus bent above the mass, and saw his companion's limbs move as he strove to drag himself from under the great weight that lay limply upon him. A glance showed the startled Nemedian that the lion was dead, its slanting skull split in half. He laid hold of the carcass, and by his aid, Conan thrust it aside and clambered up, still gripping his dripping sword.

"Are you hurt, man?" gasped Taurus, still bewildered by the stunning swiftness of that touch-and-go episode.

"No, by Crom!" answered the barbarian. "But that was as close a call as I've had in a life noways tame. Why did not the cursed beast roar as he charged?"

"All things are strange in this garden," said Taurus. "The lions strike silently—and so do other deaths. But come—little sound was made in that slaying, but the soldiers might have heard, if they are not asleep or drunk. That beast was in some other part of the garden and escaped the death of the flowers, but surely there are no more. We must climb this cord—little need to ask a Cimmerian if he can."

"If it will bear my weight," grunted Conan, cleansing his sword on the grass.

"It will bear thrice my own," answered Taurus. "It was woven from the tresses of dead women, which I took from their tombs at midnight, and steeped in the deadly wine of the upas tree, to give it strength. I will go first—then follow me closely."

The Nemedian gripped the rope and, crooking a knee about it, began the ascent; he went up like a cat, belying the apparent clumsiness of his bulk. The Cimmerian followed. The cord swayed and turned on itself, but the climbers were not hindered; both had made more difficult climbs before. The jeweled rim glittered high above them, jutting out from the perpendicular—a fact which added greatly to the ease of the ascent.

Up and up they went, silently, the lights of the city spreading out further and further to their sight as they climbed, the stars above them more and more dimmed by the glitter of the jewels along the rim. Now Taurus reached up a hand and gripped the rim itself, pulling himself up and over. Conan paused a moment on the very edge, fascinated by the great frosty jewels whose gleams dazzled his eyes—diamonds, rubies, emeralds, sapphires, turquoises, moonstones, set thick as stars in the shimmering silver. At a distance their different gleams had seemed to merge into a pulsing white glare; but now, at close range, they shimmered with a million rainbow tints and lights, hypnotizing him with their scintillations.

"There is a fabulous fortune here, Taurus," he whispered; but the Nemedian answered impatiently. "Come on! If we secure the Heart, these and all other things shall be ours."

Conan climbed over the sparkling rim. The level of the tower's top was some feet below the gemmed ledge. It was flat, composed of some dark blue substance, set with gold that caught the starlight, so that the whole looked like a wide sapphire flecked with shining gold-dust. Across from the point where they had entered there seemed to be a sort of chamber, built upon the roof. It was of the same silvery material as the walls of the tower, adorned with designs worked in smaller gems; its single door was of gold, its surface cut in scales, and crusted with jewels that gleamed like ice.

Conan cast a glance at the pulsing ocean of lights which spread far below them, then glanced at Taurus. The Nemedian was drawing up his cord and coiling it. He showed Conan where the hook had caught—a fraction of an inch of the point had sunk under a great blazing jewel on the inner side of the rim.

"Luck was with us again," he muttered. "One would think that our combined weight would have torn that stone out. Follow me; the real risks of the venture begin now. We are in the serpent's lair, and we know not where he lies hidden."

Like stalking tigers they crept across the darkly gleaming floor and halted outside the sparkling door. With a deft and cautious hand Taurus tried it. It gave without resistance, and the companions looked in, tensed for anything. Over the Nemedian's shoulder Conan had a glimpse of a glittering chamber, the walls, ceiling and floor of which were crusted with great white jewels which lighted it brightly, and which seemed its only illumination. It seemed empty of life.

"Before we cut off our last retreat," hissed Taurus, "go you to the rim and look over on all sides; if you see any soldiers moving in the gardens, or anything suspicious, return and tell me. I will await you within this chamber."

Conan saw scant reason in this, and a faint suspicion of his companion touched his wary soul, but he did as Taurus requested. As he turned away, the Nemedian slipped inside the door and drew it shut behind him. Conan crept about the rim of the tower, returning to his starting-point without having seen any suspicious movement in the vaguely waving sea of leaves below. He turned toward the door—suddenly from within the chamber there sounded a strangled cry.

The Cimmerian leaped forward, electrified—the gleaming door swung open and Taurus stood framed in the cold blaze behind him. He swayed and his lips parted, but only a dry rattle burst from his throat. Catching at the golden door for support, he lurched out upon the roof, then fell headlong, clutching at his throat. The door swung to behind him.

Conan, crouching like a panther at bay, saw nothing in the room behind the stricken Nemedian, in the brief instant the door was partly open—unless it was not a trick of the light which made it seem as if a shadow darted across the gleaming door. Nothing followed Taurus out on the roof, and Conan bent above the man.

The Nemedian stared up with dilated, glazing eyes, that somehow held a terrible bewilderment. His hands clawed at his throat, his lips slobbered and gurgled; then suddenly he stiffened, and the astounded Cimmerian knew that he was dead. And he felt that Taurus had died without knowing what manner of death had stricken him. Conan glared bewilderedly at the cryptic golden door. In that empty room, with its glittering jeweled walls, death had come to the prince of thieves as swiftly and mysteriously as he had dealt doom to the lions in the gardens below.

Gingerly the barbarian ran his hands over the man's half-naked body, seeking a wound. But the only marks of violence were between his shoulders, high up near the base of his bull-neck—three small wounds, which looked as if three nails had been driven deep in the flesh and withdrawn. The edges of these wounds were black, and a faint smell as of putrefaction was evident. Poisoned darts? thought Conan—but in that case the missiles should be still in the wounds.

Cautiously he stole toward the golden door, pushed it open, and looked inside. The chamber lay empty, bathed in the cold, pulsing glow of the myriad jewels. In the very center of the ceiling he idly noted a curious design—a black eight-sided pattern, in the center of which four gems glittered with a red flame unlike the white blaze of the other jewels. Across the room there was another door, like the one in which he stood, except that it was not carved in the scale pattern. Was it from that door that death had come?—and having struck down its victim, had it retreated by the same way?

Closing the door behind him, the Cimmerian advanced into the chamber. His bare feet made no sound on the crystal floor. There were no chairs or tables in the chamber, only three or four silken couches, embroidered with gold and worked in strange serpentine designs, and several silver-bound mahogany chests. Some were sealed with heavy golden locks; others lay open, their carven lids thrown back, revealing heaps of jewels in a careless riot of splendor to the Cimmerian's astounded eyes. Conan swore beneath his breath; already he had looked upon more wealth that night than he had ever dreamed existed in all the world, and he grew dizzy thinking of what must be the value of the jewel he sought.

He was in the center of the room now, going stooped forward, head thrust out warily, sword advanced, when again death struck at him soundlessly. A flying shadow that swept across the gleaming floor was his only warning, and his instinctive sidelong leap all that saved his life. He had a flashing glimpse of a hairy black horror that swung past him with a clashing of frothing fangs, and something splashed on his bare shoulder that burned like drops of liquid hellfire. Springing back, sword high, he saw the horror strike the

130

floor, wheel and scuttle toward him with appalling speed—a gigantic black spider, such as men see only in nightmare dreams.

It was as large as a pig, and its eight thick hairy legs drove its ogreish body over the floor at headlong pace; its four evilly gleaming eyes shone with a horrible intelligence, and its fangs dripped venom that Conan knew, from the burning of his shoulder where only a few drops had splashed as the thing struck and missed, was laden with swift death. This was the killer that had dropped from its perch in the middle of the ceiling on a strand of its web, on the neck of the Nemedian. Fools that they were not to have suspected that the upper chambers would be guarded as well as the lower!

These thoughts flashed briefly through Conan's mind as the monster rushed. He leaped high, and it passed beneath him, wheeled and charged back. This time he evaded its rush with a sidewise leap, and struck back like a cat. His sword severed one of the hairy legs, and again he barely saved himself as the monstrosity swerved at him, fangs clicking fiendishly. But the creature did not press the pursuit; turning, it scuttled across the crystal floor and ran up the wall to the ceiling, where it crouched for an instant, glaring down at him with its fiendish red eyes. Then without warning it launched itself through space, trailing a strand of slimy grayish stuff.

Conan stepped back to avoid the hurtling body—then ducked frantically, just in time to escape being snared by the flying web-rope. He saw the monster's intent and sprang toward the door, but it was quicker, and a sticky strand cast across the door made him a prisoner. He dared not try to cut it with his sword; he knew the stuff would cling to the blade, and before he could shake it loose, the fiend would be sinking its fangs into his back.

Then began a desperate game, the wits and quickness of the man matched against the fiendish craft and speed of the giant spider. It no longer scuttled across the floor in a direct charge, or swung its body through the air at him. It raced about the ceiling and the walls, seeking to snare him in the long loops of sticky gray web-strands, which it flung with a devilish accuracy. These strands were thick as ropes, and Conan knew that once they were coiled about him, his desperate strength would not be enough to tear him free before the monster struck.

All over the chamber went on that devil's game, in utter silence except for the quick breathing of the man, the low scuff of his bare feet on the shining floor, the castanet rattle of the monstrosity's fangs. The gray strands lay in coils on the floor; they were looped along the walls; they overlaid the jewel-chests and silken couches, and hung in dusky festoons from the jeweled ceiling. Conan's steel-trap quickness of eye and muscle had kept him untouched, though the sticky loops had passed him so close they rasped his naked hide. He knew he could not always avoid them; he not only had to watch the strands swinging from the ceiling, but to keep his eye on the floor, lest he trip in the coils that lay there. Sooner or later a gummy loop would writhe about him, python-like, and then, wrapped like a cocoon, he would lie at the monster's mercy.

The spider raced across the chamber floor, the gray rope waving out behind it. Conan leaped high, clearing a couch—with a quick wheel the fiend ran up the wall, and the strand, leaping off the floor like a live thing, whipped about the Cimmerian's ankle. He caught himself on his hands as he fell, jerking frantically at the web which held him like a pliant vise, or the coil of a python. The hairy devil was racing down the wall to complete its capture. Stung to frenzy, Conan caught up a jewel chest and hurled it with all his strength. It was a move the monster was not expecting. Full in the midst of the branching black legs the massive missile struck, smashing against the wall with a muffled sickening crunch. Blood and greenish slime spattered, and the shattered mass fell with the burst gem-chest to the floor. The crushed black body lay among the flaming riot of jewels that spilled over it; the hairy legs moved aimlessly, the dying eyes glittered redly among the twinkling gems.

Conan glared about, but no other horror appeared, and he set himself to working free of the web. The substance clung tenaciously to his ankle and his hands, but at last he was free, and taking up his sword, he picked his way among the gray coils and loops to the inner door. What horrors lay within he did not know. The Cimmerian's blood was up, and since he had come so far, and overcome so much peril, he was determined to go through to the grim finish of the adventure, whatever that might be. And he felt that the jewel he sought was not among the many so carelessly strewn about the gleaming chamber.

Stripping off the loops that fouled the inner door, he found that it, like the other, was not locked. He wondered if the soldiers below were still unaware of his presence. Well, he was high above their heads, and if tales were to be believed, they were used to strange noises in the tower above them—sinister sounds, and screams of agony and horror.

Yara was on his mind, and he was not altogether comfortable as he opened the golden door. But he saw only a flight of silver steps leading down, dimly lighted by what means he could not ascertain. Down these he went silently, gripping his sword. He heard no sound, and came presently to an ivory door, set with blood-stones. He listened, but no sound came from within; only thin wisps of smoke drifted lazily from beneath the door, bearing a curious exotic odor unfamiliar to the Cimmerian. Below him the silver stair wound down to vanish in the dimness, and up that shadowy well no sound floated; he had an eerie feeling that he was alone in a tower occupied only by ghosts and phantoms.

III

Cautiously he pressed against the ivory door and it swung silently inward. On the shimmering threshold Conan stared like a wolf in strange surroundings, ready to fight or flee on the instant. He was looking into a large chamber with a domed golden ceiling; the walls were of green jade, the floor of ivory, partly covered by thick rugs. Smoke and exotic scent of incense floated up from a brazier on a golden tripod, and behind it sat an idol on a sort of marble couch.

Conan stared aghast; the image had the body of a man, naked, and green in color; but the head was one of nightmare and madness. Too large for the human body, it had no attributes of humanity. Conan stared at the wide flaring ears, the curling proboscis, on either side of which stood white tusks tipped with round golden balls. The eyes were closed, as if in sleep.

This then, was the reason for the name, the Tower of the Elephant, for the head of the thing was much like that of the beasts described by the Shemitish wanderer. This was Yara's god; where then should the gem be, but concealed in the idol, since the stone was called the Elephant's Heart?

As Conan came forward, his eyes fixed on the motionless idol, the eyes of the thing opened suddenly! The Cimmerian froze in his tracks. It was no image—it was a living thing, and he was trapped in its chamber!

That he did not instantly explode in a burst of murderous frenzy is a fact that measures his horror, which paralyzed him where he stood. A civilized man in his position would have sought doubtful refuge in the conclusion that he was insane; it did not occur to the Cimmerian to doubt his senses. He knew he was face to face with a demon of the Elder World, and the realization robbed him of all his faculties except sight.

The trunk of the horror was lifted and quested about, the topaz eyes stared unseeingly, and Conan knew the monster was blind. With the thought came a thawing of his frozen nerves, and he began to back silently toward the door. But the creature heard. The sensitive trunk stretched toward him, and Conan's horror froze him again when the being spoke, in a strange, stammering voice that never changed its key or timbre. The Cimmerian knew that those jaws were never built or intended for human speech.

"Who is here? Have you come to torture me again, Yara? Will you never be done? Oh, Yag-kosha, is there no end to agony?"

Tears rolled from the sightless eyes, and Conan's gaze strayed to the limbs stretched on the marble couch. And he knew the monster would not rise to attack him. He knew the marks of the rack, and the searing brand of the flame, and tough-souled as he was, he stood aghast at the ruined deformities which his reason told him had once been limbs as comely as his own. And suddenly all fear and repulsion went from him, to be replaced by a great pity. What this monster was, Conan could not know, but the evidences of its sufferings were so terrible and pathetic that a strange aching sadness came over the Cimmerian, he knew not why. He only felt that he was looking upon a cosmic tragedy, and he shrank with shame, as if the guilt of a whole race were laid upon him.

"I am not Yara," he said. "I am only a thief. I will not harm you."

"Come near that I may touch you," the creature faltered, and Conan came near unfearingly, his sword hanging forgotten in his hand. The sensitive trunk came out and groped over his face and shoulders, as a blind man gropes, and its touch was light as a girl's hand.

"You are not of Yara's race of devils," sighed the creature. "The clean, lean fierceness of the wastelands marks you. I know your people from of old, whom I knew by another name in the long, long ago when another world lifted its jeweled spires to the stars. There is blood on your fingers."

"A spider in the chamber above and a lion in the garden," muttered Conan.

"You have slain a man too, this night," answered the other. "And there is death in the tower above. I feel; I know."

"Aye," muttered Conan. "The prince of all thieves lies there dead from the bite of a vermin."

"So—and so!" The strange inhuman voice rose in a sort of low chant. "A slaying in the tavern and a slaying on the road—I know; I feel. And the third will make the magic of which not even Yara dreams—oh, magic of deliverance, green gods of Yag!"

Again tears fell as the tortured body was rocked to and fro in the grip of varied emotions. Conan looked on, bewildered.

Then the convulsions ceased; the soft, sightless eyes were turned toward the Cimmerian, the trunk beckoned.

"Oh man, listen," said the strange being. "I am foul and monstrous to you, am I not? Nay, do not answer; I know. But you would seem as strange to me, could I see you. There are many worlds besides this earth, and life takes many shapes. I am neither god nor demon, but flesh and blood like yourself, though the substance differ in part, and the form be cast in a different mold.

"I am very old, oh man of the waste countries; long and long ago I came to this planet with others of my world, from the green planet Yag, which circles for ever in the outer fringe of this universe. We swept through space on mighty wings that drove us through the cosmos quicker than light, because we had warred with the kings of Yag and were defeated and outcast. But we could never return, for on earth our wings withered from our shoulders. Here we abode apart from earthly life. We fought the strange and terrible forms of life which then walked the earth, so that we became feared, and were not molested in the dim jungles of the east, where we had our abode.

"We saw men grow from the ape and build the shining cities of Valusia, Kamelia, Commoria and their sisters. We saw them reel before the thrusts of the heathen Atlanteans and Picts and Lemurians. We saw the oceans rise and engulf Atlantis and Lemuria, and the isles of the Picts, and the shining cities of civilization. We saw the survivors of Pictdom and Atlantis build their stone-age empires, and go down to ruin, locked in bloody wars. We saw the Picts sink into abysmal savagery, the Atlanteans into apedom again. We saw new savages drift southward in conquering waves from the Arctic circle to build a new civilization, with new kingdoms called Nemedia, and Koth, and Aquilonia and their sisters. We saw your people rise under a new name from the jungles of the apes that had been Atlanteans. We saw the descendants of the Lemurians who had survived the cataclysm, rise again through savagery and ride westward as Hyrkanians. And we saw this race of devils, survivors of the ancient civilization that was before Atlantis sank, come once more into culture and power—this accursed kingdom of Zamora.

"All this we saw, neither aiding nor hindering the immutable cosmic law, and one by one we died; for we of Yag are not immortal, though our lives are as the lives of planets and constellations. At last I alone was left, dreaming of old times among the ruined temples of jungle-lost Khitai, worshipped as a god by an ancient yellow-skinned race. Then came Yara, versed in dark knowledge handed down through the days of barbarism, since before Atlantis sank.

"First he sat at my feet and learned wisdom. But he was not satisfied with what I taught him, for it was white magic, and he wished evil lore, to enslave kings and glut a fiendish ambition. I would teach him none of the black secrets I had gained, through no wish of mine, through the eons.

"But his wisdom was deeper than I had guessed; with guile gotten among the dusky tombs of dark Stygia, he trapped me into divulging a secret I had not intended to bare; and turning my own power upon me, he enslaved me. Ah, gods of Yag, my cup has been bitter since that hour!

"He brought me up from the lost jungles of Khitai where the gray apes danced to the pipes of the yellow priests, and offerings of fruit and wine heaped my broken altars. No more was I a god to kindly jungle-folk—I was slave to a devil in human form."

Again tears stole from the unseeing eyes.

"He pent me in this tower which at his command I built for him in a single night. By fire and rack he mastered me, and by strange unearthly tortures you would not understand. In agony I would long ago have taken my own life, if I could. But he kept me alive—mangled, blinded, and broken—to do his foul bidding. And for three hundred years I have done his bidding, from this marble couch, blackening my soul with cosmic sins, and staining my wisdom with crimes, because I had no other choice. Yet not all my ancient secrets has he wrested from me, and my last gift shall be the sorcery of the Blood and the Jewel

"For I feel the end of time draw near. You are the hand of Fate. I beg of you, take the gem you will find on yonder altar."

Conan turned to the gold and ivory altar indicated, and took up a great round jewel, clear as crimson crystal; and he knew that this was the Heart of the Elephant.

"Now for the great magic, the mighty magic, such as earth has not seen before, and shall not see again, through a million million of millenniums. By my life-blood I conjure it, by blood born on the green breast of Yag, dreaming far-poised in the great blue vastness of Space.

"Take your sword, man, and cut out my heart; then squeeze it so that the blood will flow over the red stone. Then go you down these stairs and enter the ebony chamber where Yara sits wrapped in lotus-dreams of evil. Speak his name and he will awaken. Then lay this gem before him, and say, 'Yag-kosha gives you a last gift and a last enchantment.' Then get you from the tower quickly; fear not, your way shall be made clear. The life of man is not the life of Yag, nor is human death the death of Yag. Let me be free of this cage of broken blind flesh, and I will once more be Yogah of Yag, morning-crowned and shining, with wings to fly, and feet to dance, and eyes to see, and hands to break."

Uncertainly Conan approached, and Yag-kosha, or Yogah, as if sensing his uncertainty, indicated where he should strike. Conan set his teeth and drove the sword deep. Blood streamed over the blade and his hand, and the monster started convulsively, then lay back quite still. Sure that life had fled, at least life as he understood it, Conan set to work on his grisly task and quickly brought forth something that he felt must be the strange being's heart, though it differed curiously from any he had ever seen. Holding the pulsing organ over the blazing jewel, he pressed it with both hands, and a rain of blood fell on the stone. To his surprise, it did not run off, but soaked into the gem, as water is absorbed by a sponge.

Holding the jewel gingerly, he went out of the fantastic chamber and came upon the silver steps. He did not look back; he instinctively felt that some transmutation was taking place in the body on the marble couch, and he further felt that it was of a sort not to be witnessed by human eyes.

He closed the ivory door behind him and without hesitation descended the silver steps. It did not occur to him to ignore the instructions given him. He halted at an ebony door, in the center of which was a grinning silver skull, and pushed it open. He looked into a chamber of ebony and jet, and saw, on a black silken couch, a tall, spare form reclining. Yara the priest and sorcerer lay before him, his eyes open and dilated with the fumes of the yellow lotus, far-staring, as if fixed on gulfs and nighted abysses beyond human ken.

"Yara!" said Conan, like a judge pronouncing doom. "Awaken!"

The eyes cleared instantly and became cold and cruel as a vulture's. The tall silken-clad form lifted erect, and towered gauntly above the Cimmerian.

"Dog!" His hiss was like the voice of a cobra. "What do you here?"

Conan laid the jewel on the ebony table.

"He who sent this gem bade me say, 'Yag-kosha gives you a last gift and a last enchantment.'"

Yara recoiled, his dark face ashy. The jewel was no longer crystal-clear; its murky depths pulsed and throbbed, and curious smoky waves of changing color passed over its smooth surface. As if drawn hypnotically, Yara bent over the table and gripped the gem in his hands, staring into its shadowed depths, as if it were a magnet to draw the shuddering soul from his body. And as Conan looked, he thought that his eyes must be playing him tricks. For when Yara had risen up from his couch, the priest had seemed gigantically tall; yet now he saw that Yara's head would scarcely come to his shoulder. He blinked, puzzled, and for the first time that night, doubted his own senses. Then with a shock he realized that the priest was shrinking in stature—was growing smaller before his very gaze.

With a detached feeling he watched, as a man might watch a play; immersed in a feeling of overpowering unreality, the Cimmerian was no longer sure of his own identity; he only knew that he was looking upon the external evidence of the unseen play of vast Outer forces, beyond his understanding.

Now Yara was no bigger than a child; now like an infant he sprawled on the table, still grasping the jewel. And now the sorcerer suddenly realized his fate, and he sprang up, releasing the gem. But still he dwindled, and Conan saw a tiny, pygmy figure rushing wildly about the ebony table-top, waving tiny arms and shrieking in a voice that was like the squeak of an insect.

Now he had shrunk until the great jewel towered above him like a hill, and Conan saw him cover his eyes with his hands, as if to shield them from the glare, as he staggered about like a madman. Conan sensed that some unseen magnetic force was pulling Yara to the gem. Thrice he raced wildly about it in a narrowing circle, thrice he strove to turn and run out across the table; then with a scream that echoed faintly in the ears of the watcher, the priest threw up his arms and ran straight toward the blazing globe.

Bending close, Conan saw Yara clamber up the smooth, curving surface, impossibly, like a man climbing a glass mountain. Now the priest stood on the top, still with tossing arms, invoking what grisly names only the gods know. And suddenly he sank into the very heart of the jewel, as a man sinks into a sea, and Conan saw the smoky waves close over his head. Now he saw him in the crimson heart of the jewel, once more crystal-clear, as a man sees a scene far away, tiny with great distance. And into the heart came a green, shining winged figure with the body of a man and the head of an elephant—no longer blind or crippled. Yara threw up his arms and fled as a madman flees, and on his heels came the avenger. Then, like the bursting of a bubble, the great jewel vanished in a rainbow burst of iridescent gleams, and the ebony table-top lay bare and deserted—as bare, Conan somehow knew, as the marble couch in the chamber above, where the body of that strange transcosmic being called Yag-kosha and Yogah had lain.

The Cimmerian turned and fled from the chamber, down the silver stairs. So amazed was he that it did not occur to him to escape from the tower by the way he had entered it. Down that winding, shadowy silver well he ran, and came into a large chamber at the foot of the gleaming stairs. There he halted for an instant; he had come into the room of soldiers. He saw the glitter of their silver corselets, the sheen of their jeweled sword-hilts. They sat slumped at the banquet board, their dusky plumes waving somberly above their drooping helmeted heads; they lay among their dice and fallen goblets on the wine-stained lapis-lazuli floor. And he knew that they were dead. The promise had been made, the word kept; whether sorcery or magic or the falling shadow of great green wings had stilled the revelry, Conan could not know, but his way had been made clear. And a silver door stood open, framed in the whiteness of dawn.

Into the waving green gardens came the Cimmerian, and as the dawn wind blew upon him with the cool fragrance of luxuriant growths, he started like a man waking from a dream. He turned back uncertainly, to stare at the cryptic tower he had just left. Was he bewitched and enchanted? Had he dreamed all that had seemed to have passed? As he looked he saw the gleaming tower sway against the crimson dawn, its jewel-crusted rim sparkling in the growing light, and crash into shining shards.

SECRET CHAMBER

The Song of Swords

Fred Saberhagen (1930-2007)

Who holds Coinspinner knows good odds
Whichever move he make
But the Sword of Chance, to please the gods
Slips from him like a snake.

The Sword of Justice balances the pans
Of right and wrong, and foul and fair.
Eye for an eye, Doomgiver scans
The fate of all folk everywhere.

Dragonslicer, Dragonslicer, how d'you slay?
Reaching for the heart in behind the scales.
Dragonslicer, Dragonslicer, where do you stay?
In the belly of the giant that my blade impales.

Farslayer howls across the world
For thy heart, for thy heart, who hast wronged me!
Vengeance is his who casts the blade
Yet he will in the end no triumph see.

Whose flesh the Sword of Mercy hurts has drawn no breath;
Whose soul it heals has wandered in the night,

THE SONG OF SWORDS

Has paid the summing of all debts in death
Has turned to see returning light.

The Mindsword spun in the dawn's gray light
And men and demons knelt down before.
The Mindsword flashed in the midday bright
Gods joined the dance, and the march to war.
It spun in the twilight dim as well
And gods and men marched off to hell.

I shatter Swords and splinter spears;
None stands to Shieldbreaker.
My point's the fount of orphans' tears
My edge the widowmaker.

The Sword of Stealth is given to
One lonely and despised.
Sightblinder's gifts: his eyes are keen
His nature is disguised.

The Tyrant's Blade no blood hath spilled
But doth the spirit carve
Soulcutter hath no body killed
But many left to starve.

The Sword of Siege struck a hammer's blow
With a crash, and a smash, and a tumbled wall.
Stonecutter laid a castle low
With a groan, and a roar, and a tower's fall.

Long roads the Sword of Fury makes
Hard walls it builds around the soft
The fighter who Townsaver takes
Can bid farewell to home and croft.

FRED SABERHAGEN

Who holds Wayfinder finds good roads
Its master's step is brisk.
The Sword of Wisdom lightens loads
But adds unto their risk.

KEY TO LOWER LEVEL

The Dreaming City

Michael Moorcock (1939-)

Introduction

For ten thousand years did the Bright Empire of Melniboné flourish—ruling the world. Ten thousand years before history was recorded—or ten thousand years after history had ceased to be chronicled. For that span of time, reckon it how you will, the Bright Empire had thrived. Be hopeful, if you like, and think of the dreadful past the Earth has known, or brood upon the future. But if you would believe the unholy truth—then Time is an agony of Now, and so it will always be.

Ravaged, at last, by the formless terror called Time, Melniboné fell and newer nations succeeded her: Ilmiora, Sheegoth, Maidahk, S'aaleem. Then memory began: Ur, India, China, Egypt, Assyria, Persia, Greece, and Rome—all these came after Melniboné. But none lasted ten thousand years.

And none dealt in the terrible mysteries, the secret sorceries of old Melniboné. None used such power or knew how. Only Melniboné ruled the Earth for one hundred centuries—and then she, shaken by the casting of frightful runes, attacked by powers greater than men; powers who decided that Melniboné's span of ruling had been overlong—then she crumbled and her sons were scattered. They became wanderers across an Earth which hated and feared them, siring few offspring, slowly dying, slowly forgetting the secrets of their mighty ancestors. Such a one was the cynical, laughing Elric, a man of bitter brooding and gusty humor, proud prince of ruins, lord of a lost and humbled people; last son of Melniboné's sundered line of kings.

Elric, the moody-eyed wanderer—a lonely man who fought a world, living by his wits and his runesword Stormbringer. Elric, last lord of Melniboné, last worshipper of its grotesque and beautiful gods—reckless reaver and cynical slayer—torn by great griefs and with knowledge locked in his skull which would turn lesser men to babbling idiots. Elric, molder of madnesses, dabbler in wild delights...

I

"What's the hour?" The black-bearded man wrenched off his gilded helmet and flung it from him, careless of where it fell. He drew off his leathern gauntlets and moved closer to the roaring fire, letting the heat soak into his frozen bones.

"Midnight is long past," growled one of the other armored men who gathered around the blaze. "Are you still sure he'll come?"

"It's said that he's a man of his word, if that comforts you."

It was a tall, pale-faced youth who spoke. His thin lips formed the words and spat them out maliciously. He grinned a wolf-grin and stared the new arrival in the eyes, mocking him.

The newcomer turned away with a shrug. "That's so—for all your irony, Yaris. He'll come." He spoke as a man does when he wishes to reassure himself.

There were six men, now, around the fire. The sixth was Smiorgan—Count Smiorgan Baldhead of the Purple Towns. He was a short, stocky man of fifty years with a scarred face partially covered with a thick, black growth of hair. His morose eyes smoldered and his lumpy fingers plucked nervously at his rich-hilted longsword. His pate was hairless, giving him his name,

152

and over his ornate, gilded armor hung a loose woolen cloak, dyed purple.

Smiorgan said thickly, "He has no love for his cousin. He has become bitter. Yyrkoon sits on the Ruby Throne in his place and has proclaimed him an outlaw and a traitor. Elric needs us if he would take his throne and his bride back. We can trust him."

"You're full of trust tonight, count," Yaris smiled thinly, "a rare thing to find in these troubled times. I say this—" He paused and took a long breath, staring at his comrades, summing them up. His gaze flicked from lean-faced Dharmit of Jharkor to Fadan of Lormyr who pursed his podgy lips and looked into the fire.

"Speak up, Yaris," petulantly urged the patrician-featured Vilmirian, Naclon. "Let's hear what you have to say, lad, if it's worth hearing."

Yaris looked towards Jiku the dandy, who yawned impolitely and scratched his long nose.

"Well!" Smiorgan was impatient. "What d'you say, Yaris?"

"I say that we should start now and waste no more time waiting on Elric's pleasure! He's laughing at us in some tavern a hundred miles from here—or else plotting with the Dragon Princes to trap us. For years we have planned this raid. We have little time in which to strike—our fleet is too big, too noticeable. Even if Elric has not betrayed us, then spies will soon be running eastwards to warn the Dragons that there is a fleet massed against them. We stand to win a fantastic fortune—to vanquish the greatest merchant city in the world—to reap immeasurable riches—or horrible death at the hands of the Dragon Princes, if we wait overlong. Let's bide our time no more and set sail before our prize hears of our plan and brings up reinforcements!"

"You always were too ready to mistrust a man, Yaris." King Naclon of Vilmir spoke slowly, carefully—distastefully eyeing the taut-featured youth. "We could not reach Imrryr without Elric's knowledge of the maze-channels which lead to its secret ports. If Elric will not join us—then our endeavor will be fruitless—hopeless.

We need him. We must wait for him—or else give up our plans and return to our homelands."

"At least I'm willing to take a risk," yelled Yaris, anger lancing from his slanting eyes. "You're getting old—all of you. Treasures are not won by care and forethought but by swift slaying and reckless attack."

"Fool!" Dharmit's voice rumbled around the fire-flooded hall. He laughed wearily. "I spoke thus in my youth—and lost a fine fleet soon after. Cunning and Elric's knowledge will win us Imrryr—that and the mightiest fleet to sail the Dragon Sea since Melniboné's banners fluttered over all the nations of the Earth. Here we are— the most powerful sea-lords in the world, masters, every one of us, of more than a hundred swift vessels. Our names are feared and famous—our fleets ravage the coasts of a score of lesser nations. We hold power!" He clenched his great fist and shook it in Yaris's face. His tone became more level and he smiled viciously, glaring at the youth and choosing his words with precision.

"But all this is worthless—meaningless—without the power which Elric has. That is the power of knowledge—of dream-learned sorcery, if I must use the cursed word. His fathers knew of the maze which guards Imrryr from sea-attack. And his fathers passed that secret on to him. Imrryr, the Dreaming City, dreams in peace—and will continue to do so unless we have a guide to help us steer a course through the treacherous waterways which lead to her harbors. We need Elric—we know it, and he knows it. That's the truth!"

"Such confidence, gentlemen, is warming to the heart." There was irony in the heavy voice which came from the entrance to the hall. The heads of the six sea-lords jerked towards the doorway.

Yaris's confidence fled from him as he met the eyes of Elric of Melniboné. They were old eyes in a fine featured, youthful face. Yaris shuddered, turned his back on Elric, preferring to look into the bright glare of the fire.

Elric smiled warmly as Count Smiorgan gripped his shoulder. There was a certain friendship between the two. He nodded condescendingly to the other four and walked with lithe grace towards the fire. Yaris stood aside and let him pass. Elric was tall, broad-shouldered and slim-hipped. He wore his long hair bunched and pinned at the nape of his neck and, for an obscure reason, affected the dress of a Southern barbarian. He had long, knee-length boots of soft doe-leather, a breastplate of strangely wrought silver, a jerkin of chequered blue-and-white linen, britches of scarlet wool and a cloak of rustling green velvet. At his hip rested his runesword of black iron—the feared Stormbringer, forged by ancient and alien sorcery.

His bizarre dress was tasteless and gaudy, and did not match his sensitive face and long-fingered, almost delicate hands, yet he flaunted it since it emphasized the fact that he did not belong in any company—that he was an outsider and an outcast. But, in reality, he had little need to wear such outlandish gear—for his eyes and skin were enough to mark him.

Elric, last lord of Melniboné, was a pure albino who drew his power from a secret and terrible source.

Smiorgan sighed. "Well, Elric, when do we raid Imrryr?"

Elric shrugged. "As soon as you like; I care not. Give me a little time in which to do certain things."

"Tomorrow? Shall we sail tomorrow?" Yaris said hesitantly, conscious of the strange power dormant in the man he had earlier accused of treachery.

Elric smiled, dismissing the youth's statement. "Three days' time," he said, "Three—or more."

"Three days! But Imrryr will be warned of our presence by then!" Fat, cautious Fadan spoke.

"I'll see that your fleet's not found," Elric promised. "I have to go to Imrryr first—and return."

"You won't do the journey in three days—the fastest ship could not make it." Smiorgan gaped.

"I'll be in the Dreaming City in less than a day," Elric said softly, with finality.

Smiorgan shrugged. "If you say so, I'll believe it—but why this necessity to visit the city ahead of the raid?"

"I have my own compunctions, Count Smiorgan. But worry not—I shan't betray you. I'll lead the raid myself, be sure of that." His dead-white face was lighted eerily by the fire and his red eyes smoldered. One lean hand firmly gripped the hilt of his runesword and he appeared to breathe more heavily. "Imrryr fell, in spirit, five hundred years ago—she will fall completely soon—forever! I have a little debt to settle. This is my sole reason for aiding you. As you know I have made only a few conditions—that you raze the city to the ground and a certain man and woman are not harmed. I refer to my cousin Yyrkoon and his sister Cymoril..."

Yaris's thin lips felt uncomfortably dry. Much of his blustering manner resulted from the early death of his father. The old sea-king had died—leaving the youthful Yaris as the new ruler of his lands and his fleets. Yaris was not at all certain that he was capable of commanding such a vast kingdom—and tried to appear more confident than he actually felt. Now he said: "How shall we hide the fleet, Lord Elric?"

The Melnibonéan acknowledged the question. "I'll hide it for you," he promised. "I go now to do this—but make sure all your men are off the ships first—will you see to it, Smiorgan?"

"Aye," rumbled the stocky count.

He and Elric departed from the hall together, leaving five men behind; five men who sensed an air of icy doom hanging about the overheated hall.

"How could he hide such a mighty fleet when we, who know this fjord better than any, found nowhere?" Dharmit of Jharkor said bewilderedly.

None answered him.

They waited, tensed and nervous, while the fire flickered and died untended. Eventually Smiorgan returned, stamping noisily on the boarded floor. There was a haunted haze of fear surrounding him; an almost tangible aura, and he was shivering, terribly. Tremendous,

156

racking undulations swept up his body and his breath came short.

"Well? Did Elric hide the fleet—all at once? What did he do?" Dharmit spoke impatiently, choosing not to heed Smiorgan's ominous condition.

"He has hidden it." That was all Smiorgan said, and his voice was thin, like that of a sick man, weak from fever.

Yaris went to the entrance and tried to stare beyond the fjord slopes where many campfires burned, tried to make out the outlines of ships' masts and rigging, but he could see nothing.

"The night mist's too thick," he murmured, "I can't tell whether our ships are anchored in the fjord or not." Then he gasped involuntarily as a white face loomed out of the clinging fog. "Greetings, Lord Elric," he stuttered, noting the sweat on the Melnibonéan's strained features.

Elric staggered past him, into the hall. "Wine," he mumbled, "I've done what's needed and it's cost me hard."

Dharmit fetched a jug of strong Cadsandrian wine and with a shaking hand poured some into a carved wooden goblet. Wordlessly he passed the cup to Elric who quickly drained it. "Now I will sleep," he said, stretching himself into a chair and wrapping his green cloak around him. He closed his disconcerting crimson eyes and fell into a slumber born of utter weariness.

Fadan scurried to the door, closed it and pulled the heavy iron bar down.

None of the six slept much that night and, in the morning, the door was unbarred and Elric was missing from the chair. When they went outside, the mist was so heavy that they soon lost sight of one another, though scarcely two feet separated any of them.

Elric stood with his legs astride on the shingle of the narrow beach. He looked back at the entrance to the fjord and saw, with satisfaction, that the mist was still thickening, though it lay only over the fjord itself, hiding the mighty fleet. Elsewhere, the weather was clear and overhead a pale winter sun shone sharply on the black rocks of the rugged cliffs which dominated the coastline. Ahead of him the sea rose and fell monotonously, like the chest of a sleeping water-giant, grey and pure, glinting in the cold sunlight. Elric fingered the raised runes on the hilt of his black broadsword and a steady north wind blew into the voluminous folds of his dark green cloak, swirling it around his tall, lean frame.

The albino felt fitter than he had done on the previous night when he had expended all his strength in conjuring the mist. He was well-versed in the arts of nature-wizardry, but he did not have the reserves of power which the Sorcerer Emperors of Melniboné had possessed when they had ruled the world. His ancestors had passed their knowledge down to him—but not their mystic vitality and many of the spells and secrets that he had were unusable, since he did not have the reservoir of strength, either of soul or of body, to work them. But for all that, Elric knew of only one other man who matched his knowledge—his cousin Yyrkoon. His hand gripped the hilt tighter as he thought of the cousin who had twice betrayed his trust, and he forced himself to concentrate on his present task—the speaking of spells to aid him on his voyage to the Isle of the Dragon Masters whose only city, Imrryr the Beautiful, was the object of the sea-lords' massing.

Drawn up on the beach, a tiny sailing boat lay. Elric's own small craft, sturdy, oddly wrought and far stronger, far older, than it appeared. The brooding sea flung surf around its timbers as the tide withdrew, and Elric realized that he had little time in which to work his helpful sorcery.

His body tensed and he blanked his conscious mind, summoning secrets from the dark depths of his dreaming soul. Swaying, his eyes staring unseeingly, his arms jerking out ahead of him and making unholy signs in the air, he began to speak in a sibilant monotone. Slowly the pitch of his voice rose, resembling the scarcely heard shriek of a distant gale as it comes closer—then, quite suddenly, the voice rose higher until it was howling wildly to the skies and the air began to tremble and quiver. Shadow-shapes began slowly to form and they were never still but darted around Elric's body as, stiff-legged, he started forward towards his boat.

His voice was inhuman as it howled insistently, summoning the wind elementals—the sylphs of the breeze; the sharnahs, makers of gales; the h'Haarshanns, builders of whirlwinds—hazy and formless, they eddied around him as he summoned their aid with the alien words of his forefathers who had, in dream-quests taken ages before, made impossible, unthinkable pacts with the elementals in order to procure their services.

Still stiff-limbed, Elric entered the boat and, like an automaton, ran his fingers up the sail and set its ropes, binding himself to his tiller. Then a great wave erupted out of the placid sea, rising higher and higher until it towered over the vessel. With a surging crash, the water smashed down on the boat, lifted it and bore it out to sea. Sitting blank-eyed in the stern, Elric still crooned his hideous song of sorcery as the spirits of the air plucked at the sail and sent the boat flying over the water faster than any mortal ship could speed. And all the while, the deafening, unholy shriek of the released elementals filled the air about the boat as the shore vanished and open sea was all that was visible.

II

So it was, with wind-demons for shipmates, that Elric, last prince of the royal line of Melniboné, returned to the last city still ruled by his own race—the last city and the final remnant of extant Melnibonéan architecture. All the other great cities lay in ruins, abandoned save for hermits and solitaries. The cloudy pink and subtle yellow tints of the old city's nearer towers came into sight within a few hours of Elric's leaving the fjord and just offshore of the Isle of the Dragon Masters the elementals left the boat and fled back to their secret haunts among the peaks of the highest mountains in the world. Elric awoke, then, from his trance, and regarded with fresh wonder the beauty of his own birthplace's delicate towers which were visible even so far away, guarded still by the formidable sea wall with its great gate, the five-doored maze and the twisting, high-walled channels, of which only one led to the inner harbor of Imrryr.

Elric knew that he dare not risk entering the harbor by the maze, though he understood the route perfectly. He decided, instead, to land the boat further up the coast in a small inlet of which he had knowledge. With sure, capable hands, he guided the little craft towards the hidden inlet which was obscured by a growth of shrubs loaded with ghastly blue berries of a type decidedly poisonous to men since their juice first turned one blind and then slowly mad. This berry, the noidel, grew only on Melniboné, as did other rare and deadly plants whose mixture sustained the frail prince.

Light, low-hanging cloud wisps streamed slowly across the sun-painted sky, like fine cobwebs caught by a sudden breeze. All the world seemed blue and gold and green and white, and Elric, pulling his boat up on the beach, breathed the clean, sharp air of winter and savored the scent of decaying leaves and rotting undergrowth. Somewhere a bitch-fox barked her pleasure to her mate and Elric regretted the fact that his depleted race no longer appreciated natural beauty, preferring to stay close to their city and spend many of their days in drugged slumber; in study. It was not the city which dreamed, but its overcivilized inhabitants. Or had they become one and the same? Elric, smelling the rich, clean winter-scents, was wholly glad that he had renounced his birthright and no longer ruled the city as he had been born to do.

Instead, Yyrkoon, his cousin, sprawled on the Ruby Throne of Imrryr the Beautiful and hated Elric because he knew that the albino, for all his disgust with crowns and rulership, was still the rightful king of the Dragon Isle and that he, Yyrkoon, was an usurper, not elected by Elric to the throne, as Melnibonéan tradition demanded.

But Elric had better reasons for hating his cousin. For those reasons the ancient capital would fall in all its magnificent splendor and the last fragment of a glorious empire would be obliterated as the pink, the yellow, the purple and white towers crumbled—if Elric had his vengeful way and the sea-lords were successful.

On foot, Elric strode inland, towards Imrryr, and as he covered the miles of soft turf, the sun cast an ochre pall over the land and sank, giving way to a dark and moonless night, brooding and full of evil portent.

At last he came to the city. It stood out in stark black silhouette, a city of fantastic magnificence, in conception and in execution. It was the oldest city in the world, built by artists and conceived as a work of art rather than a functional dwelling-place, but Elric knew that squalor lurked in many narrow streets and that the lords of Imrryr left many of the towers empty and uninhabited rather than let the bastard population of the city dwell therein. There were few Dragon Masters left; few who would claim Melnibonéan blood.

Built to follow the shape of the ground, the city had an organic appearance, with winding lanes spiraling to the crest of the hill where stood the castle, tall and proud and many-spired, the final, crowning masterpiece of the ancient, forgotten artist who had built it. But there was no life-sound emanating from Imrryr the Beautiful, only a sense of soporific desolation. The city slept—and the Dragon Masters and their ladies and their special slaves dreamed drug-induced dreams of grandeur and incredible horror, learning unusable skills, while the rest of the population, ordered by curfew, tossed on straw-strewn stone and tried not to dream at all.

Elric, his hand ever near his sword hilt, slipped through an unguarded gate in the city wall and began to walk cautiously through the ill-lit streets, moving upwards, through the winding lanes, towards Yyrkoon's great palace.

Wind sighed through the empty rooms of the Dragon towers and sometimes Elric would have to withdraw into places where the shadows were deeper when he heard the tramp of feet and a group of guards would pass, their duty being to see that the curfew was rigidly obeyed. Often he would hear wild laughter echoing from one of the towers, still ablaze with bright torchlight which flung strange, disturbing shadows on the walls; often, too, he would hear a chilling scream and a frenzied, idiot's yell as some wretch of a slave died in obscene agony to please his master.

Elric was not appalled by the sounds and the dim sights. He appreciated them. He was still a Melnibonéan—their rightful leader if he chose to regain his powers of kingship—and though he had an obscure urge to wander and sample the less sophisticated pleasures of the outside world, ten thousand years of a cruel, brilliant and malicious culture were behind him, its wisdom gained as he slept, and the pulse of his ancestry beat strongly in his deficient veins.

Elric knocked impatiently upon the heavy, blackwood door. He had reached the palace and now stood by a small back entrance, glancing cautiously around him, for he knew that Yyrkoon had given the guards orders to slay him if he entered Imrryr.

A bolt squealed on the other side of the door and it moved silently inwards. A thin, seamed face confronted Elric.

"Is it the king?" whispered the man, peering out into the night. He was a tall, extremely thin individual with long, gnarled limbs which shifted awkwardly as he moved nearer, straining his beady eyes to get a glimpse of Elric.

"It's Prince Elric," the albino said. "But you forget, Tanglebones, my friend, that a new king sits on the Ruby Throne."

Doctor Tanglebones shook his head and his sparse hair fell over his face. With a jerking movement he brushed it back and stood aside for Elric to enter. "The Dragon Isle has but one king—and his name is Elric, whatever usurper would have it otherwise."

Elric ignored this statement, but he smiled thinly and waited for the man to push the bolt back into place.

"She still sleeps, sire," Tanglebones murmured as he climbed unlit stairs, Elric behind him.

"I guessed that," Elric said. "I do not underestimate my good cousin's powers of sorcery."

Upwards, now, in silence, the two men climbed until at last they reached a corridor which was aflare with dancing torchlight. The marble walls reflected the flames and showed Elric, crouching with Tanglebones behind a pillar, that the room in which he was interested was guarded by a massive archer—a eunuch by the look of him—who was alert and wakeful. The man was hairless and fat, his blue-black gleaming armor tight on his flesh, but his fingers were curled round the string of his short, bone bow and there was a slim arrow resting on the string. Elric guessed that this man was one of the crack eunuch archers, a member of the Silent Guard, Imrryr's finest company of warriors.

Tanglebones, who had taught the young Elric the arts of fencing and archery, had known of the guard's presence and had prepared for it. Earlier he had placed a bow behind the pillar. Silently he picked it up and, bending it against his knee, strung it. He fitted an arrow to the string, aimed it at the right eye of the guard and let fly—just as the eunuch turned to face him. The shaft missed. It clattered against the man's helmet and fell harmlessly to the reed-strewn stones of the floor.

So Elric acted swiftly, leaping forward, his runesword drawn and its alien power surging through him. It howled in a searing arc of black steel and cut through the bone bow which the eunuch had hoped would deflect it. The guard was panting and his thick lips were wet as he drew breath to yell. As he opened his mouth, Elric saw what he had expected, the man was tongueless and was a mute. His own shortsword came out and he just managed to parry Elric's next thrust. Sparks flew from the iron and Stormbringer bit into the eunuch's finely edged blade; he staggered and fell back before the nigromantic sword which appeared to be endowed with a life of its own. The clatter of metal echoed loudly up and down the short corridor and Elric cursed the fate which had made the man turn at the crucial moment. Grimly, silently, he broke down the eunuch's clumsy guard.

The eunuch saw only a dim glimpse of his opponent behind the black, whirling blade which appeared to be so light and which was twice the length of his own stabbing sword. He wondered, frenziedly, who his attacker could be and he thought he recognized the face. Then a scarlet eruption obscured his vision, he felt searing agony at his face and then, philosophically, for eunuchs are necessarily given to a certain fatalism, he realized that he was to die.

Elric stood over the eunuch's bloated body and tugged his sword from the corpse's skull, wiping the mixture of blood and brains on his late opponent's cloak. Tanglebones had wisely vanished. Elric could hear the clatter of sandaled feet rushing up the stairs. He pushed the door open and entered the room which was lit by two small candles placed at either end of a wide, richly tapestried bed. He went to the bed and looked down at the raven-haired girl who lay there.

Elric's mouth twitched and bright tears leapt into his strange red eyes. He was trembling as he turned back to the door, sheathed his sword and pulled the bolts into place. He returned to the bedside and knelt down beside the sleeping girl. Her features were as delicate and of a similar mould as Elric's own, but she had an added, exquisite beauty. She was breathing shallowly, in a sleep induced not by natural weariness but by her own brother's evil sorcery.

Elric reached out and tenderly took one fine-fingered hand in his. He put it to his lips and kissed it.

"Cymoril," he murmured, and an agony of longing throbbed in that name. "Cymoril—wake up."

The girl did not stir, her breathing remained shallow and her eyes remained shut. Elric's white features twisted and his red eyes blazed as he shook in terrible and passionate rage. He gripped the hand, so limp and nerveless, like the hand of a corpse; gripped it until he had to stop himself for fear that he would crush the delicate fingers.

A shouting soldier began to beat at the door.

Elric replaced the hand on the girl's breast and stood up. He glanced uncomprehendingly at the door.

A sharper, colder voice interrupted the soldier's yelling.

"What is happening? Who disturbs my poor sleeping sister?"

"Yyrkoon, the black hellspawn," said Elric to himself.

Confused babblings from the soldier and Yyrkoon's voice raised as he shouted through the door. "Whoever is in there—you will be destroyed a thousand times when you are caught. You cannot escape. If my good sister is harmed in any way—then you will never die, I promise you that. But you will pray to your gods that you could!"

"Yyrkoon, you paltry bombast—you cannot threaten one who is your equal in the dark arts. It is I, Elric—your rightful master. Return to your rabbit hole before I call down every power upon, above, and under the earth to blast you!"

Yyrkoon laughed hesitantly. "So you have returned again to try to waken my sister. Any such attempt will not only slay her— it will send her soul into the deepest hell—where you may join it, willingly!"

"You offspring of a festering worm, Yyrkoon. You'll have cause to repent this vile spell before your time is run! And by Arnara's six breasts—you it will be who samples the thousand deaths before long."

"Enough of this." Yyrkoon raised his voice. "Soldiers—I command you to break this door down—and take that traitor alive. Elric—there are two things you will never again have—my sister's love and the Ruby Throne. Make what you can of the little time available to you, for soon you will be groveling to me and praying for release from your soul's agony!"

Elric ignored Yyrkoon's threats and looked at the narrow window to the room. It was just large enough for a man's body to pass through. He bent down and kissed Cymoril upon the lips, then he went to the door and silently withdrew the bolts.

There came a crash as a soldier flung his weight against the door. It swung open, pitching the man forward to stumble and fall on his face. Elric drew his sword, lifted it high and chopped at the warrior's neck. The head sprang from its shoulders and Elric yelled loudly in a deep, rolling voice.

"Arioch! Arioch! I give you blood and souls—only aid me now! This man I give you, mighty Duke of Hell—aid your servant, Elric of Melniboné!"

Three soldiers entered the room in a bunch. Elric struck at one and sheared off half his face. The man screamed horribly.

"Arioch, Lord of the Darks—I give you blood and souls. Aid me, great one!"

In the far corner of the gloomy room, a blacker mist began, slowly, to form. But the soldiers pressed closer and Elric was hard put to hold them back.

He was screaming the name of Arioch, Lord of the Higher Hell, incessantly, almost unconsciously as he was pressed back further by the weight of the warriors' numbers. Behind them, Yyrkoon mouthed in rage and frustration, urging his men, still, to take Elric alive. This gave Elric some small advantage. The runesword was glowing with a strange black light and its shrill howling grated in the ears of those who heard it. Two more corpses now littered the carpeted floor of the chamber, their blood soaking into the fine fabric.

"Blood and souls for my lord Arioch!"

The dark mist heaved and began to take shape, Elric spared a look towards the corner and shuddered despite his inurement to hell-born horror. The warriors now had their backs to the thing in the corner and Elric was by the window. The amorphous mass, that was a less than pleasant manifestation of Elric's fickle patron god, heaved again and Elric made out its intolerably alien shape. Bile flooded into his mouth and, as he drove the soldiers towards the thing which was sinuously flooding forward, he fought against madness.

Suddenly, the soldiers seemed to sense that there was something behind them. They turned, four of them, and each screamed insanely as the black horror made one final rush to engulf them. Arioch crouched over them, sucking out their souls. Then, slowly, their bones began to give and snap and still shrieking bestially the men flopped like obnoxious invertebrates upon the floor: their spines broken, they still lived. Elric turned away, thankful for once that Cymoril slept, and leapt to the window ledge. He looked down and realized with despair that he was not going to escape by that route after all. Several hundred feet lay between him and the ground. He rushed to the door where Yyrkoon, his eyes wide with fear, was trying to drive Arioch back. Arioch was already fading.

Elric pushed past his cousin, spared a final glance at Cymoril, then ran the way he had come, his feet slipping on blood. Tanglebones met him at the head of the dark stairway.

"What has happened, King Elric—what's in there?"

Elric seized Tanglebones by his lean shoulder and made him descend the stairs. "No time," he panted, "but we must hurry while Yyrkoon is still engaged with his current problem. In five days' time Imrryr will experience a new phase in her history—perhaps the last. I want you to make sure that Cymoril is safe. Is that clear?"

"Aye, Lord, but…"

They reached the door and Tanglebones shot the bolts and opened it.

"There is no time for me to say anything else. I must escape while I can. I will return in five days—with companions. You will realize what I mean when that time comes. Take Cymoril to the Tower of D'a'rputna—and await me there."

Then Elric was gone, soft-footed, running into the night with the shrieks of the dying still ringing through the blackness after him.

III

Elric stood unsmiling in the prow of Count Smiorgan's flagship. Since his return to the fjord and the fleet's subsequent sailing for open sea, he had spoken only orders, and those in the terset of terms. The sea-lords muttered that a great hate lay in him, that it festered his soul and made him a dangerous man to have as comrade or enemy; and even Count Smiorgan avoided the moody albino.

The reaver prows struck eastward and the sea was black with light ships dancing on the bright water in all directions; they looked like the shadow of some enormous seabird flung on the water. Over half a thousand fighting ships stained the ocean—all of them of similar form, long and slim and built for speed rather than battle, since they were for coast-raiding and trading. Sails were caught by the pale sun; bright colors of fresh canvas—orange, blue, black, purple, red, yellow, light green or white. And every ship had sixteen or more rowers—each rower a fighting man. The crews of the ships were also the warriors who would attack Imrryr—there was no wastage of good manpower since the sea-nations were underpopulated, losing hundreds of men each year in their regular raids.

In the center of the great fleet, certain larger vessels sailed. These carried massive catapults on their decks and were to be used for storming the sea wall of Imrryr. Count Smiorgan and the other lords looked at their ships with pride, but Elric only stared ahead of him, never sleeping, rarely moving, his white face lashed by salt spray and wind, his white hand tight upon his sword hilt.

The reaver ships ploughed steadily eastwards—forging towards the Dragon Isle and fantastic wealth—or hellish horror. Relentlessly, doom-driven, they beat onwards, their oars splashing in unison, their sails bellying taut with a good wind.

Onwards they sailed, towards Imrryr the Beautiful, to rape and plunder the world's oldest city.

Two days after the fleet had set sail, the coastline of the Dragon Isle was sighted and the rattle of arms replaced the sound of oars as the mighty fleet hove to and prepared to accomplish what sane men thought impossible.

Orders were bellowed from ship to ship and the fleet began to mass into battle formation, then the oars creaked in their grooves and ponderously, with sails now furled, the fleet moved forward again.

It was a clear day, cold and fresh, and there was a tense excitement about all the men, from sea-lord to galley-hand, as they considered the immediate future and what it might bring. Serpent prows bent towards the great stone wall which blocked off the first entrance to the harbor. It was nearly a hundred feet high and towers were built upon it—more functional than the lacelike spires of the city which shimmered in the distance, behind them. The ships of Imrryr were the only vessels allowed to pass through the great gate in the center of the wall, and the route through the maze—the exact entrance, even—was a well-kept secret from outsiders.

On the sea wall, which now loomed tall above the fleet, amazed guards scrambled frantically to their posts. To them, threat of attack was well-nigh unthinkable, yet here it was—a great fleet, the greatest they had ever seen—come against Imrryr the Beautiful! They took to their posts, their yellow cloaks and kilts rustling, their bronze armor rattling, but they moved with bewildered reluctance as if refusing to accept what they saw. And they went to their posts with desperate fatalism, knowing that even if the ships never entered the maze itself, they would not be alive to witness the reavers' failure.

Dyvim Tarkan, Commander of the Wall, was a sensitive man who loved life and its pleasures. He was high-browed and handsome, with a thin wisp of beard and a tiny moustache. He looked well in the bronze armor and high-plumed helmet; he did not want to die. He issued terse orders to his men and, with well-ordered precision, they obeyed him. He listened with concern to the distant shouts from the ships and he wondered what the first move of the reavers would be. He did not wait long for his answer.

A catapult on one of the leading vessels twanged throatily and its throwing arm rushed up, releasing a great rock which sailed, with every appearance of leisurely grace, towards the wall. It fell short and splashed into the sea which frothed against the stones of the wall.

Swallowing hard and trying to control the shake in his voice, Dyvim Tarkan ordered his own catapult to discharge. With a thudding crash the release rope was cut and a retaliatory iron ball went hurtling towards the enemy fleet. So tight-packed were the ships that the ball could not miss—it struck full on the deck of the flagship of Dharmit of Jharkor and crushed the timbers in. Within seconds, accompanied by the cries of maimed and drowning men, the ship had sunk and Dharmit with it. Some of the crew were taken aboard other vessels but the wounded were left to drown.

Another catapult sounded and this time a tower full of archers was squarely hit. Masonry erupted outwards and those who still lived fell sickeningly to die in the foam-tipped sea lashing the wall. This time, angered by the deaths of their comrades, Imrryrian archers sent back a stream of slim arrows into the enemy's midst. Reavers howled as red-fletched shafts buried themselves thirstily in flesh. But reavers returned the arrows liberally and soon only a handful of men were left on the wall as further catapult rocks smashed into towers and men, destroying their only war machine and part of the wall besides.

Dyvim Tarkan still lived, though red blood stained his yellow tunic and an arrow shaft protruded from his left shoulder. He still lived when the first ram-ship moved intractably towards the great wooden gate and smashed against it, weakening it. A second ship sailed in beside it and, between them, they stove in the gate and glided through the entrance. Perhaps it was outraged horror that tradition had been broken which caused poor Dyvim Tarkan to lose his footing at the edge of the wall and fall screaming down to break his neck on the deck of Count Smiorgan's flagship as it sailed triumphantly through the gate.

Now the ram-ships made way for Count Smiorgan's craft, for Elric had to lead the way through the maze. Ahead of them loomed five tall entrances, black gaping maws all alike in shape and size. Elric pointed to the second from the left and with short strokes the oarsmen began to paddle the ship into the dark mouth of the entrance. For some minutes, they sailed in darkness.

"Flares!" shouted Elric. "Light the flares!"

Torches had already been prepared and these were now lighted. The men saw that they were in a vast tunnel hewn out of natural rock which twisted in all directions.

"Keep close," Elric ordered and his voice was magnified a score of times in the echoing cavern. Torchlight blazed and Elric's face was a mask of shadow and frisking light as the torches threw up long tongues of flame to the bleak roof. Behind him, men could be heard muttering in awe and, as more craft entered the maze and lit their own torches, Elric could see some torches waver as their bearers trembled in superstitious fear. Elric felt some discomfort as he glanced through the flickering shadows and his eyes, caught by torchflare, gleamed fever-bright.

With dreadful monotony, the oars splashed onwards as the tunnel widened and several more cave mouths came into sight. "The middle entrance," Elric ordered. The steersman in the stern nodded and guided the ship towards the entrance Elric had indicated. Apart from the muted murmur of some men and the splash of oars, there was a grim and ominous silence in the towering cavern.

Elric stared down at the cold, dark water and shuddered.

Eventually they moved once again into bright sunlight and the men looked upwards, marveling at the height of the great walls above them. Upon those walls squatted more yellow-clad, bronze-armored archers and as Count Smiorgan's vessel led the way out of the black caverns, the torches still burning in the cool winter air, arrows began to hurtle down into the narrow canyon, biting into throats and limbs.

"Faster!" howled Elric. "Row faster—speed is our only weapon now."

With frantic energy the oarsmen bent to their sweeps and the ships began to pick up speed even though Imrryrian arrows took heavy toll of the reaver crewmen. Now the high-walled channel ran straight and Elric saw the quays of Imrryr ahead of him.

"Faster! Faster! Our prize is in sight!"

Then, suddenly, the ship broke past the walls and was in the calm waters of the harbor, facing the warriors drawn up on the quay. The ship halted, waiting for reinforcements to plunge out of the channel and join them. When twenty ships were through, Elric gave the command to attack the quay and now Stormbringer howled from its scabbard. The flagship's port side thudded against the quay as arrows rained down upon it. Shafts whistled all around Elric but, miraculously, he was unscathed as he led a bunch of yelling reavers onto land. Imrryrian axemen bunched forward and confronted the reavers, but it was plain that they had little spirit for the fight—they were too disconcerted by the course which events had taken.

Elric's black blade struck with frenzied force at the throat of the leading axeman and sheared off his head. Howling demoniacally now that it had again tasted blood, the sword began to writhe in Elric's grasp, seeking fresh flesh in which to bite. There was a hard, grim smile on the albino's colorless lips and his eyes were narrowed as he struck without discrimination at the warriors.

He planned to leave the fighting to those he had led to Imrryr, for he had other things to do—and quickly. Behind the yellow-garbed soldiers, the tall towers of Imrryr rose, beautiful in their soft and scintillating colors of coral pink and powdery blue, of gold and pale yellow, white and subtle green. One such tower was Elric's objective—the Tower of D'a'rputna where he had ordered Tanglebones to take Cymoril, knowing that in the confusion this would be possible.

Elric hacked a blood-drenched path through those who attempted to halt him and men fell back, screaming horribly as the runesword drank their souls.

Now Elric was past them, leaving them to the bright blades of the reavers who poured onto the quayside, and was running up through the twisting streets, his sword slaying anyone who attempted to stop him. Like a white-faced ghoul he was, his clothing tattered and bloody, his armor chipped and scratched, but he ran speedily over the cobblestones of the twisting streets and came at last to the slender tower of hazy blue and soft gold—the Tower of D'a'rputna.

Its door was open, showing that someone was inside, and Elric rushed through it and entered the large ground-floor chamber. No-one greeted him.

"Tanglebones!" he yelled, his voice roaring loudly even in his own ears. "Tanglebones—are you here?" He leapt up the stairs in great bounds, calling his servant's name. On the third floor he stopped suddenly, hearing a low groan from one of the rooms. "Tanglebones—is that you?" Elric strode towards the room, hearing a strangled gasping. He pushed open the door and his stomach seemed to twist within him as he saw the old man lying upon the bare floor of the chamber, striving vainly to stop the flow of blood which gouted from a great wound in his side.

"What's happened man—where's Cymoril?"

Tanglebones's old face twisted in pain and grief. "She—I—I brought her here, master, as you ordered. But..." he coughed and blood dribbled down his wizened chin, "but—Prince Yyrkoon—he—he apprehended me—must have followed us here. He—struck me down and took Cymoril back with him—said she'd be—safe in the Tower of B'aal'nezbett. Master—I'm sorry..."

"So you should be," Elric retorted savagely. Then his tone softened. "Do not worry, old friend—I'll avenge you myself. I can still reach Cymoril now I know where Yyrkoon has taken her. Thank you for trying, Tanglebones—may your long journey down the last river be uneventful."

He turned abruptly on his heel and left the chamber, running down the stairs and out into the street again.

The Tower of B'aal'nezbett was the highest tower in the Royal Palace. Elric knew it well, for it was there that his ancestors had studied their dark sorceries and conducted frightful experiments. He shuddered as he thought what Yyrkoon might be doing to his own sister.

The streets of the city seemed hushed and strangely deserted, but Elric had no time to ponder why this should be so. Instead he dashed towards the palace, found the main gate unguarded and the main entrance to the building deserted. This too was unique, but it constituted luck for Elric as he made his way upwards, climbing familiar ways towards the topmost tower.

Finally, he reached a door of shimmering black crystal which had no bolt or handle to it. Frenziedly, Elric struck at the crystal with his sorcerous blade but the crystal appeared only to flow and re-form. His blows had no effect.

Elric racked his mind, seeking to remember the single alien word which would make the door open. He dared not put himself in the trance which would have, in time, brought the word to his lips, instead he had to dredge his subconscious and bring the word forth. It was dangerous but there was little else he could do. His whole frame trembled as his face twisted and his brain began to shake. The word was coming as his vocal cords jerked in his throat and his chest heaved.

He ripped the word from his throat and his whole mind and body ached with the strain. Then he cried:

"I command thee—open!"

He knew that once the door opened, his cousin would be aware of his presence, but he had to risk it. The crystal expanded, pulsating and seething, and then began to flow out. It flowed into nothingness, into something beyond the physical universe, beyond time. Elric breathed thankfully and passed into the Tower of B'aal'nezbett. But now an eerie fire, chilling and mind-shattering, was licking around Elric as he struggled up the steps towards the central chamber. There was a strange music surrounding him, uncanny music which throbbed and sobbed and pounded in his head.

Above him he saw a leering Yyrkoon, a black runesword also in his hand, the mate of the one in Elric's own grasp.

"Hellspawn!" Elric said thickly, weakly, "I see you have recovered Mournblade—well, test its powers against its brother if you dare. I have come to destroy you, cousin."

Stormbringer was giving forth a peculiar moaning sound which sighed over the shrieking, unearthly music accompanying the licking, chilling fire. The runesword writhed in Elric's fist and he had difficulty in controlling it. Summoning all his strength he plunged up the last few steps and aimed a wild blow at Yyrkoon. Beyond the eerie fire bubbled yellow-green lava, on all sides, above and beneath. The two men were surrounded only by the misty fire and the lava which lurked beyond it—they were outside the Earth and facing one another for a final battle. The lava seethed and began to ooze inwards, dispersing the fire.

The two blades met and a terrible shrieking roar went up. Elric felt his whole arm go numb and it tingled sickeningly. Elric felt like a puppet. He was no longer his own master—the blade was deciding his actions for him. The blade, with Elric behind it, roared past its brother sword and cut a deep wound in Yyrkoon's left arm. He howled and his eyes widened in agony. Mournblade struck back at Stormbringer, catching Elric in the very place he had wounded his cousin. He sobbed in pain, but continued to move upwards, now wounding Yyrkoon in the right side with a blow strong enough to have killed any other man. Yyrkoon laughed then—laughed like a gibbering demon from the foulest depths of hell. His sanity had broken at last and Elric now had the advantage. But the great sorcery which his cousin had conjured was still in evidence and Elric felt as if a giant had grasped him, was crushing him as he pressed his advantage, Yyrkoon's blood spouting from the wound and covering Elric, also. The lava was slowly withdrawing and now Elric saw the entrance to the central chamber. Behind his cousin another form moved. Elric gasped. Cymoril had awakened and, with horror on her face, was shrieking at him.

The sword still swung in a black arc, cutting down Yyrkoon's brother blade and breaking the usurper's guard.

"Elric!" cried Cymoril desperately. "Save me—save me now, else we are doomed for eternity."

Elric was puzzled by the girl's words. He could not understand the sense of them. Savagely he drove Yyrkoon upwards towards the chamber.

"Elric—put Stormbringer away. Sheathe your sword or we shall part again."

But even if he could have controlled the whistling blade, Elric would not have sheathed it. Hate dominated his being and he would sheathe it in his cousin's evil heart before he put it aside.

Cymoril was weeping, now, pleading with him. But Elric could do nothing. The drooling, idiot thing which had been Yyrkoon of Imrryr turned at its sister's cries and stared leeringly at her. It cackled and reached out one shaking hand to seize the girl by her shoulder. She struggled to escape, but Yyrkoon still had his evil strength. Taking advantage of his opponent's distraction Elric cut deep through his body, almost severing the trunk from the waist.

And yet, incredibly, Yyrkoon remained alive, drawing his vitality from the blade which still clashed against Elric's own runecarved sword. With a final push he flung Cymoril forward and she died screaming on the point of Stormbringer.

Then Yyrkoon laughed one final cackling shriek and his black soul went howling down to hell.

The tower resumed its former proportions, all fire and lava gone. Elric was dazed—unable to marshal his thoughts. He looked down at the dead bodies of the brother and the sister. He saw them, at first, only as corpses—a man's and a woman's.

Dark truth dawned on his clearing brain and he moaned in grief, like an animal. He had slain the girl he loved. The runesword fell from his grasp, stained by Cymoril's lifeblood, and clattered unheeded down the stairs. Sobbing now, Elric dropped beside the dead girl and lifted her in his arms.

"Cymoril," he moaned, his whole body throbbing. "Cymoril—I have slain you."

IV

Elric looks back at the roaring, crumbling, tumbling, flame-spewing ruins of Imrryr and drove his sweating oarsmen faster. The ship, sail still unfurled, bucked as a contrary current of wind caught it and Elric was forced to cling to the ship's side lest he be tossed overboard. He looked back at Imrryr and felt a tightness in his throat as he realized that he was truly rootless, now; a renegade and a womanslayer, though involuntarily the latter. He had lost the only woman he had loved in his blind lust for revenge. Now it was finished—everything was finished. He could envisage no future, for his future had been bound up with his past and now, effectively, that past was flaming in ruins behind him. Dry sobs eddied in his chest and he gripped the ship's rail yet more firmly.

His mind reluctantly brooded on Cymoril. He had laid her corpse upon a couch and had set fire to the tower. Then he had gone back to find the reavers successful, straggling back to their ships loaded with loot and girl-slaves, jubilantly firing the tall and beautiful buildings as they went.

He had caused to be destroyed the last tangible sign that the grandiose, magnificent Bright Empire had ever existed. He felt that most of himself was gone with it.

Elric looked back at Imrryr and suddenly a greater sadness overwhelmed him as a tower, as delicate and as beautiful as fine lace, cracked and toppled with flames leaping about it.

He had shattered the last great monument to the earlier race—his own race. Men might have learned again, one day, to build strong, slender towers like those of Imrryr, but now the knowledge was dying with the thundering chaos of the fall of the Dreaming City and the fast-diminishing race of Melniboné.

But what of the Dragon Masters? Neither they nor their golden ships had met the attacking reavers—only their foot soldiers had been there to defend the city. Had they hidden their ships in some secret waterway and fled inland when the reavers overran the city? They had put up too short a fight to be truly beaten. It had been far too easy. Now that the ships were retreating, were they planning some sudden retaliation? Elric felt that they might have such a plan—perhaps a plan concerning dragons. He shuddered. He had told the others nothing of the beasts which Melnibonéans had controlled for centuries. Even now, someone might be unlocking the gates of the underground Dragon Caves. He turned his mind away from the unnerving prospect.

As the fleet headed towards open sea, Elric's eyes were still looking sadly towards Imrryr as he paid silent homage to the city of his forefathers and the dead Cymoril. He felt hot bitterness sweep over him again as the memory of her death upon his own sword point came sharply to him. He recalled her warning, when he had left her to go adventuring in the Young Kingdoms, that by putting Yyrkoon on the Ruby Throne as regent, by relinquishing his power for a year, he doomed them both. He cursed himself. Then a muttering, like a roll of distant thunder, spread through the fleet and he wheeled sharply, intent on discovering the cause of the consternation.

Thirty golden-sailed Melnibonéan battle-barges had appeared on both sides of the harbor, issuing from two mouths of the maze. Elric realized that they must have hidden in the other channels, waiting to attack the fleet when they returned, satiated and depleted. Great war-galleys they were, the last ships of Melniboné and the secret of their building was unknown. They had a sense of age and slumbering might about them as they rowed swiftly, each with four or five banks of great sweeping oars, to encircle the raven ships.

Elric's fleet seemed to shrink before his eyes as though it were a bobbing collection of wood-shavings against the towering splendor of the shimmering battle-barges. They were well-equipped and fresh for a fight, whereas the weary reavers were intensely battle-tired. There was only one way to save a small part of the fleet, Elric knew. He would have to conjure a witch-wind for sailpower. Most of the flagships were around him and he now occupied that of Yaris, for the youth had got himself wildly drunk and had died by the knife of a Melnibonéan slave wench. Next to Elric's ship was Count Smiorgan's and the stocky sea-lord was frowning, knowing full well that he and his ships, for all their superior numbers, would not stand up to a sea-fight.

But the conjuring of winds great enough to move many vessels was a dangerous thing, for it released colossal power and the elementals who controlled the winds were apt to turn upon the sorcerer himself if he was not more than careful. But it was the only chance, otherwise the rams which sent ripples from the golden prows would smash the reaver ships to driftwood.

Steeling himself, Elric began to speak the ancient and terrible, many-voweled names of the beings who existed in the air. Again, he could not risk the trance-state, for he had to watch for signs of the elementals turning upon him. He called to them in a speech that was sometimes high like the cry of a gannet, sometimes rolling like the roar of shorebound surf, and the dim shapes of the Powers of the Wind began to flit before his blurred gaze. His heart throbbed horribly in his ribs and his legs felt weak. He summoned all his strength and conjured a wind which shrieked wildly and chaotically about him, rocking even the huge Melnibonéan ships back and forth. Then he directed the wind and sent it into the sails of some forty of the reaver ships. Many he could not save for they lay outside even his wide range.

But forty of the craft escaped the smashing rams and, amidst the sound of howling wind and sundered timbers, leapt on the waves, their masts creaking as the wind cracked into their sails. Oars were torn from the hands of the rowers, leaving a wake of broken wood on the white salt trail which boiled behind each of the reaver ships.

Quite suddenly, they were beyond the slowly closing circle of Melnibonéan ships and careering madly across the open sea, while all the crews sensed a difference in the air and caught glimpses of strange, soft-shaped forms around them. There was a discomforting sense of evil about the beings which aided them, an awesome alienness.

Smiorgan waved to Elric and grinned thankfully.

"We're safe, thanks to you, Elric!" he yelled across the water. "I knew you'd bring us luck!"

Elric ignored him.

Now the Dragon Lords, vengeance-bent, gave chase. Almost as fast as the magic-aided reaver fleet were the golden barges of Imrryr, and some reaver galleys, whose masts cracked and split beneath the force of the wind driving them, were caught.

Elric saw mighty grappling hooks of dully gleaming metal swing out from the decks of the Imrryrian galleys and thud with a moan of wrenched timber into those of the fleet which lay broken and powerless behind him. Fire leapt from catapults upon the Dragon Lords' ships and careered towards many a fleeing reaver craft. Searing, foul-stinking flame hissed like lava across the decks and ate into planks like vitriol into paper. Men shrieked, beating vainly at brightly burning clothes, some leaping into water which would not extinguish the fire. Some sank beneath the sea and it was possible to trace their descent as, flaming even below the surface, men and ships fluttered to the bottom like blazing, tired moths.

Reaver decks, untouched by fire, ran red with reaver blood as the enraged Imrryrian warriors swung down the grappling ropes and dropped among the raiders, wielding great swords and battle-axes and wreaking terrible havoc amongst the sea-ravens. Imrryrian arrows and Imrryrian javelins swooped from the towering decks of Imrryrian galleys and tore into the panicky men on the smaller ships.

All this Elric saw as he and his vessels began slowly to overhaul the leading Imrryrian ship, flag-galley of Admiral Magum Colim, commander of the Melnibonéan fleet.

Now Elric spared a word for Count Smiorgan. "We've outrun them!" he shouted above the howling wind to the next ship where Smiorgan stood staring wide-eyed at the sky. "But keep your ships heading westwards or we're finished!"

Smiorgan did not reply. He still looked skyward and there was horror in his eyes; in the eyes of a man who, before this, had never known the quivering bite of fear. Uneasily, Elric let his own eyes follow the gaze of Smiorgan. Then he saw them.

They were dragons, without doubt! The great reptiles were some miles away, but Elric knew the stamp of the huge flying beasts. The average wingspan of these near-extinct monsters was some thirty feet across. Their snakelike bodies, beginning in a narrow-snouted head and terminating in a dreadful whip of a tail, were forty feet long and although they did not breathe the legendary fire and smoke, Elric knew that their venom was combustible and could set fire to wood or fabric on contact.

Imrryrian warriors rode the dragon backs. Armed with long, spearlike goads, they blew strangely shaped horns which sang out curious notes over the turbulent sea and calm blue sky. Nearing the golden fleet, now half a league away, the leading dragon sailed down and circled towards the huge golden flag-galley, its wings making a sound like the crack of lightning as they beat through the air.

The grey-green, scaled monster hovered over the golden ship as it heaved in the white-foamed turbulent sea. Framed against the cloudless sky, the dragon was in sharp perspective and it was possible for Elric to get a clear view of it. The goad which the Dragon Master waved to Admiral Magum Colim was a long, slim spear upon which the strange pennant of black and yellow zigzag lines was, even at this distance, noticeable. Elric recognized the insignia on the pennant.

Dyvim Tvar, friend of Elric's youth, Lord of the Dragon Caves, was leading his charges to claim vengeance for Imrryr the Beautiful.

Elric howled across the water to Smiorgan. "These are your main danger, now. Do what you can to stave them off!" There was a rattle of iron as the men prepared, near-hopelessly, to repel the new menace. Witch-wind would give little advantage over the fast-flying dragons. Now Dyvim Tvar had evidently conferred with Magum Colim and his goad lashed out at the dragon throat. The huge reptile jerked upwards and began to gain altitude. Eleven other dragons were behind it, joining it now.

With seeming slowness, the dragons began to beat relentlessly towards the reaver fleet as the crewmen prayed to their own gods for a miracle.

THE DREAMING CITY

They were doomed. There was no escaping the fact. Every reaver ship was doomed and the raid had been fruitless.

Elric could see the despair in the faces of the men as the masts of the reaver ships continued to bend under the strain of the shrieking witch-wind. They could do nothing, now, but die…

Elric fought to rid his mind of the swirling uncertainty which filled it. He drew his sword and felt the pulsating, evil power which lurked in runecarved Stormbringer. But he hated that power now— for it had caused him to kill the only human he had cherished. He realized how much of his strength he owed to the black-iron sword of his fathers and how weak he might be without it. He was an albino and that meant that he lacked the vitality of a normal human being. Savagely, futilely, as the mist in his mind was replaced by red fear, he cursed the pretensions of revenge he had held, cursed the day when he had agreed to lead the raid on Imrryr and most of all he bitterly vilified dead Yyrkoon and his twisted envy which had been the cause of the whole doom-ridden course of events.

But it was too late now for curses of any kind. The loud slapping of beating dragon wings filled the air and the monsters loomed over the fleeing reaver craft. He had to make some kind of decision— though he had no love for life, he refused to die by the hands of his own people. When he died, he promised himself, it would be by his hand. He made his decision, hating himself.

He called off the witch-wind as the dragon venom seared down and struck the last ship in line.

He put all his powers into sending a stronger wind into the sails of his own boat while his bewildered comrades in the suddenly becalmed ships called over the water, enquiring desperately the reason for his act. Elric's ship was moving fast, now, and might just escape the dragons. He hoped so.

He deserted the man who had trusted him, Count Smiorgan, and watched as venom poured from the sky and engulfed him in blazing green-and-scarlet flame. Elric fled, keeping his mind from thoughts of the future, and sobbed aloud, that proud prince of ruins;

and he cursed the malevolent gods for the black day when idly, for their amusement, they had spawned sentient creatures like himself.

Behind him, the last reaver ships flared into sudden appalling brightness and, although half-thankful that they had escaped the fate of their comrades, the crew looked at Elric accusingly. He sobbed on, not heeding them, great griefs racking his soul.

A night later, off the coast of an island called Pan Tang, when the ship was safe from the dreadful recriminations of the Dragon Masters and their beasts, Elric stood brooding in the stern while the men eyed him with fear and hatred, muttering of betrayal and heartless cowardice. They appeared to have forgotten their own fear and subsequent safety.

Elric brooded and he held the black runesword in his two hands. Stormbringer was more than an ordinary battle-blade, this he had known for years, but now he realized that it was possessed of more sentience than he had imagined. Yet he was horribly dependent upon it; he realized this with soul-rending certainty. But he feared and resented the sword's power—hated it bitterly for the chaos it had wrought in his brain and spirit. In an agony of uncertainty he held the blade in his hands and forced himself to weigh the factors involved. Without the sinister sword, he would lose pride—perhaps even life—but he might know the soothing tranquility of pure rest; with it he would have power and strength—but the sword would guide him into a doom-racked future. He would savor power—but never peace.

He drew a great, sobbing breath and, blind misgiving influencing him, threw the sword into the moon-drenched sea.

Incredibly, it did not sink. It did not even float on the water. It fell point forwards into the sea and stuck there, quivering as if it were embedded in timber. It remained throbbing in the water, six inches of its blade immersed, and began to give off a weird devil-scream—a howl of horrible malevolence.

With a choking curse Elric stretched out his slim, white, gleaming hand, trying to recover the sentient hellblade. He stretched further, leaning far out over the rail. He could not grasp it—it lay some feet from him, still. Gasping, a sickening sense of defeat overwhelming him, he dropped over the side and plunged into the bone-chilling water, striking out with strained, grotesque strokes, towards the hovering sword. He was beaten—the sword had won.

He reached it and put his fingers around the hilt. At once it settled in his hand and Elric felt strength seep slowly back into his aching body. Then he realized that he and the sword were interdependent, for though he needed the blade, Stormbringer, parasitic, required a user—without a man to wield it, the blade was also powerless.

"We must be bound to one another then," Elric murmured despairingly. "Bound by hell-forged chains and fate-haunted circumstance. Well, then—let it be thus so—and men will have cause to tremble and flee when they hear the names of Elric of Melniboné and Stormbringer, his sword. We are two of a kind—produced by an age which has deserted us. Let us give this age cause to hate us!"

Strong again, Elric sheathed Stormbringer and the sword settled against his side; then, with powerful strokes, he began to swim towards the island while the men he left on the ship breathed with relief and speculated whether he would live or perish in the bleak waters of that strange and nameless sea...

The Doom that Came to Sarnath

H. P. Lovecraft (1890-1937)

There is in the land of Mnar a vast still lake that is fed by no stream and out of which no stream flows. Ten thousand years ago there stood by its shore the mighty city of Sarnath, but Sarnath stands there no more.

It is told that in the immemorial years when the world was young, before ever the men of Sarnath came to the land of Mnar, another city stood beside the lake; the grey stone city of Ib, which was old as the lake itself, and peopled with beings not pleasing to behold. Very odd and ugly were these beings, as indeed are most beings of a world yet inchoate and rudely fashioned. It is written on the brick cylinders of Kadatheron that the beings of Ib were in hue as green as the lake and the mists that rise above it; that they had bulging eyes, pouting, flabby lips, and curious ears, and were without voice. It is also written that they descended one night from the moon in a mist; they and the vast still lake and grey stone city Ib. However this may be, it is certain that they worshipped a sea-green stone idol chiseled in the likeness of Bokrug, the great water-lizard; before which they danced horribly when the moon was gibbous. And it is written in the papyrus of Ilarnek, that they one day discovered fire, and thereafter kindled flames on many ceremonial occasions. But not much is written of these beings, because they lived in very ancient times, and man is young, and knows little of the very ancient living things.

THE DOOM THAT CAME TO SARNATH

After many aeons men came to the land of Mnar; dark shepherd folk with their fleecy flocks, who built Thraa, Ilarnek, and Kadatheron on the winding river Ai. And certain tribes, more hardy than the rest, pushed on to the border of the lake and built Sarnath at a spot where precious metals were found in the earth.

Not far from the grey city of Ib did the wandering tribes lay the first stones of Sarnath, and at the beings of Ib they marveled greatly. But with their marveling was mixed hate, for they thought it not meet that beings of such aspect should walk about the world of men at dusk. Nor did they like the strange sculptures upon the grey monoliths of Ib, for those sculptures were terrible with great antiquity. Why the beings and the sculptures lingered so late in the world, even until the coming of men, none can tell; unless it was because the land of Mnar is very still, and remote from most other lands both of waking and of dream.

As the men of Sarnath beheld more of the beings of Ib their hate grew, and it was not less because they found the beings weak, and soft as jelly to the touch of stones and spears and arrows. So one day the young warriors, the slingers and the spearmen and the bowmen, marched against Ib and slew all the inhabitants thereof, pushing the queer bodies into the lake with long spears, because they did not wish to touch them. And because they did not like the grey sculptured monoliths of Ib they cast these also into the lake; wondering from the greatness of the labor how ever the stones were brought from afar, as they must have been, since there is naught like them in all the land of Mnar or in the lands adjacent.

Thus of the very ancient city of Ib was nothing spared save the sea-green stone idol chiseled in the likeness of Bokrug, the water-lizard. This the young warriors took back with them to Sarnath as a symbol of conquest over the old gods and beings of Ib, and a sign of leadership in Mnar. But on the night after it was set up in the temple a terrible thing must have happened, for weird lights were seen over the lake, and in the morning the people found the idol gone, and the high-priest Taran-Ish lying dead, as from some fear unspeakable. And before he died, Taran-Ish had scrawled upon the altar of chrysolite with coarse shaky strokes the sign of DOOM.

After Taran-Ish there were many high-priests in Sarnath, but never was the sea-green stone idol found. And many centuries came and went, wherein Sarnath prospered exceedingly, so that only priests and old women remembered what Taran-Ish had scrawled upon the altar of chrysolite. Betwixt Sarnath and the city of Ilarnek arose a caravan route, and the precious metals from the earth were exchanged for other metals and rare cloths and jewels and books and tools for artificers and all things of luxury that are known to the people who dwell along the winding river Ai and beyond. So Sarnath waxed mighty and learned and beautiful, and sent forth conquering armies to subdue the neighboring cities; and in time there sate upon a throne in Sarnath the kings of all the land of Mnar and of many lands adjacent.

The wonder of the world and the pride of all mankind was Sarnath the magnificent. Of polished desert-quarried marble were its walls, in height 300 cubits and in breadth 75, so that chariots might pass each other as men drave them along the top. For full 500 stadia did they run, being open only on the side toward the lake; where a green stone sea-wall kept back the waves that rose oddly once a year at the festival of the destroying of Ib. In Sarnath were fifty streets from the lake to the gates of the caravans, and fifty more intersecting them. With onyx were they paved, save those whereon the horses and camels and elephants trod, which were paved with granite. And the gates of Sarnath were as many as the landward ends of the streets, each of bronze, and flanked by the figures of lions and elephants carven from some stone no longer known among men. The houses of Sarnath were of glazed brick and chalcedony, each having its walled garden and crystal lakelet. With strange art were they builded, for no other city had houses like them; and travelers from Thraa and Ilarnek and Kadatheron marveled at the shining domes wherewith they were surmounted.

THE DOOM THAT CAME TO SARNATH

But more marvelous still were the palaces and the temples, and the gardens made by Zokkar the olden king. There were many palaces, the least of which were mightier than any in Thraa or Ilarnek or Kadatheron. So high were they that one within might sometimes fancy himself beneath only the sky; yet when lighted with torches dipt in the oil of Dothur their walls shewed vast paintings of kings and armies, of a splendor at once inspiring and stupefying to the beholder. Many were the pillars of the palaces, all of tinted marble, and carven into designs of surpassing beauty. And in most of the palaces the floors were mosaics of beryl and lapis-lazuli and sardonyx and carbuncle and other choice materials, so disposed that the beholder might fancy himself walking over beds of the rarest flowers. And there were likewise fountains, which cast scented waters about in pleasing jets arranged with cunning art. Outshining all others was the palace of the kings of Mnar and of the lands adjacent. On a pair of golden crouching lions rested the throne, many steps above the gleaming floor. And it was wrought of one piece of ivory, though no man lives who knows whence so vast a piece could have come. In that palace there were also many galleries, and many amphitheaters where lions and men and elephants battled at the pleasure of the kings. Sometimes the amphitheaters were flooded with water conveyed from the lake in mighty aqueducts, and then were enacted stirring sea-fights, or combats betwixt swimmers and deadly marine things.

Lofty and amazing were the seventeen tower-like temples of Sarnath, fashioned of a bright multi-colored stone not known elsewhere. A full thousand cubits high stood the greatest among them, wherein the high-priests dwelt with a magnificence scarce less than that of the kings. On the ground were halls as vast and splendid as those of the palaces; where gathered throngs in worship of Zo-Kalar and Tamash and Lobon, the chief gods of Sarnath, whose incense-enveloped shrines were as the thrones of monarchs. Not like the eikons of other gods were those of Zo-Kalar and Tamash and Lobon, for so close to life were they that one might swear the graceful bearded gods themselves sate on the ivory thrones. And up unending steps of shining zircon was the tower-chamber, wherefrom the high-priests looked out over the city and the plains and the lake by day; and at the cryptic moon and significant stars and planets, and their reflections in the lake, by night. Here was done the very secret and ancient rite in detestation of Bokrug, the water-lizard, and here rested the altar of chrysolite which bore the DOOM-scrawl of Taran-Ish.

Wonderful likewise were the gardens made by Zokkar the olden king. In the center of Sarnath they lay, covering a great space and encircled by a high wall. And they were surmounted by a mighty dome of glass, through which shone the sun and moon and stars and planets when it was clear, and from which were hung fulgent images of the sun and moon and stars and planets when it was not clear. In summer the gardens were cooled with fresh odorous breezes skillfully wafted by fans, and in winter they were heated with concealed fires, so that in those gardens it was always spring. There ran little streams over bright pebbles, dividing meads of green and gardens of many hues, and spanned by a multitude of bridges. Many were the waterfalls in their courses, and many were the lilied lakelets into which they expanded. Over the streams and lakelets rode white swans, whilst the music of rare birds chimed in with the melody of the waters. In ordered terraces rose the green banks, adorned here and there with bowers of vines and sweet blossoms, and seats and benches of marble and porphyry. And there were many small shrines and temples where one might rest or pray to small gods.

Each year there was celebrated in Sarnath the feast of the destroying of Ib, at which time wine, song, dancing, and merriment of every kind abounded. Great honors were then paid to the shades of those who had annihilated the odd ancient beings, and the memory of those beings and of their elder gods was derided by dancers and lutanists crowned with roses from the gardens of Zokkar. And the kings would look out over the lake and curse the bones of the dead that lay beneath it. At first the high-priests liked not these festivals, for there had descended amongst them queer tales of how the sea-green eikon had vanished, and how Taran-Ish had died from fear and left a warning. And they said that from their high tower they sometimes saw lights beneath the waters of the lake. But as many years passed without calamity even the priests laughed and cursed and joined in the orgies of the feasters. Indeed, had they not themselves, in their high tower, often performed the very ancient and secret rite in detestation of Bokrug, the water-lizard? And a thousand years of riches and delight passed over Sarnath, wonder of the world and pride of all mankind.

Gorgeous beyond thought was the feast of the thousandth year of the destroying of Ib. For a decade had it been talked of in the land of Mnar, and as it drew nigh there came to Sarnath on horses and camels and elephants men from Thraa, Ilarnek, and Kadatheron, and all the cities of Mnar and the lands beyond. Before the marble walls on the appointed night were pitched the pavilions of princes and the tents of travelers, and all the shore resounded with the song of happy revelers. Within his banquet-hall reclined Nargis-Hei, the king, drunken with ancient wine from the vaults of conquered Pnath, and surrounded by feasting nobles and hurrying slaves. There were eaten many strange delicacies at that feast; peacocks from the isles of Nariel in the Middle Ocean, young goats from the distant hills of Implan, heels of camels from the Bnazic desert, nuts and spices from Cydathrian groves, and pearls from wave-washed Mtal dissolved in the vinegar of Thraa. Of sauces there were an untold number, prepared by the subtlest cooks in all Mnar, and suited to the palate of every feaster. But most prized of all the viands were the great fishes from the lake, each of vast size, and served up on golden platters set with rubies and diamonds.

Whilst the king and his nobles feasted within the palace, and viewed the crowning dish as it awaited them on golden platters, others feasted elsewhere. In the tower of the great temple the priests held revels, and in pavilions without the walls the princes of neighboring lands made merry. And it was the high-priest Gnai-Kah who first saw the shadows that descended from the gibbous moon into the lake, and the damnable green mists that arose from the lake to meet the moon and to shroud in a sinister haze the towers and the domes of fated Sarnath. Thereafter those in the towers and without the walls beheld strange lights on the water, and saw that the grey rock Akurion, which was wont to rear high above it near the shore, was almost submerged. And fear grew vaguely yet swiftly, so that the princes of Ilarnek and of far Rokol took down and folded their tents and pavilions and departed for the river Ai, though they scarce knew the reason for their departing.

Then, close to the hour of midnight, all the bronze gates of Sarnath burst open and emptied forth a frenzied throng that blackened the plain, so that all the visiting princes and travelers fled away in fright. For on the faces of this throng was writ a madness born of horror unendurable, and on their tongues were words so terrible that no hearer paused for proof. Men whose eyes were wild with fear shrieked aloud of the sight within the king's banquet-hall, where through the windows were seen no longer the forms of Nargis-Hei and his nobles and slaves, but a horde of indescribable green voiceless things with bulging eyes, pouting, flabby lips, and curious ears; things which danced horribly, bearing in their paws golden platters set with rubies and diamonds containing uncouth flames. And the princes and travelers, as they fled from the doomed city of Sarnath on horses and camels and elephants, looked again upon the mist-begetting lake and saw the grey rock Akurion was quite submerged.

Through all the land of Mnar and the lands adjacent spread the tales of those who had fled from Sarnath, and caravans sought that accursed city and its precious metals no more. It was long ere any traveler went thither, and even then only the brave and adventurous young men of distant Falona dared make the journey; adventurous young men of yellow hair and blue eyes, who are no kin to the men of Mnar. These men indeed went to the lake to view Sarnath; but though they found the vast still lake itself, and the grey rock Akurion which rears high above it near the shore, they beheld not the wonder of the world and pride of all mankind. Where once had risen walls of 300 cubits and towers yet higher, now stretched only the marshy shore, and where once had dwelt fifty millions of men now crawled only the detestable green water-lizard. Not even the mines of precious metal remained, for DOOM had come to Sarnath.

But half buried in the rushes was spied a curious green idol of stone; an exceedingly ancient idol coated with seaweed and chiseled in the likeness of Bokrug, the great water-lizard. That idol, enshrined in the high temple at Ilarnek, was subsequently worshipped beneath the gibbous moon throughout the land of Mnar.

Tower of Darkness

David Madison (1951-1978)

For those who after some tomorrow stare
And those who for today alike prepare
A muezzin from the Tower of Darkness cries
Fools, your end is neither here not there.
—Omar Khayyam

The purplish-red glob of the setting sun was sinking into an ominously dramatic wall of blood-colored cloud when the two riders came out of the desert and brought up their horses at the towering wooden gates of Nysa. The dark, bearded guardsmen in uniforms of black and scarlet eyed their visitors with ill-concealed hostility.

Times were hard in the anarchy of the five kings, and the inhabitants of the walled cities therein were distrustful of strangers. Nysa was more so than most. Far from the common ways, it brooded behind its granite walls and kept its secrets well.

The captain of the guards stepped out and raised his long hardwood spear regarding the riders narrowly.

They bestrode beautifully matched dapple-gray horses, with red leather saddles and silver fittings. Bulging canvas packs hung from their saddle horns like ripe fruit.

The woman was tall and lithe, muscular without being awkward. Her heavy square-cut blond hair was confined by a circlet of beaten gold; other than that she wore not ornaments. A narrow white scar creased the perfection of her tan, pulling her right eyelid down slightly and giving her face a faint look of sleepy cynicism. A fantastically jeweled and embroidered peacock cape hung from her shoulders, contrasting oddly with her masculine linen blouse, rudely patched canvas pants, and the notched and rusty sabre in her belt.

The guard-captain had no great love of foreigners, but could not help but be impressed by her.

Her male companion was small, although supple and compactly built. He was blond, like the woman, with a pretty, faintly childish face and deep black eyes.

He was dressed in peach-colored satin trousers, soft white boots, and a shirt that was alive with needlepoint dragons. His mascara and eyeshadow had begun to run from perspiration, and there was a blue butterfly painted on his left cheek.

The captain, whose only concession to ornament was a silver bar through his nose, sneered openly at such affectation. He spat out a formal challenge in the city's native dialect, which got him an uncomprehending stare. He then addressed them in badly broken Lyonese, assuming, from the cut of their clothing, that they were from the City of Lyon. They weren't; the last store they had robbed was.

Marcus fortunately knew enough Lyonese to get by, and replied in kind. "He says Nysa has no great love for foreigners," he translated for the woman, "and he suspects we may be bandits."

"They always say that," Diana replied, "in hopes of increasing the bribe we have to give them to get in." She reached into her belt and, with a slightly contemptuous gesture, tossed him three pieces of silver: Stars, from Lyon.

The guardsman examined them carefully before putting them in his belt. He came forward to say something to Marcus in low, conspiratorial tones.

"What does he want, an extra bribe for his poor wife and children?" Diana said sardonically.

194

"I can't quite follow his Lyonese, but first he thanked us for our generosity and then said something about our being fools to come here, because the city of Nysa is damned."

"They really don't like strangers, do they?" Diana said as the guardsmen stood back and let them ride into the narrow streets.

The business at the gates had taken some time and the sun was on the edge of the horizon by then. The guardsmen drew shut the brassbound gates with a chorus of "heave-ho"s and a deafening clang. The city walls were high and thick, so high that it was already very dark in the narrow, twisting streets. The same mode of fortified architecture was carried out in the blocky stone buildings. There were few entrances, and these were fitted with massive bars. The windows had all been bricked shut, leaving only peepholes. The brickwork was quite recent and unweathered.

All the doors were already locked and there was not a soul on the streets except for the two adventurers.

"Where is everybody?" Marcus asked rhetorically.

"Home hiding under their beds, it looks like. This place is going to be about as much fun as a cheap funeral. Why couldn't we have pushed on to Shazir?"

"At night, across the desert... do you really want to end up as a midnight snack for a pack of hyenas?"

"I know, but it's so dull here, and in Shazir there are wine shops and bazaars and dances..."

"And my cousin Beatrice's whorehouse, and we could have made it if you hadn't spent half the morning nursing your hangover."

"You picked out that foul wine, as I recall, and you can tell your fat cousin that if I ever wake up and find her in bed with me again, I'll split her skull!"

This provoked a fit of giggling on Marcus's part, interrupted by a dull echoing clang, like the single stroke of a fune bell, which made the dark air vibrate.

TOWER OF DARKNESS

After the echoes of that long stroke whimpered and died, the silence fell like a blow. No one could have laughed after hearing that sound.

Diana tightened her cape and shuddered. She started to speak, but was silenced by a long mournful cry swelling into a chant as hollow and sadly directionless as the bell. Neither of them understood a word of it, but the tone was unmistakable. There was sorrow in it, sorrow and the grave. When the silence fell again, it was like the dropping of a pall.

"What was that?" Diana asked, in a voice that was oddly small.

Marcus looked up at the purpling sky and said, in a voice almost as quiet, "I have heard that in Nysa they worship the sun and fear the night for reasons they won't explain. It's taboo even to say the word 'night' here."

He pointed to a square, ugly watchtower that rose out of the center of the city like a stump of a broken tree. "That's where the bell and the chanting came from. It is called the Tower of the Dying Sun. A priest lives there whose job is to ring the bell every hour between sunset and sunrise."

"A real fun town…"

"Well, it's a place to stay. When they open the gates first thing in the morning, we can go on to Shazir."

"And your cousin Beatrice… but I refuse to sleep in the streets when I have enough money in my saddlebags to buy this place."

"I wouldn't go around announcing it, if I were you. There may be a few others around here in our profession."

Diana patted the hilt of her cutlass and smiled silently. The same low, massive architecture continued throughout the city. The streets were clean and well-paved, but depressingly narrow. They wandered at random, confronted by the bland stare of bricked windows and bolted gates. The sky was become a blue-black strip overhead, clawed by buttresses and weather beaten gargoyles. A stray beam of moonlight sometimes found its way into these black pits, but only if it had come there to die.

196

They spoke little, and for the next three strokes of the hour there was little sound except the clink of their equipment and the clatter of hooves on paving stones.

Finally they found what was undeniably an inn; locked up, of course, but still an inn. Marcus pulled the bell rope and got no response.

Diana took the direct approach and rattled her sword back and forth across the bars of the front door.

"I'll teach a bunch of grown men to be afraid of the dark!" she shouted over the hellish din. "If this doesn't wake them up, they're dead!"

At first it seemed they might be, but a few minutes more of the deafening clatter brought a response in the form of a bloodshot eye at a peephole in a brass shutter. The eye surveyed them doubtfully for a moment, then blinked and vanished just as Diana was feeling strongly tempted to poke it out. The shutters opened a few inches, although still fastened by a chain, revealing a fat, bearded and extremely angry innkeeper. He held a lamp in one hand and in the other, a curious silver medal on a chain, bearing the image of the sun.

"What seek you?" he spat in Lyonese, along with a few words in his native tongue which, though untranslatable, were obviously not complimentary.

"Wine, meat, and a bed," Marcus snarled, his own temper wearing a bit thin.

The innkeeper shouted something over his shoulder and told them to wait. After a few minutes, a skin of wine and a cloth bag of food changed hands at a somewhat inflated price.

"Now, what about a bed?"

"No. Go now. If you're still alive come morning, then I give you bed. Go!"

He slammed the shutter.

"I wish I spoke their gobbledygook, I'd tell that fat sow a thing or two about his ancestors," Diana fumed.

Marcus shrugged and said, "Superstitious. Did you see that silver medal he had?"

"I saw. So what was it?"

"It's a sun disk. They keep it with them all the time after dark, to frighten off evil spirits."

"I prefer a sword," Diana said. "Now pass me the wine."

With no place else to go, they continued toward the center of the city. The wine passed between them with friendly frequency. The food, unfortunately, consisted of black bread and a small round cheese that made up in rankness what it lacked in size, so that they ate little but drank much.

Diana, whose singing voice left a bit to be desired, struck up a bawdy old chorus about the king of Shazir and his mother-in law, with Marcus accompanying on a set of reed pipes.

Toward the center of the city the streets widened, and there were fewer buildings. Such buildings as there were grew more massive and low, like blockhouses, and the sign of the sun was everywhere, painted on walls and windows and even worked into the pattern of paving stones.

The sixth hour of night struck.

Someone a little less brave, or a little less numbed by alcohol, might have felt the fear that hung so thick in the air near the city's center, a deep abiding fear of Night and the children of darkness.

Night is very old, older than the day; night was before day was even a dream in the mind of the creator.

Where light and life are, night and death were and will be again.

They came at last to the center of the city, a flat and desolate-looking park ornamented by two appallingly ugly edifices and a number of skeletal trees.

The two buildings were the Tower of the Dying Sun, and a low and equally unattractive step-pyramid with a grotesque temple on its flat summit.

198

Around these structures lay nothing but flat parkland, sparsely vegetated. The seventh hour rang, hollow and empty sounding, but in this dead place it was singularly appropriate.

Diana's song fell to a whisper and was still, followed by Marcus's piping. This was not a place where songs were sung, or pipes played. They both knew it, without knowing why.

The ground was flat and parched, and the grass the color of putty. All the trees were leafless.

Diana crossed the low curb to the park and made arrangements to stake her horse out on its tether.

"There's probably not much nourishment in this grass," she said, working the stake into the ground, "but you can bet you're not going to find a stable that will open until sunrise."

Marcus nodded agreement and dismounted to make his horse similarly secure. Diana unslung the wineskin from the saddle and took an immoderately long pull at it.

"Here we are," she announced with mocking expansiveness. "Nysa, the garden spot of the five kingdoms."

"I'd give five kingdoms to get out of it right now," Marcus said quietly.

"Frightened, little doll?" Diana continued drunkenly. "What's to be frightened of? Everything in Nysa has crawled into its hole for the night."

"You had better eat something, and find a place to sit before you fall down," he said, not without sympathy. He put his arm around her waist.

Prudently leaving the wineskin hung from his saddle, he took the food and, tearing out a handful of bread and cheese for his intoxicated love, he pressed it into her hand. She ate with remarkably quiet obedience.

"Tired... want to sleep..." she muttered vaguely as they walked. Then, more awake, "Where are we going?"

"To the pyramid," he replied. "I think it's a temple of some sort. Perhaps the priests will put us up for the night."

"The horses…"

"I left them to graze. There's certainly nobody here to steal them."

"The money…"

"I've got it. Don't worry."

"I'm not worried, Terence."

She sometimes called him Terence when she was a glass or two the better for it. He had the good sense not to object, and never asked who Terence was when she sobered up.

The earth of the park grew powdery and dry as they approached the buildings; it shifted and swirled under their feet like ashes. There were many trees, and low benches and decorative pagodas, but all the trees were dead, clawing at the sky with oddly bent limbs. They became progressively smaller and more dwarfish until at last they were no longer trees but blind, maimed stumps of less than Marcus's height, cancerous with livid fungi.

The Tower of Dying Sun was much larger than it had seemed from outside the park. Even Diana's numbed sensibilities recoiled from its tremendous blind mass.

Shuddering a little, Marcus rattled the formidably locked gates. For a long time there was no response, but they heard a hinge shriek and had the disturbing feeling that they were being observed through a hidden peephole.

Several doors clanged in the depths of the tower, and a tall figure in dark, heavy robes descended the stairs to the gate. The robe was hooded and the voluminous cloth cast a deep shadow over his face. His hands were broad and strong, and they held a silver mallet graven with the sign of the sun.

He stopped at the gate and spoke questioningly in the city's tongue. Marcus replied that he didn't understand, in Lyonese, which got him an empty look.

The two of them tried every language they could think of, to no result. The figure on the other side of the massive bars slowly shook his head.

200

Diana stamped her foot and swore venomously. "Can't you tell this thick-headed son of an aardvark that all we want is a place to sleep?" she ranted.

"He cannot help you," a silken voice purred.

She was seated on a low stone bench beside the gate, as calmly as if she had been there all the time. She might have been, for neither of them had seen her approach.

They watched slightly awed as she bowed with old-fashioned elegance. She was as small as Marcus and much more slender, like a child of the elf-people. Though the night was growing cold, she wore only a short toga of some filmy white cloth, through which her body was clearly visible. She was thin to the point of being skeletal, and her long red hair brushed a skin so pale it almost glowed.

"I will speak with him for you," she said, laying a hand on Marcus's arm and stepping up to the gate.

The figure on the other side of the bars raised the silver hammer and stepped back as if faced with something repulsive. The woman spat at him.

She paced in front of the door with mincing, catlike steps while she and the robed man carried on a furious argument in their purring, hissing language. The man was violently angry, the woman by turns whining, seductive, and taunting. The man tried repeatedly to speak to Marcus and Diana, but without success.

Finally, the woman gave a low mocking laugh and turned away from him. "Come with me," she said, leading them away from the tower. Behind them, the man continued to speak in the unknown tongue. A note of pleading had entered his voice.

Soon they were out of range of the sound.

"As I said," the pale creature continued, "he cannot help you. He is the priest whose duty it is to strike the hours, and he is forbidden by law to leave his tower, or to open its gates after sunset."

Diana was becoming more sober, and beginning to have her doubts about this woman. Something about her pallor and the oddly mesmerizing quality of her low sleepy voice was disturbing.

"What are you doing out?" she asked. "Aren't you afraid of the dark, like everyone else?"

"Not all the inhabitants of Nysa fear the darkness. Some of us love the night. I am Cassilda, high priestess of the worshippers of the moon."

"I didn't know there was a moon-cult in these parts. Did you, Marcus?"

Marcus said nothing. His eyes were half closed, and he seemed almost asleep. If his gaze was focused at all, he might have been staring at Cassilda.

"And I thought I was the one who was drunk," she said.

"Your friend looks as if he could use a rest," Cassilda murmured.

"If he keeps looking at you that way, he's going to need the services of a surgeon," Diana said, prodding him sharply.

"Cassilda is a beautiful name..." he said vaguely.

Diana ignored that.

"We worshippers of the gentle moon are more hospitable to strangers than those who worship... than our opposition. In our temple there is food and drink aplenty, and rest for the weary traveler. Would you like to go there with me?"

"Certainly. If the food is good, I might even make a sizeable contribution to your religion."

"You might at that," Cassilda said. She laughed oddly.

Still rather unsteady, Diana rose to her feet and pulled at Marcus. He came without resistance, as if drugged.

"Poor little doll," Diana said. "He never could hold his liquor."

"Let me help you with him," Cassilda purred, putting an arm around his waist.

"I can manage," Diana replied sharply. She took the small woman's wrist to lift it from Marcus, but let go with a shudder. Cassilda's pale flesh was as cold as a day old corpse.

Cassilda only smiled.

Diana felt that she should decline this sinister moonchild's offer of hospitality, but somehow she couldn't say it. Nor look at her. Cassilda's eyes turned her soul to water.

Like figures in a dream, they threaded their way among the diseased trees toward the massive step-pyramid that Cassilda explained was the temple of the moon-worshippers.

"We are not a numerous sect," she explained. "There are at present less than fifty of us, although we hope to gain converts."

"I'm not very religious," Diana said non-committally.

Like everything else in Nysa, the entrance to the pyramid's interior was fitted with a set of gates that could have withstood an army. These, however, stood wide open, and within there was light and music.

They passed through a low, dank tunnel that sloped sharply downward and entered a room lit with hundreds of candles.

The air was thick with spicy incense, but under it Diana caught a scent that no amount of perfume could hide.

"This is a damned crypt!" she snapped, drawing up short at the doorway.

Marcus said nothing.

Cassilda laid an icy hand on Diana's arm and looked at her intently. Diana's terror and revulsion fled instantly. A limp, drugged calm enveloped her mind. She would have done anything Cassilda said.

"It is a crypt, of course," the priestess whispered, "but there is no need to be frightened. There is no other building in the city we could use for our temple. We sleep during the day, and this building is safe from those who are hostile to us."

Diana nodded and smiled. She understood. Yet somewhere at the base of the brain was a knot of fear that refused to go away, to be totally drowned in the mephitic calm of Cassilda's soothing voice. It was a raw animal sense of something wrong.

Still, she followed Cassilda and Marcus into the crypt.

TOWER OF DARKNESS

The room was huge and brilliantly lit by candles, torches and glowing braziers from which arose colored vapors tainted with the sick-sweet stench of hemp and the poppy. Great heaps of yellow-green bones in the corners stirred and rattled as rats moved among them.

Some thirty or forty persons reclined about the room on pillows, couches and divans, reading scrolls, talking languidly, or halfheartedly making love. Most of them were young, but they were not attractive. They seemed bony and ill-nourished, with the waxy color of plants grown in a dark cellar. Their rich, gaudy clothing was strangely fretted and tattered.

When Marcus and Diana entered the room, all talk ceased for a moment. They regarded their visitors with curiously fixed and glassy eyes. Then they looked away and muttered excitedly among themselves in their sibilant tongue.

Diana's attention passed lightly over the party and riveted itself on the man who sat at the head of the group on a heavy throne-like chair of dark oak. He was almost a giant, wrapped in a flowing, high collared black robe like a pall. His long hair was dead black, with broad white streaks running through it. There was an empty wine-cup in his hand and an air of brooding, hateful melancholy hung around him like a cloud.

He slowly focused his gaze on Diana. She looked into his eyes as if into an abyss. They seemed lidless, vast black pools of sorrow mingled strangely with hate and lust.

Somewhere very far away, Cassilda was saying "...and this is my husband, Gaius. We are the high priest and priestess of the moon children. This is our jester, whose name is Frog."

Diana felt something clammy brush her thigh and started in sudden revulsion. If anything human had ever deserved the name Frog, it was the wretch at her feet. He was the most deformed human being she had ever seen, a hunchbacked cripple whose legs were drawn up under him into useless knots. He dragged himself along the dusty floor by his arms, which were abnormally long.

He ran a mutilated hand across Diana's boot, touched his forehead to the floor as if bowing, and then croaked something in the city's tongue which provoked a round of hollow mirth.

Diana felt her gaze drawn away from the monster, back to Gaius, as if by a lodestone. His eyes were wells of darkness in a face whose pallor was luminous.

Diana felt herself being led to a pile of cushions by his chair. She sat, unresisting, and looked vaguely at Cassilda while the priestess took Diana's wrist and placed her hand in Gaius's. A calm, deep as that of the grave, flowed over her, although his hand was very cold. "Yours…" Cassilda said.

Questions were asked and answered about their lives, their past, how they had come to Nysa. When Marcus mentioned the horses he had left to graze, there was a great excitement and hideous laughter that penetrated even Diana's stupor.

Gaius selected four of his disciples to tend to the horses. The rest seemed disappointed.

The stale air suddenly vibrated with the ringing of the eighth hour. A silence fell over the party.

"It grows late," Gaius said. Diana knew he was speaking the tongue of Nysa, but she understood him. That troubled her dim consciousness.

"The time of feasting is come," he announced. "Frog, give us a song to accompany our meal."

Frog dragged his mutated body to the foot of a huge gilded harp, looking like a spider behind the web of strings. He stroked the harp obscenely and began to sing. His voice was as deep and hollow as the bell in the tower.

"Bring me sweet drink and I'll sing you a song
For life is short, but death is long
I'll drink to the bones that lie buried here
And the bones they will laugh and wish me good cheer
I'll drink to the vermin and drink to the worm

For while I'm alive they'll do me no harm
And when I am dead it won't matter to me
Who frets my bones or sings songs to me..."

She watched Frog's crippled paws swarm across the harp. The song flowed and writhed in her brain like a fat corpse-worm. She learned the secrets of the moon children, and they were dark secrets indeed, old secrets caked in old dry blood.

Still she felt no fear. She was utterly calm, even when Gaius put out a cold white hand and drew her up into his lap with no more effort than had she been a child.

His mouth was cold on her face, on her throat. There was pain somewhere. Someone was hurt. Someone was bleeding. Somewhere.

Her dimming gaze settled on Marcus. He was lying across Cassilda's legs and she was kidding the hollow of his neck. Her jaws were working convulsively and her pale mouth was abnormally red. A slow, thick stream of blood oozed past her lips and stained his shirt.

Vampire!

The word burst in Diana's brain like a lightning bolt. In one horrible instant, all the night-fears of her childhood came true.

She was growing weak but she could still think, and this was one situation in which her strength would avail her nothing. If she were to escape now, it would depend on her wits.

She knew that vampires, being for all practical purposes dead, could not truly be killed, but they could be mangled and destroyed by fire, by the light of the sun, by a wooden stake, or by a weapon made of silver.

Silver... her free hand sought her money pouch and brought out a fistful of the star-shaped silver coins of Lyon. With her remaining strength she raised and ground them fiercely into Gaius's eyes. It felt as though she had shoved her hand into a bucket of cold mud. His flesh reverted to rotten putrescence at the touch of the metal. Diana's long fingers sank deep into his skull and wrenched a good deal of it out.

With a roar like a wounded bear, he flung her to the floor and lurched to his feet. He staggered across the room, blindly raging.

Diana was on her feet in an instant, turning on Cassilda like a tigress. The flat of her boot crunched sickeningly against the creature's skull. Her mouth parted from Marcus's throat with a bubble of blood and an obscene, sucking noise.

Diana busied herself with stomping Cassilda's ribs for a moment until she realized that the creature felt no pain, then turned to see to Marcus.

He was already on his feet, tying a scarf around his gashed neck.

"They're... they're..." he croaked, spitting blood.

"I know what they are," she replied. "Let's get out of here."

The vampires, dropping all pretense at humanity, were hissing and snapping around them like a dog pack but afraid to advance because of what had happened to Gaius.

They suddenly divided their forces into two groups to circle around. The iron gates closed behind them with a chillingly final clang, leaving the two no direct exit from the pyramid.

"The coins in your belt." Diana whispered. "These things are afraid of silver."

Marcus threw a handful of money among them. They ran, howling, as if from a shower of hot coals.

He then reached up his sleeve and withdrew a wavy-bladed throwing knife whose silvered edge gleamed wickedly in the torchlight. Diana's long cutlass rattled out of its sheath. She grimly surveyed the situation and said, "There's no chance of taking the gate. Let's go for the other door."

"All right... now!"

They moved for the rear of the room, slowly at first, then more quickly as the vampires began to gather against the rear wall. Another scattering of silver broke their formation for a moment.

Cassilda, her face sagging from its crushed bones lurched to the wall and drew a hot poker from a brazier. She began to flail the cowering monsters with the glowing end. The stench of burning flesh soured the air.

"Up, you wretches! Kill them, you cowards!" she hissed. Then, more softly, "They have blinded your master... they have hurt my love."

She bent to Gaius, cowering at her feet with an arm over his wrecked face, and began to stroke his hair.

For a long moment, no one moved. Then, all at once, they were upon them. It was two against thirty, but none of the vampires was armed, and all were deathly afraid of Marcus's silver knife.

He moved toward the door, slashing anything that got in his way. Diana covered him with her cutlass, hacking insanely wherever flesh showed. Heads shattered, arms fell, entrails were ripped, but nothing bled and no one cried out in pain. She might have been cleaving the flesh of corpses. The only sound was their own frantic breathing. Diana could feel the coldness of them seeping into her flesh, the way warm-blooded animals radiate heat.

She had flung the peacock cape around her left arm in lieu of a shield. Each time her stroke fell late, a set of teeth met her wrist.

There were teeth everywhere, and blazing blood-tinted eyes, hands long and white with clotted nails, hands that sought her thighs, her breasts, her throat. She was going mad, killing right and left but without anyone's dying. As long as there was bone enough for them to stand on, they stood and fought.

She resisted the impulse to vomit as a headless, one-armed carcass rammed the cold stump of its neck into her belly.

Then, suddenly, it was over. They were through the door and into a narrow tunnel jammed with bones. She threw her shoulder into the chest of the dismembered torso and sent it sprawling into the thrashing mob. While they were untangling themselves, she put her weight against the door, slamming it.

The door immediately began buckling, as if being hit with a ram. "I can't hold this thing," she shrieked. "Get something to bar it!"

There were iron loops in the door for a bar, but the oaken bar was rotted away.

Marcus snatched a long thigh bone from the floor and shoved it through the loops. It held, creaking ominously from the thudding blows.

Distantly, the ninth hour struck. The hammering ceased for a moment, then began with redoubled fury.

"Nine..." Diana panted. "The sun will rise by twelve, if we can hold them."

"The sun will rise whether we can hold them or not, but I'd like to be here to see it. I think that bone is cracking."

Diana looked around them. The light coming under the door was dim, but she could see that they were in a narrow zig-zag catacomb walled on either side with masses of shored-up bones from floor to ceiling. She seized a protruding timber and began to tug frantically.

"Pull on this!" she shouted.

"You're mad! You'll bury us!"

"I hope not, but better buried than eaten."

Marcus wrapped his arms around the timber, and began to jerk savagely. It slipped about a foot. There came a shower of putrid dust followed by an ominous groaning.

"Duck!" Marcus roared, flinging himself headlong down the corridor, followed by Diana.

The lights went out with a crash and a strangling cloud of dust as they found themselves neck-deep in a river of bones. They struggled to their feet, coughing and retching. "If that doesn't hold them, nothing will," Diana gasped.

The vampires seemed to be of the same opinion. The fierce hammering faded to an occasional thud and then ceased altogether.

Marcus groped for Diana's hand in the inky darkness. After encountering a few other parts of her anatomy, he found it.

"Are you all right?" he panted.

TOWER OF DARKNESS

"I've been bitten in a few places, but I'm all right."

"Then we'd better try to find a way out of here. There must be an exit into that temple on the top of the pyramid. From there we can climb down the side."

"Good idea, but hang onto my hand. I don't want you to get lost in here."

Her palm was sweating profusely, and he suspected she was holding his hand more out of fear than a desire for safety, but he said nothing.

It was totally dark in the corridor. The air was cold and stale. Bones pressed in around them, unseen but still breathing out the pestilent silence of the centuried dead. Kings, harlots, witches, philosophers... all made equal by death.

Diana took the lead, using her long sword like a blind man's stick to search the walls and uneven floor, although she whimpered every time they encountered a spiderweb. Neither of them spoke after a while, because the horrible feeling that they were being listened to had grown in their minds.

The interior of the pyramid was a warren of tunnels. They moved through twisted corridors less than a yard wide, among mountains of bones. Sometimes the tunnel they had taken ended in a wall or the tumbled mass of a cave-in, so that they had to feel their way backward to get out.

Whenever the tunnel forked, they took the branch that slanted upward, hoping finally to reach the top of the pyramid. Several times, Diana claimed she saw light, but there was never anything there.

After what seemed hours of wandering, they came to a rusty brass ladder set in an upward-slanting stone drain.

"Where do you think it will take us?" Marcus asked.

"Anywhere... as long as it goes up."

It did go up, and very steeply, but there was light at the end, or at least a sort of lesser darkness.

They went hand over hand up the slimy rails, through cobwebs thick as fishermen's nets, hearing the sullen rustle of the spiders as they protested the destruction of their handiwork.

Suddenly the climb was over. Diana encountered a moldy wooden trap door. She flung it open and stepped out.

"The sky..." she said, almost reverently.

"It is beautiful," Marcus whispered. "But it's still night."

They were in the temple on the top of the pyramid. It was large but stripped of all its ornaments, and partially ruined. The roof had collapsed, and lay in fragments across the floor with the leering heads of gargoyles and scraps of brass roof plates. The sky above was overcast and threatening.

The windows were barred peepholes and it was fitted with doors that could have done for a fortress.

"We can go down the outside of the building and then get the hell out of here," Diana said, throwing the bolts and dragging open one of the door halves, hinges screaming.

"Oh no..." she added, very softly.

The vampires had left the pyramid by the main gate and come up the side. As Diana opened the temple door, they were just coming over the edge onto the flat roof, most of them wounded, some of them in pieces. Gaius led, his black robes streaming in the rising wind, a broad-axe clutched in both hands; he used its long handle for a staff. He advanced, blind and hideous. Then Cassilda, naked now, with one arm limp and useless.

The rest came swarming over the rim in a mass, with rusty burial armor thrown over their gaudy rags, armed with gilded swords that had been laid to rest in the hands of warriors.

Diana was unable to move. She leaned on the door, watching her doom approach. "It isn't fair..." she whispered.

Pushing her, unresisting, to one side, Marcus slammed the door and threw back the bolts, an action followed by cries of outrage and a thudding succession of hammer blows.

Diana was crying. It hurt her to cry, and she hated it, but there was no stopping it.

"They ought to die," she choked. "Why don't they die? Haven't I killed enough of them?"

She drew the long sword out of her belt, grasped it by the blunt edge of the blade. In a frightening burst of strength, she broke it in two and flung it to the floor.

"I've been betrayed..." she said to no one.

"You did the best you could," Marcus replied. "Now all we can do is wait for the sun,"

"Or for them."

Outside, Gaius was at work on the brass-bound door with his axe. The iron crescent rose and fell with mechanical persistence, splitting the wood and smashing the fittings. Gaius had the strength of a giant, and his cold flesh would never tire. The door would yield, in time.

The others crouched around him, their armor rattling with slight movements like the clatter of deathwatch beetles. Frog tugged at the hem of Gaius's robe with his crooked claws.

"Master," he whined, "it grows late. I fear the sun."

"Don't be a fool," Gaius said, surveying a horizon that he could not see. "The tenth hour has not even rung."

Diana and Marcus sat together on a heap of fallen roofing alternately watching the door and sky.

"We could go back down the tunnel," Marcus suggested.

"No. I'm not going to fight them in the dark. Besides, if the sun ever comes up, it wouldn't help us in that hole."

"You're right. What time do you think it is?"

"I don't know... I remember hearing the ninth hour ring, but it seems like we were in the tunnels for years."

Her voice was shaking, and that frightened him. He looked into her face. Tears had made tracks in the dirt. Her new clothes were ruined, and there was a mass of coagulated blood on her throat.

He kissed her very softly. She began to cry again.

"Marcus," she said, "when they come through the door, it's all over. With their swords and armor, we haven't got a chance against

212

them. Is it true what my grandmother used to tell me, that when one of those things kills you, you come back as one of them?"

"It's true." There was a world of hopelessness in those two words.

She took his small right hand, now with nails broken and blood-splattered. He wore a heavy gold ring set with a broad turquoise. She lifted the stone on its tiny hinges. In the hollow underneath lay a thin glass ampule filled with a red liquid.

"There's only enough poison in there for one person, isn't there?" she whispered.

"I wanted to get one for you, but you wouldn't hear of it." Now Marcus was the one who was crying.

"Somehow I just never thought I'd come to any situation I couldn't cut my way out of."

She was silent for a long moment, watching the sky. Then she took both of his hands, and dabbed at his eyes with the hem of her blouse.

"Your make-up is ruined." She tried to laugh, and failed. "When they come… I want you to use your knife."

He choked briefly. "The heart or the throat?"

"In the back of the neck. It's quicker and I won't have to see it."

"The sun might still rise." Outside, the thudding was joined by a sound of ripping planks. "Do you think it would help if we prayed?"

"I don't think the creator would hurry the sunrise just to please us."

Fittings shrieked. A panel was wrung out of the door and a long white arm groped in to struggle with the bolt. Marcus placed the ampule of poison under his tongue where he could crush the glass with his teeth when the time came.

The bolt rattled and fell. Diana put her arms around Marcus's waist, her head on his shoulder. He slid his left arm around her waist and drew the dagger with his right.

"Don't wait too long," she whispered.

The door ground open. Cassilda and Gaius entered, with Frog and the headless thing.

"The time of feasting is come at last," Cassilda hissed in slavering Lyonese.

"Sweet drink," Frog rasped.

Diana's grip tightened around Marcus. "Please…" she said.

There was a harsh chorus of agonized screams from outside the door. Frog threw himself at Gaius's feet, tugging frantically at his robes.

"Master!" he shrieked. "The sun!"

"Impossible," Gaius said, turning to the door. "The tenth hour…"

An instant later the glare of the rising sun filled the doorway. Gaius's robes began to smolder.

"NO!" he roared, flinging an arm across his gouged eyes as the intolerable light burned into the dead nerves. His robes were flaming now. Flesh began to run from his hands and arms like putrid wax. He brought up the broad axe in a rotting, streaming claw, and turned back to face them.

Cassilda, Frog, and the headless thing were cowering outside the advancing rectangle of light. Gaius turned the edge of the axe toward them and raised it. His face was entirely gone. The robe was a mass of blue flame.

The fleshless jaws opened. A word that might have been "Die!" came forth. The axe fell, cleaving the headless carcass to the waist. It floundered obscenely into the sunlight before finally dying.

Marcus spat out the poison capsule and pulled Diana down with him behind a mound of rubble as the ghastly drama played out before them.

The thing that had been Gaius then buried the axe in Frog's twisted spine, hooking him like a fish and heaving him back against the door with a last despairing howl of "Master…" as the light began to eat him.

"Gaius… NO!" Cassilda begged.

The flaming thing staggered forward, crumbling, and caught her arm.

"Die… now…" it croaked.

The thing was on its knees, crushing her wrist in its skeletal grip, dragging her toward the light. She shot Marcus a look of mingled horror and sorrow as she entered the sun. Marcus looked away.

There was a sound like meat frying, and a stench that defied description. When Marcus looked up, they were alone in the room.

"Is it over?" Diana asked.

"They're gone."

They stood up shakily, holding onto each other, and went out into the light.

Their descent of the pyramid attracted a considerable crowd of the locals, who had come out to investigate the silence of the morning bell.

The answer to that puzzle lay in the dusty park, in a pool of blood. It was the priest from the Tower of the Dying Sun. Without the hood, he was very young. He was the keeper of the hour-bell; the silver hammer was still in his hand. His throat was torn out. He had been dead several hours.

Their horses lay nearby, similarly killed. There were a few scraps of armor and some scorched rags in the dust near them.

Diana gently reached down and covered staring eyes.

"He must have come out of the tower to try to help," she said.

"And they caught him."

A crowd gathered around them, excited, questioning.

Diana seemed to see them from a great distance. The noise of their talk was like the beating of the surf...

Marcus found someone who spoke Lyonese, and translated. "It seems we've become local heroes. They credit us with ridding them of the vampires."

"That's more hospitality than they saw fit to give us last night."

"They say we can have anything we want..."

"Tell them we want our money gathered up, new clothes, and fresh horses. And we want them to get out of here."

"They want to know what they should do with the priest."

"Give him a good burial, but first drive a stake through his heart."

The fat, bearded innkeeper, profuse with apology, pressed a sack of coins into Diana's hands. She took it with a withering look that would haunt the man's dreams for weeks.

As they mounted their new horses and drew on their traveling cloaks, Marcus asked, "Shazir?"

"For a long stay," Diana replied. "I've got a lot of forgetting to do."

Straggler From Atlantis

Manly Wade Wellman (1903-1986)

Then he knew, or maybe he dreamed he knew, that he wasn't sea-driven, wind-driven, anymore. Those hours or eternities that had thrown him high like a stone from a sling, plunged him into strangling abysses of ocean, hurtled him in a drench and rattle of rain with the wreckage to which he clung, they were past. He was alive and out of the sea, lying peacefully face down on sand and pebbles. The waves only murmured, as though to comfort him.

He could feel the sun's warm caress on his naked back, after the wind and storm and dark clouds like smothering robes. He had not died and gone wherever one goes when one dies. He was alive and ashore—somewhere. He might even be safe.

Rolling over, he opened his eyes to see where he had been flung by the tempest that couldn't kill him. He sprawled on a white beach. Inland showed clumps of rich-leaved trees; in the sky overhead were scattered soft clouds, green and rose and pearl, like the feathers of softly tinted birds. Almost within reach of his hand lodged the splintered wooden gate that had served him in some measure as a raft, the great gate that had earlier stood in the garden wall of Theona, queen of Atlantis.

Of Atlantis. He, too, was of Atlantis—wait; of Atlantis no more. For Atlantis was lost Atlantis now, sunk to ocean's deep bottom, with Queen Theona and all her people. How he had survived he could not imagine, nor where, nor on what unknown shore.

STRAGGLER FROM ATLANTIS

Shakily, creakily he stood up, feeling the soreness in his battered muscles. He wore only sandals and a drenched rag of blue loincloth. His tanned flesh was soaked into ridges on his lean legs, his broad, panting chest, the bunchy brawn of his arms. He put up a hand to shove back his mane of dark, drenched hair. That hand shook, like an old man's. He sensed hunger within him. How long since he had eaten the delicately roasted bird and white bread and drunk the perfumed wine in Queen Theona's garden? Days ago, a lifetime ago?

Among a scatter of shoreside rocks, limpets clung. Stooping, he managed to pry loose two of them. With a big stone he broke their shells and ate them. Almost at once, they seemed to give him back a trifle of strength. He knelt to tug more strongly at a third limpet—and a shadow slid across him.

He started up. A foot was planted beside him, a vast, flat foot clad in laced leather. Its leg was like a tree trunk, meaty of calf, knuckle-kneed. Over him leaned a huge face, set on shoulders twice the height of his. Its bearded lips drew back from square cobbles of teeth. It leaned almost down on him.

"Where did you come from?" asked a thundering voice, in a language he knew.

A mighty hand fell upon his arm.

Gathering the strength from·somewhere, he whirled free of it. The great head still hung close to him, and he threw a fist, with all the boxer's skill that was his. It slammed home on the bearded jaw and he heard the giant howl out in surprised pain. But then his quivering legs gave under him and he fell down, not even feeling the sand as it came up to meet him. Something like sleep flowed over him.

Again he roused, to a tingling taste of wine in his mouth. He made himself sit up, rubbing his eyes. The giant was there; no, half a dozen were there, looming around him like crags. They were all twice as broad as he and, sitting, were as tall as he would be standing. They were leather-clad, shaggy, staring. One of them propped him against a monstrous upflung knee and proffered a big stone bottle. He drank again, deeply. His head cleared.

"Thank you," he said huskily. "What people are you?"

A giant leaned forward. His shield-wide face was tufted with coarse black hair. His lower lip looked puffy, as though bruised.

"We ask you the same, little one," he rumbled. "What people are you, and what are you doing in our country where little ones dare not come for fear of us?"

"My name is Kardios."

"Kardios," repeated the one who held him against that big knee. A free hand, big as a basket, clamped a ruddy-bearded chin. "What sort of name is that?"

Kardios grinned. "I was brought up to think it was a good one. It means the heart."

The bruise-lipped giant grunted, and Kardios looked at him. "When it comes to that, what about your name?"

"I am Yod," boomed the other. "Kardios—the heart, eh? A heart can be wounded."

"I've the head and the hand to protect my heart," said Kardios, feeling better with every moment.

"Ha!" Yod roared his gigantic scorn. "A head no bigger than a fist, a hand like a forked twig."

Kardios shoved aside the bottle and made himself stand up quickly. He glared into Yod's big, bulging eyes.

"Get a weapon to fit your hand and give me one to fit mine," he said evenly. "You're a giant, but you're clumsy to the look. I'll wager that before you raised your arm to strike, I'd have you cut open and your tripes shed out on the ground."

Silence all around at that. The giants squatted and gazed at him. He made a show of ignoring them, glancing this way and that beyond the circle to see where they had brought him. He must have been carried well inland, for the sea was not visible at all. Grass grew richly underfoot, with here and there a tuft of trees, palms and what seemed to be orchard growth. At some distance loomed a row of tawny bluffs, in which he thought he saw flecks of darkness like caves. Then he gazed all around at the giants, and grinned, showing his teeth to the gum.

"Bold words, dwarf," said another of the group at last. This one sat on a lump of rock, as though he presided. His great face was deeply folded in wrinkles, but there was no weakness of age in it. His white beard flowed like a blizzard. Over his shoulders hung a cloak of shaggy black skin, perhaps from an immense wild bull. On the knuckly hand that stroked his beard shone a gold ring set with jewels—this people knew metals and the fashioning of them. He gazed at Kardios from under white-tufted brows.

"Bold words," he said again, "from a man all alone among many bigger than he."

"I've spoken bolder than that, against dangers more worth fearing," replied Kardios. "What will you do to punish my boldness? Kill me and eat me, or just kill me? There are enough of you to try."

A grumble went up from several, but the white bearded one lifted a spadelike hand.

"Be patient, you know we may need him," he quieted his companions. Then, not unkindly: "Think, Kardios, if you know how. My name is Enek, and these people of mine, the Nephol, look to me for command and judgment. Why should we give you wine to strengthen you if we meant to kill you?"

"Wine," Kardios said after him. "Let me help my wits with more of it."

The bottle was given him. He took a long pull and wiped his mouth.

"You've said that people my size are afraid to come here," he reminded them. "I didn't come here, I was washed here by the sea. Now you say that there's a reason to keep me alive. That sounds as if my size will be of help, though you're all about eight times bigger than I am, and think bigness is a good thing."

"Not always good," said Enek gravely. "You've guessed wisely,

Kardios. There's a place the smallest of us can't go, and we want you to go there."

Kardios sat down again in the midst of them. Yod still scowled, and Kardios cocked his head and grinned.

"Yod doesn't seem anxious for anything I can do," he suggested.

"Leave Yod alone," Enek bade him. "It was Yod who found you fainting, and brought you here to us after you'd hit him when he tried to help."

"Then stop trying to frighten me, Yod," said Kardios. "I didn't live through the swallowing of Atlantis by the sea to be frightened by anything."

"We've heard speak of Atlantis," said the red bearded giant who had given Kardios wine. "Some sort of strange, shining island kingdom, they say."

"It was," amended Kardios. "You Nephol are looking at a rare specimen. Maybe a few of our ships were out in safe waters, but I doubt if anyone other than myself got away from the end of Atlantis itself."

They all goggled again, and Kardios laughed. He was feeling better all the time.

"What are you trying to tell us?" asked Enek. "What happened?"

"Well," said Kardios, "I suppose I was more or less responsible."

At that, they stared at him the more fixedly, and he laughed again.

"I wasn't a citizen of the capitol at the shore," he said. "I lived back in the hills, cutting wood and growing grapes, and I was young enough to want to better myself. So I strapped on my sword and slung my harp on my shoulder. I took the trail right down to the gold and jasper palace of Queen Theona, where she'd ruled longer than anybody ever could accurately tell. I thought she might want me for her palace guard, or to make music for her, or perhaps both."

"So you're a harper, too," grumbled Yod. "You seem to value yourself for that as well as for being a fighter."

"I've always done what I could to harp and fight well. I had surpassed all the country harpers and fighters I knew, and in my part of Atlantis there are—there were good harpers and fighters. But at the palace, and it was big enough to be a palace even for people your size, the guards at the gate laughed at me. After I'd stopped them from laughing—"

"How did you stop them?" broke in one of the listeners.

"The only way. Queen Theona came out on a balcony and watched me stop the laughter of the second one. Then she ordered the bodies carried away and the widows comforted. And she said for me to come into her garden and show if I was equally good with my harp."

"Perhaps Kardios should have a harp," said Enek. "His story sounds as if it should be sung, here and there."

A harp appeared from somewhere and was thrust into Kardios's hand. It was a big one, of course, made from the horned skull of an antelope, with strings of silver wire. Kardios tuned it expertly and struck a chord. It sounded well.

"In her garden, her women and her advisers listened while I played and sang," he said. "After a while, Theona told them they could go and leave me alone with her. She poured wine—good wine, though I'm not disparaging the wine you've given me—and offered me some food."

"This queen, older than anyone could remember," put in Enek. "What was she like?"

"I can say only that she was more beautiful than the stars, or the moon," said Kardios. "Than the sun at morning or evening. Than the jewels and gold she wore. She looked at me and told me she would like me to make a song about her."

"Did you?" prompted Enek. "What was the song?"

"I'll try to remember."

Kardios plucked the strings until he found his tune. He cleared his throat and sang:

"Atlantis, Atlantis has flowered forever,
Forever Theona has reigned as her queen,
Worshipped and honored and loved,
    but kissed never—So is Theona, and always has been.

"Fairer Theona than moon or than sun,
Fairer than stars in the vault of the skies;
No man can say when her reign was begun,
Lovely and queenly and regal and wise.

"So it was told by the gods in high heaven,
Atlantis shall live and forever prevail
Until her sweet lips in a love-kiss are given;
So runs the prophecy, so says the tale.

"Forever Atlantis has flowered, but this
Is told of Theona—the moment that she
Grants to a lover the boon of a kiss,
Atlantis, Theona, will drown in the sea."

He muted the strings. "I'm afraid I'm not in my best voice," he apologized.

"That was a good song, and well sung," Enek praised him. "What then, Kardios? What when you'd finished?"

"Theona sat beside me and said, 'Kiss me.'"

All their great lungs breathed deeply, drawing air like bellows.

"I told her to remember the prophecy. She laughed, more sweetly than music, and again she said, 'Kiss me.' So I kissed her."

"Huh?" grunted Yod. "You kissed her."

"And Atlantis sank," said Kardios.

"If that's true, how did you live?" Enek demanded.

"Ask the gods," replied Kardios. "Ask the sea and the storm. But don't ask me. If some god was making a joke on me, it was a rough one. I got hold of the garden gate somehow, and I don't know how long I spun and churned over the sea, in rain, in hail. Days? It must have been days. I don't know. But here I am."

"Do you believe him, Enek?" asked Yod.

"I believe him," Enek made answer, so quietly that he sounded almost casual. "It's a strange story, but it sounds true. It was no joke of a god, Kardios. You lived and came here because there's something here for you to do."

"You've already said that," Kardios reminded him. "What is it, and why should I do it?"

"Because we helped you back to life," Enek answered at once. "We came out today, to see in what state the storm had left our shore. It was Yod who was going ahead, found you half fainting, and got his lip bruised for his pains. Now, if you're not grateful enough to help us in return for helping you, be practical enough to think how we'd act if we were ungrateful for anything."

Kardios laughed, and this time several of the giants laughed with him. It was like rolling thunder.

"What is it I am to do?" he asked again.

"You'll need strength to hear about it," said Enek. "It's nearly sundown, and night hasn't been a happy time hereabouts in recent months. Come home with us and eat and sleep."

"I'll be grateful for those chances, at least."

They all got up and walked ponderously toward the distant bluffs.

Kardios walked among them. His first impression had been a correct one. These giants were powerful creatures, but they moved slowly. Even in his weakened condition he could have run from them easily, but he did not. As they tramped along together, Enek told Kardios what troubled them.

Moons ago, there had been a great bolt of fire from heaven, and the Nephol were sure the gods spoke to them. Some of them saw the bolt strike, not far from where they lived in caves. These reported that it seemed to burst into a great shattered spray of blazing embers, which flew in all directions. But from its very midst, a living, moving thing came away safe.

"We call him Fith," said Enek.

"Why?" asked Kardios.

224

"It is like the noise he makes," said the ruddy bearded giant who had given Kardios wine, and whose name was Jipi.

Enek continued the story. Fith had seemed to be daunted, or at least uncomfortable in the light of day, and had scrambled shapelessly away to where an ancient dry well opened. He slid himself into it, out of sight. That well, said Enek, had been thought enchanted, once the home of spirits. The Nephol had come at twilight to sing and burn sweet herbs at the well's opening, to honor what surely must be some thing sent from the gods.

"Then Fith came out," said Enek. "He flowed out—I saw him flow out like a torrent of foam. He pulled one of us down and... *flowed* over him. We ran, we were sick with fear. We did not come back until the next sunrise. There were only bones there, as clean and dry as though they had lain beside the well for a year."

"Now you're telling a story as strange to me as my story of the drowning of Atlantis seemed to you," said Kardios. "You thought this Fith was heaven sent—"

"Did he not come from the sky?" Enek pointed out. "Isn't that the home of gods?"

"I've heard our priests say there isn't any particular home of gods," Kardios remembered. "Anyway, Fith went into a well that you thought of as a sort of home of underground spirits."

"And he makes his home there."

"Where is that well?"

"There," said Enek, pointing with a finger like a bludgeon.

They were approaching a stream, with the cave-pocked bluffs on its far side. A grassless level lay before them, extending to the near bank. Upon this lay what appeared to be a tumble of pale rocks, around a dark blotch of emptiness. Two spotted goats were tethered to pegs nearby.

"You will understand," said Enek, "that, however Fith's flying chariot was destroyed, he managed to land safely at a convenient place for him. That well was very close to where he came free of the wreck."

"Do you think he knew it would be there?" suggested Kardios.

"Possibly, even though he came here from the stars. It didn't seem haphazard."

The giants sidled away from the place as they walked, and Kardios suddenly broke from among them and trotted toward the dark spot. As he came close, he saw that the strew of pale objects was made up of bones—animal bones, great and small. The goats bleated plaintively and Kardios smiled at them, for he liked animals. At the very brink of the hole he knelt. Enek was right, it was a smallish round opening. Kardios might slide his own sinewy body into it, but it was too narrow for any of the giants. He peered down. Far below, like a distant coin of silver, showed a disk of pallid light. It reminded Kardios of the phosphorescent glow of certain kinds of fungus.

He rose and came quickly back to the giants as they approached the stream. "What are those goats doing there?" he asked.

"They are for Fith," replied Enek. "Living things are what he wants. Offerings keep him from hunting us. But dead meat he will not touch."

"At least you haven't made a god of him as yet, with these sacrifices," said Kardios.

Enek sighed unhappily, and Jipi and Yod sighed with him.

"For all practical purposes, he might as well be a god, and a downright evil one at that," said Jipi. "He's here. He takes prey. But let's get on to the caves. The sun has almost set."

So it had, somewhere to seaward behind them. The giants speeded their heavy feet to the margin of the stream and crossed, one by one, on an arrangement of rough rocks. On the other side stretched a level open space, tramped hard by big feet, below the bluffs and their tiers of caves. Kardios saw fires at the mouths of those caves above and below, and giant heads peered out, like dwellers at the windows of a great tenement building such as Atlantis had known.

His escorting party split up, heading for caves here and there. Enek and Jipi guided Kardios to a ladder. Its sides were great tree trunks with the bark long worn away. Up went Enek, then Kardios, and Jipi last of all.

They reached a shelf of rock. Enek led the way along it, to a tall, broad cave opening. Inside glowed a fire. The cave was a tall roomy one and appeared to have been enlarged by powerful chippings into the rock. A giant woman leaned above the fire, clad in a loose garment of rough weave that fell to her feet. She had gray hair, in two cable-like braids, and Kardios thought her seamed face was a kindly one. She looked up from her cooking.

"Enek," she cried. "I'm glad you've come back safe." Then she stared down at Kardios. "Who's this small one?"

"He's Kardios, a friend and a helper," said Enek. "Kardios, my wife's name is Lotay. She's going to give us some supper. You eat with us, Jipi."

Lotay brought out wide clay platters. From the fire she lifted a spit with savory-smelling collops of roast meat strung on it, and poked in the ashes for roots backed in wrappings of charred leaves. Enek drew a bronze knife as long as a sword and sliced meat into a dish for Kardios. Lotay filled pottery cups with wine from a leather bag. But before they sat down to eat, Enek and Jipi went to the door of the cave. Kardios watched as they carefully lifted into place a sort of barrier, of thorny branches and tendrils woven into a close network. It filled the opening from side to side and from top to bottom. They pegged it stoutly, making sure that no gaps were left anywhere. Then, at last, all four sat down at the fireside and took up their well-filled plates.

"This meat is excellent," said Kardios. "What is it, Enek?"

"The hind foot of an elephant, if you know what elephants are."

"We had them in Atlantis, for parades and for hauling stones and timbers, but I never ate elephant before." Kardios took another mouthful. "It's as tender and juicy as fine pork."

The baked root, when broken open, presented a tasty accompaniment. The wine was better than what Kardios had awakened to among the giants. As they ate, Enek told Kardios more things. The Nephol were an ancient people but not a numerous one; those in this cave community numbered perhaps fifty. But other human races, peoples of Kardios's size, feared them and left them alone. Only on certain days were there meetings at the boundaries of the Nephol territory, where the giants traded tanned hides and uncut gems for woven fabrics and tools of bronze and polished stone.

"You see, those other peoples know that we are heaven-born," put in Jipi. "We are descended from the sons of the gods, who mated with the strongest and most beautiful daughters of men."

After the meal was finished, Lotay shyly asked Kardios to take off his salt-encrusted sandals. She sat beside the fire with them, rubbing them with pieces of fat and working them back to suppleness. Enek and Jipi and Kardios found seats on blocks of stone near a rear wall. A great store of various weapons was kept there. They were stacked against the rock or hung from pegs driven into cracks. Enek found a beautifully tanned leopard skin.

"Perhaps this can replace that poor rag of a loin cloth," he said.

"Thank you." Kardios put it on, admiring the spots on the fur. "Now, suppose you tell me more about how I am supposed to deal with Fith."

"Which means your mind is made up to do it," said Jipi, smiling.

"I made it up almost at once. You've said that Fith eats the living sacrifices you put out there."

"He would rather catch us to eat, but he takes the beasts we give him every night," said Enek. "We've given him very many of those. Goats, hogs, cows—he takes them, even bears and tigers we have trapped and tied up at the doorway of his hole. Once even an elephant, though he spent a while sucking the flesh from that."

"I've been wondering why you never just stopped up that hole, by daytime, with him inside it," said Kardios.

"We've done that. With earth and rocks. He throws them out, or somehow burrows through them. When he wants to come out and eat, he comes out."

"I see. All right, when you've given him all your beasts, what's going to happen then?"

"How often we've taken council about that," said Enek sadly. "Fith will come for us then. I've said that when that happens, I must be the first to be given him." He stroked his white beard. "I'll go out to him. Jipi will be chief after me."

"As the chief, I'd have to be the prey for him on the next night," declared Jipi.

The two boulderlike heads nodded at each other. It had been agreed upon, then, long ago.

"And you've never been able to fight him," said Kardios.

"Oh, we've tried fighting," said Enek. "Our bravest have tried. But he moves too quickly for any of the Nephol. And he - he's of no shape, and of all shapes. He changes like a cloud, like a bad dream."

"That's a new sort of creature to me," confessed Kardios—. "Indeed, he must be from the stars. We had monsters on Atlantis, but they kept honestly to one shape. You Nephol have had advantages we haven't. But you say he can devour big beasts, big men. What teeth he must have."

"No teeth," declared Jipi. "We told you that he flows away on the other side, leaving the bones."

Kardios grinned drily. "Are you sure you're not offering me as a sacrifice?"

Enek shook his great head. "If we began to give him men, even men of your size, then I'm afraid he'd truly become a god. And what benefit would that sacrifice be to us? He'd only come back the next night, seeing his way by the light he himself sheds."

"Can he climb as high as this cave?"

Enek nodded. Lotay, working on the sandals, seemed to shudder.

"We can't have Fith for a god," said Jipi stubbornly. "The sun has been our god, and Fith stays out of the sun's light. The sun is kind. Kindness is stronger than fear."

"Not always," Kardios told him. "Fear doesn't have pity. I feel like saying, you're lucky I'm here to dispose of Fith for you."

"How will you do that?" wondered Jipi. "You've said you'd go down into his hole to him, but what then?"

"Leave that to me," said Kardios, wondering in his own heart how he would manage. "I'll need a good weapon of course. The best."

"Ah," and Enek actually smiled with his great teeth, "now you bargain."

"I'm in a position where I must bargain. Look at me, I wasn't left more than a rag or two by that ride through the stormy ocean."

"Clothes, too?" asked Enek. "All right, Kardios, our women will make clothes for you. And take any weapon you want." He pointed to the arsenal stacked against the wall. "Just what sort of a weapon would hurt Fith?"

"He knows what pain is," said Kardios, gazing toward the front of the cave. "Your fabric of thorns yonder seems to keep him out. In other words, thorns pain him. And if he has a sense of pain, it's there to warn him away from injury."

"That's true," said Jipi. "You're wise, Kardios."

"I'm practical," amended Kardios.

Enek tramped over to the weapons and fumbled among them. "Here, Kardios," he said. "If you think thorns may be bad for him, how about this?"

He held it out. A great, stout pole of dark wood, and from the end hung, on a length of plaited leather cord, a ball as big as Kardios's two fists. This was cased in rawhide, and all over it projected ugly bronze spikes. Enek wagged it in his hand. The spiked ball swung like the end of a flail.

"Could you strike him with that?" he asked. "And another stroke, and more strokes until—"

But Kardios was not watching the play with the flail-weapon. He had come quickly to Enek 's side. Stooping, he picked up something else from the display.

230

"This sword," he said.

Its icy-blue blade was as long as his leg, and three fingers broad at the point where it was set in a handle of leather lashings. He inspected it carefully. It was not of bronze, not of silver. Its two edges, his practiced eye told him, were keen enough to shave with. Its point tapered leanly as a needle.

"That's a curiosity," said Jipi, joining them. "It came out of the fire when Fith's chariot smashed and flamed up on the ground."

"And the heat blistered all the ground there," added Enek. "We scouted later, and there lay that blade you're holding. At first we thought it was a snake. But Jipi picked it up and brought it here to work on and sharpen. But it's not big enough for a grown man's weapon, and we don't let children play with it; they can easily cut themselves."

"It's big enough for me," said Kardios, poising it.

The balance was excellent. He took the point in his other hand. The blade bent springily, like a tough withe. "And the temper of the metal," he said. "This wouldn't break like a bronze sword. It's harder than silver." He held it to his nose and sniffed. "It has a smell like brine. What is it?"

"We never saw any other like it," replied Jipi. "It came out of the earth under that heat. The earth was a red, crumbly sort. Sometimes we use that earth for paint."

Kardios whipped the sword through the air. It sang musically. He whirled it around his head, listening.

"Let me have this to fight Fith," he said.

"Not these thorns?" said Enek, holding out the flail.

"This is a thorn that might spike down your terrible Fith like a beetle on a pin." Kardios tested the point with his thumb. "I like it."

"Remember, Fith is quick," warned Jipi. "We've tried to throw spears at him. He only dodges away."

"Perhaps you don't throw quickly enough. Let him dodge with me. I can dodge, too."

STRAGGLER FROM ATLANTIS

He swept the sword above his head in a twinkle of light from the fire, then slashed it down at his ankles. He leaped over the blade as it slashed, spun it in the air to slash again while he jumped again. Enek grunted. Kardios paced lightly across the rocky floor.

"You," he said suddenly to Jipi, "take a spear and throw it at me."

"What are you asking?" cried Enek, and Lotay, too, looked up in amazement.

"If Jipi can strike me with a thrown spear, I'd be too slow for Fith," said Kardios. He walked out into the center of the floor and stood with bare feet apart, springy-legged, the sword half lifted in his hand. "Throw, Jipi."

Jipi grimaced. From the stand of weapons he selected a spear. It was as long as he, with a shaft made of a tall hardwood sapling, bound with rings of copper wire. The head was of beautifully polished blue flint, as long as Kardios's forearm, bound into the cleft end of the wood with lashings of sinew. Jipi balanced it on his palm and nodded above it as one who knows his weapon.

"You're sure you want this?" he asked Kardios.

"I'm sure, Jipi. Try me, I say."

Jipi's tall body flexed itself smoothly. The spear drove through the firelight.

Kardios writhed to his left. The spear hurtled past. He made a lightning slash with the sword. It bit the shaft in two, and the pieces clattered on the rock. Kardios laughed as he came to salute with his blade.

Enek drew a long amazed breath. "You'll do, Kardios. If you were twice as tall—"

"If I were twice as tall, I'd be about ten times slower. I couldn't go down and fight Fith tomorrow."

He carefully leaned the sword back in its place against the wall and sat down by the fire. He yawned. "Yes, let's sleep," said Enek. "It will do all of us good to sleep."

"It will do me a good in particular," said Kardios.

Lotay brought him his sandals and spread the spotted hide of a cow for him, then offered him a woolen coverlet. He stretched out gratefully. Enek and Lotay lighted a big candle in a sconce of baked clay and plodded to where a dark opening led to an inner cave, their sleeping quarters. Jipi found bedding and relaxed near where the weapons were gathered. Almost at once, Kardios heard Jipi's deep, regular breathing as he drifted into slumber.

Kardios did not close his own eyes. Stealthily he put on his sandals and stole to where the screen of thorns blocked the mouth of the outer cave. Crouching there, he listened. At last, with the utmost care, he twitched back a comer of the screen and slipped through. A thorn scraped his side, but he did not care. He tucked the screen in place and tiptoed along the ledge to the ladder, swung quickly down, and stood up in the open space before the caves.

Half a moon hovered above the eastern horizon. That was light enough. Kardios stole across the hard earth to the stream. He could make out the rocks at the crossing, and he stepped carefully from each to the next until he had gained the far bank. He stood and looked toward the place where bones littered the ground at the mouth of the well, and where the two goats had been tethered.

But he could not see the goats. They seemed to be cloaked in a softly glowing mist. It lay over them, a sort of half-defined clump of it. As Kardios watched, the mist stirred and churned. It seemed to thicken, to become more solid there. Then it rolled across the earth; it stole as though with a rhythmic motion. It came clear of where the goats had been. And where the goats had been there showed only another scatter of bones in the moonlight.

That had been Fith, in the act of feeding.

Even as Kardios told himself these things, Fith also seemed to come to a conclusion. Fith's substance stirred and humped itself. A point rose in the midst of that substance, grew taller and made a lumpy ball at the top. The lump swung around toward Kardios, like a head looking at him. In that lump glowed a rosy light, stronger than the blur of Fith's radiance.

"Here I am, Fith!" cried Kardios.

Instantly the luminous mass rushed at him, ponderously swift.

Kardios whirled and ran. If he had brought a weapon—but he had not. Ahead of him showed a dark, brushy clump, and into it he dived like a rabbit, exulting as he felt the rake of brambles. Fith was there close behind him, but stopped as Kardios wallowed out on the other side of the brush.

Goats eaten or not, Fith wanted Kardios. Kardios ran again, to the streamside this time, straddling quickly from rock to rock. He had barely gained the far bank before Fith was catching up. Fith had changed shape, as Enek said that shapeless shape could be changed. Kardios heard a panting behind him. The pallid mass had lengthened itself, to come writhing along like a snake after a lizard.

Like a lizard Kardios ran, as fast as he had ever run. None of the big Nephol could outrun Fith, but Kardios could. He reached the bluffs, the big ladder, and lizard-like he swarmed up. Fith was at the bottom. Kardios dashed along the- ledge, slid in past the thorny screen, feeling the rake of more sharp points. He worked the screen back into place. Outside, Fith slithered along the ledge and scraped and panted, but could not come in.

"Your dark world must be a sad world," Kardios addressed Fith. "You must go out at night and hunt for food. I'm glad I'm not you."

Fith subsided. Maybe Fith went away. Kardios paid no more attention. Again he sought his cowskin pallet and pulled the coverlet over himself. Jipi, sound asleep, did not stir. Kardios stretched at full length and crossed his arms behind his head.

He had seen Fith, he had tested Fith's speed and, to some extent, Fith's pursuit methods. He wondered again if he could have made a stand in the night if he had brought along that sword Enek had granted him. Maybe. He drew deep breaths, and went sound asleep.

Sleeping, he dreamed. He was back in the palace garden on Atlantis. Theona sat on the bench with him. Her beauty was music, there so close and so sweet. Her mouth closed on his, a yearning, seeking mouth, as though she found in him the perfect triumph of her timeless existence. Then came the abrupt rush and churning of water all around, and the water fell away and became Fith, a flow and wriggle of pursuing movement. After that came wakening, to the sound of heavy feet. Enek was awake in the cave and so was Lotay, who stooped by the fire to brown flat cakes on a tilted stone.

"Good morning," said Kardios, coming to his feet. "When do we go after Fith?"

"Eat first," said Enek, beckoning also to the wakened Jipi.

"A little," agreed Kardios. "I eat lightly before a fight, and perhaps I have reason to feast later."

He washed his face in a clay pot of water.

Breakfast was grilled fish and those cakes. They were of barley meal, coarse but palatable. Lotay gave him a dish of honey to trickle upon them. Kardios was hungry but he took only a few mouthfuls, and a sip or two of wine.

"If you are ready now—" said Enek.

"I'm ready." Kardios took the sword from its place. "Let me have cord, to swing this to my wrist so I won't lose it."

The cord was given him.

"And what kind of light for the bottom of that well? I don't mean to trust Fith's light, it might go out."

Enek brought a chunk of green cane, as long as Kardios's arm. Within it were nested live coals, closely swaddled in dry moss. The open end was plugged with clay, and holes had been bored through the tough outer substance of the cane. Kardios took it, examined it, then swung it through the air. Tiny flames burst out through the holes, then died down as he held it still.

"That will be splendid," Kardios approved.

Outside the cave, the bright morning was around them. Enek and Jipi went down the ladder with Kardios. Lofty shapes of the Nephol were abroad and came after them—men only, perhaps all the men of the community. Kardios estimated about twenty. They followed Kardios and his companions across the stepping stones. Their journey was watched by women, and by children small only by comparison with their mothers.

They reached the mouth of the well, strewn around with polished bones. Kardios peered down again, and again he saw the coinlike spot of soft light far below. He made fast the lanyard from the sword hilt to his right wrist, took the torch in his left, and sat down. "Now," he told them, "I want to go down headfirst. Tie a cord to my left ankle."

A coil of line, braided of tanned leather thongs, was produced by Jipi. "We'd better tie both ankles," he said. "This cord will cut deep into one ankle."

"No, only my left," demurred Kardios. "I don't want to land down there with my feet tied together and Fith coming. Do as I say, Jipi."

Jipi shrugged. He tore a furred strip from the edge of his mantle and wound it around Kardios's left ankle. Around this padding he drew a loop of the cord and knotted it. Kardios stood up. Enek touched his shoulder, with fingers like great ridged roots.

"Luck go with you, Kardios," he said solemnly. "You're small enough to go into the well, but your heart is as great as any of ours." He considered the praise he had spoken. "Greater," he amended.

"Thank you," said Kardios. "Hold fast to the cord and let me go down fairly fast."

He rose to his knees and yet again he looked into the deep shaft. Once more he saw, seeping from far below, the ghost of light.

"Here I go," he said.

He thrust in both torch and sword and slid after them headfirst, like a fox gliding into its burrow.

The noose clutched bitingly at his ankle. They were lowering him like a bucket. He twiddled the torch into a rosy glow. The shaft, he saw, was like a chimney, a straight, perpendicular tube into which his body could slide, easily but not roomily. The sides of it were almost glossily smooth. The rock looked volcanic, but

236

its smoothness must be something that Fith had done. He had had months in which to accomplish it, for his own sliding ease.

Down. Down. Kardios wondered how many lengths of his own body he had descended. Blood beat in his ears, but he felt no fuzziness of the wits. He was healthy, thank whatever gods must be thanked. He remembered men he had seen, men called wise in Atlantis back when anybody called things anything in Atlantis. They stood on their heads for long spaces, bringing the blood there to spur their minds. Then they sat up and prophesied or gave advice. Kardios could not remember anything that any of them said that was worth remembering.

The pale patch of light grew wider below him. He must be approaching it. Where that light would be, Fith would be. Kardios let the sword dangle from the lanyard and put out his right hand to touch the smooth wall of the tubelike shaft. The touch slowed his descent a trifle, so that the drag of the cord on his ankle slackened. Now, there, down there, he caught a glimpse of slaty rock flooring. That was where he was coming to, where he was to meet Fith and make a battle.

"I'll do it," he promised himself, half aloud.

And then he was coming into open space at the bottom of the well. As his head cleared the bottom of the shaft, he saw that there was a considerable grotto of some sort. He came to the bottom, landing on one hand and the free foot. Writhing around, he caught the hilt of the sword again and with a flick of it severed the rope that was tied to his left ankle. He stood up quickly in the middle of the floor, and whirled the torch for light to see better where he was.

There was already light to show him that, without the torch. It was a place of rough rock, plenty of level expanse underfoot, as much as a fairsized hall. All around were jagged, dull walls, slanting inward to where, overhead, they came into a curved roof like the inside of a slipshod dome. As much room here, Kardios thought, as had been in the garden of Theona, now sunk to where it was sunken. Looking swiftly this way and that, he judged that this place had been fashioned somehow, though he could not guess just now what that somehow was. The hazy light showed him a darker blotch to the side, where a corridor seemed to lead away. Opposite this, in a jagged corner, lay the light's source.

It looked like a bank of soft sand heaped in among the rocks, palely glowing, as an unpolished jewel might glow under a directed radiance. That softness spread widely, farther across than the tallest of the Nephol people. He thought the glow pulsated, then wondered if this was not a sort of motion, a stir in that substance. There was sound, too, like breathing: *fith, fith*. Then it was Fith, plainer to see here than last night by the glow of half a moon. As Kardios looked, Fith paid attention to him in turn.

For the mass moved, it defined itself. It was not slackness, giving off that blur of light. It began to move itself out from among the rocks where it nested, and it seemed to take on form. It spread like a great, flattened ray, such as once he had seen swimming under water, when he had looked over the side of a fishing boat off his home shore that was shore no longer. Fith crept on outflung projections like flukes that reached right and left. At the center, the expanse rose into a crest. Deep within that center shone the stronger light Kardios had seen the night before, rosy tinged with a thought of green. Even as Kardios stared, the central light moved within the inner mass, moved forward in it as though to face him.

"Here I am again, Fith," Kardios addressed it. "They sent me down here to fight you. Let's make it a good one."

It seemed able to hear him. It crept toward him across the floor. Its inner bulk humped forward. Its flukes moved gropingly ahead, its substance flowed into them. It took a new position and headed toward him from that one, coming, coming.

Kardios poised, fencer-fashion, on light feet. He brought his sword to center guard position, point to the fore, ready for thrust or cut. Fith approached faster, rising and swelling and breathing, *fith, fith*. Out came a flaplike projection, like a questing tentacle.

238

Kardios slid his right foot forward and swiftly stooped his long body into a smooth, skillful lunge. The swordpoint licked out, and at the very wink of the right time he brought the blade down for a sweeping, slicing cut. That extension of pale substance parted before the razory edge like a strand of wool. The severed piece went squirming away. The pale hummock of substance recoiled upon itself, almost as swiftly as Kardios recovered from his lunge, drawing his extended foot backward and falling on guard again.

"Did you taste it, Fith?" he cried. "Can you taste as well as hear? Come on, try me again."

Fith knew what he said. For Fith came on to try him again. This time the pale bulk flowed out like foamy water, seemed to blanket the floor. It stole suddenly into action. As it did so, it bunched again, and now it seemed to be moving on bumpy protuberances beneath, moved on them as on legs. The rosy light within glowed stronger. It pulsed. Other parts of the body extended, questing like feelers, like arms. Kardios nipped one of them off with a quick, slicing cut, ducked low to escape another. Fith came charging.

So fast did Fith squatter forward that for a moment Kardios was backed almost against a jagged wall. He couldn't let himself be trapped there. Again he struck at a questing length of Fith's substance. It barely flicked him as he severed it, and its touch was like a tongue of flame upon his forearm. Desperately he crouched, then hurled himself in a great, flying leap above the oncoming bulk of Fith. He landed on his feet just beyond, ran half a dozen steps and faced around.

"I'm not one of those clumsy giants, Fith," he cried. "You didn't catch me. Here I am. You must keep me amused."

Fith was drawing into a new shape. This shape rose up. It grew to the height of one of the Nephol, higher than that. It was giving itself legs, two clumsy bolsters on which it stood. It put forth arms. It was imitating the form of man. At the top, in the blob that might simulate a head, the rosy glow throbbed at him. *Fith, fith,* the creature panted.

STRAGGLER FROM ATLANTIS

"You've been observing things," said Kardios. "But you're clumsy at sculpture. Well, why do we wait?"

The giant shape came at him in a squattering run. Kardios thrust, backed away, thrust again, and then Fith was all over him. Fith had shot out in all directions and had fallen upon him like a blanket.

The sword drove into Fith's midmost part and Kardios drew it up, with a strong, full-armed rake of a sweep. The edge divided the enveloping tissue like canvas. Next instant, Kardios scrambled and floundered through that great gash, won clear like a netted bird slipping out at a gap in the mesh. He danced away, tingling as though hot water had been thrown upon him. The mass he had escaped tried to draw itself together again, there almost at his knee. He looked down to where the red light flickered, close within reach.

At once he sped his blade in a mighty drawing cut. The edge sank deep into the soft pallor, seemed to grate as it struck something more solid inside. He drew it to him with all his strength, cutting the redness in two.

The close air hummed, shrieked all around them. The red glow of awareness in Fith's tissue blinked out.

Kardios backed clear, his sword ready. But Fith was dying. The panting breath labored, then stopped. The great sprawl of substance seemed to slacken, to shrivel, before Kardios's very eyes. The pale light dimmed, grew faint.

Kardios whirled his torch. The flames jumped out to show that Fith sprawled motionless and shrunken there. The grotto was silent.

Stepping close, Kardios prodded with his sword point, poked again. There was no responding movement.

He had done it.

Moving the torch to keep its flame bright, he looked around him. There hung the cut end of the rope that had let him down. He went to it and drew it into a loop under his arms and knotted it securely. Then he took hold of the slack and tugged on it strongly. After a moment, he pulled again. The rope tightened. High above, at the surface of the ground, they were pulling to lift him.

He hung limp in the noose, barely clutching the torch in his left hand and dangling the sword from his right wrist. He was more weary than he had had time to realize, and he felt blistered and singed from where Fith had touched him. It seemed to take far longer to be drawn up than it had taken to be let down.

They were all there at the top, the Nephol. Enek put out a hand to Kardios, then drew it back. "Fith burnt you," he said.

"He scorched me here and there, but I killed him," announced Kardios, and mustered his grin with it. "He was all you said he was, and more. Killing him, I felt sorry for him a little—that foreign thing, alone and hungry and hunting. But fighting men should be careful about being sorry. Anyway, he's dead, fading into nothing down there. Close up that hole again. This time it will stay closed."

"How did you fight him?" asked Yod.

"As I've fought you, getting out of his way and countering. That's how I'd beat you."

"Of course you could beat me," Yod grated, as though the words were dragged out of him. "How could I raise a hand to you now?"

"How, indeed?" wondered Kardios. "You and I are friends."

They wanted to carry Kardios in triumph back to the caves, but he would not let them. In the space before the bluff, the giant women gathered to anoint his scald-like wounds with pleasant balms. Jipi brought him another stone bottle of what was the best wine Kardios had tasted among the Nephol. When the night came down, all sat fearlessly in the open. They sang, like gigantic birds.

"You may live among us as long as you like, Kardios," said Enek, presiding over a supper cooked on a dozen fires. "Since Atlantis is gone, let this be your home. You will be a chief, as I am. All of us will bow to you."

"That's why I'd better be going somewhere else," said Kardios. "You and I talked about religion yesterday evening, discussed how sometimes ordinary things get to be gods. I don't feel ambitions to be bowed to. Bowing to someone grows into stranger notions about holiness and supreme powers and so on."

"But where will you go?" asked Yod, gnawing the thigh bone of a boar. "We can't tell you much of the countries inland, except that there are small peoples, like you."

"I'll have to find out for you."

"The sword is yours, as we agreed," said Enek.

That night Kardios slept the sleep of exhaustion and triumph. In the morning the women brought the garments they had made. There was a short tunic of blue with white points, that fitted him as though made to his measure, and a cape of soft black wool worked with gold. He put these things on and Enek offered him the sword, for which overnight had been made a bronze-studded leather scabbard and a belt just right for Kardios's lean waist.

"You'll need provisions," said Jipi, fetching a pouch with a band to sling it to the shoulders. "Here are bread and roast meat and dried fruit. And this flask, you liked our wine. Drink on your journey, and remember us as friends."

There was no visible trail inland. Kardios said his farewells and struck out across a field shagged with coarse grass. On the far side, under the shade of a belt of trees, he stopped and turned.

The Nephol stood back there, a throng of huge men and women, with big children among them. Enek towered to the front of them. When he saw that Kardios was looking, he raised his mighty hand as thought in blessing. The other Nephol flung up their hands, too, a forest of hands.

Kardios waved back to them, full-armed. His heart felt all the warmer as he plunged in among the unknown trees.

The sword he had won jogged against his thigh as he strode. He dropped his hand to the hilt. That hilt fitted his hand as though made for it. And who could say? Perhaps it had been made for his hand, in readiness for what it had done for him and the Nephol against Fith, in readiness for what it would do in future. No man was alone and friendless if he had a proper sword.

Walking past the trunks, Kardios felt a happy surge of expectation within him, a sense of adventure perhaps waiting in the next clearing. He began to hum a tune. He hummed it again, until he had the melody and the tempo to suit the words he was putting together in his mind. At last he began to sing:

"My sword, what wonders shall we twain not do?
The world is ours, to roam and render clean.
Against whatever peril comes in view
My arm is strong, your point and edge are keen.

"For storming citadels, for holding clear
From soil and sloth, for glory in the sun,
For showing enemies the face of fear,
My good companion, you and I are one."

The Man Who Sold Rope to the Gnoles

Margaret St. Clair (1911-1995)

The gnoles have a bad reputation, and Mortensen was quite aware of this. But he reasoned, correctly enough, that cordage must be something for which the gnoles had a long unsatisfied want, and he saw no reason why he should not be the one to sell to them. What a triumph such a sale would be! The district sales manager might single out Mortensen for special mention at the annual sales-force dinner. It would help his sales quota enormously. And, after all, it was none of his business what the gnoles used cordage for.

Mortensen decided to call on the gnoles on Thursday morning. On Wednesday night he went through his Manual of Modern Salesmanship, underscoring things.

"The mental states through which the mind passes in making a purchase," he read, "have been catalogued as; 1) arousal of interest 2) increase of knowledge 3) adjustment to needs..." There were seven mental states listed, and Mortensen underscored all of them. Then he went back and double-scored No. 1, arousal of interest, No. 4, appreciation of suitability, and No. 7, decision to purchase. He turned the page.

"Two qualities are of exceptional importance to a salesman," he read. "They are adaptability and knowledge of merchandise." Mortensen underlined the qualities. "Other highly desirable attributes are physical fitness, a high ethical standard, charm of manner, a dogged persistence, and unfailing courtesy." Mortensen underlined these too. But he read on to the end of the paragraph without underscoring anything more, and it may be that his failure to put "tact and keen power of observation" on a footing with the other attributes of a salesman was responsible for what happened to him.

The gnoles live on the very edge of Terra Cognita, on the far side of a wood which all authorities unite in describing as dubious. Their house is narrow and high, in architecture a blend of Victorian Gothic and Swiss chalet. Though the house needs paint, it is kept in good repair. Thither on Thursday morning, sample case in hand, Mortensen took his way.

No path leads to the house of the gnoles, and it is always dark in the dubious wood. But Mortensen, remembering what he had learned at his mother's knee concerning the odor of gnoles, found the house quite easily. For a moment he stood hesitating before it. His lips moved as he repeated, "Good morning. I have come to supply your cordage requirements," to himself. The words were the beginning of his sales talk. Then he went up and rapped on the door.

The gnoles were watching him through the holes they had bored in the trunks of trees; it is an artful custom of theirs to which the prime authority on gnoles attests. Mortensen's knock almost threw them into confusion, it was so long since anyone had knocked at their door. Then the senior gnole, the one who never leaves the house, went flitting up from the cellars and opened it.

The senior gnole is a little like a Jerusalem artichoke made of India rubber, and he has small red eyes which are faceted in the same way that gemstones are. Mortensen had been expecting something unusual, and when the gnole opened the door he bowed politely, took off his hat, and smiled. He had got past the sentence about cordage requirements and into an enumeration of the different types of cordage his firm manufactured when the gnole, by turning his head to the side, showed him that he had no ears. Nor was there anything on his head which could take their place in the conduction of sound. Then the gnole opened his little fanged mouth and let Mortensen look at his narrow, ribbony tongue. As a tongue it was no more fit for human speech than was a serpent's. Judging from his appearance, the gnole could not safely be assigned to any of the four physio-characterological types mentioned in the Manual; and for the first time Mortensen felt a definite qualm.

Nonetheless, he followed the gnole unhesitatingly when the creature motioned him within. Adaptability, he told himself, adaptability must be his watchword. Enough adaptability, and his knees might even lose their tendency to shakiness.

It was the parlor the gnole led him to. Mortensen's eyes widened as he looked around it. There were whatnots in the corners, and cabinets of curiosities, and on the fretwork table an album with gilded hasps; who knows whose pictures were in it? All around the walls in brackets, where in lesser houses the people display ornamental plates, were emeralds as big as your head. The gnoles set great store by their emeralds. All the light in the dim room came from them.

Mortensen went through the phrases of his sales talk mentally. It distressed him that that was the only way he could go through them. Still, adaptability! The gnole's interest was already aroused, or he would never have asked Mortensen into the parlor; and as soon as the gnole saw the various cordages the sample case contained he would no doubt proceed of his own accord through "appreciation of suitability" to "desire to possess."

Mortensen sat down in the chair the gnole indicated and opened his sample case. He got out henequen cable-laid rope, an assortment of ply and yarn goods, and some superlative slender abaca fiber rope. He even showed the gnole a few soft yarns and twines made of cotton and jute.

On the back of an envelope he wrote prices for hanks and cheeses of the twines, and for 550-foot lengths of the ropes. Laboriously he added details about the strength, durability, and resistance to climatic conditions of each sort of cord. The senior gnole watched him intently, putting his little feet on the top rung of his chair and

THE MAN WHO SOLD ROPE TO THE GNOLES

poking at the facets of his left eye now and then with a tentacle. In the cellars from time to time someone would scream.

Mortensen began to demonstrate his wares. He showed the gnole the slip and resilience of one rope, the tenacity and stubborn strength of another. He cut a tarred hemp rope in two and laid a five-foot piece on the parlor floor to show the gnole how absolutely "neutral" it was, with no tendency to untwist of its own accord. He even showed the gnole how nicely some of the cotton twines made up in square knotwork.

They settled at last on two ropes of abaca fiber, 3/16 and 5/8 inch in diameter. The gnole wanted an enormous quantity. Mortensen's comment on these ropes' "unlimited strength and durability" seemed to have attracted him.

Soberly Mortensen wrote the particulars down in his order book, but ambition was setting his brain on fire. The gnoles, it seemed, would be regular customers; and after the gnoles, why should he not try the Gibbelins? They too must have a need for rope.

Mortensen closed his order book. On the back of the same envelope he wrote, for the gnole to see, that delivery would be made within ten days. Terms were 30 percent with order, balance on receipt of goods.

The senior gnole hesitated. Slyly he looked at Mortensen with his little red eyes. Then he got down the smallest of the emeralds from the wall and handed it to him.

The sales representative stood weighing it in his hands. It was the smallest of the gnoles' emeralds, but it was as clear as water, as green as grass. In the outside world it would have ransomed a Rockefeller or a whole family of Guggenheims; a legitimate profit from a transaction was one thing, but this was another; "a high ethical standard"—any kind of ethical standard—would forbid Mortensen to keep it. He weighed it a moment longer. Then with a deep, deep sigh he gave the emerald back.

He cast a glance around the room to see if he could find something which would be more negotiable. And in an evil moment he fixed on the senior gnole's auxiliary eyes.

The senior gnole keeps his extra pair of optics on the third shelf of the curiosity cabinet with the glass doors. They look like fine dark emeralds about the size of the end of your thumb. And if the gnoles in general set store by their gems, it is nothing at all compared to the senior gnole's emotions about his extra eyes. The concern good Christian folk should feel for their soul's welfare is a shadow, a figment, a nothing, compared to what a thoroughly heathen gnole feels for those eyes. He would rather, I think, choose to be a mere miserable human being than that some vandal should lay hands upon them.

If Mortensen had not been elated by his success to the point of anesthesia, he would have seen the gnole stiffen, he would have heard him hiss, when he went over to the cabinet. All innocent, Mortensen opened the glass door, took the twin eyes out, and juggled them sacrilegiously in his hand; the gnole could feel them clink. Smiling to evince the charm of manner advised in the Manual, and raising his brows as one who says, "Thank you, these will do nicely," Mortensen dropped the eyes into his pocket.

The gnole growled.

The growl awoke Mortensen from his trance of euphoria. It was a growl whose meaning no one could mistake. This was clearly no time to be doggedly persistent. Mortensen made a break for the door.

The senior gnole was there before him, his network of tentacles outstretched. He caught Mortensen in them easily and wound them, flat as bandages, around his ankles and his hands. The best abaca fiber is no stronger than those tentacles; though the gnoles would find rope a convenience, they get along very well without it. Would you, dear reader, go naked if zippers should cease to be made? Growling indignantly, the gnole fished his ravished eyes from Mortensen's pockets, and then carried him down to the cellar to the fattening pens.

But great are the virtues of legitimate commerce. Though they fattened Mortensen sedulously, and, later, roasted and sauced him and ate him with real appetite, the gnoles slaughtered him in quite a humane manner and never once thought of torturing him. That is unusual, for gnoles. And they ornamented the plank on which they served him with a beautiful border of fancy knotwork made out of cotton cord from his own sample case.

The Pit of Wings

Ramsey Campbell (1946-)

Since before dawn Ryre had been riding through the forest. Except that he disliked sleeping on the move, he would have trusted himself to his steed. Instead he sought calm at the center of himself, as he'd begun to learn to do. But the oppression of the forest clung to him. Time had drowned in the green depths.

Great leaves sailed by above him. Each was shaped like an inverted ribbed umbrella spiked on a massive trunk, and each was broader than the stretch of his body from toes to fingertips. As the trunk mounted, so the leaves dwindled; the highest would be no wider than Ryre's head. But he could see none of this. Beneath the unbroken canopy of the lowest leaves, even the dawn had been no more than a greening of the dimness.

The forest road was a tunnel formed by cutting leaves; once cut, they never grew again. They rustled, withered, beneath his steed's pads. The constant sound distracted him as he listened for a hint of the sea, a breeze to stir the stagnant air.

Sometimes, especially before dawn, he'd heard a flapping high above him. It must be the gliders—the highest leaves which, having shed scales of themselves, drifted away bearing seeds. But could those leaves make such a large lethargic sound?

Now he was caged by a lingering clamor of rain. He'd heard the storm coming, high and distant at first, advancing and descending through the forest. He could only shelter close to a trunk while deafening rain poured down the trees, turning the leaves into basins of fountains. Above him the great leaf had shivered repeatedly beneath the onslaught; he'd feared drowning. Drips seeped through the foliage to water the roots, to tap Ryre on the shoulder, to stream down his face, to coat and choke him with humidity.

He shook his head, snarling like a trapped beast—like the beast whose emblem was the V-shaped mane which widened from his shaved crown to his shoulders. He felt helplessly frustrated by the eternity of the forest, the suffocating luxuriance that seemed triumphant as a mocking conqueror, the sounds whose sources he could never glimpse. He yearned for an adversary to fight.

Suddenly he put his hands over his mount's eyes. The creature halted obediently. Ryre strained his ears; impatience gripped his brow. Yes, he had heard the sound. Amid the creaking of leaves, the soft plop of rain on the decayed forest floor, the chorus of descending splashes as high leaves drooped beneath the weight of rain, there was a distant jaggedly rhythmic thudding: axes cutting trees.

So he was nearly free of the forest. Yet the sound was not altogether heartening. As he rode forward he began to hear the dragging of chains, the cut of a whip. The oppression was lifting with the leaves, but now it was anger that shortened his breath.

Where the road dipped, he saw them. Young men whose arms looked massive as the trunks they chopped, older men whose skin was more scarred, a few brawny women, all naked except for a strip of hide protecting the genitals: there must have been a hundred of them, toiling in small groups at the edge of the forest. From their fetters, long chains trailed towards the town which Ryre glimpsed beyond the trees. Beyond the town the sea burned calmly as sunlight trailed over the horizon.

Men, dressed like the slaves but bearing whips and swords, stalked about or squatted in shade. Most looked bored, and flicked their victims as they might lazily have fingered an itch. One stood over a fallen slave. A fresh weal glistened rawly on the victim's back; his ankles were bruised by a tangle of chain. He looked old, exhausted, further aged by suffering.

Ryre hated slavery as only a man who has been enslaved can. Fury parched his throat. Yet he could not fight a town, or its customs, however deplorable. He made to ride by, past the corpse of one of the immense almost brainless crawlers of the forest, which must have wormed too close to the swordsman. Chunks of its flesh had been stripped from the bone; its eye gazed emptily at Ryre from the center of the lolling head. The slaves must have eaten the flesh raw.

The standing man grew tired of kicking his victim. He said loudly "I'm wasting my strength. You're past your usefulness. Tonight you'll ride above the trees."

The effect of his words was immediate and dismaying. His victim soiled himself in terror. The other slaves glanced upward, and shuddered; Ryre heard a distant flapping. All at once unable to bear his inability to intervene, he urged his steed to canter.

But the slave-driver had seen his glare of contempt. "Yes, ride on, unless you're seeking honest toil. We've a place for you, and chains to fit." His slow voice was viciously caressing as a whip. As he gazed up at Ryre, he licked his lips.

Ryre's grin was leisurely and mirthless. Though he could not battle slavery, he would enjoy responding to this challenge. He stared at the man as though peering beneath a stone. "Ridding the world of vermin? Yes, I'd call that honest."

The man's tongue flickered like a snake's. His smile twitched, as did his hand: nervous, or beckoning for reinforcements? "What kind of swordsman is it who lets his words fight for him?" he demanded harshly.

"No man fights with vermin. He crushes them."

Swordsmen were advancing stealthily. "Perhaps his words are a sheath to keep his sword from rusting," one said.

Let them think Ryre's awareness was held by the duel of words. He would cut down his challenger when he was ready, together with

253

anyone else who dared attack him. Unhurriedly he withdrew his sword from its sheath.

A third man spoke, drawing Ryre's attention to the far tip of the advancing crescent of men. "He'll wear our bracelet well."

His steed's uneasy movement warned Ryre. He glanced back in time to see why they were trying to distract him: a man was creeping carefully over the decayed leaves, ready to drag Ryre down and club him with a sword-hilt.

Discovered, the man leapt back—but not swiftly enough. The quick slash of Ryre's blade failed to cleave his skull; instead, the sword bit lower. The man staggered away moaning, trying to hold his cheek to his face.

The others rushed at Ryre. When the original challenger flinched back from the whooping arc of the sword, however, they retreated too. The man seemed wary not only of Ryre but also of the darkening sky. "Let him go," he snarled, trying to sound undaunted. "We've no time to waste on him—not now."

The drivers tugged the chains. It was clearly a signal, for the chains drew loudly taut and dragged their victims into the town like strings of struggling fish. Ryre saw the old man stumbling to keep up. The slaves were pulled staggering into a large wooden barn, which resounded with an uproar of metal links. The great doors thudded shut.

The sight infuriated Ryre. He was scarcely heartened by the agony of the slave-driver, clutching his face as companions aided him into a structure like a barracks next to the barn. Shrugging beneath the weight of frustration, Ryre rode into the port of Gaxanoi.

In the streets men were lighting lamps. Flames fluttered in vases of thick glass which dangled from poles sprouting next to the central gutters. The entire small town was built of wood; the dim narrow streets reminded him of the forest. But at least a chill salt wind blew through the town, which creaked like an enormous ship. Above the forest the flapping was louder.

Like the streets, the dockside was almost deserted. Ryre's

mounted shadow accompanied him, jerking hugely over logs that formed walls. Seamen were entering taverns beside the wharf. On the dock, next to a lone ship, timber lay waiting to be loaded in trade for, among other commodities, chains. He grinned sourly. Gaxanoi had summed itself up.

Eventually he found the harbor-master's house, overlooking the wharf. The man proved reluctant to open the door, and taciturn when he did so. At last he admitted grudgingly that there might be ships tomorrow on which Ryre could work his passage. "Stay near the wharf," he advised, already closing the door.

Ryre did so, in a tavern, once he had stabled his steed nearby. The streets resembled decks of a ship of the dead. The only sounds of life were the clatter and panting of a boy who ran from tavern to tavern, apparently bearing a message. As Ryre entered the tavern the boy ran out, flinching wild-eyed from him.

A few sailors sat on benches, drinking morosely. Each stared into the steady flame in the glass vase before him. Frequently one or other of them would glance up like a wary beast. They seemed to resent having to spend a night in Gaxanoi—or, Ryre suspected, this particular night. He wished he knew more about the town than its name.

Was it their resentment that made the seamen dangerous? One demanded of the taverner why the door was unlocked. When his companions tried to restrain him he fought savagely; the floorboards made it sound that giants were wrestling. The fight spilled out of the tavern, and Ryre observed that the sailors quickly stunned the drunken man and dragged him hastily inside. "What is out there?" Ryre asked one—but the man glared, seeming almost to blame him for the fracas. When Ryre asked the question of the taverner, he shook his head nervously. "Nothing that I care to speak of."

Ryre had his wooden tankard refilled, and sat by a window. Let whatever was abroad in the night stay out there. He wasn't about to blind himself with drink and glassed flame: if a threat was approaching, he meant to see it before it came too near.

Still, there seemed to be little to see. Beside the ship, vases flickered on their poles. Waves lapped sleepily at the dock; light snaked in the water. A thin chill wind swung the vases. Shadows of poles danced, advancing, retreating. The ship rocked; it creaked, muffled and monotonous. Ryre shook himself free of its wooden lullaby—for suddenly there was something to watch.

At first he could hardly make out the swimming shapes below the far end of the wharf: a pack of white rats, advancing through black water? Then the vases swayed, and showed him the figures whose cowled heads he'd glimpsed reflected in the sea.

Their robes were pale as fungus. They emerged two by two from a wide dark street at the edge of the dock. The slow pallid emergence reminded Ryre of worms dropping from a gap. There seemed no end to the procession; surely it would fill the wharf.

Despite its size, the procession was unnervingly silent. A distant flapping could be heard. There was violence amid the ceremony: figures struggling desperately but mutely, which seemed to hover in the air among their robed captors. Ryre distinguished that the victims were bound and gagged, and kept aloft by taut ropes held by robed men. The sight made him think of insects in a web.

As the vanguard came abreast of the window, Ryre saw that the first victim was the slave he had seen struck down. The old man looked too exhausted to struggle; he hung slack in the air

—but his eyes were lurid with terror. The procession halted as though to display him. A seaman muttered nervously "What do they want?"

At once Ryre knew, and sprang to his feet, cursing. He drew his sword as the tavern door crashed open. Six hooded men came in, swift and silent as predators. Only their robes whispered and glimmered like marsh light in the dimness. One man pointed at Ryre, and his companions imitated him. The foremost and tallest intoned "He is to fly."

His voice was low, yet seemed as massive as the creaking that had caged Ryre in the forest. No doubt his ritual words terrified slaves, and perhaps the whole of Gaxanoi. But to Ryre the six were only men who had to hide their faces in cowls—and one of them, the man who had pointed him out and whose cowl now sagged back treacherously, was the slave-driver who had challenged him. The high priest—presumably the tall man called himself something of the kind—stood aside.

Three men stepped forward; swords snaked from beneath their robes. The slave-driver and another man hung back, ready with ropes to bind their victim.

One swordsman advanced, while his companions began to circle their prey. They meant to trap Ryre in the cramped maze of the tables and benches, which were fastened securely to the floor. But the furniture helped Ryre. He leapt backward onto a bench; then, as his adversary lunged at him, sprang onto the bench behind the man. Before the swordsman could react, a blow of Ryre's sword had split his skull. He sprawled over a table, his head spilling like an overturned tankard of blood.

Ryre leapt from table to table, heading for the door. Wood thundered around him. As he reached the door, the priest retreated hastily along the wall. One stroke of the blade severed the web of ropes—but four men came running from the procession, swords gleaming eagerly. Could Ryre hold the priest hostage? Perhaps—but as he made to seize the man, a blade came hissing towards Ryre's neck. Only a desperate leap sideways saved him from the blow, which bit deep into a log of the wall. He whirled; his movement added force to his blade's sweep.

The second swordsman crumpled, bowing his half-severed head.

Ryre had been driven back into the tavern. He stared about wildly. The seamen had withdrawn into the shadows, and clearly wanted no part of the fight; the same appeared true of the taverner. Beyond the vats of wine, Ryre glimpsed a rough staircase. If he reached an upper window, he could escape through the alley—if it was unguarded.

THE PIT OF WINGS

He dodged backwards between the tables. His scything blade cleared a race around him. By the time the swordsmen saw his plan and rushed towards the stairs, Ryre was nearly at the vats. As he reached them, the taverner grabbed a heavy wooden scoop from beside one. Before Ryre could turn, the taverner had clubbed him down.

The swordsmen were on Ryre at once. One knocked the sword from his hand, another inserted the point of his blade beneath Ryre's chin to lever him to his feet. "Come," he said with cruel tenderness, "they are hungry. Can't you hear them?"

Ryre heard only the taverner's fearful muttering. "Take him out. I got him for you. Take him out and let me lock the doors."

Belatedly Ryre understood why the boy had been running from tavern to tavern. He turned on the taverner, snarling—but at once four sword-points pricked his neck. The points, a lethal collar, urged him out onto the wharf.

The procession and the bared swords closed around him. His captors unbelted their robes, which they had gathered up in order to pursue him. The gliding robes helped muffle the advance of the procession. Ryre was silent too: not from awe, but because all his being was alert for a chance to make his escape.

If he so much as moved his head to ease his cramped neck, a sword-point drew his blood. At least they had been unable to remove his armor, whose leaves would simply tighten about him unless he first relaxed. He trudged onward, a puppet strung by its neck. Vases swung their lights, and made the town sway. Houses floated by, rocking with shadow, locking up fear. The flapping was closer, and sounded impatient.

Soon they entered the forest. At the edge of the town, robed men had seized vases; the light groped amid the gigantic leaves, or wandered away vaguely into the reaches of the forest. This was not the road Ryre had followed, and which he had assumed to be the sole track. Where did this road lead, and to what evil purpose?

The multitude of trees rose above him. They glistened like pillars of a submerged temple, secret and threatening. Smells of warm luxuriance and decay oppressed him. Huge dim leaves twitched as stored rain fell; the dark dripping avenues sounded like an infinity of moist caves. Somewhere was a leathery fluttering sluggish and restless. Once he had heard such a clamor deep in a cave that stank of beasts and blood.

Far down the leafy tunnel the dimness was shifting. It fluttered pallidly. Ahead the leathery restlessness grew louder, peremptory. Sword-points bit into Ryre's neck. Were his captors ensuring that he could not escape, or making him the scapegoat of their own fears?

They prodded him forward into the open. As he stumbled from beneath the trees, he saw that the pale stirring was only of moonlight and shade. The moon had risen above distant forested mountains, and showed him a wide glade, bare except for unstable shadows. Above the trees hovered a host of dry eager flapping.

Ryre felt a sword reach for his jugular vein. He tensed: if he was to die here, he'd leave a few agonizing memories among his captors. But the sword relaxed as the slave-driver said gloating "Save him for last. Let him watch."

The trussed victims were carried into the glade. Ryre saw how hastily they were dropped, and how the robed men scurried out of the glade, glancing fearfully at the sky. Despite the size of the procession, there were only four victims. One did not struggle—because he was already dead, Ryre saw; he looked days dead. Presumably this rite served as funeral in Gaxanoi.

All at once the flapping was violent above the glade. Ryre could not lift his head to see, but he glimpsed nightmare shadows roaming over the ground. "Now," the slave-driver hissed.

As swords rose to tap his veins, Ryre sprang. He had slumped a little, bending his knees, as though crushed by despair. Now he leapt to his full height, a head taller than any of them, and launched himself at the slave-driver. Sword-points ripped tracks down his neck—but his soldiers knocked two blades aside, while the others thudded against his armor, bruising his torso. Before the man's exultant grin had time to collapse into panic, Ryre had smashed his fist into the slave-driver's face.

The man staggered backwards into the glade, flailing the air with his sword, and fell. The shock failed to jar the hilt from his grasp. Ryre rushed at him to grapple for the weapon. The sword sprang up. Had Ryre not dodged aside, he would have been emasculated.

The hooded men hung back, daunted by the flapping. How much time had Ryre to gain himself a weapon? The sound of great dry wings descended; shadows swallowed the glade. As he circled the prone man, staying just out of reach of the sweeps of the sword while he tried to dizzy his victim, Ryre glanced up—and gasped, appalled.

Flapping down from the pale sky, in a flock which stank of caverns and worse, came wings. Their span was greater than the spread of his arms. They were the blotchy white of decay; between their bony fingers, skin fluttered lethargically as drowned sails. All this was frightful

—but there was no body to speak of between each pair of wings, only a whitish rope of flesh thin as a child's arm. Yet as a pair of wings sailed down near him, Ryre saw a mouth gape along the whole length of the scrawny object. Its lips resembled a split in fungus, and it was crammed with teeth.

The slave-driver scrabbled backwards towards the trees, mumbling in terror. One pair of wings settled on a bound victim, like a carelessly flung shroud; then they rose, lifting their prey towards the moon. Ryre's spirit sickened, for the mouth was embedded in the length of the man's chest. The lips worked, sucking.

Enraged and dismayed, Ryre forced his adversary away from the trees. But neither could Ryre flee that way, for the shade bristled with swords. The man twisted on the ground, moaning—then made a vicious lunge with his sword. It was too violent. It hurled the sword from his grip, to impale the ground beside Ryre.

Ryre seized the hilt. Now he could defend himself as best he might, though the weapon was less well-balanced than his own, and heavier. He heard the thud of another sword, thrown to his adversary. The watchers barred the way into the forest. They intended the man to finish Ryre rather than risk combat themselves.

Somewhere behind him, far too numerous and close, Ryre heard wings. They would be enough to contend with when he tried to cross the glade. Before the slave-driver could reach the thrown sword, a slash of Ryre's blade hamstrung him.

Ryre was turning, ready to dash for the far side of the glade, when a shadow engulfed the earth around him. He had no time to react before he was flung to the ground. Once, on board ship, he had been crushed by a fallen sail. He was as helpless now—but this burden felt as though it had been dragged from a swamp. A stench as of something dead and disinterred filled his nostrils. Though he had clung to the sword, his sword-arm was pinned down, useless. He could only snarl and writhe impotently as teeth bit through his armor and fastened in his back, beside his spine.

He felt the lips tear his armor like paper, widening the gap. He lay in wait, and forced himself to suffer the sucking of the mouth embedded in his flesh. As soon as the wings lifted him, he began to chop at the nearest. But they were tougher than his armor. The sword hardly marked them.

He was being lifted, as he might have caught up an infant. The glade whirled away below him; the forest was a moonlit whirlpool, dizzying. He felt himself dangling from teeth clenched deep in his flesh. He hacked at the wings haphazardly and frenziedly—until he felt the sword grow heavier. The feaster was draining his strength with his blood.

The shrieks of the slave-driver afforded Ryre grim satisfaction. He saw the man borne upward struggling by avid wings. Then the sight dwindled; Ryre's wings were carrying him above the trees. He hurled himself about, trying to force the wings towards the leaves, to entangle them. But he could not control their flight; he was merely wasting his strength.

The forest plummeted below him. Deafening winds grabbed his breath. A chill seized him—because of the giddy height, or the leathery fans of wings, or the ebbing of his vitality? The swaying moon steadied; it seemed unnaturally close, perhaps because the wings crowded the sky with its color.

Beneath him, the world consisted of nothing but trees. The shrunken forest drifted by, a dense mosaic formed by countless concentric patterns of leaves. It looked unreal; his sense of perspective was floating away, into something like a dream. Among the flock of wings, a few seed-bearing leaves glided by.

Was the mouth poisoning him as well as drinking his blood? Perhaps, for as his wings swooped higher he was possessed by a kind of insidious delirium. He felt he had sprouted wings and obeyed his dreams. They had transformed him. No longer was he doomed to earthbound plodding. He was a creature of the air, with only the approaching moon, the gliding leaves, the rest of his flock for companions.

A glimpse of that flock pierced his delirium. Around him airborne mouths gaped, hungry for the leavings. His wings lifted him greedily. They were gaining height thanks to his blood, and because he was growing lighter. The other feeding pairs of wings rose exultantly. As their victims turned moon-pale, the gorged wings glowed blotchily pink. Like remains in a web, the victims hardly struggled now.

All at once Ryre saw his chance. The moon swayed like a spider's cocoon shaken by the gusts of the wings; the dwarfed forest looked insubstantial as the blanched sky. Sly waves of vertiginous ecstasy crept over him, blurring his vision further. He had seen a broad leaf gliding towards him. If it drifted sufficiently close…

It did, and at once was impaled by an upward thrust of his sword. The additional burden had no effect on his headlong flight, but that was not his plan. Instead, Ryre thrust the leaf among the fingertips of one wing, to hinder them. The wing struggled; off balance, the feaster dipped towards the trees—and the leaf ripped, almost wrenching the sword from his grasp. He had to cling to the hilt with both hands to prevent the weapon from falling with the torn leaf.

He grew frenzied. Ramming the sword into his belt, he seized the bony arms of the wings, either to break them or to wrench the mouth out of his flesh. Why had he waited so long? Though his muscles trembled with his gathered strength, the wings brushed his hands aside. In any case he would achieve only a fall to his death; yet he preferred a clean death to suffering the hunger of the wings.

Ahead, he could see their lair, a blotch of darkness, roughly circular and perhaps a hundred yards wide, among the trees. Wings circled above its rim, like witches dancing a delirious ritual. Was it another glade? As the foremost pair of burdened wings dropped its victim—the bound corpse—into the circle, Ryre saw that the lair was a pit.

His own wings bore him helplessly closer. He glimpsed the depths, and nausea giddied him. He clutched the sword-hilt. Rather than fall conscious into that pit, he would take his own life. Even that ultimate hopelessness was preferable to what waited below.

The rocky sides of the pit were dry. The place resembled the socket of a skull, a desiccated cavity amid the profusion of forest. Its floor was invisible, for the pit was piled with skeletons, tangled indistinguishably. Some of the bones were awesomely gigantic. Atop the pile lay the dropped corpse, as though on a mockery of a pyre.

As Ryre watched aghast, the enormous bony heap stirred. The corpse toppled down its slope. Had the surrounding fecundity possessed the jumble of skeletons, united them into a monstrous parody of life? Ryre's brain whirled, bereft of sense. Then he saw what was crawling out from beneath the bones.

Very slowly and feebly, old wings emerged. They were discolored as corpses, and looked as though they should have died long ago. A stench of decay welled upward. Dust, no doubt from skeletons, clung to the wings. The groping reminded him of worms in meat.

They clambered on their fingertips over the bones towards the corpse. They resembled pairs of senile hands, skeletal and webbed. Their lips sagged open, exposing teeth and stumps of teeth. The wings fumbled blindly up the shifting heap; they slid back and clambered again. One by one they reached the corpse and fastened on it. Soon it was entirely covered by a heaving of wings, which divided their victim raggedly and crawled away with their prizes.

Ryre dragged his sword free. The burdened wings hovered above the rim. He knew they were draining their victims before dropping the remnants into the pit. He saw the slave-driver fall, clenched and empty.

The sword felt leaden. Ryre clutched the hilt with his other hand, in case it fell from his enfeebled fingers. Then, snarling at his vindictive fate, he turned the point towards his belly. He meant to drive the blade upwards. Mouths hovered close to him, baring their teeth. He hoped he was weakened enough to die quickly.

Then—though perhaps it would serve only to make his death more ironic—he glimpsed his chance. Was it worth trying? Might he not use up his strength, and be unable even to die cleanly? But he refused to die while he yet had a chance to fight. Without warning he lunged with the sword at the nearest pair of empty wings, and stabbed at the mouth.

He felt the sword pierce flesh within the lips. Yes, the flesh was vulnerable there! He dug the blade deeper, embedding it—and the hilt was almost torn from his hands as the wings flapped convulsively. He managed to keep hold, though his agonized fingers were audibly straining. The hilt was his last hold on life.

Then, as he had prayed inarticulately might happen, the wounded wings became entangled with his own. The leathery struggle caged him; he choked on gusts of decay. He was falling amid the tangle of wings. But as he glimpsed the landscape he roared, enraged by the taunts of his fate. He was falling straight into the pit.

His rage twisted the sword deep in the flesh of the mouth. He heard and felt the teeth grind on the blade; he clung grimly to the flailing hilt. The uninjured mouth writhed in his own flesh. For a moment the struggling wings disengaged. He was borne upward, over the rim of the pit.

A few trees sailed by, close enough to grab, though they were withered, and might break. In any case, he dared not let go of the sword. He soared away from the pit, above the denser forest. His strength was still dwindling; the hilt shifted dangerously in his hands. He had no time to choose his moment. Closer to the pit than he would have wished, he dragged the blade towards him with all his remaining force, and entangled the wings.

Convulsed by their struggles, the hilt smashed against his fingers, bruising them. He felt his back tear as the embedded teeth gnashed. But the wings had ensnared one another, and were falling towards the trees.

They crashed through the leaves. Cupped rain inundated them. Ryre was deafened by the battle of wings and the ripping of leaves. The trunks grew close here, as though to wall off the aridity of the pit. The wings smashed through another flooded layer, and were caught between trunks. Ryre snarled with gasping mirth as he heard the struggling fingers break.

Still the canopy of leaves gave way. The twitching wings continued to fall. Ryre let go of the sword and embracing a trunk, swung his body with all the violence he could summon. He felt skeletal fingers break. Even then the mouth refused to let go of his flesh. Not until he and the wings had crashed through the lowest leaves to the ground did the teeth part, jarred open by the shock of the fall.

Half-stunned and giddy with the draining, Ryre nonetheless forced himself to his feet. The pairs of wings were hobbling away in the direction of the unseen pit. He wrenched his sword out of the injured mouth and pursued them, stabbing and hacking. The wings would not die. Though he chopped at the joints of the fingers, and thrust the blade again and again into the mouths, the wings still dragged themselves unevenly towards their lair. Long after he had exhausted the last of his strength and was sitting propped against a tree, with the sword dug into the ground before him to prevent his toppling forward, he heard a ragged flapping and saw pale things crawling lopsidedly away from him, into the dark.

THE PIT OF WINGS

He pressed his back against a drooping leaf, which was cool as balm. His back felt raw, and withered as a mummy's, but seemed to be losing little blood. He dozed, waiting for the dawn and for a hint of his strength to return to him. Nearby there might be leaves whose healing power was greater. He could hear the serpentine denizens of the forest worming their way through the dark arcades. Surely one would be stupid enough to come within reach of his blade. When he could, he would walk—and if his wanderings took him towards Gaxanoi, a few buildings might blaze and a few chains break.

Black God's Kiss

C. L. Moore (1911-1987)

They brought in Joiry's tall commander, struggling between two men-at-arms who tightly gripped the ropes which bound their captive's mailed arms. They picked their way between mounds of dead as they crossed the great hall toward the dais where the conqueror sat, and twice they slipped a little in the blood that spattered the flags. When they came to a halt before the mailed figure on the dais, Joiry's commander was breathing hard, and the voice that echoed hollowly under the helmet's confines was hoarse with fury and despair.

Guillaume the conqueror leaned on his mighty sword, hands crossed on its hilt, grinning down from his height upon the furious captive before him. He was a big man, Guillaume, and he looked bigger still in his spattered armor. There was blood on his hard, scarred face, and he was grinning a white grin that split his short, curly beard glitteringly. Very splendid and very dangerous he looked, leaning on his great sword and smiling down upon fallen Joiry's lord, struggling between the stolid men-at-arms.

"Unshell me this lobster," said Guillaume in his deep, lazy voice. "We'll see what sort of face the fellow has who gave us such a battle. Off with his helmet, you."

But a third man had to come up and slash the straps which held the iron helmet on, for the struggles of Joiry's commander were too fierce, even with bound arms, for either of the guards to release their hold. There was a moment of sharp struggle; then the straps parted and the helmet rolled loudly across the flagstones.

Guillaume's white teeth clicked on a startled oath. He stared. Joiry's lady glared back at him from between her captors, wild red hair tousled, wild lion-yellow eyes ablaze.

"God curse you!" snarled the lady of Joiry between clenched teeth. "God blast your black heart!"

Guillaume scarcely heard her. He was still staring, as most men stared when they first set eyes upon Jirel of Joiry. She was tall as most men, and as savage as the wildest of them, and the fall of Joiry was bitter enough to break her heart as she stood snarling curses up at the tall conqueror. The face above her mail might not have been fair in a woman's head-dress, but in the steel setting of her armor it had a biting, sword-edge beauty as keen as the flash of blades. The red hair was short upon her high, defiant head, and the yellow blaze of her eyes held fury as a crucible holds fire.

Guillaume's stare melted into a slow smile. A little light kindled behind his eyes as he swept the long, strong lines of her with a practiced gaze. The smile broadened, and suddenly he burst into full-throated laughter, a deep bull bellow of amusement and delight.

"By the Nails!" he roared. "Here's welcome for the warrior! And what forfeit d'ye offer, pretty one, for your life?"

She blazed a curse at him.

"So? Naughty words for a mouth so fair, my lady. Well, we'll not deny you put up a gallant battle. No man could have done better, and many have done worse. But against Guillaume—" He inflated his splendid chest and grinned down at her from the depths of his jutting beard. "Come to me, pretty one," he commanded. "I'll wager your mouth is sweeter than your words."

Jirel drove a spurred heel into the shin of one guard and twisted from his grip as he howled, bringing up an iron knee into the abdomen of the other. She had writhed from their grip and made three long strides toward the door before Guillaume caught her. She felt his arms closing about her from behind, and lashed out with both spiked heels in a futile assault upon his leg armor, twisting like a maniac, fighting with her knees and spurs, straining hopelessly at the ropes which bound her arms. Guillaume laughed and whirled her round, grinning down into the blaze of her yellow eyes. Then deliberately he set a fist under her chin and tilted her mouth up to his. There was a cessation of her hoarse curses.

"By Heaven, that's like kissing a sword-blade," said Guillaume, lifting his lips at last.

Jirel choked something that was mercifully muffled as she darted her head sidewise, like a serpent striking, and sank her teeth into his neck. She missed the jugular by a fraction of an inch.

Guillaume said nothing, then. He sought her head with a steady hand, found it despite her wild writhing, sank iron fingers deep into the hinges of her jaw, forcing her teeth relentlessly apart. When he had her free he glared down into the yellow hell of her eyes for an instant. The blaze of them was hot enough to scorch his scarred face. He grinned and lifted his ungauntleted hand, and with one heavy blow in the face he knocked her half-way across the room. She lay still upon the flags.

II

Jirel opened her yellow eyes upon darkness. She lay quiet for a while, collecting her scattered thoughts. By degrees it came back to her, and she muffled upon her arm a sound that was half curse and half sob. Joiry had fallen. For a time she lay rigid in the dark, forcing herself to the realization.

The sound of feet shifting on stone nearby brought her out of that particular misery. She sat up cautiously, feeling about her to determine in what part of Joiry its liege lady was imprisoned. She knew that the sound she had heard must be a sentry, and by the dank smell of the darkness that she was underground. In one of the little dungeon cells, of course. With careful quietness she got to her feet, muttering a curse as her head reeled for an instant and then began to throb. In the utter dark she felt around the cell. Presently she came to a little wooden stool in a corner, and was satisfied. She gripped one leg of it with firm fingers and made her soundless way around the wall until she had located the door.

The sentry remembered, afterward, that he had heard the wildest shriek for help which had ever rung in his ears, and he remembered unbolting the door. Afterward, until they found him lying inside the locked cell with a cracked skull, he remembered nothing.

Jirel crept up the dark stairs of the north turret, murder in her heart. Many little hatreds she had known in her life, but no such blaze as this. Before her eyes in the night she could see Guillaume's scornful, scarred face laughing, the little jutting beard split with the whiteness of his mirth. Upon her mouth she felt the remembered weight of his, about her the strength of his arms. And such a blast of hot fury came over her that she reeled a little and clutched at the wall for support. She went on in a haze of red anger, and something like madness burning in her brain as a resolve slowly took shape out of the chaos of her hate. When that thought came to her she paused again, mid-step upon the stairs, and was conscious of a little coldness blowing over her. Then it was gone, and she shivered a little, shook her shoulders and grinned wolfishly, and went on. By the stars she could see through the arrow-slits in the wall it must be near to midnight. She went softly on the stairs, and she encountered no one. Her little tower room at the top was empty. Even the straw pallet where the serving-wench slept had not been used that night. Jirel got herself out of her armor alone, somehow, after much striving and twisting. Her doeskin shirt was stiff with sweat and stained blood. She tossed it disdainfully into a corner. The fury in her eyes had cooled now to a contained and secret flame. She smiled to herself as she slipped a fresh shirt of doeskin over her tousled red head and donned a brief tunic of link-mail. On her legs she buckled the greaves of some forgotten legionary, relic of the not long past days when Rome still ruled the world. She thrust a dagger through her belt and took her own long two-handed sword bare-bladed in her grip. Then she went down the stairs again.

She knew there must have been revelry and feasting in the great hall that night, and by the silence hanging so heavily now she was sure that most of her enemies lay still in drunken slumber, and she experienced a swift regret for the gallons of her good French wine so wasted. And the thought flashed through her head that a determined woman with a sharp sword might work some little damage among the drunken sleepers before she was overpowered. But she put that idea by, for Guillaume would have posted sentries to spare, and she must not give her secret freedom so fruitlessly.

Down the dark stairs she went, and crossed one corner of the vast central hall whose darkness she was sure hid wine-deadened sleepers, and so into the lesser dimness of the rough little chapel that Joiry boasted. She had been sure she would find Father Gervase there, and she was not mistaken. He rose from his knees before the altar, dark in his robe, the starlight through the narrow window shining upon his tonsure.

"My daughter!" he whispered. "My daughter! How have you escaped? Shall I find you a mount? If you can pass the sentries you should be in your cousin's castle by daybreak."

She hushed him with a lifted hand.

"No," she said. "It is not outside I go this night. I have a more perilous journey even than that to make. Shrive me, father."

He stared at her. "What is it?"

She dropped to her knees before him and gripped the rough cloth of his habit with urgent fingers.

"Shrive me, I say! I go into hell tonight to pray the devil for a weapon, and it may be I shall not return."

Gervase bent and gripped her shoulders with hands that shook.

"Look at me!" he demanded. "Do you know what you're saying? You go—"

"Down!" She said it firmly. "Only you and I know that passage, father—and not even we can be sure of what lies beyond.

271

But to gain a weapon against that man I would venture into perils even worse than that."

"If I thought you meant it," he whispered, "I would waken Guillaume now and give you into his arms. It would be a kinder fate, my daughter."

"It's that I would walk through hell to escape," she whispered back fiercely. "Can't you see? Oh, God knows I'm not innocent of the ways of light loving—but to be any man's fancy, for a night or two, before he snaps my neck or sells me into slavery—and above all, if that man were Guillaume! Can't you understand?"

"That would be shame enough," nodded Gervase. "But think, Jirel! For that shame there is atonement and absolution, and for that death the gates of heaven open wide. But this other—Jirel, Jirel, never through all eternity may you come out, body or soul, if you venture—down!"

She shrugged.

"To wreak my vengeance upon Guillaume I would go if I knew I should burn in hell forever."

"But Jirel, I do not think you understand. This is a worse fate than the depths of hellfire. This is—this is beyond all the bounds of the hells we know. And I think Satan's hottest flames were the breath of paradise, compared to what may befall there."

"I know. Do you think I'd venture down if I could not be sure? Where else would I find such a weapon as I need, save outside God's dominion?"

"Jirel, you shall not!"

"Gervase, I go! Will you shrive me?" The hot yellow eyes blazed into his, lambent in the starlight.

After a moment he dropped his head. "You are my lady. I will give you God's blessing, but it will not avail you—there."

III

She went down into the dungeons again. She went down a long way through utter dark, over stones that were oozy and odorous with moisture, through blackness that had never known the light of day. She might have been a little afraid at other times, but that steady flame of hatred burning behind her eyes was a torch to light the way, and she could not wipe from her memory the feel of Guillaume's arms about her, the scornful press of his lips on her mouth. She whimpered a little, low in her throat, and a hot gust of hate went over her.

In the solid blackness she came at length to a wall, and she set herself to pulling the loose stones from this with her free hand, for she would not lay down the sword. They had never been laid in mortar, and they came out easily. When the way was clear she stepped through and found her feet upon a downward-sloping ramp of smooth stone. She cleared the rubble away from the hole in the wall, and enlarged it enough for a quick passage; for when she came back this way—if she did—it might well be that she would come very fast.

At the bottom of the slope she dropped to her knees on the cold floor and felt about. Her fingers traced the outline of a circle, the veriest crack in the stone. She felt until she found the ring in its center. That ring was of the coldest metal she had ever known, and the smoothest. She could put no name to it. The daylight had never shown upon such metal.

She tugged. The stone was reluctant, and at last she took her sword in her teeth and put both hands to the lifting. Even then it taxed the limit of her strength, and she was strong as many men. But at last it rose, with the strangest sighing sound, and a little prickle of gooseflesh rippled over her.

Now she took the sword back into her hand and knelt on the rim of the invisible blackness below. She had gone this path once before and once only, and never thought to find any necessity in life strong enough to drive her down again. The way was the strangest she had ever known. There was, she thought, no such passage in all the world save here. It had not been built for human feet to travel. It had not been built for feet at all. It was a narrow, polished shaft that corkscrewed round and round. A snake might have slipped in and gone shooting down, round and round in dizzy circles—but no snake on earth was big enough to fill that shaft. No human travelers had worn the sides of the spiral so smooth, and she did not care to speculate on what creatures had polished it so, through what ages of passage.

She might never have made that first trip down, nor anyone after her, had not some unknown human hacked the notches which made it possible to descend slowly; that is, she thought it must have been a human. At any rate, the notches were roughly shaped for hands and feet, and spaced not too far apart; but who and when and how she could not even guess. As to the beings who made the shaft, in long-forgotten ages—well, there were devils on earth before man, and the world was very old.

She turned on her face and slid feet-first into the curving tunnel. That first time she and Gervase had gone down in sweating terror of what lay below, and with devils tugging at their heels. Now she slid easily, not bothering to find toeholds, but slipping swiftly round and round the long spirals with only her hands to break the speed when she went too fast. Round and round she went, round and round.

It was a long way down. Before she had gone very far the curious dizziness she had known before came over her again, a dizziness not entirely induced by the spirals she whirled around, but a deeper, atomic unsteadiness as if not only she but also the substances around her were shifting. There was something queer about the angles of those curves. She was no scholar in geometry or aught else, but she felt intuitively that the bend and the slant of the way she went were somehow outside any other angles or bends she had ever known. They led into the unknown and the dark, but it seemed to her obscurely that they led into deeper darkness and mystery than the merely physical, as if, though she could not put it clearly even into thoughts, the peculiar and exact lines of the tunnel had been carefully angled to lead through poly-dimensional space as well as through the underground—perhaps through time, too. She did not know she was thinking such things; but all about her was a blurred dizziness as she shot down and round, and she knew that the way she went took her on a stranger journey than any other way she had ever traveled.

Down and down. She was sliding fast, but she knew how long it would be. On that first trip they had taken alarm as the passage spiraled so endlessly and with thoughts of the long climb back had tried to stop before it was too late. They had found it impossible. Once embarked, there was no halting. She had tried, and such waves of sick blurring had come over her that she came near to unconsciousness. It was as if she had tried to halt some inexorable process of nature, half finished. They could only go on. The very atoms of their bodies shrieked in rebellion against a reversal of the change.

And the way up, when they returned, had not been difficult. They had had visions of a back-breaking climb up interminable curves, but again the uncanny difference of those angles from those they knew was manifested. In a queer way they seemed to defy gravity, or perhaps led through some way outside the power of it. They had been sick and dizzy on the return, as on the way down, but through the clouds of that confusion it had seemed to them that they slipped as easily up the shaft as they had gone down; or perhaps that, once in the tunnel, there was neither up nor down.

The passage leveled gradually. This was the worst part for a human to travel, though it must have eased the speed of whatever beings the shaft was made for. It was too narrow for her to turn in, and she had to lever herself face down and feet first, along the horizontal smoothness of the floor, pushing with her hands. She was glad when her questing heels met open space and she slid from the mouth of the shaft and stood upright in the dark.

Here she paused to collect herself. Yes, this was the beginning of the long passage she and Father Gervase had traveled on that long-ago journey of exploration. By the veriest accident they had found the place, and only the veriest bravado had brought them thus far. He had gone on a greater distance than she—she was younger then, and more amenable to authority—and had come back white-faced in the torchlight and hurried her up the shaft again.

She went on carefully, feeling her way, remembering what she herself had seen in the darkness a little farther on, wondering in spite of herself, and with a tiny catch at her heart, what it was that had sent Father Gervase so hastily back. She had never been entirely satisfied with his explanations. It had been about here—or was it a little farther on? The stillness was like a roaring in her ears.

Then ahead of her the darkness moved. It was just that—a vast, imponderable shifting of the solid dark. Jesu! This was new! She gripped the cross at her throat with one hand and her sword-hilt with the other. Then it was upon her, striking like a hurricane, whirling her against the walls and shrieking in her ears like a thousand wind-devils—a wild cyclone of the dark that buffeted her mercilessly and tore at her flying hair and raved in her ears with the myriad voices of all lost things crying in the night. The voices were piteous in their terror and loneliness. Tears came to her eyes even as she shivered with nameless dread, for the whirlwind was alive with a dreadful instinct, an animate thing sweeping through the dark of the underground; an unholy thing that made her flesh crawl even though it touched her to the heart with its pitiful little lost voices wailing in the wind where no wind could possibly be.

And then it was gone. In that one flash of an instant it vanished. Only in the heart of it could one hear the sad little voices wailing or the wild shriek of the wind. She found herself standing stunned, her sword yet gripped futilely in one hand and the tears running down her face. Poor little lost voices, wailing. She wiped the tears away with a shaking hand and set her teeth hard against the weakness of reaction that flooded her. Yet it was a good five minutes before she could force herself on. After a few steps her knees ceased to tremble.

The floor was dry and smooth underfoot. It sloped a little downward, and she wondered into what unplumbed deeps she had descended by now. The silence had fallen heavily again, and she found herself straining for some other sound than the soft padding of her own boots. Then her foot slipped in sudden wetness. She bent, exploring fingers outstretched, feeling without reason that the wetness would be red if she could see it. But her fingers traced an immense outline of a footprint—splayed and three-toed like a frog's, but of monster size. It was a fresh footprint. She had a vivid flash of memory—that thing she had glimpsed in the torchlight on the other trip down. But she had light then, and now she was blind in the dark, the creature's natural habitat...

For a moment she was not Jirel of Joiry, vengeful fury on the trail of a devilish weapon, but a frightened woman alone in the unholy dark. That memory had been so vivid...Then she saw Guillaume's scornful, laughing face again, the little beard dark along the line of his jaw, the strong teeth white with his laughter; and something hot and sustaining swept over her like a thin flame, and she was Joiry again, vengeful and resolute. She went on more slowly, her sword swinging in a semicircle before every third step, that she might not be surprised too suddenly by some nightmare monster clasping her in smothering arms. But the flesh crept upon her unprotected back.

The smooth passage went on and on. She could feel the cold walls on either hand, and her upswung sword grazed the roof. It was like crawling through some worm's tunnel, blindly under the weight of countless tons of earth. She felt the pressure of it above and about her, overwhelming, and found herself praying that the end of this tunnel-crawling might come soon, whatever the end might bring.

But when it came it was a stranger thing than she had ever dreamed. Abruptly she felt the immense, imponderable oppression cease. No longer was she conscious of the tons of earth pressing about her. The walls had fallen away and her feet struck a sudden rubble instead of the smooth floor. But the darkness that had bandaged her eyes was changed too, indescribably. It was no longer darkness, but void; not an absence of light, but simple nothingness. Abysses opened around her, yet she could see nothing. She only knew that she stood at the threshold of some immense space, and sensed nameless things about her, and battled vainly against that nothingness which was all her straining eyes could see. And at her throat something constricted painfully.

She lifted her hand and found the chain of her crucifix taut and vibrant around her neck. At that she smiled a little grimly, for she began to understand. The crucifix. She found her hand shaking despite herself, but she unfastened the chain and dropped the cross to the ground. Then she gasped.

All about her, as suddenly as the awakening from a dream, the nothingness had opened out into undreamed-of distances. She stood high on a hilltop under a sky spangled with strange stars. Below she caught a glimpse of misty plains and valleys with mountain peaks rising far away. And at her feet a ravening circle of small, slavering, blind things leaped with clashing teeth.

They were obscene and hard to distinguish against the darkness of the hillside, and the noise they made was revolting. Her sword swung up of itself, almost, and slashed furiously at the little dark horrors leaping up around her legs. They died squashily, splattering her bare thighs with unpleasantness, and after a few had gone silent under the blade the rest fled into the dark with quick, frightened pantings, their feet making a queer splashing noise on the stones.

Jirel gathered a handful of the coarse grass which grew there and wiped her legs of the obscene splatters, looking about with quickened breath upon this land so unholy that one who bore a cross might not even see it. Here, if anywhere, one might find a weapon such as she sought. Behind her in the hillside was the low tunnel opening from which she had emerged. Overhead the strange stars shone. She did not recognize a single constellation, and if the brighter sparks were planets they were strange ones, tinged with violet and green and

278

yellow. One was vividly crimson, like a point of fire. Far out over the rolling land below she could discern a mighty column of light. It did not blaze, nor illuminate the dark about it. It cast no shadows. It simply was a great pillar of luminance towering high in the night. It seemed artificial—perhaps man-made, though she scarcely dared hope for men here.

She half expected, despite her brave words, to come out upon the storied and familiar red-hot pave of hell, and this pleasant, starlit land surprised her and made her more wary. The things that built the tunnel could not have been human. She had no right to expect men here. She was a little stunned by finding open sky so far underground, though she was intelligent enough to realize that however she had come, she was not underground now. No cavity in the earth could contain this starry sky. She came of a credulous age, and she accepted her surroundings without too much questioning, though she was a little disappointed, if the truth were known, in the pleasantness of the mistily starlit place. The fiery streets of hell would have been a likelier locality in which to find a weapon against Guillaume.

When she had cleansed her sword on the grass and wiped her legs clean, she turned slowly down the hill. The distant column beckoned her, and after a moment of indecision she turned toward it. She had no time to waste, and this was the likeliest place to find what she sought.

The coarse grass brushed her legs and whispered round her feet. She stumbled now and then on the rubble, for the hill was steep, but she reached the bottom without mishap, and struck out across the meadows toward that blaze of far-away brilliance. It seemed to her that she walked more lightly, somehow. The grass scarcely bent underfoot, and she found she could take long sailing strides like one who runs with wings on his heels. It felt like a dream. The gravity pull of the place must have been less than she was accustomed to, but she only knew that she was skimming over the ground with amazing speed.

BLACK GOD'S KISS

Traveling so, she passed through the meadows over the strange, coarse grass, over a brook or two that spoke endlessly to itself in a curious language that was almost speech, certainly not the usual gurgle of earth's running water. Once she ran into a blotch of darkness, like some pocket or void in the air, and struggled through gasping and blinking outraged eyes. She was beginning to realize that the land was not so innocently normal as it looked.

On and on she went, at that surprising speed, while the meadow skimmed past beneath her flying feet and gradually the light drew nearer. She saw now that it was a round tower of sheeted luminance, as if walls of solid flame rose up from the ground. Yet it seemed to be steady, nor did it cast any illumination upon the sky.

Before much time had elapsed, with her dream-like speed she had almost reached her goal. The ground was becoming marshy underfoot, and presently the smell of swamps rose in her nostrils and she saw that between her and the light stretched a belt of unstable ground tufted with black reedy grass. Here and there she could see dim white blotches moving. They might be beasts, or only wisps of mist. The starlight was not very illuminating.

She began to pick her way carefully across the black, quaking morasses. Where the tufts of grass rose she found firmer ground, and she leaped from clump to clump with that amazing lightness, so that her feet barely touched the black ooze. Here and there slow bubbles rose through the mud and broke thickly. She did not like the place.

Half-way across, she saw one of the white blotches approaching her with slow, erratic movements. It bumped along unevenly, and at first she thought it might be inanimate, its approach was so indirect and purposeless. Then it blundered nearer, with that queer bumpy gait, making sucking noises in the ooze and splashing as it came. In the starlight she saw suddenly what it was, and for an instant her heart paused and sickness rose overwhelmingly in her throat. It was a woman—a beautiful woman whose white bare body had the curves and loveliness of some marble statue. She was crouching like a frog, and as Jirel watched in stupefaction she straightened her legs abruptly and leaped as a frog leaps, only more clumsily, falling forward into the ooze a little distance beyond the watching woman. She did not seem to see Jirel. The mud-spattered face was blank. She blundered on through the mud in awkward leaps. Jirel watched until the woman was no more than a white wandering blur in the dark, and above the shock of that sight pity was rising, and uncomprehending resentment against whatever had brought so lovely a creature into this—into blundering in frog leaps aimlessly through the mud, with empty mind and blind, staring eyes. For the second time that night she knew the sting of unaccustomed tears as she went on.

The sight, though, had given her reassurance. The human form was not unknown here. There might be leathery devils with hoofs and horns, such as she still half expected, but she would not be alone in her humanity; though if all the rest were as piteously mindless as the one she had seen—she did not follow that thought. It was too unpleasant. She was glad when the marsh was past and she need not see any longer the awkward white shapes bumping along through the dark.

She struck out across the narrow space which lay between her and the tower. She saw now that it was a building, and that the light composed it. She could not understand that, but she saw it. Walls and columns outlined the tower, solid sheets of light with definite boundaries, not radiant. As she came nearer she saw that it was in motion, apparently spurting up from some source underground as if the light illuminated sheets of water rushing upward under great pressure. Yet she felt intuitively that it was not water, but incarnate light.

She came forward hesitantly, gripping her sword. The area around the tremendous pillar was paved with something black and smooth that did not reflect the light. Out of it sprang the up-rushing walls of brilliance with their sharply defined edges. The magnitude of the thing dwarfed her to infinitesimal size. She stared upward with undazzled eyes, trying to understand. If there could be such a thing as solid, no-radiating light, this was it.

IV

She was very near under the mighty tower before she could see the details of the building clearly. They were strange to her—great pillars and arches around the base, and one stupendous portal, all molded out of the rushing, prisoned light. She turned toward the opening after a moment, for the light had a tangible look. She did not believe she could have walked through it even had she dared.

When that tremendous portal arched over her she peered in, affrighted by the very size of the place. She thought she could hear the hiss and spurt of the light surging upward. She was looking into a mighty globe inside, a hall shaped like the interior of a bubble, though the curve was so vast she was scarcely aware of it. And in the very center of the globe floated a light. Jirel blinked. A light, dwelling in a bubble of light. It glowed there in midair with a pale, steady flame that was somehow alive and animate, and brighter than the serene illumination of the building, for it hurt her eyes to look at it directly.

She stood on the threshold and stared, not quite daring to venture in. And as she hesitated a change came over the light. A flash of rose tinged its pallor. The rose deepened and darkened until it took on the color of blood. And the shape underwent strange changes. It lengthened, drew itself out narrowly, split at the bottom into two branches, put out two tendrils from the top. The blood-red paled again, and the light somehow lost its brilliance, receded into the depths of the thing that was forming. Jirel clutched her sword and forgot to breathe, watching. The light was taking on the shape of a human being—of a woman—of a tall woman in mail, her red hair tousled and her eyes staring straight into the duplicate eyes at the portal...

"Welcome," said the Jirel suspended in the center of the globe, her voice deep and resonant and clear in spite of the distance between them. Jirel at the door held her breath, wondering and afraid. This was herself, in every detail, a mirrored Jirel—that was it, a Jirel mirrored upon a surface which blazed and smoldered with barely repressed light, so that the eyes gleamed with it and the whole figure seemed to hold its shape by an effort, only by that effort restraining itself from resolving into pure, formless light again. But the voice was not her own. It shook and resounded with a knowledge as alien as the light-built walls. It mocked her. It said:

"Welcome! Enter into the portals, woman!"

She looked up warily at the rushing walls about her. Instinctively she drew back.

"Enter, enter!" urged the mocking voice from her own mirrored lips. And there was a note in it she did not like.

"Enter!" cried the voice again, this time a command.

Jirel's eyes narrowed. Something intuitive warned her back, and yet—she drew the dagger she had thrust in her belt and with a quick motion she tossed it into the great globe-shaped hall. It struck the floor without a sound, and a brilliant light flared up around it, so brilliant she could not look upon what was happening; but it seemed to her that the knife expanded, grew large and nebulous and ringed with dazzling light. In less time than it takes to tell, it had faded out of sight as if the very atoms which composed it had flown apart and dispersed in the golden glow of that mighty bubble. The dazzle faded with the knife, leaving Jirel staring dazedly at a bare floor.

Jirel found her voice with an effort.

"I seek a weapon," she said, "a weapon against a man I so hate that upon earth there is none terrible enough for my need."

"You so hate him, eh?" mused the voice.

"With all my heart!"

"With all your heart!" echoed the voice, and there was an undernote of laughter in it that she did not understand. The echoes of that mirth ran round and round the great globe. Jirel felt her cheeks burn with resentment against some implication in the derision which she could not put a name to. When the echoes of the laugh had faded the voice said indifferently:

"Give the man what you find at the black temple in the lake. I make you a gift of it."

The lips that were Jirel's twisted into a laugh of purest mockery; then all about that figure so perfectly her own the light flared out. She saw the outlines melting fluidly as she turned her dazzled eyes away. Before the echoes of that derision had died, a blinding, formless light burned once more in the midst of the bubble.

Jirel turned and stumbled away under the mighty column of the tower, a hand to her dazzled eyes. Not until she had reached the edge of the black, unreflecting circle that paved the ground around the pillar did she realize that she knew no way of finding the lake where her weapon lay. And not until then did she remember how fatal it is said to be to accept a gift from a demon. Buy it, or earn it, but never accept the gift. Well—she must surely be damned by now, for having ventured down of her own will into this curious place for such a purpose as hers. The soul can be lost but once.

She turned her face up to the strange stars and wondered in what direction her course lay. The sky looked blankly down upon her with its myriad meaningless eyes. A star fell as she watched, and in her superstitious soul she took it for an omen, and set off boldly over the dark meadows in the direction where the bright streak had faded. No swamps guarded the way here, and she was soon skimming along over the grass with that strange, dancing gait that the lightness of the place allowed her. And as she went she was remembering, as from long ago in some other far world, a man's arrogant mirth and the press of his mouth on hers. Hatred bubbled up hotly within her and broke from her lips in a little savage laugh of anticipation. What dreadful thing awaited her in the temple of the lake, what punishment from hell to be loosed by her own hands upon Guillaume? And though her soul was the price it cost her, she would count it a fair bargain if she could drive that laughter from his mouth and bring terror into the eyes that mocked her.

Thoughts like these kept her company for a long way upon her journey. She did not think to be lonely or afraid in the uncanny darkness across which no shadows fell from that mighty column behind her. The unchanging meadows flew past underfoot, lightly as meadows in a dream. It might almost have been that the earth moved instead of herself, so effortlessly did she go. She was sure now that she was heading in the right direction, for two more stars had fallen in the same arc across the sky.

The meadows were not untenanted. Sometimes she felt presences near her in the dark, and once she ran full-tilt into a nest of little yapping horrors like those on the hill-top. They lunged up about her with clicking teeth, mad with a blind ferocity, and she swung her sword in frantic circles, sickened by the noise of them lunging splashily through the grass and splattering her sword with their deaths. She beat them off and went on, fighting her own sickness, for she had never known anything quite so nauseating as these little monstrosities.

She crossed a brook that talked to itself in the darkness with that queer murmuring which came so near to speech, and a few strides beyond it she paused suddenly, feeling the ground tremble with the rolling thunder of hoofbeats approaching. She stood still, searching the dark anxiously, and presently the earth-shaking beat grew louder and she saw a white blur flung wide across the dimness to her left, and the sound of hoofs deepened and grew. Then out of the night swept a herd of snow-white horses. Magnificently they ran, manes tossing, tails streaming, feet pounding a rhythmic, heart-stirring roll along the ground. She caught her breath at the beauty of their motion. They swept by a little distance away, tossing their heads, spurning the ground with scornful feet.

But as they came abreast of her she saw one blunder and stumble against the next, and that one shook his head bewilderedly; and suddenly she realized that they were blind—all running so splendidly in a deeper dark than even she groped through. And she saw too their coats were roughened with sweat, and foam dripped from their lips, and their nostrils were flaring pools of scarlet. Now and again one stumbled from pure exhaustion. Yet they ran, frantically, blindly through the dark, driven by something outside their comprehension.

As the last one of all swept by her, sweat-crusted and staggering, she saw him toss his head high, spattering foam, and whinny shrilly to the stars. And it seemed to her that the sound was strangely articulate. Almost she heard the echoes of a name—"Julienne! Julienne!"—in that high, despairing sound. And the incongruity of it, the bitter despair, clutched at her heart so sharply that for the third time that night she knew the sting of tears.

The dreadful humanity of that cry echoed in her ears as the thunder died away. She went on, blinking back the tears for the beautiful blind creature, staggering with exhaustion, calling a girl's name hopelessly from a beast's throat into the blank darkness wherein it was forever lost.

Then another star fell across the sky, and she hurried ahead, closing her mind to the strange, incomprehensible pathos that made an undertone of tears to the starry dark of this land. And the thought was growing in her mind that, though she had come into no brimstone pit where horned devils pranced over flames, yet perhaps it was after all a sort of hell through which she ran.

Presently in the distance she caught a glimmer of something bright. The ground dipped after that and she lost it, and skimmed through a hollow where pale things wavered away from her into the deep dark. She never knew what they were, and was glad. She hoped it was a lake, and ran more swiftly.

It was a lake—a lake that could never have existed outside some obscure hell like this. She stood on the brink doubtfully, wondering if this could be the place the light-devil had meant. Black, shining water stretched out before her, heaving gently with a motion unlike that of any water she had ever seen before. And in the depths of it, like fireflies caught in ice, gleamed myriad small lights. They were fixed there immovably, not stirring with the motion of the water. As she watched, something hissed above her and a streak of light split the dark air. She looked up in time to see something bright curving across the sky to fall without a splash into the water, and small ripples of phosphorescence spread sluggishly toward the shore, where they broke at her feet with the queerest whispering sound, as if each succeeding ripple spoke the syllable of a word.

She looked up, trying to locate the origin of the falling lights, but the strange stars looked down upon her blankly. She bent and stared down into the center of the spreading ripples, and where the thing had fallen she thought a new light twinkled through the water. She could not determine what it was, and after a curious moment she gave the question up and began to cast about for the temple the light-devil had spoken of.

After a moment she thought she saw something dark in the center of the lake, and when she had stared for a few minutes it gradually became clearer, an arch of darkness against the starry background of water. It might be a temple. She strolled slowly along the brim of the lake, trying to get a closer view of it, for the thing was no more than a darkness against the spangles of light, like some void in the sky where no stars shine. And presently she stumbled over something in the grass.

She looked down with startled yellow eyes, and saw a strange, indistinguishable darkness. It had solidity to the feel but scarcely to the eye, for she could not quite focus upon it. It was like trying to see something that did not exist save as a void, a darkness in the grass. It had the shape of a step, and when she followed with her eyes she saw that it was the beginning of a dim bridge stretching out over the lake, narrow and curved and made out of nothingness. It seemed to have no surface, and its edges were difficult to distinguish from the lesser gloom surrounding it. But the thing was tangible—an arch carved out of the solid dark—and it led out in the direction she wished to go. For she was naïvely sure now that the dim blot in the center of the lake was the temple she was searching for. The falling stars had guided her, and she could not have gone astray.

So she set her teeth and gripped her sword and put her foot upon the bridge. It was rock-firm under her, but scarcely more than a foot or so wide, and without rails. When she had gone a step or two she began to feel dizzy; for under her the water heaved with a motion that made her head swim, and the stars twinkled eerily in its depths. She dared not look away for fear of missing her footing on the narrow arch of darkness. It was like walking a bridge flung across the void, the stars underfoot and nothing but an unstable strip of nothingness to bear her up. Halfway across, the heaving of the water and the illusion of vast, constellated spaces beneath and the look her bridge had of being no more than empty space ahead, combined to send her head reeling; and as she stumbled on, the bridge seemed to be wavering with her, swinging in gigantic arcs across the starry void below.

Now she could see the temple more closely, though scarcely more than an outlined emptiness against the star-crowded brilliance behind it, etching its arches and columns of blankness upon the twinkling waters. The bridge came down in a long dim swoop to its doorway. Jirel took the last few yards at a reckless run and stopped breathless under the arch that made the temple's vague doorway. She stood there panting and staring about narroweyed, sword poised in her hand. For though the place was empty and very still she felt a presence even as she set her foot upon the floor of it.

She was staring about a little space of blankness in the starry lake. It seemed to be no more than that. She could see the walls and columns where they were outlined against the water and where they made darknesses in the star-flecked sky, but where there was only dark behind them she could see nothing. It was a tiny place, no more than a few square yards of emptiness upon the face of the twinkling waters. And in its center an image stood.

She stared at it in silence, feeling a curious compulsion growing within her, like a vague command from something outside herself. The image was of some substance of nameless black, unlike the material which composed the building, for even in the dark she could see it clearly. It was a semi-human figure, crouching forward with outthrust head, sexless and strange. Its one central eye was closed as if in rapture, and its mouth was pursed for a kiss. And though it was but an image and without even the semblance of life, she felt unmistakably the presence of something alive in the temple, something so alien and innominate that instinctively she drew away.

She stood there for a full minute, reluctant to enter the place where so alien a being dwelt, half conscious of that voiceless compulsion growing up within her. And slowly she became aware that all the lines and angles of the halfseen building were curved to make the image their center and focus. The very bridge swooped its long arc to complete the centering. As she watched, it seemed to her that through the arches of the columns even the stars in the lake and sky were grouped in patterns which took the image for their focus. Every line and curve in the dim world seemed to sweep round toward the squatting thing before her with its closed eye and expectant mouth.

Gradually the universal focusing of lines began to exert its influence upon her. She took a hesitant step forward without realizing the motion. But that step was all the dormant urge within her needed. With her one motion forward the compulsion closed down upon her with whirlwind impetuosity. Helplessly she felt herself advancing, helplessly with one small, sane portion of her mind she realized the madness that was gripping her, the blind, irresistible urge to do what every visible line in the temple's construction was made to compel. With stars swirling around her she advanced across the floor and laid her hands upon the rounded shoulders of the image—the sword, forgotten, making a sort of accolade against its hunched neck—and lifted her red head and laid her mouth blindly against the pursed lips of the image.

In a dream she took that kiss. In a dream of dizziness and confusion she seemed to feel the iron-cold lips stirring under hers. And through the union of that kiss—warm-blooded woman with image of nameless stone—through the meeting of their mouths something entered into her very soul; something cold and stunning;

something alien beyond any words. It lay upon her shuddering soul like some frigid weight from the void, a bubble holding something unthinkably alien and dreadful. She could feel the heaviness of it upon some intangible part of her that shrank from the touch. It was like the weight of remorse or despair, only far colder and stranger and—somehow—more ominous, as if this weight were but the egg from which things might hatch too dreadful to put even into thoughts.

The moment of the kiss could have been no longer than a breath's space, but to her it was timeless. In a dream she felt the compulsion falling from her at last. In a dim dream she dropped her hands from its shoulders, finding the sword heavy in her grasp and staring dully at it for a while before clarity began its return to her cloudy mind. When she became completely aware of herself once more she was standing with slack body and dragging head before the blind, rapturous image, that dead weight upon her heart as dreary as an old sorrow, and more coldly ominous than anything she could find words for.

And with returning clarity the most staggering terror came over her, swiftly and suddenly—terror of the image and the temple of darkness, and the coldly spangled lake and of the whole, wide, dim, dreadful world about her. Desperately she longed for home again, even the red fury of hatred and the press of Guillaume's mouth and the hot arrogance of his eyes again. Anything but this. She found herself running without knowing why. Her feet skimmed over the narrow bridge lightly as a gull's wings dipping the water. In a brief instant the starry void of the lake flashed by beneath her and the solid earth was underfoot. She saw the great column of light far away across the dark meadows and beyond it a hill-top rising against the stars. And she ran.

She ran with terror at her heels and devils howling in the wind her own speed made. She ran from her own curiously alien body, heavy with its weight of inexplicable doom. She passed through the hollow where pale things wavered away, she fled over the uneven meadows in a frenzy of terror. She ran and ran, in those long light bounds the lesser gravity allowed her, fleeter than a deer, and her own panic choked in her throat and that weight upon her soul dragged at her too drearily for tears. She fled to escape it, and could not; and the ominous certainty that she carried something too dreadful to think of grew and grew.

For a long while she skimmed over the grass tirelessly, wing-heeled, her red hair flying. The panic died after a while, but that sense of heavy disaster did not die. She felt somehow that tears would ease her, but something in the frigid darkness of her soul froze her tears in the ice of that gray and alien chill.

And gradually, through the inner dark, a fierce anticipation took form in her mind. Revenge upon Guillaume! She had taken from the temple only a kiss, so it was that which she must deliver to him. And savagely she exulted in the thought of what that kiss would release upon him, unsuspecting. She did not know, but it filled her with fierce joy to guess. She had passed the column and skirted the morass where the white, blundering forms still bumped along awkwardly through the ooze, and was crossing the coarse grass toward the nearing hill when the sky began to pale along the horizon. And with that pallor a fresh terror took hold upon her, a wild horror of daylight in this unholy land. She was not sure if it was the light itself she so dreaded, or what that light would reveal in the dark stretches she had traversed so blindly—what unknown horrors she had skirted in the night. But she knew instinctively that if she valued her sanity she must be gone before the light had risen over the land. And she redoubled her efforts, spurring her wearying limbs to yet more skimming speed. But it would be a lost race, for already the stars were blurring out, and a flush of curious green was broadening along the sky, and around her the air was turning a vague, unpleasant gray.

She toiled up the steep hillside breathlessly. When she was half-way up, her own shadow began to take form upon the rocks, and it was unfamiliar and dreadfully significant of something just outside her range of understanding.

She averted her eyes from it, afraid that at any moment the meaning might break upon her outraged brain.

She could see the top of the hill above her, dark against the paling sky, and she toiled up in frantic haste, clutching her sword and feeling that if she had to look in the full light upon the dreadful little abominations that had snapped around her feet when she first emerged she would collapse into screaming hysteria.

The cave-mouth yawned before her, invitingly black, a refuge from the dawning light behind her. She knew an almost irresistible desire to turn and look back from this vantage-point across the land she had traversed, and gripped her sword hard to conquer the pervasive longing. There was a scuffling in the rocks at her feet, and she set her teeth in her underlip and swung viciously in brief arcs, without looking down. She heard small squeakings and the splashy sound of feet upon the stones, and felt her blade sheer thrice through semi-solidity, to the click of little vicious teeth. Then they broke and ran off over the hillside, and she stumbled on, choking back the scream that wanted so fiercely to break from her lips.

She fought that growing desire all the way up to the cave-mouth, for she knew that if she gave way she would never cease shrieking until her throat went raw.

Blood was trickling from her bitten lip with the effort at silence when she reached the cave. And there, twinkling upon the stones, lay something small and bright and dearly familiar. With a sob of relief she bent and snatched up the crucifix she had torn from her throat when she came out into this land. And as her fingers shut upon it a vast, protecting darkness swooped around her. Gasping with relief, she groped her way the step or two that separated her from the cave.

Dark lay like a blanket over her eyes, and she welcomed it gladly, remembering how her shadow had lain so awfully upon the hillside as she climbed, remembering the first rays of savage sunlight beating upon her shoulders. She stumbled through the blackness, slowly getting control again over her shaking body and laboring lungs, slowly stilling the panic that the dawning day had roused so inexplicably within her. And as that terror died, the dull weight upon her spirit became strong again. She had all but forgotten it in her panic, but now the impending and unknown dreadfulness grew heavier and more oppressive in the darkness of the underground, and she groped along in a dull stupor of her own depression, slow with the weight of the strange doom she carried.

Nothing barred her way. In the dullness of her stupor she scarcely realized it, or expected any of the vague horrors that peopled the place to leap out upon her. Empty and unmenacing, the way stretched before her blindly stumbling feet. Only once did she hear the sound of another presence—the rasp of hoarse breathing and the scrape of a scaly hide against the stone—but it must have been outside the range of her own passage, for she encountered nothing.

When she had come to the end and a cold wall rose up before her, it was scarcely more than automatic habit that made her search along it with groping hand until she came to the mouth of the shaft. It sloped gently up into the dark. She crawled in, trailing her sword, until the rising incline and lowering roof forced her down upon her face. Then with toes and fingers she began to force herself up the spiral, slippery way.

Before she had gone very far she was advancing without effort, scarcely realizing that it was against gravity she moved. The curious dizziness of the shaft had come over her, the strange feeling of change in the very substance of her body, and through the cloudy numbness of it she felt herself sliding round and round the spirals, without effort. Again, obscurely, she had the feeling that in the peculiar angles of this shaft was neither up nor down. And for a long while the dizzy circling went on.

When the end came at last, and she felt her fingers gripping the edge of that upper opening which lay beneath the floor of Joiry's lowest dungeons, she heaved herself up wearily and lay for awhile on the cold floor in the dark, while slowly the clouds of dizziness passed from her mind, leaving only that ominous weight within. When the darkness had ceased to circle about her, and the floor steadied, she got up dully and swung the cover back over the opening, her hands shuddering from the feel of the cold, smooth ring which had never seen daylight.

When she turned from this task she was aware of the reason for the lessening in the gloom around her. A guttering light outlined the hole in the wall from which she had pulled the stones—was it a century ago? The brilliance all but blinded her after her long sojourn through blackness, and she stood there awhile, swaying a little, one hand to her eyes, before she went out into the familiar torchlight she knew waited her beyond. Father Gervase, she was sure, anxiously waited her return. But even he had not dared to follow her through the hole in the wall, down to the brink of the shaft.

Somehow she felt that she should be giddy with relief at this safe homecoming, back to humanity again. But as she stumbled over the upward slope toward light and safety she was conscious of no more than the dullness of whatever unreleased horror it was which still lay so ominously upon her stunned soul.

She came through the gaping hole in the masonry into the full glare of torches awaiting her, remembering with a wry inward smile how wide she had made the opening in anticipation of flight from something dreadful when she came back that way. Well, there was no flight from the horror she bore within her. It seemed to her that her heart was slowing, too, missing a beat now and then and staggering like a wary runner.

She came out into the torchlight, stumbling with exhaustion, her mouth scarlet from the blood of her bitten lip and her bare greaved legs and bare sword-blade foul with the deaths of those little horrors that swarmed around the cave-mouth. From the tangle of red hair her eyes stared out with a bleak, frozen inward look, as of one who has seen nameless things. That keen, steel-bright beauty which had been hers was as dull and fouled as her sword-blade, and at the look in her eyes Father Gervase shuddered and crossed himself.

V

They were waiting for her in an uneasy group—the priest anxious and dark, Guillaume splendid in the torchlight, tall and arrogant, a handful of men-at-arms holding the guttering lights and shifting uneasily from one foot to the other. When she saw Guillaume the light that flared up in her eyes blotted out for a moment the bleak dreadfulness behind them, and her slowing heart leaped like a spurred horse, sending the blood riotously through her veins. Guillaume, magnificent in his armor, leaning upon his sword and staring down at her from his scornful height, the little black beard jutting. Guillaume, to whom Joiry had fallen. Guillaume.

That which she carried at the core of her being was heavier than anything else in the world, so heavy she could scarcely keep her knees from bending, so heavy her heart labored under its weight. Almost irresistibly she wanted to give way beneath it, to sink down and down under the crushing load, to lie prone and vanquished in the ice-gray, bleak place she was so dimly aware of through the clouds that were rising about her. But there was Guillaume, grim and grinning, and she hated him so very bitterly—she must make the effort. She must, at whatever cost, for she was coming to know that death lay in wait for her if she bore this burden long, that it was a two-edged weapon which could strike at its wielder if the blow were delayed too long. She knew this through the dim mists that were thickening in her brain, and she put all her strength into the immense effort it cost to cross the floor toward him. She stumbled a little, and made one faltering step and then another, and dropped her sword with a clang as she lifted her arms to him.

He caught her strongly, in a hard, warm clasp, and she heard his laugh triumphant and hateful as he bent his head to take the kiss she was raising her mouth to offer. He must have seen, in that last moment before their lips met, the savage glare of victory in her eyes, and been startled. But he did not hesitate. His mouth was heavy upon hers.

BLACK GOD'S KISS

It was a long kiss. She felt him stiffen in her arms. She felt a coldness in the lips upon hers, and slowly the dark weight of what she bore lightened, lifted, cleared away from her cloudy mind. Strength flowed back through her richly. The whole world came alive to her once more. Presently she loosed his slack arms and stepped away, looking up into his face with a keen and dreadful triumph upon her own.

She saw the ruddiness of him draining away, and the rigidity of stone coming over his scarred features. Only his eyes remained alive, and there was torment in them, and understanding. She was glad—she had wanted him to understand what it cost to take Joiry's kiss unbidden. She smiled thinly into his tortured eyes, watching. And she saw something cold and alien seeping through him, permeating him slowly with some unnamable emotion which no man could ever have experienced before. She could not name it, but she saw it in his eyes—some dreadful emotion never made for flesh and blood to know, some iron despair such as only an unguessable being from the gray, formless void could ever have felt before—too hideously alien for any human creature to endure. Even she shuddered from the dreadful, cold bleakness looking out of his eyes, and knew as she watched that there must be many emotions and many fears and joys too far outside man's comprehension for any being of flesh to undergo, and live. Grayly she saw it spreading through him, and the very substance of his body shuddered under that iron weight.

And now came a visible, physical change. Watching, she was aghast to think that in her own body and upon her own soul she had borne the seed of this dreadful flowering, and did not wonder that her heart had slowed under the unbearable weight of it. He was standing rigidly with arms half bent, just as he stood when she slid from his embrace. And now great shudders began to go over him, as if he were wavering in the torchlight, some grey-faced wraith in armor with torment in his eyes. She saw the sweat beading his forehead. She saw a trickle of blood from his mouth, as if he had bitten through his lip in the agony of this new, incomprehensible emotion. Then a last shiver went over him violently, and he flung up his head, the little curling beard jutting ceilingward and the muscles of his strong throat corded, and from his lips broke a long, low cry of such utter, inhuman strangeness that Jirel felt coldness rippling through her veins and she put up her hands to her ears to shut it out. It meant something—it expressed some dreadful emotion that was neither sorrow nor despair nor anger, but infinitely alien and infinitely sad. Then his long legs buckled at the knees and he dropped with a clatter of mail and lay still on the stone floor.

They knew he was dead. That was unmistakable in the way he lay. Jirel stood very still, looking down upon him, and strangely it seemed to her that all the lights in the world had gone out. A moment before he had been so big and vital, so magnificent in the torchlight—she could still feel his kiss upon her mouth, and the hard warmth of his arms...

Suddenly and blindingly it came upon her what she had done. She knew now why such heady violence had flooded her whenever she thought of him—knew why the light-devil in her own form had laughed so derisively—knew the price she must pay for taking a gift from a demon. She knew that there was no light anywhere in the world, now that Guillaume was gone.

Father Gervase took her arm gently. She shook him off with an impatient shrug and dropped to one knee beside Guillaume's body, bending her head so that the red hair fell forward to hide her tears.

The Fortress Unvanquishable, Save For Sacnoth

Lord Dunsany (1878-1957)

In a wood older than record, a foster brother of the hills, stood the village of Allathurion; and there was peace between the people of that village and all the folk who walked in the dark ways of the wood, whether they were human or of the tribes of the beasts or of the race of the fairies and the elves and the little sacred spirits of trees and streams. Moreover, the village people had peace among themselves and between them and their lord, Lorendiac. In front of the village was a wide and grassy space, and beyond this the great wood again, but at the back the trees came right up to the houses, which, with their great beams and wooden framework and thatched roofs, green with moss, seemed almost to be a part of the forest.

Now in the time I tell of, there was trouble in Allathurion, for of an evening fell dreams were wont to come slipping through the tree trunks and into the peaceful village; and they assumed dominion of men's minds and led them in watches of the night through the cindery plains of Hell. Then the magician of that village made spells against those fell dreams; yet still the dreams came flitting through the trees as soon as the dark had fallen, and led men's minds by night into terrible places and caused them to praise Satan openly with their lips.

THE FORTRESS UNVANQUISHABLE, SAVE FOR SACNOTH

And men grew afraid of sleep in Allathurion. And they grew worn and pale, some through the want of rest, and others from fear of the things they saw on the cindery plains of Hell.

Then the magician of the village went up into the tower of his house, and all night long those whom fear kept awake could see his window high up in the night glowing softly alone. The next day, when the twilight was far gone and night was gathering fast, the magician went away to the forest's edge, and uttered there the spell that he had made. And the spell was a compulsive, terrible thing, having a power over evil dreams and over spirits of ill; for it was a verse of forty lines in many languages, both living and dead, and had in it the word wherewith the people of the plains are wont to curse their camels, and the shout wherewith the whalers of the north lure the whales shoreward to be killed, and a word that causes elephants to trumpet; and every one of the forty lines closed with a rhyme for "wasp."

And still the dreams came flitting through the forest, and led men's souls into the plains of Hell. Then the magician knew that the dreams were from Gaznak. Therefore he gathered the people of the village, and told them that he had uttered his mightiest spell—a spell having power over all that were human or of the tribes of the beasts; and that since it had not availed the dreams must come from Gaznak, the greatest magician among the spaces of the stars. And he read to the people out of the Book of Magicians, which tells the comings of the comet and foretells his coming again. And he told them how Gaznak rides upon the comet, and how he visits Earth once in every two hundred and thirty years, and makes for himself a vast, invincible fortress and sends out dreams to feed on the minds of men, and may never be vanquished but by the sword Sacnoth.

And a cold fear fell on the hearts of the villagers when they found that their magician had failed them.

Then spake Leothric, son of the Lord Lorendiac, and twenty years old was he: "Good Master, what of the sword Sacnoth?"

And the village magician answered: "Fair Lord, no such sword as yet is wrought, for it lies as yet in the hide of Tharagavverug, protecting his spine."

Then said Leothric: "Who is Tharagavverug, and where may he be encountered?"

And the magician of Allathurion answered: 'He is the dragon-crocodile who haunts the Northern marshes and ravages the homesteads by their marge. And the hide of his back is of steel, and his under parts are of iron; but along the midst of his back, over his spine, there lies a narrow strip of unearthly steel. This strip of steel is Sacnoth, and it may be neither cleft nor molten, and there is nothing in the world that may avail to break it, nor even leave a scratch upon its surface. It is of the length of a good sword, and of the breadth thereof. Shouldst thou prevail against Tharagavverug, his hide may be melted away from Sacnoth in a furnace; but there is only one thing that may sharpen Sacnoth's edge, and this is one of Tharagavverug's own steel eyes; and the other eye thou must fasten to Sacnoth's hilt, and it will watch for thee. But it is a hard task to vanquish Tharagavverug, for no sword can pierce his hide; his back cannot be broken, and he can neither burn nor drown. In one way only can Tharagavverug die, and that is by starving.'

Then sorrow fell upon Leothric, but the magician spoke on:

"If a man drive Tharagavverug away from his food with a stick for three days, he will starve on the third day at sunset. And though he is not vulnerable, yet in one spot he may take hurt, for his nose is only of lead. A sword would merely lay bare the uncleavable bronze beneath, but if his nose be smitten constantly with a stick he will always recoil from the pain, and thus may Tharagavverug, to left and right, be driven away from his food."

Then Leothric said: "What is Tharagavverug's food?"

And the magician of Allathurion said: "His food is men."

But Leothric went straightway thence, and cut a great staff from a hazel tree, and slept early that evening. But the next morning, awaking from troubled dreams, he arose before the dawn, and, taking with him provisions for five days, set out through the forest northwards towards the marshes. For some hours he moved through the gloom of the forest, and when he emerged from it the sun was above the horizon shining on pools of water in the waste land. Presently he saw the claw-marks of Tharagavverug deep in the soil, and the track of his tail between them like a furrow in a field. Then Leothric followed the tracks till he heard the bronze heart of Tharagavverug before him, booming like a bell.

And Tharagavverug, it being the hour when he took the first meal of the day, was moving towards a village with his heart tolling. And all the people of the village were come out to meet him, as it was their wont to do; for they abode not the suspense of awaiting Tharagavverug and of hearing him sniffing brazenly as he went from door to door, pondering slowly in his metal mind what habitant he should choose. And none dared to flee, for in the days when the villagers fled from Tharagavverug, he, having chosen his victim, would track him tirelessly, like a doom. Nothing availed them against Tharagavverug. Once they climbed the trees when he came, but Tharagavverug went up to one, arching his back and leaning over slightly, and rasped against the trunk until it fell. And when Leothric came near, Tharagavverug saw him out of one of his small steel eyes and came towards him leisurely, and the echoes of his heart swirled up through his open mouth. And Leothric stepped sideways from his onset, and came between him and the village and smote him on the nose, and the blow of the stick made a dint in the soft lead. And Tharagavverug swung clumsily away, uttering one fearful cry like the sound of a great church bell that had become possessed of a soul that fluttered upward from the tombs at night—an evil soul, giving the bell a voice. Then he attacked Leothric, snarling, and again Leothric leapt aside, and smote him on the nose with his stick. Tharagavverug uttered like a bell howling. And whenever the dragon-crocodile attacked him, or turned towards the village, Leothric smote him again.

So all day long Leothric drove the monster with a stick, and he drove him farther and farther from his prey, with his heart tolling angrily and his voice crying out for pain.

Towards evening Tharagavverug ceased to snap at Leothric, but ran before him to avoid the stick, for his nose was sore and shining; and in the gloaming the villagers came out and danced to cymbal and psaltery. When Tharagavverug heard the cymbal and psaltery, hunger and anger came upon him, and he felt as some lord might feel who was held by force from the banquet in his own castle and heard the creaking spit go round and round and the good meat crackling on it. And all that night he attacked Leothric fiercely, and oft-times nearly caught him in the darkness; for his gleaming eyes of steel could see as well by night as by day. And Leothric gave ground slowly till the dawn, and when the light came they were near the village again; yet not so near to it as they had been when they encountered, for Leothric drove Tharagavverug farther in the day than Tharagavverug had forced him back in the night. Then Leothric drove him again with his stick till the hour came when it was the custom of the dragon-crocodile to find his man. One third of his man he would eat at the time he found him, and the rest at noon and evening. But when the hour came for finding his man a great fierceness came on Tharagavverug, and he grabbed rapidly at Leothric, but could not seize him, and for a long while neither of them would retire. But at last the pain of the stick on his leaden nose overcame the hunger of the dragon-crocodile, and he turned from it howling. From that moment Tharagavverug weakened. All that day Leothric drove him with his stick, and at night both held their ground; and when the dawn of the third day was come the heart of Tharagavverug beat slower and fainter. It was as though a tired man was ringing a bell. Once Tharagavverug nearly seized a frog, but Leothric snatched it away just in time. Towards noon the dragon-crocodile lay still for a long while, and Leothric stood near him and leaned on his trusty stick. He was very tired and sleepless, but had more leisure now for eating his provisions. With Tharagavverug the end was coming fast, and in the afternoon his breath came hoarsely, rasping in his throat. It was as the sound of many huntsmen blowing blasts on horns, and towards evening his breath came faster but fainter, like the sound of a hunt going furious to the distance and dying away, and he made desperate rushes towards the village; but Leothric still leapt about him, battering his leaden nose. Scarce audible now at all was the sound of his heart: it was like a church bell tolling beyond hills for the death of someone unknown and far away. Then the sun set and flamed in the village windows, and a chill went over the world, and in some small garden a woman sang; and Tharagavverug lifted up his head and starved, and his life went from his invulnerable body, and Leothric lay down beside him and slept. And later in the starlight the villagers came out and carried Leothric, sleeping, to the village, all praising him in whispers as they went. They laid him down upon a couch in a house, and danced outside in silence, without psaltery or cymbal. And the next day, rejoicing, to Allathurion they hauled the dragon-crocodile. And Leothric went with them, holding his battered staff; and a tall, broad man, who was smith of Allathurion, made a great furnace, and melted Tharagavverug away till only Sacnoth was left, gleaming among the ashes. Then he took one of the small eyes that had been chiseled out, and filed an edge on Sacnoth, and gradually the steel eye wore away facet by facet, but ere it was quite gone it had sharpened redoubtably Sacnoth. But the other eye they set in the butt of the hilt, and it gleamed there bluely.

And that night Leothric arose in the dark and took the sword, and went westwards to find Gaznak; and he went through the dark forest till the dawn, and all the morning and till the afternoon. But in the afternoon he came into the open and saw in the midst of The Land Where No Man Goeth the fortress of Gaznak, mountainous before him, little more than a mile away.

And Leothric saw that the land was marsh and desolate. And the fortress went up all white out of it, with many buttresses, and was broad below but narrowed higher up, and was full of gleaming windows with the light upon them. And near the top of it a few white clouds were floating, but above them some of its pinnacles reappeared. Then Leothric advanced into the marshes, and the eye of Tharagavverug looked out warily from the hilt of Sacnoth; for Tharagavverug had known the marshes well, and the sword nudged Leothric to the right or pulled him to the left away from the dangerous places, and so brought him safely to the fortress walls.

And in the wall stood doors like precipices of steel, all studded with boulders of iron, and above every window were terrible gargoyles of stone; and the name of the fortress shone on the wall, writ large in letters of brass: "The Fortress Unvanquishable, Save For Sacnoth."

Then Leothric drew and revealed Sacnoth, and all the gargoyles grinned, and the grin went flickering from face to face right up into the cloud-abiding gables.

And when Sacnoth was revealed and all the gargoyles grinned, it was like the moonlight emerging from a cloud to look for the first time upon a field of blood, and passing swiftly over the wet faces of the slain that lie together in the horrible night. Then Leothric advanced towards a door, and it was mightier than the marble quarry, Sacremona, from which of old men cut enormous slabs to build the Abbey of the Holy Tears. Day after day they wrenched out the very ribs of the hill until the Abbey was builded, and it was more beautiful than anything in stone. Then the priests blessed Sacremona, and it had rest, and no more stone was ever taken from it to build the houses of men. And the hill stood looking southwards lonely in the sunlight, defaced by that mighty scar. So vast was the door of steel. And the name of the door was The Porte Resonant, the Way of Egress for War.

Then Leothric smote upon the Porte Resonant with Sacnoth, and the echo of Sacnoth went ringing through the halls, and all the dragons in the fortress barked. And when the baying of the remotest dragon had faintly joined in the tumult, a window opened far up among the clouds below the twilit gables, and a woman screamed, and far away in Hell her father heard her and knew that her doom was come.

THE FORTRESS UNVANQUISHABLE, SAVE FOR SACNOTH

And Leothric went on smiting terribly with Sacnoth, and the grey steel of the Porte Resonant, the Way of Egress for War, that was tempered to resist the swords of the world, came away in ringing slices.

Then Leothric, holding Sacnoth in his hand, went in through the hole that he had hewn in the door, and came into the unlit, cavernous hall.

An elephant fled trumpeting. And Leothric stood still, holding Sacnoth. When the sound of the feet of the elephant had died away in the remoter corridors, nothing more stirred, and the cavernous hall was still.

Presently the darkness of the distant halls became musical with the sound of bells, all coming nearer and nearer.

Still Leothric waited in the dark, and the bells rang louder and louder, echoing through the halls, and there appeared a procession of men on camels riding two by two from the interior of the fortress, and they were armed with scimitars of Assyrian make and were all clad with mail, and chain-mail hung from their helmets about their faces, and flapped as the camels moved. And they all halted before Leothric in the cavernous hall, and the camel bells clanged and stopped. And the leader said to Leothric:

"The Lord Gaznak has desired to see you die before him. Be pleased to come with us, and we can discourse by the way of the manner in which the Lord Gaznak has desired to see you die."

And as he said this he unwound a chain of iron that was coiled upon his saddle, and Leothric answered:

"I would fain go with you, for I am come to slay Gaznak."

Then all the camel-guard of Gaznak laughed hideously, disturbing the vampires that were asleep in the measureless vault of the roof. And the leader said:

"The Lord Gaznak is immortal, save for Sacnoth, and weareth armor that is proof even against Sacnoth himself, and hath a sword the second most terrible in the world."

Then Leothric said: "I am the Lord of the sword Sacnoth."

And he advanced towards the camel-guard of Gaznak, and Sacnoth lifted up and down in his hand as though stirred by an exultant pulse. Then the camel-guard of Gaznak fled, and the riders leaned forward and smote their camels with whips, and they went away with a great clamor of bells through colonnades and corridors and vaulted halls, and scattered into the inner darknesses of the fortress. When the last sound of them had died away, Leothric was in doubt which way to go, for the camel-guard was dispersed in many directions, so he went straight on till he came to a great stairway in the midst of the hall. Then Leothric set his foot in the middle of a wide step, and climbed steadily up the stairway for five minutes. Little light was there in the great hall through which Leothric ascended, for it only entered through arrow slits here and there, and in the world outside evening was waning fast. The stairway led up to two folding doors, and they stood a little ajar, and through the crack Leothric entered and tried to continue straight on, but could get no farther, for the whole room seemed to be full of festoons of ropes which swung from wall to wall and were looped and draped from the ceiling. The whole chamber was thick and black with them. They were soft and light to the touch, like fine silk, but Leothric was unable to break any one of them, and though they swung away from him as he pressed forward, yet by the time he had gone three yards they were all about him like a heavy cloak. Then Leothric stepped back and drew Sacnoth, and Sacnoth divided the ropes without a sound, and without a sound the severed pieces fell to the floor. Leothric went forward slowly, moving Sacnoth in front of him up and down as he went. When he was come into the middle of the chamber, suddenly, as he parted with Sacnoth a great hammock of strands, he saw a spider before him that was larger than a ram, and the spider looked at him with eyes that were little, but in which there was much sin, and said:

"Who are you that spoil the labor of years all done to the honor of Satan?"

And Leothric answered: "I am Leothric, son of Lorendiac."

And the spider said: "I will make a rope at once to hang you with."

Then Leothric parted another bunch of strands, and came nearer to the spider as he sat making his rope, and the spider, looking up from his work, said: "What is that sword which is able to sever my ropes?"

And Leothric said: "It is Sacnoth."

Thereat the black hair that hung over the face of the spider parted to left and right, and the spider frowned; then the hair fell back into its place, and hid everything except the sin of the little eyes which went on gleaming lustfully in the dark. But before Leothric could reach him, he climbed away with his hands, going up by one of his ropes to a lofty rafter, and there sat, growling. But clearing his way with Sacnoth, Leothric passed through the chamber, and came to the farther door; and the door being shut, and the handle far up out of his reach, he hewed his way through it with Sacnoth in the same way as he had through the Porte Resonant, the Way of Egress for War. And so Leothric came into a well-lit chamber, where Queens and Princes were banqueting together, all at a great table; and thousands of candles were glowing all about, and their light shone in the wine that the Princes drank and on the huge gold candelabra, and the royal faces were irradiant with the glow, and the white table-cloth and the silver plates and the jewels in the hair of the Queens, each jewel having a historian all to itself, who wrote no other chronicles all his days. Between the table and the door there stood two hundred footmen in two rows of one hundred facing one another. Nobody looked at Leothric as he entered through the hole in the door, but one of the Princes asked a question of a footman, and the question was passed from mouth to mouth by all the hundred footmen till it came to the last one nearest Leothric; and he said to Leothric, without looking at him:

"What do you seek here?"

And Leothric answered: "I seek to slay Gaznak."

And footman to footman repeated all the way to the table: "He seeks to slay Gaznak."

And another question came down the line of footmen: "What is your name?"

And the line that stood opposite took his answer back.

Then one of the Princes said: "Take him away where we shall not hear his screams."

And footman repeated it to footman till it came to the last two, and they advanced to seize Leothric.

Then Leothric showed to them his sword, saying, "This is Sacnoth," and both of them said to the man nearest: "It is Sacnoth;" then screamed and fled away.

And two by two, all up the double line, footman to footman repeated, "It is Sacnoth," then screamed and fled, till the last two gave the message to the table, and all the rest had gone. Hurriedly then arose the Queens and Princes, and fled out of the chamber. And the goodly table, when they were all gone, looked small and disorderly and awry. And to Leothric, pondering in the desolate chamber by what door he should pass onwards, there came from far away the sounds of music, and he knew that it was the magical musicians playing to Gaznak while he slept.

Then Leothric, walking towards the distant music, passed out by the door opposite to the one through which he had cloven his entrance, and so passed into a chamber vast as the other, in which were many women, weirdly beautiful. And they all asked him of his quest, and when they heard that it was to slay Gaznak, they all besought him to tarry among them, saying that Gaznak was immortal, save for Sacnoth, and also that they had need of a knight to protect them from the wolves that rushed round and round the wainscot all the night and sometimes broke in upon them through the moldering oak. Perhaps Leothric had been tempted to tarry had they been human women, for theirs was a strange beauty, but he perceived that instead of eyes they had little flames that flickered in their sockets, and knew them to be the fevered dreams of Gaznak.

THE FORTRESS UNVANQUISHABLE, SAVE FOR SACNOTH

Therefore he said:

"I have a business with Gaznak and with Sacnoth," and passed on through the chamber.

And at the name of Sacnoth those women screamed, and the flames of their eyes sank low and dwindled to sparks.

And Leothric left them, and, hewing with Sacnoth, passed through the farther door.

Outside he felt the night air on his face, and found that he stood upon a narrow way between two abysses. To left and right of him, as far as he could see, the walls of the fortress ended in a profound precipice, though the roof still stretched above him; and before him lay the two abysses full of stars, for they cut their way through the whole Earth and revealed the under sky; and threading its course between them went the way, and it sloped upward and its sides were sheer. And beyond the abysses, where the way led up to the farther chambers of the fortress, Leothric heard the musicians playing their magical tune. So he stepped on to the way, which was scarcely a stride in width, and moved along it holding Sacnoth naked. And to and fro beneath him in each abyss whirred the wings of vampires passing up and down, all giving praise to Satan as they flew. Presently he perceived the dragon Thok lying upon the way, pretending to sleep, and his tail hung down into one of the abysses.

And Leothric went towards him, and when he was quite close Thok rushed at Leothric.

And he smote deep with Sacnoth, and Thok tumbled into the abyss, screaming, and his limbs made a whirring in the darkness as he fell, and he fell till his scream sounded no louder than a whistle and then could be heard no more. Once or twice Leothric saw a star blink for an instant and reappear again, and this momentary eclipse of a few stars was all that remained in the world of the body of Thok. And Lunk, the brother of Thok, who had lain a little behind him, saw that this must be Sacnoth and fled lumbering away. And all the while that he walked between the abysses, the mighty vault of the roof of the fortress still stretched over Leothric's head, all filled

310

with gloom. Now, when the further side of the abyss came into view, Leothric saw a chamber that opened with innumerable arches upon the twin abysses, and the pillars of the arches went away into the distance and vanished in the gloom to left and right.

Far down the dim precipice on which the pillars stood he could see windows small and closely barred, and between the bars there showed at moments, and disappeared again, things that I shall not speak of.

There was no light here except for the great Southern stars that shone below the abysses, and here and there in the chamber through the arches lights that moved furtively without the sound of footfall.

Then Leothric stepped from the way, and entered the great chamber.

Even to himself he seemed but a tiny dwarf as he walked under one of those colossal arches.

The last faint light of evening flickered through a window painted in somber colors commemorating the achievements of Satan upon Earth. High up in the wall the window stood, and the streaming lights of candles lower down moved stealthily away.

Other light there was none, save for a faint blue glow from the steel eye of Tharagavverug that peered restlessly about it from the hilt of Sacnoth. Heavily in the chamber hung the clammy odor of a large and deadly beast.

Leothric moved forward slowly with the blade of Sacnoth in front of him feeling for a foe, and the eye in the hilt of it looking out behind.

Nothing stirred.

If anything lurked behind the pillars of the colonnade that held aloft the roof, it neither breathed nor moved.

The music of the magical musicians sounded from very near.

Suddenly the great doors on the far side of the chamber opened to left and right. For some moments Leothric saw nothing move, and waited clutching Sacnoth. Then Wong Bongerok came towards him, breathing.

This was the last and faithfullest guard of Gaznak, and came from slobbering just now his master's hand.

More as a child than a dragon was Gaznak wont to treat him, giving him often in his fingers tender pieces of man all smoking from his table.

Long and low was Wong Bongerok, and subtle about the eyes, and he came breathing malice against Leothric out of his faithful breast, and behind him roared the armory of his tail, as when sailors drag the cable of the anchor all rattling down the deck.

And well Wong Bongerok knew that he now faced Sacnoth, for it had been his wont to prophesy quietly to himself for many years as he lay curled at the feet of Gaznak.

And Leothric stepped forward into the blast of his breath, and lifted Sacnoth to strike.

But when Sacnoth was lifted up, the eye of Tharagavverug in the butt of the hilt beheld the dragon and perceived his subtlety.

For he opened his mouth wide, and revealed to Leothric the ranks of his sabre teeth, and his leather gums flapped upwards. But while Leothric made to smite at his head, he shot forward scorpion-wise over his head the length of his armored tail. All this the eye perceived in the hilt of Sacnoth, who smote suddenly sideways. Not with the edge smote Sacnoth, for, had he done so, the severed end of the tail had still come hurtling on, as some pine tree that the avalanche has hurled point foremost from the cliff right through the broad breast of some mountaineer. So had Leothric been transfixed; but Sacnoth smote sideways with the flat of his blade, and sent the tail whizzing over Leothric's left shoulder; and it rasped upon his armor as it went, and left a groove upon it. Sideways then at Leothric smote the foiled tail of Wong Bongerok, and Sacnoth parried, and the tail went shrieking up the blade and over Leothric's head. Then Leothric and Wong Bongerok fought sword to tooth, and the sword smote as only Sacnoth can, and the evil faithful life of Wong Bongerok the dragon went out through the wide wound.

Then Leothric walked on past that dead monster, and the

armored body still quivered a little. And for a while it was like all the ploughshares in a county working together in one field behind tired and struggling horses; then the quivering ceased, and Wong Bongerok lay still to rust.

And Leothric went on to the open gates, and Sacnoth dripped quietly along the floor.

By the open gates through which Wong Bongerok had entered, Leothric came into a corridor echoing with music. This was the first place from which Leothric could see anything above his head, for hitherto the roof had ascended to mountainous heights and had stretched indistinct in the gloom. But along the narrow corridor hung huge bells low and near to his head, and the width of each brazen bell was from wall to wall, and they were one behind the other. And as he passed under each the bell uttered, and its voice was mournful and deep, like to the voice of a bell speaking to a man for the last time when he is newly dead. Each bell uttered once as Leothric came under it, and their voices sounded solemnly and wide apart at ceremonious intervals. For if he walked slow, these bells came closer together, and when he walked swiftly they moved farther apart. And the echoes of each bell tolling above his head went on before him whispering to the others. Once when he stopped they all jangled angrily till he went on again.

Between these slow and boding notes came the sound of the magical musicians. They were playing a dirge now very mournfully.

And at last Leothric came to the end of the Corridor of the Bells, and beheld there a small black door. And all the corridor behind him was full of the echoes of the tolling, and they all muttered to one another about the ceremony; and the dirge of the musicians came floating slowly through them like a procession of foreign elaborate guests, and all of them boded ill to Leothric.

The black door opened at once to the hand of Leothric, and he found himself in the open air in a wide court paved with marble. High over it shone the moon, summoned there by the hand of Gaznak.

THE FORTRESS UNVANQUISHABLE, SAVE FOR SACNOTH

There Gaznak slept, and around him sat his magical musicians, all playing upon strings. And, even sleeping, Gaznak was clad in armor, and only his wrists and face and neck were bare.

But the marvel of that place was the dreams of Gaznak; for beyond the wide court slept a dark abyss, and into the abyss there poured a white cascade of marble stairways, and widened out below into terraces and balconies with fair white statues on them, and descended again in a wide stairway, and came to lower terraces in the dark, where swart uncertain shapes went to and fro. All these were the dreams of Gaznak, and issued from his mind, and, becoming gleaming marble, passed over the edge of the abyss as the musicians played. And all the while out of the mind of Gaznak, lulled by that strange music, went spires and pinnacles beautiful and slender, ever ascending skywards. And the marble dreams moved slow in time to the music. When the bells tolled and the musicians played their dirge, ugly gargoyles came out suddenly all over the spires and pinnacles, and great shadows passed swiftly down the steps and terraces, and there was hurried whispering in the abyss.

When Leothric stepped from the black door, Gaznak opened his eyes. He looked neither to left nor right, but stood up at once facing Leothric.

Then the magicians played a deathspell on their strings, and there arose a humming along the blade of Sacnoth as he turned the spell aside. When Leothric dropped not down, and they heard the humming of Sacnoth, the magicians arose and fled, all wailing, as they went, upon their strings.

Then Gaznak drew out screaming from its sheath the sword that was the mightiest in the world except for Sacnoth, and slowly walked towards Leothric; and he smiled as he walked, although his own dreams had foretold his doom. And when Leothric and Gaznak came together, each looked at each, and neither spoke a word; but they smote both at once, and their swords met, and each sword knew the other and from whence he came. And whenever the sword of Gaznak smote on the blade of Sacnoth it rebounded

314

gleaming, as hail from off slated roofs; but whenever it fell upon the armor of Leothric, it stripped it off in sheets. And upon Gaznak's armor Sacnoth fell oft and furiously, but ever he came back snarling, leaving no mark behind, and as Gaznak fought he held his left hand hovering close over his head. Presently Leothric smote fair and fiercely at his enemy's neck, but Gaznak, clutching his own head by the hair, lifted it high aloft, and Sacnoth went cleaving through an empty space. Then Gaznak replaced his head upon his neck, and all the while fought nimbly with his sword; and again and again Leothric swept with Sacnoth at Gaznak's bearded neck, and ever the left hand of Gaznak was quicker than the stroke, and the head went up and the sword rushed vainly under it.

And the ringing fight went on till Leothric's armor lay all round him on the floor and the marble was splashed with his blood, and the sword of Gaznak was notched like a saw from meeting the blade of Sacnoth. Still Gaznak stood unwounded and smiling still.

At last Leothric looked at the throat of Gaznak and aimed with Sacnoth, and again Gaznak lifted his head by the hair; but not at his throat flew Sacnoth, for Leothric struck instead at the lifted hand, and through the wrist of it went Sacnoth whirring, as a scythe goes through the stem of a single flower.

And bleeding, the severed hand fell to the floor; and at once blood spurted from the shoulders of Gaznak and dripped from the fallen head, and the tall pinnacles went down into the earth, and the wide fair terraces all rolled away, and the court was gone like the dew, and a wind came and the colonnades drifted thence, and all the colossal halls of Gaznak fell. And the abysses closed up suddenly as the mouth of a man who, having told a tale, will forever speak no more.

Then Leothric looked around him in the marshes where the night mist was passing away, and there was no fortress nor sound of dragon or mortal, only beside him lay an old man, wizened and evil and dead, whose head and hand were severed from his body.

And gradually over the wide lands the dawn was coming up, and ever growing in beauty as it came, like to the peal of an organ played by a master's hand, growing louder and lovelier as the soul of the master warms, and at last giving praise with all its mighty voice.

Then the birds sang, and Leothric went homeward, and left the marshes and came to the dark wood, and the light of the dawn ascending lit him upon his way. And into Allathurion he came ere noon, and with him brought the evil wizened head, and the people rejoiced, and their nights of trouble ceased.

This is the tale of the vanquishing of The Fortress Unvanquishable, Save For Sacnoth, and of its passing away, as it is told and believed by those who love the mystic days of old.

Others have said, and vainly claim to prove, that a fever came to Allathurion, and went away; and that this same fever drove Leothric into the marshes by night, and made him dream there and act violently with a sword.

And others again say that there hath been no town of Allathurion, and that Leothric never lived.

Peace to them. The gardener hath gathered up this autumn's leaves. Who shall see them again, or who wot of them? And who shall say what hath befallen in the days of long ago?

KEY TO CAVERNS

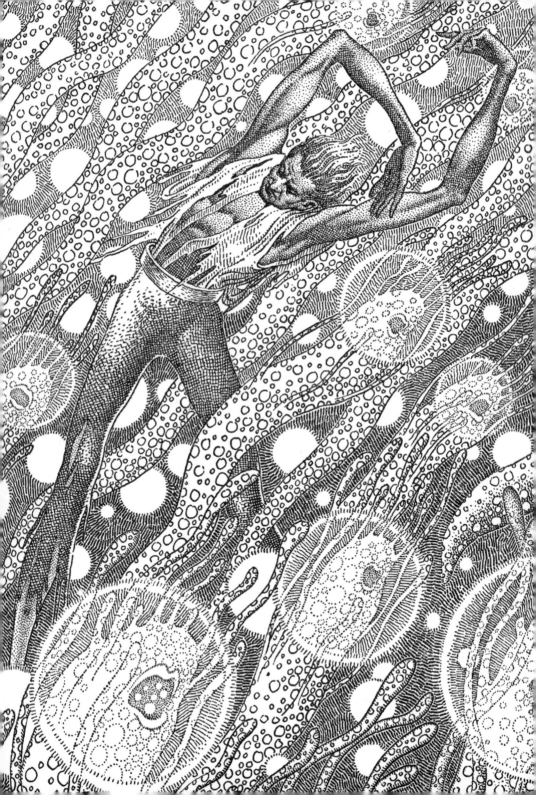

The People Of The Pit

A. Merritt (1884-1943)

North of us a shaft of light shot halfway to the zenith. It came from behind the five peaks. The beam drove up through a column of blue haze whose edges were marked as sharply as the rain that streams from the edges of a thunder cloud. It was like the flash of a searchlight through an azure mist. It cast no shadows.

As it struck upward the summits were outlined hard and black and I saw that the whole mountain was shaped like a hand. As the light silhouetted it, the gigantic fingers stretched, the hand seemed to thrust itself forward. It was exactly as though it moved to push something back. The shining beam held steady for a moment; then broke into myriads of little luminous globes that swung to and fro and dropped gently. They seemed to be searching.

The forest had become very still. Every wood noise held its breath. I felt the dogs pressing against my legs. They too were silent; but every muscle in their bodies trembled, their hair was stiff along their backs and their eyes, fixed on the falling lights, were filmed with the terror glaze. I looked at Anderson. He was staring at the North where once more the beam had pulsed upward. "It can't be the aurora," I spoke without moving my lips. My mouth was as dry as though Lao T'zai had poured his fear dust down my throat.

"If it is I never saw one like it," he answered in the same tone. "Besides who ever heard of an aurora at this time of the year?"

He voiced the thought that was in my own mind.

"It makes me think something is being hunted up there," he said, "an unholy sort of hunt—it's well for us to be out of range."

"The mountain seems to move each time the shaft shoots up," I said. "What's it keeping back, Starr? It makes me think of the frozen hand of cloud that Shan Nadour set before the Gate of Ghouls to keep them in the lairs that Eblis cut for them."

He raised a hand—listening.

From the North and high overhead there came a whispering. It was not the rustling of the aurora, that rushing, crackling sound like the ghosts of winds that blew at Creation racing through the skeleton leaves of ancient trees that sheltered Lilith. It was a whispering that held in it a demand. It was eager. It called us to come up where the beam was flashing. It drew. There was in it a note of inexorable insistence. It touched my heart with a thousand tiny fear-tipped fingers and it filled me with a vast longing to race on and merge myself in the light. It must have been so that Ulysses felt when he strained at the mast and strove to obey the crystal sweet singing of the Sirens.

The whispering grew louder.

"What the hell's the matter with those dogs?" cried Anderson savagely. "Look at them!"

The malamutes, whining, were racing away toward the light. We saw them disappear among the trees. There came back to us a mournful howling. Then that too died away and left nothing but the insistent murmuring overhead.

The glade we had camped in looked straight to the North. We had reached I suppose three hundred miles above the first great bend of the Koskokwim toward the Yukon. Certainly we were in an untrodden part of the wilderness. We had pushed through from Dawson at the breaking of the Spring, on a fair lead to the lost five peaks between which, so the Athabasean medicine man had told us, the gold streams out like putty from a clenched fist. Not an Indian were we able to get to go with us. The land of the Hand Mountain was accursed they said. We had sighted the peaks the night before, their tops faintly outlined against a pulsing glow. And now we saw the light that had led us to them.

Anderson stiffened. Through the whispering had broken a curious pad-pad and a rustling. It sounded as though a small bear were moving towards us. I threw a pile of wood on the fire and, as it blazed up, saw something break through the bushes. It walked on all fours, but it did not walk like a bear. All at once it flashed upon me—it was like a baby crawling upstairs. The forepaws lifted themselves in grotesquely infantile fashion. It was grotesque but it was—terrible. It grew closer. We reached for our guns—and dropped them. Suddenly we knew that this crawling thing was a man!

It was a man. Still with the high climbing pad-pad he swayed to the fire. He stopped.

"Safe," whispered the crawling man, in a voice that was an echo of the murmur overhead. "Quite safe here. They can't get out of the blue, you know. They can't get you—unless you go to them."

He fell over on his side. We ran to him. Anderson knelt.

"God's love!" he said. "Frank, look at this!" He pointed to the hands. The wrists were covered with torn rags of a heavy shirt. The hands themselves were stumps! The fingers had been bent into the palms and the flesh had been worn to the bone. They looked like the feet of a little black elephant! My eyes traveled down the body. Around the waist was a heavy band of yellow metal. From it fell a ring and a dozen links of shining white chain!

"What is he? Where did he come from?" said Anderson. "Look, he's fast asleep—yet even in his sleep his arms try to climb and his feet draw themselves up one after the other! And his knees—how in God's name was he ever able to move on them?"

It was even as he said. In the deep sleep that had come upon the crawler arms and legs kept raising in a deliberate, dreadful climbing motion. It was as though they had a life of their own—they kept their movement independently of the motionless body. They were semaphoric motions. If you have ever stood at the back of a train and had watched the semaphores rise and fall you will know exactly what I mean.

Abruptly the overhead whispering ceased. The shaft of light dropped and did not rise again. The crawling man became still. A gentle glow began to grow around us. It was dawn, and the short Alaskan summer night was over. Anderson rubbed his eyes and turned to me a haggard face.

"Man!" he exclaimed. "You look as though you have been through a spell of sickness!"

"No more than you, Starr," I said. "What do you make of it all?"

"I'm thinking our only answer lies there," he answered, pointing to the figure that lay so motionless under the blankets we had thrown over him. "Whatever it was—that's what it was after. There was no aurora about that light, Frank. It was like the flaring up of some queer hell the preacher folk never frightened us with."

"We'll go no further today," I said. "I wouldn't wake him for all the gold that runs between the fingers of the five peaks—nor for all the devils that may be behind them."

The crawling man lay in a sleep as deep as the Styx. We bathed and bandaged the pads that had been his hands. Arms and legs were as rigid as though they were crutches. He did not move while we worked over him. He lay as he had fallen, the arms a trifle raised, the knees bent.

"Why did he crawl?" whispered Anderson. "Why didn't he walk?" I was filing the band about the waist. It was gold, but it was like no gold I had ever handled. Pure gold is soft. This was soft, but it had an unclean, viscid life of its own. It clung to the file. I gashed through it, bent it away from the body and hurled it far off. It was—loathsome!

All that day he slept. Darkness came and still he slept That night there was no shaft of light, no questing globe, no whispering. Some spell of horror seemed lifted from the land. It was noon when the crawling man awoke. I jumped as the pleasant drawling voice sounded.

"How long have I slept?" he asked. His pale blue eyes grew quizzical as I stared at him. "A night—and almost two days," I said. "Was there any light up there last night?" He nodded to the North eagerly. "Any whispering?"

"Neither," I answered. His head fell back and he stared up at the sky.

"They've given it up, then?" he said at last.

"Who have given it up?" asked Anderson.

"Why, the people of the pit," replied the crawling man quietly.

We stared at him. "The people of the pit," he said. "Things that the Devil made before the Flood and that somehow have escaped God's vengeance. You weren't in any danger from them—unless you had followed their call. They can't get any further than the blue haze. I was their prisoner," he added simply. "They were trying to whisper me back to them!"

Anderson and I looked at each other, the same thought in both our minds.

"You're wrong," said the crawling man. "I'm not insane. Give me a very little to drink. I'm going to die soon, but I want you to take me as far South as you can before I die, and afterwards I want you to build a big fire and burn me. I want to be in such shape that no infernal spell of theirs can drag my body back to them. You'll do it too, when I've told you about them—" he hesitated. "I think their chain is off me?" he said.

"I cut it off," I answered shortly.

"Thank God for that too," whispered the crawling man.

He drank the brandy and water we lifted to his lips.

"Arms and legs quite dead," he said. "Dead as I'll be soon. Well, they did well for me. Now I'll tell you what's up there behind that hand. Hell!

"Now listen. My name is Stanton—Sinclair Stanton. Class 1900, Yale. Explorer. I started away from Dawson last year to hunt for five peaks that rise like a hand in a haunted country and run pure gold between them. Same thing you were after? I thought so. Late last fall my comrade sickened. Sent him back with some Indians. Little later all my Indians ran away from me. I decided I'd stick, built a cabin, stocked myself with food and lay down to winter it. In the Spring I started off again. Little less than two weeks ago I sighted the five peaks. Not from this side though—the other. Give me some more brandy.

"I'd made too wide a detour," he went on. "I'd gotten too far North. I beat back. From this side you see nothing but forest straight up to the base of the Hand Mountain. Over on the other side—"
He was silent for a moment.

"Over there is forest too. But it doesn't reach so far. No! I came out of it. Stretching miles in front of me was a level plain. It was as worn and ancient looking as the desert around the ruins of Babylon. At its end rose the peaks. Between me and them—far off—was what looked like a low dike of rocks. Then—I ran across the road!"

"The road!" cried Anderson incredulously.

"The road," said the crawling man. "A fine smoot stone road. It ran straight on to the mountain. Oh, it was road all right—and worn as though millions and millions of feet had passed over it for thousands of years. On each side of it were sand and heaps of stones. After a while I began to notice these stones. They were cut, and the shape of the heaps somehow gave me the idea that a hundred thousand years ago they might have been houses. I sensed man about them and at the same time they smelled of immemorial antiquity. Well—

"The peaks grew closer. The heaps of ruins thicker. Something inexpressibly desolate hovered over them; something reached from them that struck my heart like the touch of ghosts so old that they could be only the ghosts of ghosts. I went on.

"And now I saw that what I had thought to be the low rock range at the base of the peaks was a thicker litter of ruins. The Hand Mountain was really much farther off. The road passed between two high rocks that raised themselves like a gateway."

The crawling man paused.

A. MERRITT

"They were a gateway," he said. "I reached them. I went between them. And then I sprawled and clutched the earth in sheer awe! I was on a broad stone platform. Before me was—sheer space! Imagine the Grand Canyon five times as wide and with the bottom dropped out. That is what I was looking into. It was like peeping over the edge of a cleft world down into the infinity where the planets roll! On the far side stood the five peaks. They looked like a gigantic warning hand stretched up to the sky. The lip of the abyss curved away on each side of me.

"I could see down perhaps a thousand feet. Then a thick blue haze shut out the eye. It was like the blue you see gather on the high hills at dusk. And the pit—it was awesome; awesome as the Maori Gulf of Ranalak, that sinks between the living and the dead and that only the freshly released soul has strength to leap—but never strength to cross again.

"I crept back from the verge and stood up, weak. My hand rested against one of the pillars of the gateway. There was carving upon it. It bore in still sharp outlines the heroic figure of a man. His back was turned. His arms were outstretched. There was an odd peaked headdress upon him. I looked at the opposite pillar. It bore a figure exactly similar. The pillars were triangular and the carvings were on the side away from the pit. The figures seemed to be holding something back. I looked closer. Behind the outstretched hands I seemed to see other shapes.

"I traced them out vaguely. Suddenly I felt unaccountably sick. There had come to me an impression of enormous upright slugs. Their swollen bodies were faintly cut—all except the heads which were well marked globes. They were—unutterably loathsome. I turned from the gates back to the void. I stretched myself upon the slab and looked over the edge.

"A stairway led down into the pit!"

"A stairway!" we cried.

"A stairway," repeated the crawling man as patiently as before. "It seemed not so much carved out of the rock as built into it. The

325

slabs were about six feet long and three feet wide. It ran down from the platform and vanished into the blue haze."

"But who could build such a stairway as that?" I said. "A stairway built into the wall of a precipice and leading down into a bottomless pit!"

"Not bottomless," said the crawling man quietly. "There was a bottom. I reached it!"

"Reached it?" we repeated.

"Yes, by the stairway," answered the crawling man. "You see—I went down it!

"Yes," he said. "I went down the stairway. But not that day. I made my camp back of the gates. At dawn I filled my knapsack with food, my two canteens with water from a spring that wells up there by the gateway, walked between the carved monoliths and stepped over the edge of the pit.

"The steps ran along the side of the rock at a forty degree pitch. As I went down and down I studied them. They were of a greenish rock quite different from the granitic porphyry that formed the wall of the precipice. At first I thought that the builders had taken advantage of an outcropping stratum, and had carved from it their gigantic flight. But the regularity of the angle at which it fell made me doubtful of this theory.

"After I had gone perhaps half a mile I stepped out upon a landing. From this landing the stairs made a V-shaped turn and ran on downward, clinging to the cliff at the same angle as the first flight; it was a zig-zag, and after I had made three of these turns I knew that the steps dropped straight down in a succession of such angles. No strata could be so regular as that. No, the stairway was built by hands! But whose? The answer is in those ruins around the edge, I think—never to be read.

"By noon I had lost sight of the five peaks and the lip of the abyss. Above me, below me, was nothing but the blue haze. Beside me, too, was nothingness, for the further breast of rock had long since vanished. I felt no dizziness, and any trace of fear was swallowed in a vast curiosity. What was I to discover? Some ancient and wonderful civilization that had ruled when the Poles were tropical gardens? Nothing living, I felt sure—all was too old for life. Still, a stairway so wonderful must lead to something quite as wonderful I knew. What was it? I went on.

"At regular intervals I had passed the mouths of small caves. There would be two thousand steps and then an opening, two thousand more steps and an opening—and so on and on. Late that afternoon I stopped before one of these clefts. I suppose I had gone then three miles down the pit, although the angles were such that I had walked in all fully ten miles. I examined the entrance. On each side were carved the figures of the great portal above, only now they were standing face forward, the arms outstretched as though to hold something back from the outer depths. Their faces were covered with veils. There were no hideous shapes behind them. I went inside. The fissure ran back for twenty yards like a burrow. It was dry and perfectly light. Outside I could see the blue haze rising upward like a column, its edges clearly marked. I felt an extraordinary sense of security, although I had not been conscious of any fear. I felt that the figures at the entrance were guardians—but against what?

"The blue haze thickened and grew faintly luminescent. I fancied that it was dusk above. I ate and drank a little and slept. When I awoke the blue had lightened again, and I fancied it was dawn above. I went on. I forgot the gulf yawning at my side. I felt no fatigue and little hunger or thirst, although I had drunk and eaten sparingly. That night I spent within another of the caves, and at dawn I descended again.

"It was late that day when I first saw the city—."
He was silent for a time.

"The city," he said at last, "there is a city you know. But not such a city as you have ever seen—nor any other man who has lived to tell of it. The pit, I think, is shaped like a bottle; the opening before the five peaks is the neck. But how wide the bottom is I do not know—thousands of miles maybe. I had begun to catch little glints of light far down in the blue. Then I saw the tops of—trees, I suppose they are. But not our kind of trees—unpleasant, snaky kind of trees. They reared themselves on high thin trunks and their tops were nests of thick tendrils with ugly little leaves like arrow heads. The trees were red, a vivid angry red. Here and there I glimpsed spots of shining yellow. I knew these were water because I could see things breaking through their surface—or at least I could see the splash and ripple, but what it was that disturbed them I never saw.

"Straight beneath me was the—city. I looked down upon mile after mile of closely packed cylinders. They lay upon their sides in pyramids of three, of five—of dozens—piled upon each other. It is hard to make you see what that city is like—look, suppose you have water pipes of a certain length and first you lay three of them side by side and on top of them you place two and on these two one; or suppose you take five for a foundation and place on these four and then three, then two and then one. Do you see? That was the way they looked. But they were topped by towers, by minarets, by flares, by fans, and twisted monstrosities. They gleamed as though coated with pale rose flame. Beside them the venomous red trees raised themselves like the heads of hydras guarding nests of gigantic, jeweled and sleeping worms!

"A few feet beneath me the stairway jutted out into a Titanic arch, unearthly as the span that bridges Hell and leads to Asgard. It curved out and down straight through the top of the highest pile of carven cylinders and then it vanished through it. It was appalling—it was demonic—"

The crawling man stopped. His eyes rolled up into his head. He trembled and his arms and legs began their horrible crawling movement. From his lips came a whispering. It was an echo of the high murmuring we had heard the night he came to us. I put my hands over his eyes. He quieted.

"The Things Accursed!" he said. "The People of the Pit! Did I whisper. Yes—but they can't get me now—they can't!"

After a time he began as quietly as before.

"I crossed the span. I went down through the top of that—building. Blue darkness shrouded me for a moment and I felt the steps twist into a spiral. I wound down and then—I was standing high up in—I can't tell you in what, I'll have to call it a room. We have no images for what is in the pit. A hundred feet below me was the floor. The walls sloped down and out from where I stood in a series of widening crescents. The place was colossal—and it was filled with a curious mottled red light. It was like the light inside a green and gold flecked fire opal. I went down to the last step. Far in front of me rose a high, columned altar. Its pillars were carved in monstrous scrolls—like mad octopuses with a thousand drunken tentacles; they rested on the backs of shapeless monstrosities carved in crimson stone. The altar front was a gigantic slab of purple covered with carvings.

"I can't describe these carvings! No human being could—the human eye cannot grasp them any more than it can grasp the shapes that haunt the fourth dimension. Only a subtle sense in the back of the brain sensed them vaguely. They were formless things that gave no conscious image, yet pressed into the mind like small hot seals—ideas of hate—of combats between unthinkable monstrous things—victories in a nebulous hell of steaming, obscene jungles—aspirations and ideals immeasurably loathsome—

"And as I stood I grew aware of something that lay behind the lip of the altar fifty feet above me. I knew it was there—I felt it with every hair and every tiny bit of my skin. Something infinitely malignant, infinitely horrible, infinitely ancient. It lurked, it brooded, it threatened and it—was invisible!

"Behind me was a circle of blue light. I ran for it. Something urged me to turn back, to climb the stairs and make away. It was impossible. Repulsion for that unseen Thing raced me onward as though a current had my feet. I passed through the circle. I was out on a street that stretched on into dim distance between rows of the carven cylinders.

"Here and there the red trees arose. Between them rolled the stone burrows. And now I could take in the amazing ornamentation that clothed them. They were like the trunks of smooth skinned trees that had fallen and had been clothed with high reaching noxious orchids. Yes—those cylinders were like that—and more. They should have gone out with the dinosaurs. They were—monstrous. They struck the eyes like a blow and they passed across the nerves like a rasp. And nowhere was there sight or sound of living thing.

"There were circular openings in the cylinders like the circle in the Temple of the Stairway. I passed through one of them. I was in a long, bare vaulted room whose curving sides half closed twenty feet over my head, leaving a wide slit that opened into another vaulted chamber above. There was absolutely nothing in the room save the same mottled reddish light that I had seen in the Temple. I stumbled. I still could see nothing, but there was something on the floor over which I had tripped. I reached down—and my hand touched a thing cold and smooth—that moved under it—I turned and ran out of that place—I was filled with a loathing that had in it something of madness—I ran on and on blindly—wringing my hands—weeping with horror—

"When I came to myself I was still among the stone cylinders and red trees. I tried to retrace my steps; to find the Temple. I was more than afraid. I was like a new loosed soul panic-stricken with the first terrors of hell. I could not find the Temple! Then the haze began to thicken and glow; the cylinders to shine more brightly. I knew that it was dusk in the world above and I felt that with dusk my time of peril had come; that the thickening of the haze was the signal for the awakening of whatever things lived in this pit.

"I scrambled up the sides of one of the burrows. I hid behind a twisted nightmare of stone. Perhaps, I thought, there was a chance of remaining hidden until the blue lightened and the peril passed. There began to grow around me a murmur. It was everywhere—and it grew and grew into a great whispering. I peeped from the side of the stone down into the street. I saw lights passing and repassing. More and more lights—they swam out of the circular doorways and they thronged the street. The highest were eight feet above the pave; the lowest perhaps two. They hurried, they sauntered, they bowed, they stopped and whispered—and there was nothing under them!"

"Nothing under them!" breathed Anderson.

"No," he went on, "that was the terrible part of it—there was nothing under them. Yet certainly the lights were living things. They had consciousness, volition, thought—what else I did not know. They were nearly two feet across—the largest. Their center was a bright nucleus—red, blue, green. This nucleus faded off, gradually, into a misty glow that did not end abruptly. It too seemed to fade off into nothingness—but a nothingness that had under it a somethingness. I strained my eyes trying to grasp this body into which the lights merged and which one could only feel was there, but could not see.

"And all at once I grew rigid. Something cold, and thin like a whip, had touched my face. I turned my head. Close behind were three of the lights. They were a pale blue. They looked at me—if you can imagine lights that are eyes. Another whiplash gripped my shoulder. Under the closest light came a shrill whispering. I shrieked. Abruptly the murmuring in the street ceased. I dragged my eyes from the pale blue globe that held them and looked out—the lights in the streets were rising by myriads to the level of where I stood! There they stopped and peered at me. They crowded and jostled as though they were a crowd of curious people—on Broadway. I felt a score of the lashes touch me—

"When I came to myself I was again in the great Place of the Stairway, lying at the foot of the altar. All was silent. There were no lights—only the mottled red glow. I jumped to my feet and ran toward the steps. Something jerked me back to my knees. And then I saw that around my waist had been fastened a yellow ring of metal. From it hung a chain and this chain passed up over the lip of the high ledge. I was chained to the altar!

"I reached into my pockets for my knife to cut through the ring. It was not there! I had been stripped of everything except one of the canteens that I had hung around my neck and which I suppose

They had thought was—part of me. I tried to break the ring. It seemed alive. It writhed in my hands and it drew itself closer around me! I pulled at the chain. It was immovable. There came to me the consciousness of the unseen Thing above the altar. I groveled at the foot of the slab and wept. Think—alone in that place of strange light with the brooding ancient Horror above me—a monstrous Thing, a Thing unthinkable—an unseen Thing that poured forth horror—

"After awhile I gripped myself. Then I saw beside one of the pillars a yellow bowl filled with a thick white liquid. I drank it. If it killed I did not care. But its taste was pleasant and as I drank my strength came back to me with a rush. Clearly I was not to be starved. The lights, whatever they were, had a conception of human needs.

"And now the reddish mottled gleam began to deepen. Outside arose the humming and through the circle that was the entrance came streaming the globes. They ranged themselves in ranks until they filled the Temple. Their whispering grew into a chant, a cadenced whispering chant that rose and fell, rose and fell, while to its rhythm the globes lifted and sank, lifted and sank.

"All that night the lights came and went—and all that night the chant sounded as they rose and fell. At the last I felt myself only an atom of consciousness in a sea of cadenced whispering; an atom that rose and fell with the bowing globes. I tell you that even my heart pulsed in unison with them! The red glow faded, the lights streamed out; the whispering died. I was again alone and I knew that once again day had broken in my own world.

"I slept. When I awoke I found beside the pillar more of the white liquid. I scrutinized the chain that held me to the altar. I began to rub two of the links together. I did this for hours. When the red began to thicken there was a ridge worn in the links. Hope rushed up within me. There was, then, a chance to escape.

"With the thickening the lights came again. All through that night the whispering chant sounded, and the globes rose and fell. The chant seized me. It pulsed through me until every nerve and muscle quivered to it. My lips began to quiver. They strove like a man trying to cry out on a nightmare. And at last they too were whispering the chant of the people of the pit. My body bowed in unison with the lights—I was, in movement and sound, one with the nameless things while my soul sank back sick with horror and powerless. While I whispered I—saw Them!"

"Saw the lights?" I asked stupidly.

"Saw the Things under the lights," he answered. "Great transparent snail-like bodies—dozens of waving tentacles stretching from them—round gaping mouths under the luminous seeing globes. They were like the ghosts of inconceivably monstrous slugs! I could see through them. And as I stared, still bowing and whispering, the dawn came and they streamed to and through the entrance. They did not crawl or walk—they floated! They floated and were—gone!

"I did not sleep. I worked all that day at my chain. By the thickening of the red I had worn it a sixth through. And all that night I whispered and bowed with the pit people, joining in their chant to the Thing that brooded above me!

"Twice again the red thickened and the chant held me—then on the morning of the fifth day I broke through the worn links of the chain. I was free! I drank from the bowl of white liquid and poured what was left in my flask. I ran to the Stairway. I rushed up and past that unseen Horror behind the altar ledge and was out upon the Bridge. I raced across the span and up the Stairway.

"Can you think what it is to climb straight up the verge of a cleft world—with hell behind you? Hell was behind me and terror rode me. The city had long been lost in the blue haze before I knew that I could climb no more. My heart beat upon my ears like a sledge. I fell before one of the little caves feeling that here at last was sanctuary. I crept far back within it and waited for the haze to thicken. Almost at once it did so. From far below me came a vast and angry murmur. At the mouth of the rift I saw a light pulse up through the blue; die down and as it dimmed I saw myriads of the globes that are the eyes of the pit people swing downward into the abyss. Again and again the light pulsed and the globes fell. They were hunting me. The whispering grew louder, more insistent.

"There grew in me the dreadful desire to join in the whispering as I had done in the Temple. I bit my lips through and through to still them. All that night the beam shot up through the abyss, the globes swung and the whispering sounded—and now I knew the purpose of the caves and of the sculptured figures that still had power to guard them. But what were the people who had carved them? Why had they built their city around the verge and why had they set that Stairway in the pit? What had they been to those Things that dwelt at the bottom and what use had the Things been to them that they should live beside their dwelling place? That there had been some purpose was certain. No work so prodigious as the Stairway would have been undertaken otherwise. But what was the purpose? And why was it that those who had dwelt about the abyss had passed away ages gone, and the dwellers in the abyss still lived? I could find no answer—nor can I find any now. I have not the shred of a theory.

"Dawn came as I wondered and with it silence. I drank what was left of the liquid in my canteen, crept from the cave and began to climb again. That afternoon my legs gave out. I tore off my shirt, made from it pads for my knees and coverings for my hands. I crawled upward. I crawled up and up. And again I crept into one of the caves and waited until again the blue thickened, the shaft of light shot through it and the whispering came.

"But now there was a new note in the whispering. It was no longer threatening. It called and coaxed. It drew.

"A new terror gripped me. There had come upon me a mighty desire to leave the cave and go out where the lights swung; to let them do with me as they pleased, carry me where they wished. The desire grew. It gained fresh impulse with every rise of the beam until at last I vibrated with the desire as I had vibrated to the chant in the Temple. My body was a pendulum. Up would go the beam and

I would swing toward it! Only my soul kept steady. It held me fast to the floor of the cave; And all that night it fought with my body against the spell of the pit people.

"Dawn came. Again I crept from the cave and faced the Stairway. I could not rise. My hands were torn and bleeding; my knees an agony. I forced myself upward step by step. After a while my hands became numb, the pain left my knees. They deadened. Step by step my will drove my body upward upon them.

"And then—a nightmare of crawling up infinite stretches of steps—memories of dull horror while hidden within caves with the lights pulsing without and whisperings that called and called me—memory of a time when I awoke to find that my body was obeying the call and had carried me half way out between the guardians of the portals while thousands of gleaming globes rested in the blue haze and watched me. Glimpses of bitter fights against sleep and always, always—a climb up and up along infinite distances of steps that led from Abaddon to a Paradise of blue sky and open world!

"At last a consciousness of the clear sky close above me, the lip of the pit before me—memory of passing between the great portals of the pit and of steady withdrawal from it—dreams of giant men with strange peaked crowns and veiled faces who pushed me onward and onward and held back Roman Candle globules of light that sought to draw me back to a gulf wherein planets swam between the branches of red trees that had snakes for crowns.

"And then a long, long sleep—how long God alone knows—in a cleft of rocks; an awakening to see far in the North the beam still rising and falling, the lights still hunting, the whispering high above me calling.

"Again crawling on dead arms and legs that moved—that moved —like the Ancient Mariner's ship—without volition of mine, but that carried me from a haunted place. And then—your fire—and this—safety!"

The crawling man smiled at us for a moment. Then swiftly life faded from his face. He slept.

THE PEOPLE OF THE PIT

That afternoon we struck camp and carrying the crawling man started back South. For three days we carried him and still he slept. And on the third day, still sleeping, he died. We built a great pile of wood and we burned his body as he had asked. We scattered his ashes about the forest with the ashes of the trees that had consumed him. It must be a great magic indeed that could disentangle those ashes and draw him back in a rushing cloud to the pit he called Accursed. I do not think that even the People of the Pit have such a spell. No.

But we did not return to the five peaks to see.

Legacy From Sorn Fen

Andre Norton (1912-2005)

By the western wall of Klavenport on the Sea of Autumn Mists—but you do not want a bard's beginning to my tale, Goodmen? Well enough, I have no speak-harp to twang at all the proper times. And this is not altogether a tale for lords-in-their-halls. Though the beginning did lie in Klavenport right enough.

It began with one Higbold. It was after the Invaders' War and those were times when small men, if they had their wits sharpened, could rise in the world—swiftly, if fortune favored them. Which is a bard's way of saying they knew when to use the knife point, when to swear falsely, when to put hands on what was not rightfully theirs.

Higbold had his rats running to his whistle, and then his hounds to his horn. Finally no one spoke (save behind a shielding hand, glancing now and then over his shoulder) about his beginnings. He settled in the Gate Keep of Klavenport, took command there, married a wife who was hall-born (there were such to be given to landless and shieldless men then, their kin so harried by war, or dead in it, that they went gladly to anyone who offered a roof over their heads, meat in the dish, and mead in the cup before them). Higbold's lady was no more nor less than her sisters in following expediency.

Save that from the harsh days before her marriage she held memories. Perhaps it was those which made her face down Higbold himself in offering charity to those begging from door to door.

LEGACY FROM SORN FEN

Among those came Caleb. He lacked an eye and walked with a lurch which nigh spilled him sprawling every time he took a full stride. What age he was no one could say; cruel mauling puts years on a man.

It might have been that the Lady Isbel knew him from the old days, but if so neither spoke of that. He became one of the household, working mainly in the small walled garden. They say that he was one with the power of growing things, that herbs stood straight and sweet-smelling for him, flowers bloomed richly under his tending.

Higbold had nothing to interest him in the garden. Save that now and then he met someone there where they could stand well in the open, walls too often having ears. For Higbold's ambition did not end in his keepship of the Klavenport Gate. Ah, no, such a man's ambition never ceases to grow. But you can gain only so much by showing a doubled fist, or a bared sword. After a certain point you must accomplish your means more subtly, by influencing men's minds, not the enslavement of their bodies. Higbold studied well.

What was said and done in the garden one night in early midsummer was never known. But Higbold had a witness he did not learn about until too late. Only servants gossip as always about their masters, and there is a rumor that Caleb went to Lady Isbel to talk privately. Then he took his small bundle of worldly goods and went forth, not only from the gate keep, but out of Klavenport as well, heading west on the highway.

Near the port there had been repairing, rebuilding, and the marks of the Invaders' War had faded from the land. But Caleb did not keep long to the highway. He was a prudent man, and knew that roads made for swift travel can lead hunters on a man's tracks.

Cross-country was hard, doubly so for his twisted body. He came to the fringes of the Fen of Sorn. Ah, I see you shake your heads and draw faces at that! Rightly do you so, Goodmen, rightly. We all know that there are parts of High Hallack which belong to the Old Ones, where men with sense in their thick skulls do not walk.

But it was there Caleb found that others had before him. They were herdsmen who had been driving the wild hill cattle (those which ranged free during the war) to market. Something had frightened the beasts and sent them running. Now the herders, half-mad with the thought of losing all reward of their hard labor, tracked them into the fen.

However, in so doing, they came upon something else. No, I shall not try to describe what they started out of its lair. You all know that there are secrets upon secrets in places like the fen. Enough to say that this had the appearance of a woman, enough to incite the lust of the drovers who had been kept so long from the lifting of any skirt. Having cornered the creature, they were going to have their sport.

Caleb had not left Klavenport unarmed. In spite of his twisted body he was an expert with crossbow. Now he again proved his skill. Twice he fired and men howled like beasts—or worse than beasts, seeing what they had been doing—beasts do not so use their females.

Caleb shouted as if he were leading a group of men-at-arms. The herders floundered away. Then he went down to what they had left broken behind them.

No man knows what happened thereafter, for Caleb spoke of it to no one. But in time he went on alone, though his face was white and his work-hardened hands shook.

He did not venture into the fen, but traveled, almost as one with a set purpose, along its edge. Two nights did he camp so. What he did and with whom he spoke, why those came—who can tell? But on the morning of the third day he turned his back on Sorn Fen and started toward the highway.

It was odd, but as he walked his lurching skip-step was not so evident, as if, with every stride he took, his twisted body seemed straighter. By the night of the fourth day he walked near as well as any man who was tired and footsore might. It was then that he came to the burned-out shell of the Inn of the Forks.

Once that had been a prosperous house. Much silver had spun across its tables into the hands of the keeper and his family. It was built at a spot where two roads, one angling north, one south, met, to continue thereon into Klavenport. But the day of its glory passed before the Battle of Falcon Cut. For five winter seasons or more its charred timbers had been a dismal monument to the ravages of war, offering no cheer for the traveler.

Now Caleb stood looking at its sad state and—

Believe this or not as you will, Goodmen. But suddenly there was no burned-out ruin. Rather stood an inn. Caleb, showing no surprise, crossed the road to enter. Enter it as master, for as such he was hailed by those about their business within its courtyard.

Now there were more travelers up and down the western roads, for this was the season of trade with Klavenport. So it was not long before the tale of the restored inn reached the city. There were those unable to believe such a report, who rode out, curious, to prove it true.

They found it much as the earlier inn had been. Though those who had known it before the war claimed there were certain differences. However, when they were challenged to name these, they were vague. But all united in the information that Caleb was host there and that he had changed with the coming of prosperity, for prosperous he certainly now was.

Higbold heard the reports. He did not frown, but he rubbed his forefinger back and forth under his thick lower lip. Which was a habit of his when he thought deeply, considering this point and that. Then he summoned to him a flaunty, saucy piece in skirts. She had long thrown herself in his direction whenever she could. It was common knowledge that, while Higbold had indeed bedded his lady in the early days of their marriage, to make sure that none could break the tie binding them, he was no longer to be found in her chamber, taking his pleasures elsewhere. Though as yet, with none under his own roof.

Now he spoke privately with Elfra, and set in her hands a slip of parchment. Then openly he berated her loudly, had her bustled roughly, thrown into the street without so much as a cloak about her shoulders. She wept and wailed, and took off along the western road.

In time she reached the Inn at the Forks. Her journey had not been an easy one so she crept into the courtyard as much a beggar in looks as any of the stinking, shuffling crowd who hung around a merchant's door in the city. Save that when she spoke to Caleb she gave him a bit of parchment with on it a message which might have been writ in my lady's hand. Caleb welcomed her and at length he made her waiting maid in the tap room. She did briskly well, such employment suiting her nature.

The days passed. Time slid from summer into autumn. At length the Ice Dragon sent his frost breath over the land. It was then that Elfra stole away with a merchant bound for Klavenport. Caleb, hearing of her going, shrugged and said that if she thought so to better her life the choice was hers.

But Elfra stayed with the merchant only long enough to reach the gate. From there she went directly to Higbold's own chamber. At first, as he listened, there was that in his face which was not good to see. But she did not take warning, sure that he looked so only because her tale was so wild. To prove the truth of her words she held her hand over the table.

About her thumb (so large it was that she could not wear it elsewhere on her woman's hand) was a ring of green stone curiously patterned with faint red lines as if veined with blood. Holding it directly in Higbold's sight, Elfra made a wish.

Below on the table there appeared a necklace of gems, such a necklace as might well be the ransom for a whole city in the days of the war. Higbold sucked in his breath, his face gone blank, his eyes half hooded by their lids.

Then his hand shot out and imprisoned her wrist in a grim grip and he had off that ring. She looked into his face and began to whimper, learning too late that she was only a tool, and one which had served its purpose now, and having served its purpose—

She was gone!

But Higbold cupped the ring between his palms and smiled evilly.

Shortly thereafter at the Inn flames burst out. No man could fight their fierce heat as they ate away what the magic of the Old Ones had brought into being. Once more Caleb stood in the cold owning nothing. Nothing, that is, except his iron will.

He wasted no time in regrets, nor in bewailing that lack of caution which had lost him his treasure. Rather he turned and began to stride along the road. When he came to a certain place he cut away from the path of men. Though snow blew about him, and a knife-edged wind cut like a lash at his back, he headed for the fen.

Again time passed. No one rebuilt, by magic or otherwise, the Inn. But with Higbold things happened. Those who had once been firm against him became firm supporters, or else suffered various kinds of chastening misfortune. His lady kept his chamber. It was rumored that she ailed and perhaps would not live out the year.

There had never been a king of High Hallack, for the great lords held themselves all equal, one to another. None would have given support to a fellow to set him over the rest. But Higbold was not of their company, and so it might be a matter of either unite against him, or acknowledge his rulership. Still those men expected to be foremost in opposition to his rise seemed oddly hesitant to take any step to prevent it.

In the meantime there were rumors concerning a man who lived on the fringe of Sorn Fen and who was a tamer of beasts, even a seller of them. A merchant, enterprising and on the search for something unique, was enough intrigued by such tales to make a detour. He came into Klavenport from that side venture with three strange animals.

They were small, yet they had the look of the fierce snow cats of the high range. Only these were obviously tame, so tame that they quickly enchanted the merchants' wives and the ladies of the city into wanting them for pets. Twice the merchant returned to the fen fringe and bought more of the cats—well pleased each time with his bargain.

Then he needed an export permit and had to go to Higbold. So he came to the Keep bringing a "sweetener" for dealing after the custom—that being one of the cats. Higbold was not one with a liking for animals. His horses were tools to be used, and no hound ever lay in his hall or chamber. But he had the cat carried on to his lady's bower. Perhaps he thought that he would not have to consider her for long and this gift might give some coating of pretense.

Shortly after, he began to dream. Now there was certainly enough in his past to provide ill dreams for not one man but a troop. However, it was not of the past that he dreamed, but rather of the present, and perhaps a dark future. For in each of these dreams (and they were real enough to bring him staring up in bed calling for candles as he woke out of them), he had lost the ring Elfra had brought him—the ring now the core of all his schemes.

He had worn it secretly on a cord around his neck under his clothing. However, all his dreams were of it slipping from that security. So now when he slept he grasped it within his hand.

Then one morning he awoke to find it gone. Fear rode him hard until he found it among the covers on his bed. At last his night terrors drove him to putting it under his tongue as he slept. His tempers were such that those in close contact with him went in fear of their lives.

At last came the night when he dreamed again and this time the dream seemed very real. Something crouched first at the foot of his bed, and then it began a slow, slinking advance, stalking up the length of it. He could not move, but had to lie sweating, awaiting its coming.

Suddenly he roused out of that nightmare, sneezing. The ring lay where he coughed it forth. By it crouched the strange cat, its eyes glowing so that he would swear it was no cat, but something else, more intelligent and malignant, which had poured its being into the cat's small body. It watched him with cold measurement and he was frozen, unable to put forth his hand to the ring. Then, calmly, it took up that circlet of green and red in its mouth, leaped from the bed and was gone.

Higbold cried out and grabbed. But the creature was already at the door of the chamber, streaking through as the guard came in answer to his lord's call. Higbold thrust the man aside as he raced to follow.

"The cat!" His shouts alarmed the whole keep. "Where is the cat?"

But it was the hour before daybreak when the men were asleep. Those aroused by his shouting blinked and were amazed for a moment or two.

Higbold well knew that there were a hundred, no, a thousand places within that pile where such a small animal might hide, or drop to eternal loss that which it carried. That thought created frenzy in his brain, so that at first he was like one mad, racing to and fro, shouting to watch, to catch the cat.

Then came a messenger from the gate saying that the cat had been seen to leap the wall and run from the Keep, and the city, out into the country. Deep in him Higbold knew a growing cold which was like the chill of death, since it heralded the end of all his plans. For if the Keep provided such a wealth of hiding places, then what of the countryside?

He returned, stricken silent now with the fullness of his loss, to his chamber. There he battered his bare fists against the stone of the wall, until the pain of his self-bruising broke through the torment in his mind and he could think clearly again.

Animals could be hunted. He had hounds in his kennels, though he had never wasted time in the forms of the chase in which the high-born delighted. He would hunt that cat as no beast in High Hallack had ever been hunted before. Having come to his senses, he gave orders in a tone of voice that made those about him flinch and look sidewise, keeping as distant as they dared.

In the hour before dawn the hunt was up, though it was a small party riding out of the Keep. Higbold had ordered with him only the master of hounds with a brace of the best trail keepers, and his squire.

The trail was so fresh and clear the hounds ran eagerly. But they did not pad along the highway, taking at once to open ground. This speedily grew more difficult for the riders, until the dogs far outstripped the men. Only their belling voices, raised now and then, told those laboring after that they still held the track. Higbold now had his fear under tight control, he did not push his horse, but there was a tenseness in the lines of his body which suggested that, if he could have grown wings, he would have soared ahead in an instant.

Wilder and rougher grew the country. The laboring squire's horse was lamed and had to drop behind. Higbold did not even spare him a glance. The sun was up and ahead was that smooth green of the fen country. In Higbold that frozen cold was nigh his heart. If the fleeing cat took into that there would be no following.

When they reached the outer fringe of that dire land the trail turned at an angle and ran along the edge, as if the creature had willfully decided not to trust to the promised safety beyond.

At length they came upon a small hut, built of the very material of this forsaken land, boulders and stones set together for its walls, a thatch of rough branches for roof. As they approached the hounds were suddenly thrown back as if they had run into an invisible wall. They yapped and leaped, and were again hurled to the earth, their clamor wild.

Their master dismounted from his blowing horse and ran forward. Then he, too, met resistance. He stumbled and almost fell, putting out his hands and running them from right to left. He might have been stroking some surface.

Higbold came out of the saddle and strode forward.

"What is it?" For the first time in hours he spoke, his words grating on the ear.

"There—there is a wall, Lord—" quavered the master, and he shrank back from both the place and Higbold.

Higbold continued to tramp on. He passed the master and the shivering, whining hounds. The man, the dogs, were mad. There was no wall, there was only the hut and what he sought in it.

He set his hand on the warped surface of the door and slammed it open with the full force of his frustration.

Before him was a rough table, a stool. On the stool sat Caleb. On the table top crouched the cat, purring under the measured stroking of the man's gentle hand. By the animal lay the ring.

Higbold strove to put out his hand, to snatch up that treasure. From the moment he sighted it, that had his full attention. The animal, the man, meant nothing to him. But now Caleb's other hand dropped loosely over the circlet. Higbold was powerless to move.

"Higbold," Caleb addressed him directly, using no polite forms or title, "you are an evil man, but one of power—too much power. In the past year you have used that very cleverly. A crown is nigh within your grasp—is that not so?"

Soft and smooth he spoke as one entirely without fear. He had no weapon, only lounged at his ease. Higbold's hatred now outweighed his fear, so that he wanted nothing so much as to smash the other's face into crimson ruin. Yet he could not stir as much as a finger.

"You have, I think," Caleb continued, "greatly enjoyed your possession of this." He raised his hand a little to show the ring.

"Mine--!" Higbold's throat hurt as he shaped that thick word.

"No." Caleb shook his head, still gently, as one might to a child who demanded what was not and never would be his. "I shall tell you a tale, Higbold. This ring was a gift, freely given to me. I was able to ease somewhat the dying of one who was not of our kind, but had been death-dealt by those like you in spirit. Had she not been taken unawares she would have had her defenses, defenses such as you now taste. But she was tricked, and then used with such cruelty as would shame any one daring to call himself one of us. Because I tried to aid, though there was little I could do, I was left this token— and my keeping it was confirmed by her people. It can only be used for a limited time, however. I intended to use it for good. That is a thought to make you smile, isn't it Higbold?

"Then you used your lady's name to beg of me aid for one I thought badly treated. So, in my blindness, I brought about my own

346

betrayal. I am a simple man, but there are things even the simple can do. To have Higbold for High King over this land—that is wrong—beyond one's own wishes or fears.

"So I spoke again to those of the fen, and with their aid I set a trap—to bring you hither. And you came, easily enough. Now." He lifted his hand and let the ring lie. It seemed there was a glow about it and again Higbold's eyes were drawn to it and he saw nothing else. Out of sight, beyond the gleaming green and red of the ring, a voice spoke.

"Take up the ring you wish so much, Higbold. Set it on your finger once again. Then go and claim your kingdom!"

Higbold found that now he could stretch forth his hand. His fingers closed about the ring. Hurriedly, lest it be rift from him once more, he pushed it on his finger.

He did not look again at Caleb, instead he turned and went out of the hut, as if the other man had ceased to exist. The hounds lay on their muddied bellies, whimpering a little as they licked at paws sore from their long run. Their master squatted on his heels watching for his lord's return. Their two horses stood with drooping heads, foam roping their bits.

Higbold did not move toward his mount, nor did he speak to he waiting hound master. Instead he faced west and south a little. As one who marches toward a visible and long desired goal, paying no heed to that about him, he strode toward the fen. His hound master did not move to stop him. Staring drop-jawed, he watched him go, until he was swallowed up in the mists.

Caleb came forth from the hut, the cat riding on his shoulder, and stood at ease. It was he who broke silence first.

"Return to your lady, my friend, and say to her that Higbold has gone to seek his kingdom. He shall not return."

Then he, also, went to where the mists of the fen wreathed him around and he could no longer be seen.

When the master came again to Klavenport he told the Lady Isbel what he had seen and heard. Thereafter, she seemed to gather strength (as if some poison drained or shadow lifted from her) and came forth from her chamber. She set about making arrangements to give gifts from the wealth of Higbold.

When summer reached its height she rode forth before dawn, taking only one waiting maid (one who had come with her from her father's house and was tied with long bonds of loyalty). They were seen to follow the highway for a space as the guards watched. Thereafter no man marked where they went, and they were not seen again.

Whether she went to seek her lord, or another, who knows? For the Fen of Sorn renders not to our blood its many secrets.

Crom the Barbarian

Gardner Fox (1911-1986) and John Giunta (1920-1970)

IN THE EARLY DAYS OF THE EARTH, THERE WERE MANY STRANGE RACES AND TRIBES MOVING ACROSS THE LAND, MANY CITIES AND COUNTRIES NOW FORGOTTEN, UNRECORDED BY ANY HISTORY. OCCASIONALLY VAGUE LEGEND OR UNINTELLIGIBLE PARCHMENTS IN SOME TIBETAN LAMASERY GIVE A HINT. VESTIGES OF THEIR EXISTENCE STILL REMAIN AT EASTER ISLAND, IN THE DAMP JUNGLES OF BRAZIL, UNDER THE HOT SANDS OF THE SAHARA AND THE GOBI. FROM ONE OF THOSE LONG-LOST PARCHMENTS RECOVERED IN AN UNDERWATER UPHEAVAL, TRANSLATED BY A LINGUAL EXPERT, WE BRING YOU THIS TALE OF THE EARTH'S MORNING, A DAY BORN IN THE MISTS OF EARTH'S BEGINNING...

CROM WAS A BARBARIAN-A MAN BORN OF THE YELLOW-HAIRED AESIR WHO MIGRATED FROM ASIA INTO EUROPE, A MAN STRONG WITH MUSCLE, HIS BRAIN KEEN IN THOSE DAYS OF BRUTE-LIKE SUPERSTITION AND SAVAGERY. HIS SWORD WAS MADE OF IRON, AND HE LIVED AND SLEPT WITH IT ALWAYS AT HIS SIDE.

BUT CROM WAS TO BE SWEPT FROM THE CARAVANS OF HIS PEOPLE, AWAY FROM THE BIG VANS AND THE SHAGGY PONIES, INTO A WORLD WHERE GREED AND BLACK MAGIC HELD SWAY, WHERE ONLY HIS SWORD AND HIS WITS STOOD TO HELP HIM WHEN HE FACED THE HORRIBLE FATE OF...

AS THE WOODEN-WHEELED VANS OF THE AESIR STOPPED AT A MISTED WATERSIDE TO FRESHEN WARRIORS AND BEASTS ALIKE, A CYMRI BOWSTRING TWANGED....

GNNNGG!

HO, AESIR! ENEMY BOWS! OUT, SWORDS-AN ENEMY!

To Crom, all men who were not Aesir, were enemies. They must be killed, that his tribe might become rich and prosperous...

CYMRI! MONKEY-PEOPLE! KILL-KILL!

With shouts of delight, seeing but one youth facing them, the Cymri sprang forward. But they had never faced a sword that was like a dart of light, it moved so swiftly!

AIEEE! HE IS A DEVIL!

HIS SWORD IS NOT ONE-- BUT MANY!

From the broad vans of the Aesir, the yew longbows were twanging. Long shafts hurtled through the air to split the smaller Cymri bowmen...

HO! THEY REEL! THEY FALL BACK!

LOOK-A BOAT! THEY COME FOR CROM AND LALLA...

In their little bullhide boat, the Cymri swept through the mists. Hairy arms lifted Crom's sister Lalla...

DOGS! YAPPING LITTLE CURS OF CYMRI! LET GO LALLA--

MY SWORD IS DRY! IT HAS LONG BEEN THIRSTY! DRINK DEEP, SKULL-CRACKER! DRINK YOUR FILL!

Slowly, inch by inch, Crom fought his way to a footing in the boat. Unnoticed, it drifted farther and farther from shore, until it floated alone on the vast sea...

YIELD, YOU FOUL HOUNDS OF HEL! YIELD...

A shrill wail of agony from the last of the Cymri... an axe-head slamming down on Crom... and Lalla screamed in fear...

GODS BE MERCIFUL-- CROM... CROM!

ONWARD DRIFTED THE BULLHIDE BOAT. A WIND SPRANG UP, CARRIED IT SWIFTLY THROUGH THE MISTS, WHILE A SOBBING GIRL LAY OVER A FALLEN CROM...

CROM STIRRED. HE SAT UP, A HAND TO HIS HEAD. A GRIN TWISTED HIS FACE...A SAVAGE, TRIUMPHANT GRIN!

BY SET HIMSELF! IT WAS LUCKY MY FOOT SLIPPED IN A PUDDLE OF BLOOD, OR THAT AXE WOULD HAVE LIFTED THE TOP OF MY SKULL! NOW—WHERE ARE WE?

I DO NOT KNOW, A WIND HAS BEEN BLOWING, TAKING US FOWARD EVER SINCE YOU FELL!

FOR THREE DAYS THE LITTLE BOAT SPED WESTWARD BEFORE THE WIND, AND THEN, ON THE MORNING OF THE FOURTH DAY, THE MISTS CLEARED TO REVEAL A BLACK ISLAND, AND LOVELY WOMEN STANDING BEFORE IT...

CROM! I AM AFRAID! THIS IS MAGIC! WITCHCRAFT! THE WIND BROUGHT US HERE!

WHAT OF THAT? I THINK I COULD LIKE THIS ISLAND! THOR—WHAT WOMEN!

BY THE HOOVES OF NESSUS! A GOOD WIND, SISTER! HOW ARE YOU NAMED, GIRL?

CROM— LOOK!

HA! OLD ONE— IS THIS YOUR ISLAND? ARE THESE YOUR WOMEN?

ALL MINE, CROM! AH, I KNOW YOU, BARBARIAN. IN THE SMOKE OF MY HERB FIRES I HAVE WATCHED YOU FIGHT. I SENT A WIND TO BRING YOU TO ME.

TELL OTHERS THAT, MAGE! I BELIEVE NOT IN YOUR CHARMS AND MAGIC. THERE IS A TRICK TO IT. BUT NOW I'M HERE— WHAT WANT YOU OF ME?

ETERNAL YOUTH!

TO CROM'S BARBARIC MIND THE OLD MAGICIAN MEANT ONLY ONE THING—TO TAKE CROM'S YOUNG, POWERFUL BODY FOR HIS OWN, BY SOME SORCEROUS MEANS...

BACK, YOU OLD DEVIL! NO MAN TAKES MY STRENGTH FROM ME! I --

PUT DOWN YOUR BLADE, CROM. I MEAN TO DRINK OF WATER—STRANGE WATER—THAT WILL MAKE ME AS YOUNG AS YOU, AND EVEN YOUNGER. BUT YOU MUST BRING IT TO ME!

3

That night before the roaring fire in the hearth of his ancient castle, Dwelf, the magician spoke eagerly to Crom...

The fountain has been there since the beginning of the earth, when people came from the stars to build it. Some day it will be lost—buried under what men will call the Sahara Desert—but now it is there—for me!

There is a great tower in the city of Ophir that shelters the fountain. There are gold and jewels all about it. Take all the jewels and gold you want, just bring me the water of youth, in this jug you will bring with you!

With a growl of rage rumbling in his muscle-corded throat, Crom leaned across the bare wooden table. In his hand a dagger glinted red in the firelight...

If you do not agree—your sister Lalla dies by torture!

By Set! Threaten me, will you, old man? I...

Crom the barbarian staggered as his eyes locked with the burning orbs of old Dwelf! Crom did not know what hypnotism was—but it stopped him—drove him back...

You...will.. ..do..as...I ..say..!

Thor save me! Your eyes... they burn! I cannot move..

In a daze, Crom staggered down to the water's edge and clambered into the bullhide boat. Moments later, it was moving out to sea, toward fabled Ophir...

His eyes! They know some trick to sap a man's will. When I next see Dwelf, I shall not look in his eyes, but at his neck—and aim skull-cracker there!

Ophir was the richest city on the shores of the inland sea. Its women went in silks and jewels, its men wore mail foxed in silver, and bore swords fitted with gold. Toward Ophir by night crept Crom, savage eyes alert and eager...

Dwelf said there was a tower...a great black tower! That is where the fountain is!

But when he found the tower, his heart sank within him in awe. His voice rasped with annoyance—Crom knew not fear!

By the teeth of Garm the hound—it's well guarded! It would take an army to storm it!

NEAR THE SQUARE OF THE TOWER STOOD A FLAT, LONG BUILDING. CROM STARED AT IT, HIS BRAIN BUSY. AND THEN, AS A PRETTY WATER-GIRL WALKED PAST, CROM CAUGHT HER WITH AN ARM...

WORKING SO LATE, MAIDEN? DON'T THE GIRLS OF OPHIR DANCE AND SING?

WHO HAS MONEY TO DANCE IN THE TAVERNS?

I HAVE MONEY! GOLDEN PITARS! BUT TELL ME... THAT BUILDING BEYOND US— WHAT IS IT?

THE CITY JAIL, STRANGER! BUT TALK NOT OF JAIL. THE NIGHT IS YOUNG, AND GWENNA IS THIRSTY...

THE CITY JAIL! I COULD ENTER THAT EASILY ENOUGH, BY THOR! FROM THERE TO THE TOWER.. BY A CORD... STRONG ENOUGH TO BEAR MY WEIGHT...

YOU ARE SILENT, STRANGER!

WITH A CARELESS LAUGH, CROM DREW THE GIRL TO HIM, BUT HIS BRAIN WAS SCHEMING EVEN AS HE PUT HIS LIPS TO HERS...

I WILL BE ARRESTED! THROWN INTO JAIL! BUT FIRST— THE CORD AND A FILE!

CROM USED A GOLDEN PITAR TO BUY THE CORD AND FILE. HE STRAPPED THEM ABOUT A LEG AND TWISTED A BANDAGE AROUND IT, TO HIDE THEM. AND THEN HE ROARED HIS GLEE, LIFTING GWENNA HIGH ON A SHOULDER...

I'LL FIGHT ANY MAN IN THE PLACE! ANY MAN AT ALL! COME ONE— COME ALL!

THE MEN OF OPHIR ROUSED UNDER HIS TAUNTS. THEY FLUNG THEMSELVES AT HIM. JOYOUSLY CROM LAUGHED, FOR THE LOVE OF FIGHTING FLOWED IN HIS VEINS...

WHAT A MAN! ZUES! HE'S MAD!

I'LL NOT HURT YOU! THERE...I'LL TAP WITH THE FLAT OF MY BLADE!

BUT WHEN THE CITY POLICE ARRIVED, CROM MEEKLY YIELDED, AND WALKED WITH THEM TOWARD THE JAIL...

I'LL BE OUT TOMORROW, WATER GIRL! TAKE THESE COINS UNTIL THEN...

5

BUT WHILE THE CITY OF OPHIR SLEPT, CROM WORKED WITH HIS FILE AT THE OLD, WORN BARS OF HIS CELL...

A GOOD LONG CORD... WITH THE FILE ATTACHED... WILL REACH THE ROOF OF THE TOWER YONDER...

MOMENTS LATER, A FILE CLANGED ON THE STONE ORNAMENTS OF THE BLACK TOWER.. DRAGGED... THEN HELD! AND CROM SWUNG OUT INTO THE MOONLIGHT...

FREYA GUIDE ME! MAY THE CORD HOLD MY WEIGHT—

AT THAT INSTANT, TANIT, QUEEN OF OPHIR, STIRRED FROM HER COUCH AND WALKED TO THE WINDOW OF HER BEDROOM...

AM I DREAMING? OR IS THAT A MAN-SWINGING TOWARD THE BLACK TOWER?

LIKE A WEIGHTED PENDULUM, CROM CATAPULTED THROUGH THE NIGHT!

THE GODS FAVOR ME! I'M GOING TO GET A HANDHOLD ON THE ORNAMENTS!

FOOT BY FOOT, CROM MOUNTED THE TOWER, AS HE PUT A HAND ON THE EDGE OF THE ROOF AND SWUNG UP, TWO BLACK, SNARLING PANTHERS LAUNCHED THEMSELVES AT HIM!

SET! THEY'LL TOPPLE ME BACK- OFF THE TOWER- TO FALL AND BREAK MY BACK!

BUT CROM WAS HALF ANIMAL HIMSELF! HIS GREAT MUSCLES TENSED FOR THE SHOCK OF THEIR LEAP! HIS LAUGHTER RANG LOUD IN THE NIGHT!

HA! COME YOU BLACK BEAUTIES! I'VE FOUGHT YOUR KIND BEFORE, IN THE JUNGLES OF IND! HA!

SNARLS AND GROWLS RUMBLED FROM FURRY THROATS AS MAN AND BEASTS ROLLED ACROSS THE TOWER ROOF! CLAWS AND FANGS SANK DEEP, BUT CROM FOUGHT SILENTLY, CLEVERLY...

GOT MY DAGGER! NOW I WILL RETURN THOSE SCRATCHES!

6

WHILE CROM FOUGHT FOR HIS LIFE ON THE TOWER ROOF, TANIT RACED BY AN UNDERGROUND PASSAGE INTO THE TOWER...

NO NEED TO CALL THE GUARD! THE FOOL WILL BE KILLED BEFORE HE COMES TO THE TREASURE ROOM! I WANT TO SEE HIM DIE!

HIGH ABOVE, ON THE ROOF, CROM'S GREAT MUSCLES CREAKED WITH STRAIN! A PANTHER SCREAMED AS ITS BACK BROKE! ANOTHER GURGLED AS A DAGGER DRANK ITS LIFE-BLOOD!

BOTH DEAD! THE WAY LIES CLEAR FOR MY FEET!

DOWN A FLIGHT OF STAIRS CROM MOVED, AND THEN ALONG A CORRIDOR. SUDDENLY A DOOR CRASHED OPEN, AND PALACE GUARDS POURED OUT...

HO! MORE BLOOD TO DRINK, SKULL-CRACKER!

NOW, SKULL-CRACKER! NOW!

HE LEAPS LIKE A DEER!

CROM'S GORILLA-LIKE STRENGTH, THE CUNNING OF HIS SWORD-HAND, SWEPT THE SOFT, POLITICALLY APPOINTED GUARDS BEFORE HIM. ONE OF THEM SCREAMED, TOO LATE TO CALL FOR HELP...

THE PATH IS OPEN!

AAGG!

CHUCKLING HIS TRIUMPH, CROM WALKED FORWARD INTO THE CHAMBER OF THE FOUNTAIN...

I DID IT! I DID WHAT NO MAN LIVING OR DEAD COULD DO! I CAME UNAIDED TO THE FOUNTAIN OF ETERNAL YOUTH!

AND THEN—A CRY BROKE FROM HIS LIPS! A CRY OF HORROR AND REPULSION! HIS EYES WIDENED IN REALIZATION THAT HE WAS DOOMED—BUT WITH AN OATH, HE DRAGGED SKULL-CRACKER FROM HIS SCABBARD!

BY THOR'S HAMMER! IT IS THE EARTH-SPANNER! IORMUNGUNDIR IT-SELF!

7

ITH A SCRAPING OF HARD SCALES, WITH A HISS OF EXPELLED BREATH AND DARTING TONGUE, A MONSTROUS SNAKE—FROM WHICH THE LEGENDS OF THE VIKING EARTH-CIRCLING SNAKE HAS ARISEN—ROSE SLOWLY FROM ITS CIRCLED COILS ABOUT THE PLAYING FOUNTAIN. FLAT, BEADY EYES SOUGHT THE HUGE FORM OF THE BARBARIAN. ANGRILY THE MONSTER ROSE, HIGHER AND HIGHER...

ITH A HISS AND A LIGHTNING-LIKE DART OF ITS FLAT HEAD, THE MONSTER STRUCK...

BY THE ICE IN THE BEARD OF ULLER! THAT WAS— CLOSE!

HE RECOVERS SLOWLY! IF I CAN AVOID HIS NEXT LUNGE—THEN SPRING FORWARD—WHILE HE DRAWS BACK—

GAIN THE SNACK-THING STRUCK! THIS TIME, CROM JUMPED HIGH ON STEEL-THEWED LEGS!

NOW—WHILE HE IS SLOW IN RECOVERING—I MUST STRIKE!

KULL-CRACKER GLINTED RED IN THE TORCHLIGHT AS CROM SWUNG IT ONCE AROUND HIS HEAD, THEN BROUGHT IT DOWN...

YOU DIE, MONSTER!

ITH A GRIN OF CONQUEST, CROM STEPPED FORWARD. BEHIND HIM, SLIM DAGGER UPLIFTED TO SPLIT HIS BACK, CAME TANIT, ON BARE FEET THAT MADE NO SOUND ON THE MAR-BLE FLOOR!

NOW FOR THE WATERS OF ETERNAL YOUTH!

8

DIE, BARBARIAN!

HO! A SHE-CAT HUNGERS FOR MY BLOOD—

...UT BEFORE TANIT COMPLETED THE DOWNWARD SWEEP OF HER SLIM BLADE, CROM HAD SEEN HER REFLECTION IN THE UPRAISED JUG...

THERE IS BUT ONE WAY TO HANDLE PRETTY GIRLS WHO WOULD PUT A DAGGER IN A MAN'S BACK! THE BARBARIAN'S WAY!

OHHH!

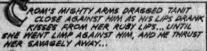

ROM'S MIGHTY ARMS DRAGGED TANIT CLOSE AGAINST HIM AS HIS LIPS DRANK KISSES FROM HER RUBY LIPS... UNTIL SHE WENT LIMP AGAINST HIM, AND HE THRUST HER SAVAGELY AWAY...

BY NESSUS' HOOVES! YOUR JEWEL! SET IN THE CROWN OF OPHIR! SO YOU MUST BE TANIT— IT'S QUEEN!

IT'S RICH! I'VE LOOTED THESE WATERS-KISSED A QUEEN-AND WILL FILL MY POUCH WITH A KING'S FORTUNE! QUITE A NIGHT, EH, PRETTY ONE?

YOU FOOL! YOU'LL NEVER GET OUT OF HERE ALIVE! MY GUARDS WILL CUT YOU TO PIECES!

OH, NO, PRETTY ONE! THEY'LL NOT PUT A HAND ON ME, BECAUSE *YOU* RIDE WITH ME - AS A *HOSTAGE!*

NEVER! I'LL DIE FIRST!

ROUD TANIT WAS A QUEEN, BUT ALSO A WOMAN. SHE THRILLED TO THE SAVAGE STRENGTH OF CROM AS HE LIFTED HER HIGH IN HIS ARMS AND BEAT DOWN HER CLAWING FINGERS.

THERE, NOW! NO HARM WILL COME TO YOU. AFTER YOU'VE SEEN ME SAFELY PAST THE GATES, I'LL LET YOU GO!

BEAST! YOU PIG! ALL RIGHT-YOU WIN, BARBARIAN!

9

KEY TO SECRET PASSAGE

SWORD OF DRAGONUS

Frank Brunner (1949-)

SWORD of DRAGONUS

"IN THE DARK DISTANCE, STOOD THE CASTLE OF THE WIZARD TALVURAS! IT WAS BUILT ON A ROCKY CRAG, AND ITS SPIRES AND TOWERS THRUST UPWARDS INTO THE CLOUDS! THIS WAS TRULY AN EVIL FORBODING- STRUCTURE! DRAGONUS SPURRED HIS MOUNT ONWARD...

A FEW DAYS EARLIER, DRAGONUS HAD BEEN IN THE CHAMBER OF BALTHUS, THE ALBINO PRINCE OF ONE OF THE STYGIAN COLONIES! THE PALE ONE, IT SEEMED HAD DESIRED A BEAUTIFUL CREATURE NAMED ZAREEN FOR HIS BRIDE! BALTHUS RELATED TO DRAGONUS HOW HE HAD SENT HIS MINIONS TO ABDUCT THIS MAIDEN......

BRUNNER '70

..."ONLY TO BE THWARTED! THE MAGICIAN TALVURAS HAD EYES FOR THE GIRL ALSO!, AND HAD HER SPIRITED AWAY FROM THE VERY CLUTCHES OF THE ALBINO'S SERVITORS!"......NOW BALTHUS WOULD ENLIST DRAGONUS TO GET HER BACK! IF DRAGONUS COULD RETRIEVE HER AND KILL TALVURAS IN THE PROCESS, HE WOULD BE REWARDED ANY OF THE ALBINO'S — —COUNTLESS TREASURES!

"DRAGONUS NOW APPROACHED THE GATES OF TALVURAS FORTRESS! SUDDENLY FROM OUT OF THE SKY APPEARED THE CASTLE'S GRISLY GUARDIANS!"

DRAGONUS PARRIED AND THRUST, BUT INSTEAD OF FLESH HIS SWORD PENETRATED AN ICY VACUUM......

....WHICH FROZE HIS BLOOD AND FOR AN INSTANT HE FELT ICY FINGERS GROPE FOR HIS WEAPONS BEFORE HE FELL INTO AN ONRUSH-ING SWATH OF DARKNESS

AZEDLY, THE WARRIOR AWOKE, THE STENCH OF ROTTING FLESH ASSAILED HIS NOSTRILS, AND THE SIGHT OF HALF DECAYED BODIES HANGING IN SHACKLES OFFENDED HIS EYES! THIS WAS THE DUNGEON OF TALVURAS!!

I AM DRAGONUS! WHO BE YE? ..ARE THERE ANY OTHER UN- -FORTUNATES HERE...ALIVE?

THERE IS ONLY ME... ... AND THE OLD ONE! I HAVE BEEN HERE BUT A SHORT TIME BUT THE OTHERS..

CROSS THE ROOM SAT THE FAT DUNGEON-KEEPER, TOSSING CRUMBS THE PRISONERS MEAL TO THE RATS, THE ONE CALLED THALD, SPAT TH DISGUST WHILE DRAGONUS NOTICED THE PILE OF WEAPONS NEAR E GUARD, AMONG THEM, HIS OWN UNMISTAKABLE BLADE, CARVED FROM THE FANG OF A DRAGON!

FEAR NOT!, I AM ON A MISSION, AS SOON AS TALVURAS' SENDS FOR ME FOR QUESTIONING...

SEND FOR YOU? YOU FOOL!! ONCE YOU ARE HERE!,... YOU ARE ONE OF THE DEAD !!!... TALVURAS QUESTIONS NO ONE!

YOU SAY YOU ARE A SORCERER! CAN YOU MUSTER UP ENOUGH WILL TO FETCH MY SWORD?

IT IS USELESS, LONG AGO I TRIED TO DESTROY TALVURAS! THAT IS WHY I AM HERE, HE HAS REMOVED ALL MY POWERS AND IT WOULD STRAIN ME GREATLY TO LIFT AN OBJECT WITH WHAT LITTLE WILL IS LEFT ME!

OU ARE MERE WARRIORS!, AND WILL T AND DIE!! LIKE ALL OUR FRIENDS RE! BUT I.... I AM A SORCERER AND L NOT AGE, I WILL STAY HERE FOR ALL ERNITY!, UNLESS TALVURAS GRANTS ME VIOLENT DEATH!

...BESIDES NO MERE SWORD WILL CUT THESE CHAINS! I HAVE TRIED IT!!

I ONLY LONG FOR DEATH!

HAVE YOU DEATH, THEN,....BUT HEAR ME, MY BLADE IS NO ORDINARY WEAPON!! BRING ME THAT WHITE SWORD BY THE STAIRS AND LEAVE THE REST TO ME!!

YOU ONLY FATIGUE YOURSELF SORCERER! AND DEATH WILL COME THAT MUCH SOONER TO THE MAN WHO WASTES HIS ENERGY HACKING AT HIS CHAINS! HA HA HA HA

IN BUT A MOMENT, THE MIRACULOUS BLADE WAS IN THE OLD ONE'S GRASP, MUCH TO THE JAILKEEPERS SHOCK!

.... THE BLADE SLASHED THROUGH THALD'S CHAIN WITH A SINGLE EFFORTLESS STROKE! AND IN A SURGE OF GALVANIZED ACTION, THALD WAS UPON THE - FAT KEEPER!

HIS PLUMP FEATURES BLUDGEONED INTO A BLOODY PULP!, THE OBESE GUARD CRA- -SHED TO THE FLOOR SCREAMING! THE HUGE RATS, DRAWN BY THE SCENT OF BLOOD SWARMED OVER THEIR FEEDER GREEDILY SAVORING THE LAST MEAL HE WOULD EVER OFFER THEM!!

...MORTALLY WOUNDED, BEELZEBUB RECEDED INTO THE BLAZING, HEALING QUAGMIRE! TALVURAS PREPARED THE ONLY DEFENSE LEFT TO HIM!!

ARMED WITH AN UNFAMILIAR WEAPON!, TALVURAS CRINGED LIKE A TRAPPED REPTILE!....

PREPARE TO DIE, SORCEROUS DOG!

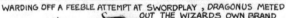

WARDING OFF A FEEBLE ATTEMPT AT SWORDPLAY, DRAGONUS METED OUT THE WIZARDS OWN BRAND OF JUSTICE!.....

.....AND CLAIMED HIS REWARD!!

ALTHOUGH THE ALBINO PRINCE NEVER SUSPECTED, DRAGONUS KNEW FROM THE OUTSET WHAT HIS FEE WOULD BE!... BY THE TIME BALTHUS FINALLY DISCOVERED THE TRUTH DRAGONUS WOULD BE FAR AWAY!

Finis

Afterword

Gary Gygax relied on his fondness of Sword and Sorcery stories when creating the original Dungeons and Dragons role playing games. His inspiration leaned towards the pulpier ones—albeit with some strangeness and weirdness—but in many ways, still the typical 'hero's journey' fantasy stories with a Northern European background and with other cultures always appearing very foreign and 'other'. As editor of *Weird Tales* in the early 2000s—tasked with bringing the magazine into the twenty-first century—I was very familiar with these stories, but I was also very aware of their limitations. That said, if you take a closer look at some of the stories that inspired Gygax you can see that it wasn't just the standard tales but often the more unusual ones in which the main characters are not necessarily the flawless heroes you might expect.

For example, Jack Vance's Dying Earth tales are unique and brilliant with a focus on a post-apocalyptic future, giving these stories a more science-fictional bent and setting than the usual medieval fantasies, so it is easy to see how this world can inform and inspire other stranger worlds (similar to the Zothique cycle of stories by Clark Ashton Smith represented here in *Appendix N* with the story 'The Empire of the Necromancers'). In addition, Vance's 'Turjan of Miir' illustrates the influence of how magic works in D&D, presenting us with a wizard who is despondent over his failures in producing new and viable beings. It is his quest for a

AFTERWORD

forbidden ancient knowledge that forces him out of his comfortable workroom into the wider world where he must find a hidden land to uncover the secret spell. He encounters all kinds of creatures in his travels, including the bad-tempered T'sais, created by the wizard Pandelume. And it is his meeting with her that motivates him to create her opposite, T'sain. The magic and the adventures are unique, but the relationships between the two artificial women are so black and white that it does beg an inevitable conversation about gender stereotypes, not to mention the overall representation of women in the story and comparable genre fictions of the period.

David Madison's 'Tower of Darkness' presents a different depiction of women that doesn't employ the usual stereotypes. The story begins with all the elements of the typical sword and sorcery story, with two travelers (marauders?), Diana and Marcus, coming upon a strange city with a secret. The pair are warned when they try to pass through the city gates that everything shuts down after dark, but they ignore these cautions, of course. But the genius is in how these two characters are described. Rarely have I seen such exacting depictions of clothing, makeup and accessories that speaks to who they are; with Diana wearing "A fantastically jeweled and embroidered peacock cape..." and Marcus "...with a blue butterfly painted on his left cheek." Even the banter between the two of them is engaging and hilarious, but the story takes a dark turn when they encounter a stranger and uncover the secret of this city.

In thinking about how Madison portrays his main characters and how this feeds into representation, I can't help but be reminded of the Alyx stories by Joanna Russ and wonder if Gygax considered these tales at all. Like other anti-heroes in earlier Sword and Sorcery, such as Moorcock's Elric and Leiber's Fafhrd and the Gray Mouser stories, Alyx has her flaws. She is a thief and a pirate. Indeed, there is a reference in one of Russ's stories that hints at a relationship between Alyx and Fafhrd. This kind of playfulness between the characters is evident in many of these stories, which allows the reading audience to imagine different possibilities. But what I find even more interesting is that Alyx comes across a time travel device, which adds an element of science fiction, similar to the blending tropes of the Vance stories.

There is a great deal of humor in these influential tales. 'The Man Who Sold Rope to the Gnoles' by Margaret St. Clair is a perfect example of this humor, introducing us as it does to Mortensen, a man who thinks he is the best salesperson around who can outsmart the gnoles! This story is a treasure and a perfect embodiment of how you can't be too careful when dealing with creatures you don't really understand. And yet, even though this story was written by a woman, all the characters are male, even the gnoles (although I am not sure how Mortensen could tell. Wouldn't it be more interesting if the gnole wasn't male? Or even female?).

The power of these stories is how they allow us to look at what the genre could be. We have a foundation from which to draw, a jumping off point. Especially when we consider how many of these stories are placed in settings that are so far-reaching and eccentric that anything can be imagined. When looking at the flawed protagonists, we can imagine flipping things around and seeing what those changes may bring to the forefront. For example, what IF the gnoles were non-binary? What if Cymoril had rescued Elric at Imrryr in Michael Moorcock's first Elric story, 'The Dreaming City'? And dare we even imagine if the necromancers from Smith's story, Mmatmuor and Sodosma, were more than just allies but partners in life as well? Or would that be blasphemous?

Overall the most successful original stories that influenced Dungeons and Dragons all have a bit of humor in them and somehow push against type for the Sword and Sorcery genre. The whimsical, ribald nature that many of these stories possess opens up a space for readers to engage with them in more immersive ways, while darker stories filled with ghastly images and over the top horror invite heated discussions and necessary debate. This may be exactly why these stories continue to entertain new generations of readers, and why players keep playing D&D while more new players feel compelled to join in. At the time of this writing the current publisher of Dungeons & Dragons, Wizards of the Coast, released a statement on diversity in which they addressed how they will resolve the errors and mistakes of representation in past books and stories, while outlining their commitment to promoting inclusivity in the future. Although a lot of the stories that originally inspired D&D feature protagonists that are almost invariably white and male— an unfortunate reflection of the limited social horizons of Gygax's target audience at the time—it's heartening to see more people from all around the world get immersed in this imaginative gameplay in ways that make it genuinely new and different, re-imagining and re-inhabiting its worlds as their own.

Ann VanderMeer, 2020

Notes On The Stories

(When appropriate, stories have been rendered into American English.)

"How Sargoth Lay Siege to Zaremm" © 1972 by Lin Carter. First appeared in *Swordsmen and Supermen* (New York: Centaur Press, 1972). Reprinted by permission of the author's literary executor, Robert M. Price.

"Tale of Hauk" © 1977 by Poul Anderson. First appeared in *Swords Against Darkness* (New York: Zebra Books, 1977). Reprinted by arrangement with The Trigonier Trust.

"Jewels in the Forest" by Fritz Leiber. First appeared as "Two Sought Adventure" in *Unknown*, August 1932. © 1995 by the Estate of Fritz Leiber, published in 2014 by Open Road Integrated Media, Inc. Reprinted with permission of the author's estate.

"Empire of the Necromancers" © 1932 by Clark Ashton Smith. First appeared in *Weird Tales*, September 1932. Reprinted with permission of CASiana Enterprises, The Literary Estate of Clark Ashton Smith.

NOTES ON THE STORIES

"Turjan of Miir" © 1950, 2002 by Jack Vance. First published in *The Dying Earth* (Hillman Periodicals No. 41: New York, 1950). Reprinted by permission of the author's agent, Spatterlight.

"A Hero at the Gates" © 1979 by Tanith Lee. First appeared in *Shayol* #3, Summer 1979. Reprinted by permission of the author's estate.

"Tower of the Elephant" by Robert E. Howard, © Conan Properties International LLC. First appeared in *Weird Tales*, March 1933. Reprinted by permission of Conan Properties International LLC.

"Song of Swords" © 1983 by Fred Saberhagen. First appeared in *The First Book of Swords* (New York: Tor, 1983). Reprinted by permission of the author's estate.

"The Dreaming City" © 1961 by Michael Moorcock. First appeared in *Science Fantasy*, June 1961. Reprinted by permission of the author.

"Doom that Came to Sarnath" by H.P. Lovecraft. First appeared in *Marvel Tales of Science and Fantasy*, March/April 1935. Available in the public domain.

"Tower of Darkness" by David Madison, © Jessica Amanda Salmonson for the estate of David Madison. First appeared in *Swords Against Darkness III* (New York: Zebra Books, 1978). Reprinted by permission of the author's literary executor, Jessica Amanda Salmonson.

"Straggler from Atlantis" © 1977 by Manly Wade Wellman. First appeared in *Swords Against Darkness* (New York: Zebra Books, 1977). Reprinted by permission of the author's literary executor, David Drake.

376

NOTES ON THE STORIES

Appendix N: Inspirational and Educational Reading

Gary Gygax's original list of "Inspirational and Educational Reading" from first edition of the 1979 *Dungeons Masters Guide*.

Anderson, Poul. THREE HEARTS AND THREE LIONS; THE HIGH CRUSADE; THE BROKEN SWORD.

Bellairs, John. THE FACE IN THE FROST.

Brackett, Leigh.

Brown, Frederic.

Burroughs, Edgar Rice. "Pellucidar" series; Mars series; Venus series.

Carter, Lin. "World's End" series.

de Camp, L. Sprague. LEST DARKNESS FALL; THE FALLIBLE FIEND; et al.

de Camp & Pratt. "Harold Shea" series; THE CARNELIAN CUBE.

Derleth, August.

Dunsany, Lord.

Farmer, P. J.: "The World of the Tiers" series; et al.

Fox, Gardner: "Kothar" series; "Kyrik" series; et al.

Howard, R. E.: "Conan" series.

Lanier, Sterling: HIERO'S JOURNEY.

Leiber, Fritz: "Fafhrd & Gray Mouser" series; et al.

Lovecraft, H. P.

Merritt, A.: CREEP, SHADOW, CREEP; MOON POOL; DWELLERS IN THE MIRAGE; et al.

Moorcock, Michael: STORMBRINGER; STEALER OF SOULS; "Hawkmoon" series (esp. the first three books).

Norton, Andre.

Offutt, Andrew J.: editor of SWORDS AGAINST DARKNESS III.

Pratt, Fletcher: BLUE STAR; et al.

Saberhagen, Fred: CHANGELING EARTH; et al.

St. Clair, Margaret: THE SHADOW PEOPLE; SIGN OF THE LABRYS.

Tolkien, J. R. R.: THE HOBBIT; "Ring trilogy".

Vance, Jack: THE EYES OF THE OVERWORLD; THE DYING EARTH; et al.

Weinbaum, Stanley.

Wellman, Manly Wade.

Williamson, Jack.

Zelazny, Roger: JACK OF SHADOWS; "Amber" series; et al.